THE DRAWING OF THE
WAITING

"EXHILARATING!"
Philadelphia Inquirer

"AN EXTRAORDINARY BOOK...
BOTH ORIGINAL AND DAZZLING!"
Cleveland Plain Dealer

"A WONDERFUL KALEIDOSCOPE OF THE
IMAGINATION...FASCINATING"
Poul Anderson

"A TREAT"   *Publishers Weekly*

"THE BEST MINGLING OF HISTORY
WITH HISTORICAL MAGIC
THAT I HAVE EVER SEEN"
Gene Wolfe

"AN EXCEEDINGLY FINE,
INTELLIGENT, POWERFUL NOVEL!"
Chicago Sun-Times

"A NOVEL TO BE READ FOR ENJOYMENT"
San Francisco Chronicle

THE DRAGON WAITING

A Masque of History

JOHN M. FORD

AVON BOOKS  NEW YORK

AVON BOOKS
A division of
The Hearst Corporation
105 Madison Avenue
New York, New York 10016

First Avon Books Printing: April 1985

AVON TRADEMARK REG. U. S. PAT. OFF. AND IN OTHER COUNTRIES, MARCA REGISTRADA, HECHO EN U.S.A.

Printed in the U.S.A.

K-R 10 9 8 7 6 5 4 3 2

To those who were there,
at the crisis.

The Empire lay in the imposed order; around
the throne the visionary zone of clear light
hummed with celestial action; there the forms
of chamberlains, logothetes, nuncios, went and came . . .
These dwelled in Byzantium. . . .
But also in the mind of the Empire another kind
of tale lay than that of the Grail.

> —Charles Williams
> *The Region of the Summer Stars*

Ahistorical Note

IN the second century C.E., Loukianos of Samosata wrote, "Everyone's writing history now, and I don't want to be left out of the furore." Loukianos, who was also known as Lucian the Scoffer, then produced a fantasy story called the *True History.*

What follows is a work of fiction, which makes use of historical characters and settings in the manner usual to drama. Some events, and all dialogues, are invented, as of course are the overtly fantastic elements. There are as few technical anachronisms as could be managed, though some of the technologies given were not known in the story's locales at the time it is set.

The quotations heading each section are from Shakespeare's *Richard III.* It, and many other works historical and otherwise, have provided atmosphere and detail for the present book, but all interpretations of character, especially of that most reinterpreted of English kings, are naturally my own.

My purpose has been to entertain, not to raise issues to the dignity of a historical controversy. As Nennius wrote twelve centuries ago, if there was such a person and that was when he wrote, "I yield to him who knows more of these things than I do."

JMF/1982

Contents

Shadows As They Pass:

HISTORICAL CHARACTERS

For those who have some difficulty following the large array of titles common to the nobility of the period, or are simply interested in such lists, the following is a nonexhaustive summary of the real historical figures appearing in the novel. Absence of a name does not necessarily mean the character is not historical, and as explained previously, some liberties have been taken with those who do appear below.

ENGLISH AND SCOTS

CECILY, DUCHESS OF YORK, and her three surviving sons:
RICHARD PLANTAGENET, DUKE OF GLOUCESTER, later King Richard III
GEORGE PLANTAGENET, DUKE OF CLARENCE
KING EDWARD IV
RICHARD, DUKE OF YORK
ANNE NEVILLE, Richard of Gloucester's wife
ELIZABETH WOODVILLE, Edward IV's Queen
JAMES TYRELL, henchman to Richard
RICHARD RATCLIFFE, ditto
FRANCIS LOVELL, ditto

ALEXANDER STUART, DUKE OF ALBANY, brother to King James III of Scotland

ANTHONY WOODVILLE, LORD SCALES, EARL RIVERS, brother to Queen Elizabeth

EDWARD, PRINCE OF WALES, later King Edward V

DOCTOR JOHN MORTON

HENRY STAFFORD, DUKE OF BUCKINGHAM

WILLIAM HASTINGS, LORD HASTINGS, King's Chamberlain to Edward IV

EDWARD OF MIDDLEHAM, son to Richard of Gloucester

HENRY TYDDER (i.e., "Tudor," given its correct period pronunciation)

FRENCH

KING LOUIS XI

FRANÇOIS VILLON, poet and ne'er-do-well

MARGARET OF ANJOU, Queen to King Henry VI of England

ITALIANS

LUIGI PULCI, poet

MARSILIO FICINO, poet and philosopher

GIULIANO DE' MEDICI, brother to

LORENZO DE' MEDICI, called The Magnificent (official title of the current head of the Medici Bank)

ALESSANDRA SCALA, theatrical designer

GIROLAMO SAVONAROLA

GALEAZZO MARIA SFORZA, DUKE OF MILAN

FEDERIGO DA MONTEFELTRO, mercenary commander, DUKE OF URBINO

DOMINIC MANCINI, diplomat

DOCTOR JOHN ARGENTINE, physician

PART ONE

Children of the Empire

Lo, at their births good stars were opposite . . . .
All unavoided is the doom of destiny.
                                    —ACT IV, SCENE 4

Chapter 1
GWYNEDD

THE road the Romans made traversed North Wales a little way inland, between the weather off the Irish Sea and the mountains of Gwynedd and Powys; past the copper and the lead that the travel-hungry Empire craved. The road crossed the Conwy at Caerhun, the Clwyd at Asaph sacred to Esus, and the Roman engineers passed it through the hills, above the shore and below the peaks, never penetrating the spine of the country. Which is not to say that there were no ways in; only that the Romans did not find them.

From Caernarfon to Chester the road remained, and at Caerhun in the Vale of Conwy there were pieces of walls and straight ditches left where the legionary fort had held the river crossing. Roman stones, but no Romans; not for a thousand years.

Beyond Caerhun the road wound upslope for a mile, to an inn called The White Hart. Hywel Peredur lived there in this his eleventh year, the nine hundred tenth year of Arthur's Triumph, the one thousand ninety-fifth year of Constantine's City. This March afternoon, Hywel stood on the Roman paving below the innyard, and was King of the Romans.

Fields all his dominion rolled out forever before and below him, lined and set with trees that from the height were no more than tufts on a cloth of patchwork greens and browns. Conwy water was a broad ribbon stitched in easy

3

curves across the cloth. The March air smelled of peat and moisture and nothing at all but its own cold cleanness on the sharp edge of spring.

The place Hywel stood was called *Pen-y-Gaer,* Head of the Fortress. There had been a fortress, even before the legions came; but of its builders too only stones were left, bits of wall and rampart. And the defense of the slope, a field of sharp-edged boulders set in ranks down the hill.

Hywel stood on the road and commanded the stones, soldiers without death or fear, like the warriors grown from dragon's teeth in the story; any assault against them would break and be scattered. Then, at Hywel's signal, his legion of horse would gallop forth from Caerhun and cut down the discomfited enemy, sparing only the nobles for ransom and tribute. His captains, in purple and gold, mounted on white horses, would drive the captive lords before him, shouting *Peredur, Peredur!* that all might know who was conqueror here. . . .

Not far up the road was a milestone; it was worn and half-legible, and Hywel knew no Latin, but he could read the name CONSTANTI. Constantine. Emperor. Founder of the Beautiful City. And now a god, like Julius Caesar, like Arthur King of Britain. Hywel would run his fingers in the carved letters of the name when he passed the marker, touching the figure of the god.

Three years ago, on the May kalend, he had stunned a sparrow with a sling pellet, bound its wings, and taken it to the milestone. It had trembled within his shirt, and then, when he set it down, become curiously still, as if waiting. But Hywel had had no knife, and was afraid to use his naked hands. By the time he had found two flat stones and done the thing, he could no longer remember his intended prayer.

Now, clouds drifted across the low sun, making shadow patterns on the ground. The river dulled to slate, then flashed blue-silver. The standing stones seemed to move, to march, beat spears on shields in salute. Sparrows were forgotten as Hywel moved his cohorts, as soldier and king and god.

Until dust rose, and men moved crosswise to the dream, light flashing on steel: real soldiers, on the road to the inn. Hywel watched and listened, knowing that if he were quite still they could not detect him. He heard the scrape of pikes on the paving stones, the stamp of booted feet, chains dragging. He let the breeze bring him their voices, not distinguishable words but rhythms: English voices, not Welsh. As they turned the last bend in the road, Hywel's eyes picked out the badge they wore. Then he turned and ran lightly to the gate of The White Hart. As he crossed the innyard, a dog sniffed and raised its head for a pat that was not coming; sparrows fluttered up from the eaves.

The cruck-beamed serving hall was dim with afternoon. A little peat smoke hung in the air. Dafydd, the innkeeper, was working at the fire while Glynis, the pretty barmaid, wiped mugs. Both looked up, Glynis smiling, Dafydd not. "Well, my lord of the north, come in, do! While you've been with your councillors, this fire nearly—"

"Soldiers on the road," Hywel said, in Welsh. "My lord of Ireland's men, from Caernarfon." He knew Dafydd's anger was only mocking; when the innkeeper was truly angry he became deadly quiet and small-spoken.

"Well, then," said Dafydd, "they'll be wanting ale. Go you and draw a kettleful."

Hywel, grinning, said "And shall I fetch some butter?"

The innkeeper smiled back. "We've none that rancid. Now draw you the ale; they'll not care to wait."

"Ie."

"And speak English when the soldiers can hear you."

"Ie."

"And give yourself a whipping, lad—I haven't time!"

Hywel paused at the top of the cellar stairs. "There's a prisoner with them. A wizard."

Dafydd put the poker down, wiped his hands on his apron. "Well then," he said quietly, "that's bad news for someone."

Hywel nodded without understanding and clumped downstairs. He drew the ale into a black iron kettle, put it on the lift and hoisted it up; and only then, standing in the

quiet cellar, did he realize just what he'd said. He had
heard the chains, right enough, but never once seen what
was in them.

Eight men, and something else, stood in the innyard.

The men wore leather jackets, carried swords and pole
axes; two had longbows across their backs. One, helmeted
and officious, had a long leather pouch at his side, and a
baldric from which little wooden bottles hung on strings.
Charges of powder, Hywel knew, for the hand-cannon in
the pouch.

The badge on the soldiers' sleeves was a snarling dog on
its hind legs; a talbot-hound, for Sir John Talbot, the latest
Lieutenant of Ireland. Talbot had smashed the Côtentin
rebels at Henry V's order; it was said the mothers of Anjou
quieted their children with threats of *Jehan Talbó*. Now
that Henry was dead, long live Henry VI, and the advisors
to the three-year-old King hoped the War Hound could
quiet the Irish as well.

Four soldiers held chains that led to the other thing,
which crouched on the ground, black and shapeless. Hywel
thought it must be some great hunting-hound, a namesake
talbot, perhaps, or a beast from Ireland across the sea;
then it put out a pale paw, spread long fingers, and Hywel
saw it was a man on hands and knees, in fantastically
ruined clothes and a black cloak.

The thin hands left blood on the earth. There was a
shackle, engraved with something, on each wrist and each
ankle, linked to the leash-chains. The head turned, and the
black hood fell back, showing dull iron around the man's
neck. The collar was engraved as well. Next to it was a
straggly gray beard, a nostril with blood dry around it.

Hywel stared at a dark eye, glassy as with fever, or madness. The eye did not blink. The cracked lips moved.

"None of that, now!" shouted a soldier, and pulled the
chain he held, dropping the man flat; another soldier
swung the butt of his axe into the man's ribs, and there
was a hint of a groan. The first soldier bent halfway down
and shook the chain. " 'Tain't beyond th' law for us to have

your tongue, an you try any chanteries." To Hywel he
sounded exactly like Dafydd's wife Nansi scolding a hen
that would not lay. The prone man was very still.

"Ale! Where's ale!" cried the others, turning away from
the prisoner, and Dafydd came behind Hywel with a tray
of tankards, hot mulled ale topped with brown foam and
steaming. "Here, Hywel. And Ogmius send us all the right
words to say." Hywel took the tray into the yard. A cheer
went up—for him, he realized, and for one passing instant
he was Caesar again—then the mugs were snatched from
him.

"Here, boy, here."

"Jove's beard, that's good!"

"Jove strike you down, it ain't English beer." The
speaker winked at Hywel. "But it's good anyway, eh boy."

Hywel barely noticed. He was staring again at the
chained man, who still did not move except to breathe raggedly. A little of the cloak had blown back, showing the
man's shirt sleeve. The fabric was embroidered in complex
patterns—not the Celtic work he knew, but similar, interlocking designs.

And The White Hart was an inn with good trade; Hywel
had seen silk twice before, on the wives of lords.

"You have a care of our dog, there, lad," said the soldier
who had winked. His tone was friendly. "He's an eastern
sorcerer, a Bezant. From the City itself, they say."

The City of Constantine. "What . . . did he do?"

"Why, he magicked, lad, what else? Magicked for th'
Irish rebels 'gainst King Harry, rest him. Five years he
hid up in them Irish hills, sorcellin' and afflictin'. But we
ketched him, anyway. Lord Jack ketched him, an' now he's
Talbot's dog."

"Tom," the serjeant said sharply, and the soldier stood
to attention for a moment. Then he winked at Hywel again
and tossed his empty tankard into Hywel's hands.

"Have a look here, boy," Tom said. The soldier reached
down and grasped the manacle around the wizard's left
wrist, pulled it up as if there were no man attached to it.
"See that serpent, cut there in th' iron? That's a Druid ser-

pent, as has power t' bind wizards. Old Irish Patrick drove all the snakes out of Ireland, for the good of his magic fellows. But we took some snakes with us. Snakes of leather, an' iron.'' The soldier let the shackle fall with a hollow clunk. The prisoner made no sound. Hywel stood fascinated, wondering.

"Innkeeper!" the serjeant said.

Dafydd came out, wiping his hands on his apron. "Yes, Captain?"

The serjeant did not correct his rank. "Have you a blacksmith here? This rebel's harmless enough, but he'll crawl off with half a chance given him. We'll want him fixed to something with weight."

"You'll be staying here for a time, then?"

"We're in no hurry. The prisoner's to be taken to York for execution."

A soldier said "The Irish Sea were deep enough."

"Not to bury his curse, man," said the serjeant curtly. "Leave killing him to his own sort of worker." He turned back to Dafydd. "Don't worry about the lads, innkeeper; they're good and they'll obey me." He weighted the last word slightly. "And they're bloody tired of minding this rebel."

"Hywel," said the innkeeper, "run you and tell Siôn Mawr he's wanted, with hammer and tongs."

A high-voiced young soldier called after Hywel, "And you tell 'im this aren't no horse wanting shod! A hammer on them chains—"

Hywel ran. He did not look back. He was afraid to. Under all the soldiers' voices, under Dafydd's, under his own breathing, he could hear another voice, whispering, insistent, like the beat of blood in his ears when all was still. He had heard it without pause since the sorcerer's lips had moved without sound.

You who can hear me, it said, *come to me. Follow my voice.*

And as Hywel ran through the gathering dark, it seemed that hands reached after him, grasping at his limbs, his throat, trying to draw him back.

* * *

Nansi touched the spit-dog's collar; it stopped walking its treadle, and Nansi carved a bit of mutton from the roasting haunch. The dog resumed turning the meat. Nansi put the mutton on a wooden plate with a spoonful of boiled corn, added a piece of soft brown bread.

"The soldiers didn't pay for no meat for him," said Dai, the kitchen boy.

"You needn't tell me what they've not paid for," Nansi said, tenting a napkin over the plate. "I hope he has his teeth; I daren't send a knife. Here, Dai, go you quick, ere it's cold."

"Why do they beat him, if he can't magic?"

"I'm sure I don't know, Dai," Nansi said, with a bitter look. "Take it, now."

"I'll take his dinner," Hywel said, from the kitchen door.

Dai's mouth opened, then shut. Nansi turned away.

"I've drawn his water," Hywel said. "And I'm not afraid of him. You're afraid, aren't you, Dai?"

Dai's pudgy hands tightened. He was a year or so older than Hywel, and also an orphan. Dafydd and Nansi, who had no children, had taken them in together, and tried to bring them up as brothers. Hywel could no longer remember what that was like, even when he tried.

Dai said *"Ie,* feared enough. You feed him." He handed the covered plate to Hywel, who took it with a nod. Hywel did not hate Dai; usually he liked Dai. But they were not brothers.

Just outside the kitchen, he picked up the hooded lantern and pot of ale he had set by the door, and crossed to the barn. Moonlight slanted across the interior. The wizard was sitting up against a post, all white and black in the light. His head turned slightly; Hywel held very still. The face was a skull's, with tiny glints in the eyesockets.

Hywel hung the lantern from a peg and opened the shutter; the wizard winced and turned his face away.

It was all he could turn. A chain went through his collar, twice around the post and his upper body, holding him upright. The chains from his ankles were fixed to two old cart wheels. Hywel had seen Siôn Mawr the smith going home, and could not have missed the murder-black look Siôn gave him; now he understood it.

"It was you after all," the chained man said, and Hywel nearly dropped the food. "Is that for me?"

Hywel took a step. The voice in his head was gone, but he still felt somehow drawn to the wizard. He stopped. "The soldiers say you can't work magic, in those chains."

"But you know better, don't you?" His English had only a little foreign sound. "Well, they're mostly right. I can't do much, and I truly can't escape. Come here, boy." He moved his hands. Hywel turned away, not to see the sign.

"At least put my supper in reach. Then you may go. Please."

Hywel moved closer, looked again at the wizard. The cloak was spread out beneath the man; it was lined with glossy black—more silk. Beneath the cloak he wore a dark green gown of heavy brocade, torn at every seam, showing the white silk shirt. Gown and shirt were embroidered all over with interlocking lines in gold and silver thread, with brighter colors worked between. The patterns drew Hywel's eye despite himself.

He set the plate down in the straw, uncovered it. The man's eyes widened, becoming very liquid, and he ran his tongue over very white teeth specked with dirt. He reached out, one-handed. Hywel saw that his wrist chains were linked behind his back. The wizard set the plate in his lap, and his delicate fingers hovered over it, talonlike, straining; there was not enough chain for his two hands to touch.

Hywel thought of offering to feed him, but could not say it.

The hands ceased to strain then. The wizard groped for and reached the napkin, shook it out, and arranged it as best he could over his shiny, filthy shirt. Then the thin fingers picked up a single kernel of corn and raised it to the swollen mouth. He chewed it very slowly.

Trying not to watch the wizard's hands or eyes, Hywel uncapped the pot of ale. He took a twist of greasy paper from his belt pouch, opened it, and slipped the white butter within into the blood-warm ale. He stirred the pot with a clean straw and pushed it as close to the man as he dared. The wizard waited for Hywel to draw back, then picked up the ale and took a small sip. His eyes closed and he pressed his head back against the post, loosening the iron at his throat just slightly.

"Nectar and ambrosia," he said. "Thank you, boy." He put the ale down and picked up the mutton, took small, worrying bites.

Finally Hywel said, "You called me by magic. No one else could hear. . . . Why?"

The man paused, sighed, wiped his hands and lips. "I thought you were . . . someone else. Someone who could help."

"You thought I was a wizard?"

"I called to the talent. . . . It spent me before I heard the answer. Hard to work with a boot in your ribs." He reached for the bread, nibbled.

"I'm not a wizard," Hywel said.

"No. I'm sorry. But I am glad you brought me this supper."

They sat for a little while like that, the wizard eating slowly, Hywel crouched, watching him. To Hywel it seemed the man wanted to make his supper last all night. He said, "You thought I was a wizard."

"I believe I explained that," the man said patiently. "Isn't it late for you to be awake still?"

"Dafydd doesn't care, long as the fire doesn't go out. You said it was somebody else you called. But I heard you. You called *me.*"

The man swallowed, licked his damaged lips. "I called to the talent. The power. It . . . radiates, like the light from a candle. I felt it, and answered back. That's all."

"Then I *am* a wizard," Hywel said, breathless, triumphant.

The man shook his head, rattling iron. *"Magus latens* . . . no. Someday you could be, if you were taught. But now . . ." There was a noise within his throat that might have been a laugh. "Now you're catalyzed. And I did it, now that I would not do it."

Hywel said "Could you teach me?"

Again the choked laugh. "Why do you think I'm in chains, boy? I'd be dead now if they didn't fear my death-curse so, and my tongue and eyes aren't sure through tomorrow. Go to bed, boy."

Hywel put his foot against one of the cartwheels chained to the wizard's feet. He pushed. The chain shifted; in a moment it would be taut. It was astonishingly easy.

"Please," the man said, "don't." There was no pleading in it, nor command. Hywel turned, saw the dark eyes ringed white and red, the face white as bare bone. And he stopped pushing. Perhaps if sparrows had voices . . .

"I am very tired," the man said. "Please come tomorrow, and I will walk with you."

"Will you tell me about magic?" Hywel's foot was still on the wheel, but it had suddenly become very heavy and hard to move.

The man's voice was weak, but his eyes were black and burning. "Come back tomorrow and I will tell you all I know about magic."

Hywel picked up the plate and napkin, the ale pot. He stood, moved away backwards.

"My name," said the wizard, "is Kallian Ptolemy. With the letter *pi,* if you can write."

Hywel said nothing. Everyone knew that wizards gained power by knowing names. He took the lantern from its peg, shuttered it.

Kallian Ptolemy said "Good night, Hywel Peredur."

Hywel did not know whether to shudder or cry for joy.

Hywel did not sleep much. *All he knew,* Ptolemy had said. Maybe Ptolemy was not a very strong wizard. A few soldiers had caught and chained him, after all.

Owain Glyn Dŵr had been a mighty wizard, Hywel knew. Everyone in Wales did. Glyn Dŵr and a few English lords had almost taken the crown from King Henry IV. And he really had taken Wales away from Henry V, though that Henry was a Monmouthshire man; Glyn Dŵr sat for years as King in Harlech, with his own lords and armies.

The English had finally scattered Owain's soldiers, but they never took Owain, and no one ever saw Owain die. It was said he never died; that he slept like Arthur; that he would come back when the time was right.

Hywel could remember Owain's son, Meredydd, visiting The White Hart; a tall man with big shoulders, much more like a warrior than a great sorcerer. But he *was* a wizard. He made a glass marble out of the empty air and gave it to Hywel, holding Hywel's hand, treating him just as if Hywel were a great chief of Wales.

And Dafydd had been angry, very silently angry, after Meredydd ap Owain had gone.

Hywel dressed before dawn. The air was calm and cold, the moon down and the sky like black glass; Hywel made his way mostly by touch and memory. He looked to the fire in the serving hall, poking ashes and evening out the peat covering. The red glow beneath seemed full of mysteries and power. *All he knew of magic.* Hywel wondered if he would be able to turn lead to gold. If he could fly.

Just at daybreak he looked in on Ptolemy. The wizard was awake, looking disturbed.

"You've come early to lessons," he said tightly.

"No—I—uh"

"I am about to soil myself. If you could be of some help, perhaps . . ."

Hywell fetched a pail, then made some slack in Ptolemy's ankle chains, allowing the wizard, with Hywel's help, to slide up the post enough to squat.

"What's the noise?" Tom, the soldier who had spoken to Hywel, stuck his head inside. He saw Ptolemy, his hose down and his gown lifted, straining with gravity and iron; and Hywel behind, with his hands in Ptolemy's armpits.

"Why, you filthy pair of—"

Then the truth dawned, and the soldier burst out with snorting laughter. Hywel got the bucket into place and the wizard used it, noisily. The soldier sniffed the air as if

smelling sweet flowers, turned, and went out still choking
with laughter.

Hywel helped Ptolemy with his clothes, neither of them
speaking. Settled again, the sorcerer said "I'm sorry."

Hywel shook his head, picked up the pail.

Ptolemy said "These are the only clothes I have. I—"

"You tell me, next time," Hywel said, and went out to
the dungheap.

The sun was brilliant on the hills, the sky a perfect blue.
It was going to be the longest day of Hywel's life.

"An' then I thought, I knew 'e was a Greek, but—"

The soldiers howled with laughter, pounding their mugs
on the table, splashing beer. Annie, the ugly barmaid,
went around filling the mugs again; she was pinched and
groped as she passed. Dafydd had sent Glynis to Caerhun
for "a while."

"An' the boy, Tom? Did 'e look pleased?"

"Ah," Tom said, "just like an English wife; not pleased
but workin' with a will."

Hywel, his cheeks burning, turned away—though they
were not looking at him—and went down to the cellar,
hearing behind him, "No wonder Welsh rebels fight so
foul—"

Downstairs, Dafydd was cleaning a fish packed in ice
and sawdust. He looked up for a moment as Hywel appeared, then went back to his work.

"I did nothing," Hywel said in Cymric. His eyes hurt
and his voice kept catching.

"I know what you did," said Dafydd, in English. Hywel
waited, struggling against tears; Dafydd said no more.

Hywel finally said "He was looking for a wizard, here. I
wonder if he was looking for Glyn Dŵr, to help him."

Dafydd stopped cutting at the fish. He held the knife
lightly, looked at the flash from the blade. "Did he say
that?"

"He—" Hywel's anger was all turned to fear by Dafydd's
sudden softness. "He said he was looking for a wizard."

"Well then. Let's hope his friend finds him. Somewhere

other than here, gods willing." Dafydd took a few more strokes at the fish, then tossed it onto the kitchen lift and stomped up the stairs, wiping his hands furiously on his apron.

Hywel wept.

The sun was below the hills; Hywel was headed toward the kitchen to get Ptolemy's dinner when a hand touched his shoulder.

"Easy, boy! Didn't mean to scare you." It was Tom the soldier. His bow was over his shoulder; he slipped it off and held it out to show Hywel. "Ever drawn one of these?"

Hywel shook his head vaguely.

"Takes practice," Tom said. "We say, to make a bowman, start with his grandfather. I'm going to shoot a bit while there's light left. . . . Would you like to come along? Yew Alice is long for you, but . . ."

"No," Hywel said. "I . . . can't." The bow was white and beautiful. Hywel had seen longbows before, of course, but never been offered the chance to shoot one.

"I shouldn't'a laughed at you. Serjeant said so. I . . . didn't mean anything." Hywel realized suddenly that Tom was only four or five years older than himself.

All I know of magic.

"Tomorrow?" Hywel said, in a small voice.

"I'll be gone tomorrow. Serjeant said."

Then Ptolemy would be gone, and there really was no choice. Hywel tried to hate the soldier, for his mockery, but it was impossible; like hating Dai, or Dafydd more than two hours after a whipping, or . . .

"I have work," Hywel said, and left Tom and his beautiful Alice behind. When he came back from the kitchen, they were not in the yard.

Ptolemy ate not quite so slowly as the night before. When he had finished, wiped his mouth, pissed into the bucket, he motioned Hywel around to sit facing him, and arranged his ruined clothing.

"These seemed like such finery in Ireland," he said. "When I knew they must take me at last, I put on my best.

They did not seem impressed. Are English lords so fabu-
lous?"

"They wear silk," Hywel said.

"Oh, I know. Our silk. All silk passes through Byzantium at some time, did you know that?"

Hywel shook his head.

"Do you think my clothes are fine . . . were, I mean?"

"Yes, very fine."

"Ordinary stuff, on the streets of the City."

"Constantine's City? Byzantium?"

"There is no other City in the world."

"Are there many wizards there?"

"There is everything there. Wizards, merchants, priests
. . . kings come to the City, and they say that they would
rather be beggars in Byzantium than kings in their own
country. . . ."

Ptolemy talked on of the City Beautiful. Hywel listened,
dutifully at first, then willingly, then rapt, hearing of the
miles of triple walls, patrolled by men in armor of ham-
mered gold, pierced by seven times seven gates plus one,
but never the engines of an enemy army. There were
armies within, of gladiators, who fought at an arena in the
Roman style but larger than any in Rome.

Byzantium's wide streets met at forums set with columns of porphyry and ivory and gold, passed beneath
arches proclaiming the greatness and wisdom of the City
and its builders, wound into bazaars at which all the fruits
of Earth and the crafts of Man could be purchased, with
coins that British and Chinese, Slav and African, German
and Portuguese and Dane all accepted as true currency
. . . and for which all their traders brought goods to the
gates and the seven walled harbors.

Stone-arched aqueducts brought pure water to the City.
Manmade tunnels carried its waste away. In Byzantium
were more palaces than most cities had temples, and more
temples than cities had houses. And at the heart of the
conurbation, glory among glories, stood the Pantheon
Kyklos Sophia, the Circle of Wisdom.

"Its dome could cover any temple in Britain; it reaches

to the sky, the stars. It contains the stars: a thousand lanterns of gold, each one the sacred light of a different deity. To enter it is itself worship."

"Who is your god?" Hywel said, nearly whispering.

"The same as the builders of Kyklos Sophia worshiped. The perfection of the curve. The meeting of the stones. Time and energy and precision; those are the wizard's true gods, though I daresay we find others more convenient to curse by."

Hywel's thoughts were drawn suddenly back. "Teach me about magic."

Ptolemy sighed. "They are taking me to Eboracum . . . your York, where there is a Pantheon, to kill me. Perhaps York will cause me to think of the City before I die."

"You said you would teach me."

"I said that I would tell you all I know."

Hywel nodded.

"Magic destroys," Ptolemy said. "Every spell, enchantment, effect, ruins the worker a little more. If you are strong-willed, the wrecking takes a little longer . . . but it happens in the end, just the same."

Ptolemy was silent. Hywel waited, suddenly fearing Ptolemy would say what indeed he did: "That is all I know."

Hywel trembled. This time there was no difficulty in hating. He looked at the chains. Ptolemy's eyes shut tight and his face went white.

Hywel felt a rumbling, not physical but mental. He stared at the iron wrapping Ptolemy's chest. His eyes felt hot. He moved his hands, fingers curling.

The chain clinked and slithered tight, squeezing the wizard's chest. Little creases formed in his shirt and gown, like cracks.

Hywel gaped. His fingers tightened. So did Ptolemy's chains, without the touch of hands.

Ptolemy's head turned. "If you kill me—" Then his air ran out.

Hywel relaxed his fingers. The chain slackened. Ptolemy gulped a breath.

Hywel's head hurt. His limbs felt weak, limp, and his heart beat fast, as if he had been running very hard. He tried to stand, but his legs only flopped on the straw. He knew that Ptolemy would kill him now; still, he tried to crawl away with arms that were soft tallow.

I will not hurt you, novice, said the voice inside his head. *Your strength will return. This is your first lesson.*

Hywel turned back to Ptolemy, who sat back, head cocked to one side, eyes dark and very deep.

"Time and energy," Ptolemy said quietly, "never energy alone. Spirit is to matter at . . . I've forgotten the numbers; some astounding ratio. You cannot push down a stone wall with your hands . . . but if you will wait, find the keystone of the wall, the effort you can make will produce the result you want. So with magic. And the stones, falling, will crush something. So with magic.

"Can you walk now, Hywel?"

Hywel found that he could.

"Then good night . . . novice."

Hywel staggered from the barn without taking the plate or lantern. He looked back once at Ptolemy; the wizard was smiling at him, teeth bare and white, and there was nothing like love in the look.

Dafydd and Nansi were in the kitchen when Hywel came in; the room was lit poorly by a tallow-dip. Dafydd was drinking from a glass goblet; Hywel could smell the strong brandy.

Nansi said, "You ought be in bed."

"I did . . ." Hywel was unsteady, as when he drank too much beer. "I did a magic."

"The Bezant?" Dafydd said, and Hywel saw his hand tighten on the glass, as if he might throw it.

"I did. I'm a . . . wizard."

Dafydd tensed further. Nansi touched his wrist, and he relaxed . . . no, collapsed, as if he were dying right there in his chair. "Your uncle," he said weakly.

"My . . . uncle was a wizard?" Dafydd had not ever spoken on Hywel's ancestors, except to say they were all dead fighting.

Nansi said "Your grandmother was Owain Glyn Dŵr's sister." Just like that. Just as if it were nothing at all.

"Listen, Hywel . . . son," Dafydd said, in a thick, tired voice. "Glyn Dŵr allied with the Bezants. They sent wizards, soldiers. They said they'd help Owain make Wales free. He trusted 'em . . . and Owain's trust wasn't earned light, I know."

He drank more brandy. "I don't know if they ever meant to help . . . or if they did, but turned their coats . . . or if they just honest lost; but the fact is, they aided Owain. And Owain's gone. And that Empire's surely not.

"Ogmius choke me if I offer love to English soldiers, Sucellus break my head if I bow to an English king . . . but if they want to cut off that wizard's head they can have my axe and Esus bless the blow."

Hywel was in no danger of tears this time, tired as he was; now at last he knew whom he could trust.

No one; no one at all.

Without another word, he went to his bed, sat down on it and pulled off his boots, and toppled over asleep.

Serpents coiled around Hywel, tightening around his arms and legs, trying to drag him down and crush the life from him.

There was a sword in his hand; a white sword that shone in the enveloping darkness. The snakes drew their fanged heads back from the light, an instant before Hywel severed those heads with a stroke.

Chop, swish, and his left foot was free; slash, his right. Short strokes, as at a kidney for pie, and bits of snake fell wriggling from his left arm. But still they hung on his sword arm, squeezing the blood out, scales scraping the flesh.

Light sparked from a dagger hilt at Hywel's belt. He drew it with his left hand. His right arm was a writhing mass of knotted green. He put in the knife and skinned them off like skinning a hare, not even creasing his bare arm beneath.

There was a tug at his neck. The largest snake yet, a

green and black monster yards long, had wrapped itself
around Hywel's throat. The sleek head came around, staring with black eyes into Hywel's, showing fangs like
curved daggers. A drop of venom, red as blood and boiling,
fell from each fang.

Hywel brought up sword and knife at once, catching the
serpent's head where the steels crossed. The coil tightened. Hywel felt his eyes bulge, his air stop. He levered the
two blades. Smoking blood ran down to his hands and
burned them. The snake's half-severed head turned sidewise, flicked its two-pointed tongue to brush Hywel's lips.

A bone cracked and the head flew off. Its body spasmed,
crushing Hywel's throat, and he thought they would die
together—then he dropped the blades and pulled at the
suddenly limp coils, and was free—

Hywel awoke soaked with cold sweat. His arms were
flung out on the bed; they moved, but slowly, without
strength. He put a hand to his crotch; no, not that. He felt
as if he had been swimming, buoyed by the water until his
muscles had forgotten how to work. . . .

As he had felt after the magic.

He tried to get up, and could not, and was afraid; the
harder he tried, the less he did, the more afraid he became. He had seen horses ridden to death: sodden with foam,
on the ground trembling and heaving, beautiful horses
turned in one heedless ride to grunting dying *things* with
something terrible in their eyes.

Somehow he tugged his boots on, got to his feet. The
world floated and spun and screamed in his ears.

Some of the lights and noise, he knew after a moment,
were real: torches and the shouts of soldiers in the innyard.

Dafydd came in, in shirt and hose, carrying a fish-oil
lamp that guttered and stank. "You are here," he said unevenly. "Well, then, that's something."

"What . . . ?"

"The wizard's gone. Broke loose somehow." Dafydd
looked Hywel up and down, and his voice fell. "Did you
free him?"

"No," Hywel said, and as he spoke knew that he had lied.

Dafydd nodded. "No, of course. I'm sorry, son. I've been—"

Afraid, Hywel thought.

"Your uncle Owain was . . ." Dafydd did not finish that sentence either. He wiped his free hand on his shirttail and walked out.

Hywel waited, listening for the innkeeper's steps to die away. Then he began stuffing his pouch with things from his keep-box. He put on his best cloak and went, softly, softly, down to the innyard.

The serjeant was shouting, trying to form his men and decide on a pattern of search. Lanterns bobbed and metal shone yellowly. The men stamped and breathed fog in the chill night air. Hywel pulled his cloak around himself and sidled past unseen.

He was not certain himself how to find Ptolemy. Up to the mountains, or down to the river, or along the roads, hiding at the roadside when anyone passed? He held very still.

Along the valley, he thought, *to Aberconwy and the sea. A ship, however I can, but a ship out of this vile country—*

Hywel blinked; it was not his thought, though it had been in his head.

"Like the light from a candle," Hywel said silently, and swallowed a burst of giggles. He knew this part of Dyffryn Conwy better than any English soldiers. And he would find Ptolemy. He would follow the talent.

Hywel was cold very soon. His wet clothes were icy and stiff, and every breeze froze him again. The ground he had been so sure of was another country by night, the moon-shadows black consuming voids. He had no lantern, no fire. Only Ptolemy's candle-light.

If he was very calm, and thought very hard, it seemed he could see it as a light, dancing slowly above the bushes and stones ahead. *Fairy fire,* Hywel thought, and then very clearly thought that he followed fairy fire, and when he returned, years would have gone by; everyone he knew here would be long dead. But he would come back a wizard.

He was sorry that he would never see Nansi and Dafydd, Dai and Glynis and Annie, ever again. He put a hand on his bulging pouch, and was sorry he could not have taken more things with him; the tin plate that Siôn Mawr had stamped with Hywel's name, the woolen sweater and scarf Annie had made him when Nasi taught her to knit—lopsided but warm; he wanted them very much just now. The innyard dog would have been good company, worthless old hound that he was.

But you had to give things up. Like the offerings you put on the altar, when you wanted Ogmius to help with your letters or Esus to bless the wood you cut: you could not have those back again. If you cheated the gods they would hate you, and curse you forever.

And in all the stories, wizards and heroes had to be—had to be—

Shriven. That was the word. Hywel thanked Ogmius for it. Then he stopped, took Meredydd ap Owain's glass marble from his pouch. He made a hole in the ground with his thumb, dropped in the marble, covered it over. Hywel was certain the offering was proper, remembering the story of the Greek who talked with a mouthful of marbles.

The light, or voice, or whatever it was he was following, was growing stronger. Kallian Ptolemy seemed to have stopped moving. The wizard might have fallen, been hurt. Hywel didn't know what he would do in that event, unless Ptolemy's magic could heal. Surely it could; old village women could do that much! And maybe—though he hardly dared think it—maybe Ptolemy had paused to let Hywel catch up.

"Yes," said Ptolemy's voice, right out loud and just ahead, "I am waiting. Hurry along, Hywel ap Owain."

Startled by the voice, and the name Ptolemy had called him, Hywel scrambled on, to a small cleft in the hillside. There, against a rock, sat Ptolemy in moonlight.

"Did you bring me late supper, boy?" Ptolemy said. He spoke Cymric, for the first time.

Hywel came close, knelt. "Please, sir . . . I came to follow you. To Contantine's City, if you go there. To be your student."

"That's absurd," Ptolemy said flatly.

"My lord sir," said Hywel, trying to be defiant and respectful at once, "you said I could be a wizard. I wish to be."

"Why? Because the life attracts you? The romance, the adventure? The chains and the filthy straw, and the soldiers' spit in your face?" Ptolemy looked at the ground, shook his head. "They do not worship Thoth in Ireland; perhaps he does not go there. He deserted me, certainly." The wizard stared at Hywel, his face half-lit. "I went there for the purposes of the Empire. But I ate their food, and drank their whiskey, and lived in their houses, and slept with any number of their women . . . and then one day I found I was fighting their war. In time I cared for those . . . barbarians . . . so much that I actually ceased to do any magics that might injure them . . . which meant, any magics at all. . . . And soon enough the English soldiers put the iron on me. You don't understand a word of what I'm saying, do you, boy?"

Hywel crawled closer. "I set you free, my lord Ptolemy."

"I had my fill of that phrase in Ireland," Ptolemy said. "If you ever reach Byzantium, do not as you value— oh, whatever you call freedom—let them hear you say that. . . . To free someone, you see, is the ultimate human act. And in the City they know the difference between actors and directors. It is the Empire's heart and brain, that difference. This country is full of actors, I know very well; and did one of them move to aid me, any more than Thoth whom I worshiped?"

"Bezants like you . . . here, my lord sir?" Hywel thought about what Dafydd had said, about Glyn Dŵr and the Byzantines.

"Why, this is Britain, isn't it, and not a part of Byzantium? So of course they're here, to change that. As I was in Ireland, until I was no longer of use to my directors."

"If you won't teach me, sir, at least take me to the City with you. I set you free—"

"Of course there's no use," Ptolemy said wearily. "You aren't enough aware that you have a soul to understand a threat to it. And if you were, you still couldn't leave the power alone. I wonder if there's any power any human can leave alone. Old Claudius tried to refuse godhood, and failed. . . ."

Ptolemy rested his head in his hands for just a moment. "Ah, there's no use. If I'd changed in Ireland, I'd never even have called you. Just let them throw me in the sea, and blessed them as I sank. And that crude bowman was right; you're a tempting boy. Come here, novice."

Hywel got up. Ptolemy stood as he approached. The wizard's face went wholly into shadow as he turned and put a hand around the back of Hywel's neck. He spoke in clear and perfect Cymric.

"Will you, Hywel Peredur ap Owain, swear by every god you honor and fear that you will concentrate upon the lessons I give you, that you will take the meaning of each lesson fully, forgetting it never?"

"I swear," Hywel said, hearing himself very shrill.

Ptolemy's voice went cold and dead. "Then here is your lesson in the nature of sorcery, and wizards, and the truth about every magic that is done."

The grip on Hywel's neck tightened painfully. Hywel tried to turn, but could not move at all. The end of Ptolemy's forefinger glowed in the darkness, red and hot as a poker in the fire. Hywel's eyes went wide, and he was as helpless to close them as in a dream.

The burning finger pierced his eye, hissing like a snake when it strikes.

Chapter 2
GAUL

DIMITRIOS Ducas was ten years old when the Emperor of Byzantium made Dimi's father the governor of a province on the frontier. The day was carved into Dimi's memory forever: the clear sunlight outside the family villa, the blueness of the Aegean below, breeze scented by sea and olive groves.

His father had let him touch the Imperial order, and he remembered the authority and weight of the paper, the red wax seal on a ribbon of purple silk. The seal smelled of cinnamon, and showed the Emperor with a big nose and tiny eyes (though perhaps the wax had not properly filled the seal) and the Year of the City: 1135.

There was another seal, much smaller, in golden wax, imprinted with a three-pointed thing Dimi's father said was the flower of Gaul, and the inscription 300TH YEAR OF PARTITION.

Most of all Dimitrios remembered his parents. His father Cosmas stood in the slanting light of the atrium, his casual gown worn loose, looking like Apollo. "I am to be a *strategos* in the West. It is an honor. The province is an important one; the eastern part of the old *Provincia Lugudunensis,* which the Gauls call *Burgundy.* Our capital"—he looked straight at Dimi—"will be Alesia."

If Cosmas Ducas was Apollo, then Dimi's mother Iphigenia was surely Hera. *"Gaul?* How can you call that an

honor, when you know very well what it is? The Paleologi
Emperors are still afraid of the Ducai; to steal the Throne
of the World from our line was never enough for them.
Now they're purging their righteous fears, by purging *us*—
sending us to die of cold and isolation. If we're not murdered by trousered barbarians, or stricken with a plague
. . . We're being sent away, never to return!"

"If that is my Emperor's order," Cosmas said.

"Emperor? Usurper! You are more an Emperor than
he—you, Ducas. . . ."

The argument went on for a long time; Dimitrios recalled it as lasting hours, though perhaps his memory
stretched that. *Alesia*, he had thought, *Julius Caesar*. . . .

And in the end, both Cosmas and Iphigenia were proven
right, in their ways. The family Ducas went to Gaul; and
no one bearing that name ever returned to Greece.

Dimitrios was first over the hill. He shot a glance back,
making sure the others could not see him, then bent his
head on his horse's neck and talked her to a canter.

There are times when you must use the spurs, son,
Cosmas Ducas said, *but remember, you lead with your voice
and your body, not the metal.*

Dimi was well down the valley before his companions
topped the rise; he heard their shouts, their horses' pro-
tests, then finally the rumble of hooves far behind. He
laughed and whispered to white Luna beneath him, "We'll
feed them a little dust before supper, won't we, girl."

To either side of him, endless ranks of green vines on
wooden arbors flashed past. The smallholders were out,
wooden-shod, broad-brimmed hats shading their faces. A
few bowed as the Governor's son rode by, dazzling in his
armor of bright steel scales.

Dimi heard another horse, closer behind than it should
have been. He looked back; a dapple gray was gaining on
him. The rider had streaming black hair and a grin visible
across the distance.

Dimitrios laughed and waved. Charles, of course. Only
Charles could have come so close to catching him.

"But no closer, eh, Luna," Dimi said. "The gallop, now, girl."

Luna responded, swift as a white cloud aross the wide blue sky.

The dirt road met the Imperial road just ahead. "Enough, Luna." Dimi knew better than to drive a horse too hard, and he also knew better than to gallop down an Imperial road, scattering the common traffic, without a very good reason.

Luna slowed to a walk just as her hooves hit the paving stones. Then Dimi heard hoofbeats to his left and rear, and turned in the saddle.

Charles bore down on him, standing in the stirrups. Dimi shouted, Luna stepped sidewise; the Frenchman brought his horse around at an amazingly acute angle. Then he leaped.

Dimitrios let himself be taken down, and the two of them rolled in the dust at the roadside. As Charles tried to pin his shoulders, Dimi got a toe hooked behind Charles's knee, put out his other leg for leverage, and flipped them both over; he put his knee on Charles's chest and drew his thumbnail swiftly across the other youth's throat.

Charles panted, then laughed. *"Ave, Caesar,"* he said, *"morituri salutandum."*

"You're *already* dead," Dimi said, and then he was laughing too. He stood, pulling Charles up with him, and they knocked dust from each other's clothing as their horses looked on.

The others, all of them boys of Dimi's age, rode up shortly: tall thin Robert, noisy Jean-Luc, and quiet León; the Rémy twins, dissimilar as twins could be—Alain, hairy and bearish, and Michel, small and acrobatic as a circus dwarf. They wore linen shirts and leather vests like Charles's, and sashes of purple silk Dimitrios had filched from his mother's sewing; they were his Praetorians, his *cohors equitata.* "Who won?" Jean asked, in French. "If not for Dimi's armor, we couldn't have told you apart at all."

"And it was all dusty," Robert added.

Charles said "The race, I won."

"Like a Cantabrian!" they all shouted, Dimi as well.

"The fight, Dimitrios won." .

"Like a Caesar!"

Charles and Dimi remounted, and the cohort rode up the Imperial road to town, through the Ozerain valley. Ahead of them rose the Plateau d'Alise, thirteen hundred feet high, the lesser hills around it faded in the summer haze. Sun flashed from the heliostat atop the plateau, new Empire built on the site of old Empire's triumph. For this was Alesia, where Vercingetorix had stood for the last time against the divine Julius. To Dimi's left was Mont Réa, where Julius had himself ridden to the relief of his cohorts, his bodyguard behind him . . . just as Dimitrios rode now.

They reached the town wall, slowing their horses to a walk at the gate. The men at the gate wore bronze dress armor and scarlet cloaks, and carried gilded spears with eagles as cross guards; they saluted the Governor's son, and he and his fellows drew up straight in their saddles, trooping by.

They passed trim houses of wood and whitewashed clay, sloped roofs shingeld with wood, or tile, or even lead, for Alesia prospered; the two wealthiest vintners in town and the Jewish banker were rebuilding in stone from Narbo to the south—*Lyon,* as the French called it. The streets were broad enough for two carts to pass without crowding a pedestrian to each side, and had gutters that drained down to vaulted sewers underground. There were smells of cooking, and sawdust and stone dust, and now of sweating horses, but none of the latrine stinks of the little provincial villages.

Smoke rose in white feathers from pottery chimneys. Along the roof peaks were set barrels and troughs of water, an idea of one of Cosmas Ducas's engineers. Should a fire start, and burn through the roof, the water would fall on the blaze and drown it. The tests with models were disappointing, but someone pointed out that the little house was more rapidly consumed by flame than a real one, and the model barrel contained vastly less water—the cube root of its dimension. After the engineer had proposed the construction and burning of a real house, the Governor let him put his barrels on the rooftops of consenting citizens, to wait for empirical proof.

Jean-Luc reined in as the party passed his house. *"Ave atque vale,"* he said, and the others hailed him farewell. One by one—two, counting the Rémys—they separated, until at the base of the Mont-Alise slope, the gates to the Governor's Palace, only Dimitrios and Charles were left.

"I know we passed your house," Dimi said, trying to sound careless.

"I want you to ask your father," Charles said. "I want you to ask him today, Dimi."

"Why today? December's half a year off. . . ."

"Don't you want to ask him?" Charles was not laughing now, nor even smiling.

"Of course." *What I don't want,* Dimi thought, *is to hear him say no; and until I ask him, he can't say no.* He looked up at the sun, and prayed directly that his fear did not show. "Come with me, then."

"What? No, I—I'll see you tomorrow." And Charles clucked to his dappled horse, turned, and rode off down the street at an unlawful speed.

Then Dimitrios knew that his friend was just as afraid as he was, and somehow that made everything—even the refusal itself—all right in Dimi's mind. He rode through the palace gates, to find his father.

Dimi's mother was in the front hall, the tall windows open to admit light on samples of carpet that lay all around. When Dimi came in, Iphigenia Ducas was in conversation with a merchant; the man wore silk hose and a liripipe hat piled up on his head, and his accent was Portuguese. The household's interpreter stood a little behind his mistress, listening patiently.

Dimitrios waited for a pause. He wondered if the trader knew anything of the new lands the Portuguese Empire had discovered beyond the Western Sea; but of course it would be rude to ask. Or at least his mother would call it that. Finally he said "Where's Father?"

"At the construction—what have you been *doing?*"

"Riding, Mother."

"Riding through what, the city sewers?" Iphigenia narrowed her eyes, and Dimi knew what was coming next. "With those . . . Gauls, I suppose."

Frenchmen, Mother, Dimi thought, but there was no point in saying anything.

"I wish you'd spend more time with the *Roman* boys. You're their natural leader, you know; they respect you. Those Gauls are just seeking advancement, favors."

She had it just backwards, of course. "The Imperials are all clerks' sons, growing up to be clerks"—Dimi watched his mother's face—"and eunuchs."

That did it; it was the one point that stopped all argument with Iphigenia. A eunuch could rise to any office or honor in the Empire, except one; could hold any title but Emperor. And many noble fathers castrated their sons for their future security, since the Emperor then need not fear them as usurpers.

But usurpation—always called "restoration"—had obsessed the family Ducas since the last Ducas emperor was deposed over three centuries ago. Iphigenia Ducas could have kept her own respectable family name when she married, but she had bound herself fully to a dream. To mention the cutting to her, or to Dimi's uncle Philip, was to remind them that dreams could die.

There was a silence. Iphigenia's nails picked at the swatch of Persian carpet in her lap. The Portuguese trader was politely deaf and mute. The interpreter, himself a eunuch, stood calm, a faint smile on his babyish face.

"Pardon me, Mother; and you, sir." Dimitrios stepped back.

"You'll bathe before dinner."

"Of course, Mother." He went out.

Above the old palace, a new one was rising: higher, greater, grander in every respect, and more Byzantine, complexly vaulted and buttressed, than the plain lines of the old house. A legion of workmen moved on the face of the hill digging and conveying and stacking and truing. Sawdust and lime mortar mingled in the air.

Cosmas Ducas stood near a partial wall, talking with his chief military engineer; his hands moved as he spoke, tracing palace in the air. Both men wore white capes, breastplates, and high greaves, all very dusty; they had plain steel caps with cloth to shade the neck. Cosmas turned, and Dimi saw the flash of the Imperial eagle inlaid in gold on his chest.

"Father!"

"Come up, son!" Dimitrios climbed the embankment.

"Well, Tertullian," Cosmas Ducas said to the engineer, "what do you think of him?"

Tertullian was broader than Cosmas, big-muscled, not as tall. "I'd have him as a captain, when he's . . ." Dimi did not need to guess the rest of the sentence. It was the same reason he was here.

"Bull's blood, Tully, I know that. So would Caractacus. What I want to know is, would he be a better captain of engineers, or of horse?"

Tertullian paused, though he did not fidget. "I hear his numbers are good. And as many times as I've chased him off this site, it's clear he can handle himself around works without getting killed."

Cosmas crossed his bare arms across the golden eagle. He nodded slowly, looking straight at his son. Part of Dimi rebelled at this, almost angry at being discussed as the men might discuss a yearling colt or a marriageable woman; but another part knew that he could follow any of his father's knights in any art of war, and he was fiercely proud that Cosmas Ducas knew it.

Tertullian said, "I've only one qualm, General."

Cosmas stopped nodding, but that was all that changed. "Yes?"

"Siegework's slow going, General. Even cannon peck slow at the walls they're building now. Looking at the boy just now, I wonder if he's got the patience for contravallations and latrines."

Cosmas laughed, loud enough to turn heads among the

workers. "By my brand, Tully, now I know why engineers are rarer than generals, and prized higher.

"Come here, Dimi. It seems you may be doomed to be a general after all. Look, down from here. This will be the Governor's office, right where we're standing; there'll be a big window, with just this view."

It was a glorious view of the town, the meeting of three valleys, the plains rich with vineyards; and it was a clever location too, on the western point of the plateau. A window here would not weaken the palace defenses, unless the attacker could fly.

"Now, son. What's your news?"

Dimi turned back to his father. Tertullian stood silent to the rear. "I want to ask about . . ." *Don't look away, don't look at your toes. Say it now.* ". . . the initiations. Into the Mysteries."

"Dimi, the Emperor himself can't bring December any sooner."

"Lord remind him of that," Tertullian said softly.

Dimitrios shook his head. "I want . . . that is, Charles wants to be initiated. To become a Raven, with me."

Cosmas looked serious. "Is this Charles's idea, or yours?" Comas said the name properly—*Sharl,* not *Karolus* as the other Imperials pronounced it.

"His, sir."

"And do his people worship Mithras, or Cybele?"

"No, sir. Charles says they do not worship much at all, except a goddess called Sequana, when they are sick. And the divine Julius, and Claudius too."

"May I speak, Lion?" Tertullian said.

Cosmas said "I hear you, Persian." Dimi was puzzled for just a moment, because the engineer was of course not from Persia; then he realized that they had used the titles of the fourth and fifth ranks of the Mysteries, *Leo* and *Perses.* Dimitrios was startled to hear that Tertullian outranked his father, but he hoped he did not show it.

Tertullian said "Our Lord sees a man's heart, not his nation. The Mysteries are for those brave enough."

"I know that," Cosmas said. "And I also know . . ." He

put his hand on Dimi's shoulder, gently, firmly. Dimi could see the sacred brand on his wrist, put there when Cosmas had reached the third rank of the Mysteries. "Do you understand, son, that the Empire has ruled these people since the divine Julius?"

"Of course, Father."

"And do you understand how the Empire rules, when it is not of the population ruled?"

Dimi knew the words from his lessons. Now, for the first time, they began to mean something, and he did not think he liked the meaning. "We rule because we force nothing but the law. None need worship our gods, speak our languages, adopt our ways, even walk our roads, given only that they obey the law."

Cosmas nodded. "And what is the first among Imperial laws?"

"The Doctrine of Julian the Wise: All faiths are equal: no faith shall forbid another, nor shall the Empire champion any faith."

Cosmas said, "And here, I *am* the Empire; and as my son, so are you. If Charles abandons his people's religion for ours, they will say we beguiled him, or perhaps even forced him, to do it. That is how rebellion begins. . . We say we rule from Julius's time, but it is not true. When Western Rome fell to the invaders, we lost these people. It was centuries before New Rome recovered the lands, with the help of the English King. And even after we had the lands again, we had to win the people again. Do you understand?"

"Yes," Dimi said, and supposed that in fact he did. And he also began to understand something of his father's office.

Tertullian spoke, without any note of criticism. "And does the young Gaul live without Mithras, then, for the sake of appearances?"

"For the sake of the Empire, perhaps," said Cosmas, calmly.

"If he were my son's friend—"

"If you had a son, and he had a friend, I would most hap-
pily see him come to us, and be tested to the Mysteries."

Dimi was confused. He had stopped being afraid of the
denial—and also ceased believing a denial was possible.
Now he wondered what else he might be about to lose.
"Father—are you saying—the law is not the same for all?"

Cosmas looked very hard for a moment, then very sad.
"No, son. The law is equal for all. But duty is not."

For a long moment the two men and the boy stood silent,
removed from the motion around them. Then Cosmas took
his hand from Dimi's shoulder, with an awkward pat, and
went away with Tertullian.

Dimitrios looked westward from the hill, saw rainclouds
approaching. After four years in this country he had come
to love its frequent rains, and especially that miraculous
winter rain called snow. But now the breeze that led the
rain was a change wind, a voice telling him that from now
on, nothing would be as it had been.

Dinner that evening was unpleasantly tense. Dimi said
nothing, supposing he had said too much already today.
Cosmas gave only the smallest comments, and seemed
somewhere far away. Iphigenia talked a bit about the car-
pets she had purchased, but no one else was interested and
she soon stopped. Zoë and Livia, Dimi's little sisters, knew
better than to speak in such an atmosphere.

That left the forum open to Cosmas's brother Philip,
which was worse than all the silences put together. Iphigenia Ducas had a dream of the Imperial throne; Philip
Ducas had a vision. Sometimes he literally had visions,
falling to the floor chewing his tongue.

Many years ago, Cosmas had told Dimi, Philip was a
fine captain of cavalry; but he had fallen from his horse
and struck his head. Now he talked in circles and crooked
paths. For some years he had worn togas instead of decent
gowns and hose, but no one minded because the togas were
easier to clean.

If Fortune was a goddess, as some said, then there was
no defying her. And Philip would always be Cosmas's elder

brother. And (Dimi's father would add, in a different voice) it was well recorded, in Rome and the City and even in Gaul and Britain, that the divine Emperor Julius had himself had a falling sickness.

But sometimes Philip was awful.

"And then I said, ho, you Paleologue, twice presumptuous, I call you, first to the name of divine Constantine, then to the title Emperor—ho, Paleologus, *Dipleonektis,* you think you have done for the Ducai, don't you, making them kings of the Gaulish mud." Rain spattered the narrow windows, and the lights wavered. Philip's eyes went wide, then he went on: "But seed put living into soil takes root, yes, and vines grow long, and you watch that a vine does not crawl across your bed of stolen purple, Paleologus Usurper, and twine round your crooked neck.

"All this I said. Would have said, had I been there. Oh, Cosmas, brother, youth, why did you not take me with you to confront the creature in his marble lair?"

Philip was looking directly at Dimitrios. Dimi said nothing. He was beginning to wonder if there was any use in speaking to any of his family.

"That is enough, brother," Cosmas said levelly. "Enough of strangling Emperors, enough of stealing the purple."

It had no effect. It never did. But Dimi remembered his father saying that at certain times one must charge regardless, even uphill.

"Ah, you can't fool me, Cosmas, young brother!" Philip slapped his half-bare thigh and rolled on his couch, so that Dimi was afraid he was about to have a fit again. "Philip's bold, but Cosmas is clever, just as our mother said! He'll catch the Paleologi napping in their false-dyed silk, and with his son, Digenes—"

Dimi sat up on his dining couch, told a servant to clear his place. He spoke French; the dinner servants were discharged if they showed any sign of understanding Greek or Latin. "Excuse me, Father?"

Cosmas nodded grimly. Iphigenia looked distracted. Philip noticed nothing. Dimitrios pushed his feet into leather pattens and walked out of the dining room, as silently, as invisibly, as he could.

The corridors were dim, and the skylights rattled with rain. Dimi passed a fresco of Caesar's defeat of Vercingetorix, the pigments a dozen times renewed. Farther on was a tapestry depicting the Partition of Gaul, the Emperor Manuel the Comnene and King Henry II of Britain dividing the country from North Sea to Mediterranean, three hundred and four hundred years ago.

Dimitrios did not understand how a war could end like that, with a streak drawn across a map. England was such a little country; how could it have stood against the Empire, had only Manuel chosen to send the Legions?

There had been Legions in Britain during the Old Empire, Dimi knew. The Divine Julius of the fresco had led them. There had been a Caesar of the Narrow Seas, when the Legions and not the lawyers were the Empire's strength.

Dimi's mother had already chosen a place in the new palace for the Partition tapestry, but the engineers believed the fresco was too old and fragile to be moved. Dimitrios thought that he would have to come back here occasionally, after they all lived up the hill, to see the painted Caesar.

Victories of the New Empire, he thought, running a hand across the tapestry fabric, nails picking at the threads. *Clerks' victories. Lawyers' victories. But I will remember thee, O Caesar.*

Perhaps there would even be a Caesar—or a *strategos*—of the Narrow Seas once again. If his father was right, if he was destined to be a general . . . But that was too much to quite imagine, on a bellyful of dinner and the aftertaste of Uncle Philip.

A light was burning in the next room, the library. Dimi knew it must be Lucian, his father's deputy administrator; still, for some reason, or no reason, he slipped his feet from the leather sandals and walked on hose, silent, into the room.

Lucian sat on a high stool before a sloped desk, his white

gown bunched up in his lap. At his elbow was a rack of pens and inkwells, and a stone to grind the points. A lensatic lamp threw bright light on his writing, and his eyes were intent behind lenses of their own. A black ribbon tied the eyeglasses around his head.

Dimi knew he must be silent now. A noise, making Lucian blot a word or twist a letter, and he'd be wishing he'd heard out Uncle Philip.

Lucian was an Egyptian, with doctorates from the University at Alexandria; it was customary for a *strategos* to have a civilian as deputy. His real name sounded odd in Greek—"like an obscenity," he said—and he had changed it. He was brown, and dry as a stick, and the thinnest eunuch Dimitrios had ever seen; he didn't seem ever to eat, and drank boiled herbs instead of wine. His religion was a weirdly complicated thing called "Knowingism."

Dimi stood entirely still, watching Lucian's goose-quill stroke gracefully across the paper, forming the angular characters of the formal Byzantine alphabet, Cyril's alphabet. Dimi read, *A 14th Report to the University Authority. To Be Destroyed After Reading.*

I remind my lord that the theories of (the scribe's hand hid a part) *in the actual case; these are human beings, not ciphers. However, I believe*

Lucian's nose twitched. Lifting the pen carefully, he turned his head. "Good evening, Dimitrios." He smiled, his mouth a sharp V. "Did you require a book, or myself?"

"Neither, Lucian. I was just . . . walking. What are you writing?"

Lucian looked at the sheet, sighed, then reached to the top of the desk and rolled down a sheet to cover the work. "Another in an endless series of self-justifying explanations of myself, to people who demand but never understand them."

Dimitrios understood that sort of thing perfectly. "Lucian . . . why have there been so many emperors named Constantine? Isn't it . . . well, disrespectful to the Divine one?" It was a silly sort of question, Dimi knew, especially since the tenth Constantine had been a Ducas. But it kept him from asking the question he wanted—about the obligations of a frontier governor—and getting the answer that he very much supposed he did not want.

Lucian looked thoughtful. He had at times refused to answer Dimi's questions, or sent Dimi to his father for an answer, but he had never dismissed a question as childish or stupid. "I don't know if eleven Constantines in eleven centuries is so many. There have been a lot of Johns, too. But. You know that we have no law of Imperial succession; anyone who can get to the throne and stay there, whether by dynasty or force or inertia or . . . anything else . . . is the true Emperor. With a few exceptions." The eunuch looked at his lap.

"Yes. I know that." If there was anything Dimitrios knew much too well, that was it.

"And you can read in any book that the first Constantine died of old age, in the Imperial bed, with his eyes still in his head. Now, discounting his son Constantius, who could hardly help it, I suspect they were trying to bring back the better aspects of the Divine Founder's reign. Name-magic, if you will. That hardly seems disrespectful. Even if it did not help the Third Constantine, or the Sixth or the Seventh."

Dimitrios nodded. "Thank you, Lucian."

"Not at all, Dimitrios." They each had elaborate formal titles of address, but those had never been necessary in private.

Dimi turned to go.

"Dimitrios . . ." Dimi turned. The administrator sat perched on his stool like a skinny white bird. The lamp made stars of light in his eyeglasses. ". . . would be an entirely acceptable name for an Emperor."

Dimi nodded and went to his room, wondering if Lucian knew what had really been in his mind, when he himself was unsure.

"Down! *Vite!* Quick!"

Dimitrios dropped onto his chest at Charles's whisper,

at once wishing he wore his brigandine jacket; but the leather was lighter, easier to move in.

Beside Dimi, Charles slowly raised his head over the half-built wall they hid behind. "I think it's clear now. Ready?"

Dimi got to hands and knees. "Ready."

"Now, then," and they were over the wall, two moving shadows in the autumn afternoon.

Today the two of them were playing the Great Raid: the unfinished palace was a sorcerer's castle in Middle Africa, Dimi was Richard Lionheart, and Charles was Yusuf al-Nasir. Dimi had wanted to be the Eastern King, but Charles wouldn't be an Englishman, even a great Englishman.

The rest of the game was simple. The workmen were the black wizard's enchanted guards, who had basilisk eyes; if the Kings were spotted they were dead. The Governor's Office was the wizard's sanctum; if they could reach that alive, then good Damascus steel, the broadsword and the scimitar, would slay the fiend.

They moved down and across the slope, stepping over wooden falsework and discarded tools, freezing at the sound of a voice or a shadow across their path. A stairway had been left unguarded, and silently they descended, kings in soft-soled boots.

"Now, Yusuf my brother," Dimi whispered, "we must part, lest we be slain together this near our goal."

"Oui, Coeur-de-Lion." It was not Arabic, but that scarcely mattered now; and Charles's hair was dark enough for a Turk's, dark as Dimi's own. "Your hand, my brother of the West?"

Dimi took Charles's hand. They were really quite alike, he thought. Charles had been hurt by the denial of the Mysteries, but it had not separated them. Richard Lionheart worshipped Apollo, and Yusuf Sala-ud-Din was the bounty of Ormazd's faith, yet they had lived and warred and died together as brothers in glory.

Their hands parted and they moved off, Charles left, Dimi right.

Dimi crept along the wall. The ground was soft, and the smell of wet grass was sweet and strong. He flicked stone dust from beneath his fingernails.

Just ahead, the wall turned away from him, and the ground fell away. Around the corner would be the office's bay window. There was a small side window, just another step to the right. . . .

No, he thought, King Richard would not use side windows, like a thief. Dimi moved on around the corner, to the angle of the bay. A shape moved up ahead. Now, before the guard's eyes struck him dead. He put a hand on the sill and vaulted through the high opening.

Charles came through the other side of the bay in just the same fashion; the two of them landed on the bare floor within in the same ready crouch. They pointed fingers, said as one, "I thought you were—" and fell back laughing.

Charles sprang to his feet. "Ah, wizard of the black country, the Kings of East and West are come to end your vile reign! After you, *Coeur-de-Lion.*"

Dimi mimed drawing a broadsword. He paused. "Together."

Charles smiled, drew his curved sword. Dimi could see the patterned blade as clearly as he saw his own. "Now."

Dimitrios thrust to the vitals. Charles sliced off the head. They raised swords in salute, cleaned them on the sorcerer's cloak, and sheathed them, their tongues providing the snick of blade into scabbard.

Charles said *"Mon ami Coeur-de-Lion . . ."*

"Yes, O King of Jerusalem?"

"Don't wizards curse their killers?"

Dimitrios looked down at the imaginary corpse. "I'd forgotten about that. Maybe it's not true."

They heard voices, steps approaching.

"It's true," Dimi said.

"The window?"

"Maybe they'll go on past." The two boys moved a little toward the door, flattened themselves against the wall, and listened.

"It's my father," Dimi said. "And—"

"The wall's moving," said Charles.

Where they leaned, a stone panel, blended with the rest of the surface, swung away on hidden hinges.

Charles and Dimi looked at each other for barely a heartbeat before going through.

It was quite dark within. Dimi's foot moved back, felt no floor behind him; he put his hands against the wall to steady himself. Then his eyes began to adjust; there was a little light from narrow slits overhead. He saw a staircase leading down into darkness.

"A dungeon?" Charles whispered.

"I don't think so—the dungeons should be on the other side of the building. It could be . . . a Mithraeum."

"Then I shouldn't go down."

"Then neither should I. But we can't stay here. And besides, it can't be ready yet, whatever it is."

They descended, silently except for a faint shuffling and the rush of blood in their ears.

"I think it turns," Dimi said.

But it did not turn; the stairway ended in blank walls to all sides. "A trap," Charles said, breathless. "As the pyramid-builders made for robbers. Do you suppose stones fall to crush us, or smother . . . ?"

"There's light, and air," Dimi said, pointing at the slits in the ceiling. But pyramids made him think of Lucian, and he realized what else could come through those openings.

Above, there was a bright flare of lanternlight, and voices. The light washed the walls, dazzling the boys. Dimi heard his father's voice again, and that of Tertullian the engineer.

"What—" Cosmas said, echoing. "Tully, someone's down there."

"Sir?" Tertullian took a step, playing his lantern. He drew his shortsword and advanced down the steps.

Dimitrios felt as if he were choking as the two men came into view.

"What in the name of the Bull and the Dog," said Cosmas Ducas, "are you two doing in here?" There was something like anger in his voice, and something like bewilderment.

"I ordered Charles to come with me," Dimi said. "He's not responsible."

"Please, General sir, I am," said Charles, in excellent barracks Greek. "We are marching behind the same ass."

Dimitrios thought he was going to die. The Governor's eyebrows rose. Dimi said, "We didn't mean to be trapped"—Tertullian barked a laugh—"We'll go now, if you will please let us out."

Cosmas Ducas looked very stern, yet thoughtful, as Apollo must have looked when Hermes stole his cattle. Dimi only hoped they got away as lightly.

"Tertullian," Cosmas said, in a chilling voice, "this passage was to be our secret alone, was it not?"

"Till now it was, General."

Cosmas nodded slowly. "Tertullian . . . make sure they keep the secret."

"General." The engineer advanced on the boys, holding his sword straight out at waist height. Dimi looked at the blade, then at his father's face, and saw no pity in either.

Dimi stepped back and to the side, standing in front of Charles. *"Non,"* his friend said, and they stood side by side against the wall.

Tertullian's sword thrust into a crack in the stone wall. He lifted the blade, and there was a faint click from within the stones.

Another panel, like the one overhead, swung inward.

"Go on, Castor, Pollux," Cosmas said, laughing almost too hard to speak.

Charles and Dimi bowed slightly and dashed through the door, into an unfinished lower gallery, and out of the palace.

Not a word of what had happened was spoken over dinner, but Cosmas Ducas was voluble and pleased-looking, talking of plans for the winter and spring to come among the French. He called them that; not *Gauli* but *Franciscoi.* And the look that he gave to Dimitrios across the room was like the sun after a month of rain.

* * *

"The bull must die," said the voice in darkness.

Dimitrios stood entirely still, suppressing the urge to shiver. A strip of red silk had been wound around his eyes, blocking out every scrap of sight; then hands had stripped him, bound his hands behind his back with soft, tough gut. He was lifted, carried, put on his feet again, on cold stone . . . but where he was he did not know, except that they had gone down stairs. The places of the Mysteries were always subterranean.

"But who shall kill the bull?" another voice said. Dimi could not identify the voices, though he knew they must be men he knew; his concentration was hurt by trying to remain still, to keep his balance with his hands tied.

"Mithras," said the first voice. "Mithras is the friend to all cattle; he shall kill the bull."

"Shall he kill his friend?" said the second man. "He will not do it."

Heat bathed Dimitrios from all sides, flames thundering very close. He smelled sulfur and naphtha. Sweat started all over his body, the drops drying in moments, leaving the skin stiff. He was in the presence of the Sun.

"Mithras will kill the bull," said the voice of the Sun; the punishing heat seemed to pulse with the words. "For it is at my order, and he is a soldier who obeys. . . . Where is the Raven?"

"Here, O Sun," Dimitrios said, trying not to gulp the furnace air.

"You must take this order to Mithras, on the Earth below us," said the Sun. "He must slay the bull, for without a little death there can be no new life. Will you take this order?"

"I will."

"Then, Raven, spread your wings."

There was a touch of fire at Dimi's wrists, and his hands were freed. He raised his arms, arched them above his head.

"Raven, you are the lord of the upper air. Wings bear you truly, down to the Earth."

The fires went out with a *whoosh*. Then wind struck Dimitrios, cold air, burning cold.

He shifted a foot; his toes felt nothing but air blasting
upward. He spread his arms and moved with the currents,
not knowing how deep the void might be. The wind made
him deaf and dizzy, and the cold was worse than the fires
had been, drawing and searing his skin. Somewhere it was
December, he knew, somewhere above him in the ordinary
world.

The wind died down. Dimitrios felt himself swaying, but
he had lost all other orientation, even of one limb to another. *Hermes, you protect the Raven,* he thought, *aid me
now;* but in his ringing ears he heard only the laughter of
the trickster-god.

A hand touched his shoulder; a strong hand, a warrior's
hand, thick with the calluses a sword-hilt makes. "Raven,
I see you have come on a ray of light from the Sun himself;
why do you come to me?"

For a terrible, weak-kneed instant Dimi thought he
would not be able to speak, but the strength came. "You
are Mithras, and you must slay the bull."

The hand held firm. "Who says this? Are you a messenger of Ahriman, who would have the bull destroyed?"

"I bring orders from the Sun," Dimitrios said. "He says
the bull must die."

"Then it is done," said the voice of Mithras, and though
Dimi had been taught the legend well, still he was surprised by the anguish in the Lord's words.

The hand left Dimi's shoulder, and he stood for a moment again naked and alone. Then a robe was tossed over
his shoulders, his feet were guided into slippers. The cloth
was unwound from his eyes, and he blinked in firelight.

He stood at one end of a long vaulted hall, with a hearth
at each end and pillars down the sides; between the pillars,
the initiates reclined on couches, as if at dinner.

One group wore black belted gowns and black feathered
hoods with beaks shading their eyes. Two of these Ravens
stood by Dimitrios, tying his gown, lowering a beaked cowl
onto his head.

The Father stood nearby, in his red gown and curled Phrygian cap; he put a hand on the sickle in his belt and struck his staff on the floor. *"Chaīre, hieros corax!"* said the Father of all those gathered, and the brothers answered as one: "Hail, divine Raven!" The Ravens attending Dimitrios led him to a couch with the others, and the next initiation began.

Dimitrios watched the mechanisms in the dais with fascination: vents in the floor blew first Greek fire, then cold air, around the supplicant. The platform that had seemed so dizzyingly high was less than a handsbreadth from the floor when fully raised.

Two potential Ravens failed, one losing his balance during the passage of air, one fainting in the Sun's presence. The fires went out instantly as the boy toppled toward them. Both supplicants were picked up, still blindfolded, by two initiates of the third, Soldier, rank, and carried out without a word being spoken. They would have another chance in a year's time, if they so wished. The Mysteries were for those brave enough.

When all were admitted and seated, the sacred meal was served; the flesh of the slain bull, roasted on long daggers, and the bull's blood to drink, followed by a strong red wine.

It was the day of brotherhood, the day Mithras was born to bring new life to all men; the twenty-fifth of December, Year of the City 1139.

August, Year of the City 1140, 305th Year of Partition.

Cosmas Ducas stared at the bedroom ceiling with eyes that were dull as pebbles; his hair was matted and his cheeks were hollow, and the hand that clutched the sheet showed vein and bone right through the skin.

It was not possible, Dimitrios thought, even as he looked at the man in the bed; this could not be the Lion of Mithras, and Apollo was immortal.

But the doctors had been with Cosmas Ducas, and poked him and listened to his body sounds and stared for hours at vials of his fluids, and all they said was that the end would be soon. Dimitrios thought that, if there could be no recovery, he hoped they were right; and he hated himself for the thought.

There were spice-smelling candles lighted in the corners of the room day and night, warding against evil magic; charms hung at doors and windows to prevent the entry of killing spirits. Iphigenia had spent a fortune on the town apothecaries' entire stock of alicorn; a pinch went into all the food Cosmas ate, all the wine he drank. At that rate their supply would last a century. Dimitrios thought it was no wonder that one never saw a living unicorn, not at the price their horns brought in a poisonous world.

Last week a young man claiming to be a wizard had passed through Alesia; he promised a cure, for gold and the use of a servant girl in a midnight ritual. Cosmas's sickness did not cease. Caractacus's light cavalry caught the sorcerer and brought him back. He was still splashed with the girl's blood.

Just one month ago . . . the workmen were fitting glass to the new palace windows, Cosmas directing them from the side of the hill. Dimitrios was coming down the slope, and called to his father; Cosmas turned . . . and held his head . . . and sank down, down, kneeling to some Invisible. . . .

They thought it was just a touch of sun, the Governor working too long, dressed too closely in the summer day. But he could not speak. Shortly he could not stand, and then not sit up. Now only his eyes could move, and when Dimitrios saw them staring at him he felt something was being demanded of him.

There was a scream outside. Dimi looked out the window; two soldiers were dragging the wizard away from where Tertullian stood, holding a fire-heated dagger. One more person who would never be Emperor of Byzantium.

Dimitrios went out of the room just as his mother came in. She led his sisters. Zoë carried a little tambourine, Livia a silver cymbal, and Dimi knew they had come from the temple of Cybele. He hoped something had been said for the servant girl's soul.

Out in the hall, alone, he reached within his shirt,

touched the silver medallion that hung around his neck; he felt the Raven and Caduceus. The disc felt cold, as if it were only a piece of metal. Mithras was eternal, they said, and all who worshipped Him were touched with eternity. Last December, in fire and air, there had seemed to be such a thing as eternity; now it was August, in damp heat and the smell of sickness, and if Cosmas Ducas was dying then so could any other god.

Dimi went downstairs, looked in the library for Lucian. But Uncle Philip was there instead, going over the only two books Dimi had ever known him to read: Michael Psellus's *Chronographia*, with its glowing word-portraits of the Ducas Emperors Constantine X and Michael VII, and the epic poem *Digenes Akritas*, five hundred years old, in which the son of a Ducas woman and a Syrian king conquered armies of barbarians and founded a magical princedom on the Euphrates River.

Dimitrios went outside. A group of men was dismounting at the palace gates: French nobles from town. Some of them were his friends' fathers. Dimi looked around.

Sure enough, Charles and Jean-Luc and the Rémys and the rest were approaching; Dimi waved and walked to them. Somehow he didn't feel like running today. Perhaps it was the sun.

"Good day, *bonjour,* good to see you, men."

"Our fathers got the Governor's message," Alain Rémy said. "Is he much better, Dimi?"

Jean-Luc said "We made an offering to Sequana for him. All of us, together."

Dimitrios had no idea what to say. "You mean . . . a message came from Lucian."

"Not the deputy," Charles said. "I saw the letter, and it said 'Ducas, *strategos.'* The script was very shaky, but we knew of course that the Governor was sick."

"I don't . . . understand." Dimi turned back toward the house, trying to think. Cosmas Ducas could not lift a pen to sign his name, however shakily. Lucian had authority of his own. Who then would have presumed to the power, *pleonektis—*

Philip.

"Wait for me," Dimi said, and started toward the house. As he reached the steps, his mother came stumbling out the door, onto the portico. She clutched her cap in her hands, and her hair hung loose. Dimitrios ran to her, horrified. "Mother," he said, "come inside—where's Uncle Philip, Mother?"

"Busy," she said unevenly, "in men's affairs, with the trousered lords of Gaulish hell. . . . Are these your barbarian friends?" She had been crying, and was starting again. She did not smell of wine. "Ask them—" She raised her head, shouted "You! Gauls!" She pushed past Dimi, walking toward the boys; Dimi reached toward her but was afraid to touch her.

Iphigenia said loudly, "I want a vampire."

There was no movement at all. The dust in the air hung still, smelling of dung.

"Well, are you deaf? Do you not understand language? Dimi, translate; tell them I need a vampire, and will pay in gold coin of the Empire."

"Mother, what are you saying?"

She turned on him, the cap crumpled in her fingers, her eyes dripping. "Is your head made of wood? Your father is dying. Will you let him die, or will you help me to save him?"

"By Ahriman's Serpent?" Dimi said, gasping.

Iphigenia slapped him. It did not hurt, but he stared at her, his cheek and eyes stinging, knowing that if he blinked he would begin to cry.

Dimitrios walked past her to his men. Quietly he said, in French, "Do any of you know of . . . a diseased one?"

They were all very quiet for a moment. Then Charles said, "Near Seigny. Up the Imperial road."

Dimi nodded. "All right." He looked around at his Praetorian Guard. "No one has to follow me—"

"We're going," Jean-Luc said. No one disagreed. Charles just drew the purple sash from inside his shirt and tied it across his shoulder and chest.

They rode without speaking, up the valley to the northwest, horseshoes striking sparks from the Roman paving. *Riding like demons,* Dimi thought, tasting irony on his tongue.

A few miles up the road, when he knew unaided eyes could not spot them from the house, Dimi signaled a halt.

"We'll have to ride hard for Seigny," Alain said.

"We're not going any further." Dimi swung out of the saddle and led Luna from the road, talking softly to the white mare. He found some grass for her, then sat down on a rock. He could see the top of Mont-Alise, golden-bright against the eastern sky. The others watched him, then followed him.

"Captain . . ." said León, who almost never spoke.

"When Mithras slew the bull," Dimi said slowly, "he cut its throat, so its blood would give life to all the Earth. But Ahriman . . . the Enemy . . . sent his servant the snake, to drink the bull's blood up." Dimi looked around. Surely the Mysteries would not be damaged by this. He told them for the sake of Mithras, after all. And for his father's soul. "The Raven saw the snake, though, and pecked at it. And the Dog, who is friend to men, bit the snake. And Mithras crushed it with his heel. Still the snake swallowed a mouthful of the bull's blood, and crawled away alive . . . but its wounds came from a god and the friends of a god, and ever after it must drink blood to stay alive."

Dimi said "My father would have cursed us all—" and he stopped, because his voice was trembling.

Charles said "Then I suppose it is a good thing that there is no vampire in Seigny."

They all stared at him. Then Dimi smiled. So did the others. *They understand,* Dimi thought. That was enough.

"How long shall we wait?" Jean-Luc asked.

Dimi looked to the east. "Till sunset, I think . . ." Then, sharply, "No. Mount up now."

Atop Vercingetorix's redoubt, the heliostat was flashing, the whirling mirror sending to the channels of the Empire that one of its *strategoi* was dead.

* * *

The artificial cavern glowed with firelight, echoed with the voice of the Solar Courier, initiate just below the Father: "O Lord! I have been born again and pass away in exaltation. In exaltation I die. Birth that produces life brings me into being and frees me for death. I go my way as you have ordered. . . ."

The casket hung in a net of wires, suspended above the dais at the end of the Mithraeum. Inside his robe and black Raven hood, Dimitrios smelled naphtha and his own sweat.

The Courier of the Sun read the Invocation of Julian the Wise, Emperor of Byzantium: ". . . a fiery chariot shall bear you to Olympus, tossing in a whirlwind; you shall be free from the curse and weariness of your mortal limbs. You shall reach your father's courts of ethereal light, from which you wandered to enter a human body."

Fire blossomed up from the floor, mixed with wind that made the flames dance and roar, like lions devouring the casket and the dead Lion within it.

Dimi gave silent thanks for the cowl that hid his eyes.

The Empire was far too organized to be severely disturbed by the death of any one man. Caractacus, the commander of horse, became general military commander; Lucian took over the Governor's administrative tasks. The treasurers and clerks mourned for three days and went back to work. A new *strategos* would be dispatched by the City as soon as possible. And that was all, on the Imperial level.

On a lower level, Dimitrios saw less of his family and more of his friends. His mother went daily to the temple of Cybele; she insisted on preparing her own meals, and sprinkled every dish with the gritty alicorn, more precious than gold dust. Uncle Philip smiled darkly when he saw Dimi, and was silent and secretive—easier to live with than his wildness had been, but not reassuring.

And in December, Charles and Robert would become Ravens. There was no longer any reason against it.

In October the new palace was finished enough for occu-

pancy. Lucian had arranged for the Ducases and their personal servants to stay in the old house as long as they desired; there seemed to be an administrative delay in
reoccupying their Greek estates.

Of course, many of the old palace's furnishings were already destined for the new building, but the family did not
need more than a few of the rooms. The tapestries, including the Partition of Gaul, were rolled and removed; plain
cloths kept out draft and chill in the rooms still in use.
Lucian needed direct access to much of the library, and
rather than disturb the Ducases at all hours the books
were taken up the hill. Thanks to an architectural quirk,
the one privy it was found convenient to keep in use was
also the least pleasant one.

On the last night in November, Dimitrios had gone from
his room to the kitchen for a piece of bread and a little
warm wine. Coming back, he paused before the Alesia
fresco. The single light in the hall was low and wavering,
and shadows seemed to animate the painted figures. The
Gauls fought, in broken ranks, with their crude farmers'
weapons. The Legionaries marched, hammer of Empire.
Vercingetorix stood on the mountain, wind wild in his
hair, leading his men on to death as free men; Julius's cape
fluttered in the same wind, as with infinite patience he
tore down all his enemy's defenses.

A black shadow fell across the divine general. Dimi
turned, saw Philip standing there. A book, the *Digenes
Akritas*, was open in his hands, and in the bad light he
looked like his dead brother.

"You hair is dark, like a Syrian's or a Gaul's, yet I know
you are a Ducas," Philip said. His voice was firm, not like
his usual babbling, though the words were just the same.
"Come with me."

Dimi followed. He did not know why. Perhaps it was the
resemblance to his father.

They went to the old Governor's Office. The room
had been empty for weeks, the door unopened. So Dimi
thought.

He was wrong. Within were chests, and armor, and

weapons piled up; on the walls were military maps of the area around Alesia, and a copy of the plan of the new palace.

"What is this?" Dimi said, not quite believing what he saw, feeling as if he had walked into a bad, bad dream.

"This is the great work of this house," Philip said. "The work my young brother could not finish." He put down the book, pointed to one of the maps. "This is the restoration of a Ducas to the Throne of the World . . . starting here, in the same mud where the divine Julius began."

Dimitrios shook his head. It was a dream in fact, the old insane dream, and now Cosmas Ducas was sleeping as well, and there was no one to end it.

"Cosmas won them with words, and I won them with gold and words." Philip opened a chest, picked up a handful of coins, let them run through his fingers. He seemed like some kind of demon from a legend, showing the hero his magic, evil wealth.

Dimi wondered where all the gold had come from . . . if there was still a white villa on the blue Aegean Sea.

Philip said "Do you know what he said, of you? He said, 'This is my son, whom the Gauls love. He will be a king, my son, if he must begin as a king in Gaul.' And you will. But it will not end in Gaul. It will not end in Greece. It will end in the City of Constantine . . . and perhaps not there.

"Your father and I read to the leaders of the Gauls, from the book of Digenes; and they believed us."

Dimi did not, would not believe his father had had anything to do with this; he tried to think what Cosmas could really have said about him that crazy Philip was twisting so.

Cosmas Ducas had stopped calling the people *Gauls.*

Philip was saying ". . . they will rise at your command, Dimitrios Ducas, Digenes."

Dimi turned away, walked out of the room. The bread in his hand tore, and the wine sloshed over his fingers onto the floor.

"I know why you turn down the crown on the sword," Philip said from the doorway. "Of course Mithras is your crown." His voice was calm and reasonable as he blasphemed the Mysteries, and so like Cosmas's that Dimi's neck prickled. "But there are kings and emperors on Earth, and our Lord was their second crown. The divine Julian the Wise—"

Three figures stood before Dimi in the dark hall: his mother and his sisters, fully dressed in the middle of the night.

"You may have denied him while he lived," Iphigenia said, "and deserted him at his death, but you will honor your father now, or I swear by Ishtar I will cut your throat and bathe in your blood as the bull's—for you are no man at all, but a beast sent to me for sacrifice."

Dimitrios looked down. Livia and Zoë clutched their mother's gown, and Dimi could see their terror rising like heat. He stood barefoot and cold and ridiculous in the hallway, crumbs and wine spilling from his hands, and knew that he was weak. He closed his eyes, saw in his mind's darkness the battle fresco: Vercingetorix standing with his Gauls alone.

But I will remember thee, O Caesar.

The *cohors equitata* met on foot, on the top of Mont-Alise, on a December night that was cold and hard and clear. They wore their leather, for silence and speed: they must enter past basilisks, seeking out the enemy sorcerer in his fortress.

"But it'll be different from the game," Dimitrios said, his breath white. "The guards can't really knock us down with just a look, so our best chance is to stay together. And they've only been in the new palace for a little while; we know every block and corner, and especially all the good hiding places. And we know one place they don't know about at all." Charles smiled. The others had been told of the secret stairs but had never actually seen them.

"We'll go in through the upper apartments, by the door to escape fire. Lucian's is the end room. If he's not there, he must be in either the library or the office. So we go down the narrow stair to the library hall; then to the west gal-

lery, where the secret panel is." Dimi paused, his hands
frozen in a gesture. "There's a drapery in front of the panel
now, so once we're through they won't even see where
we've gone."

Dimitrios was aware of his friends' nervousness; he had
compared it to his own and thought nothing further. But
now there was something else present, something more
than worry.

Jean-Luc said, "When we've taken the deputy . . . he'll
stop all the soldiers?"

"Of course, or we'll—" Dimi came up short. The idea of
killing Lucian had never really entered his mind, and it
did not come easily now. "But by then the townspeople will
be at the gates, calling for a new governor. . . ."

Looking at their faces, long and grave in the light of
their small lantern, Dimi realized what that strange emotion was. He had only just been fully introduced to it himself. It was guilt.

"My father . . . was not arming when I left the house."
Charles sounded as had Mithras, when he agreed to kill
his friend the Bull.

"Nor ours," Michel Rémy said, in his piping voice.

Robert said "I was told to stay at home tonight."

Dimi almost demanded to know why they had all still
come, but he knew the answer, and would not insult them
by asking it.

You do not lead men with metal, Cosmas Ducas had told
Dimitrios; and gold was as much a metal as steel.

"If I ordered you to go home," Dimi said, "would you
obey?"

They all, one by one, swore they would. Then Charles
said "If we left you, would you still attack the palace,
alone?"

"Yes." At certain times one must charge regardless—

"Then do not order us to leave."

Dimi saw the fresco again, much clearer than something
of paint could be, Vercingetorix standing with his Gauls.
Alone.

But I will remember thee.

They swore oaths on drawn knives then, and started down the hill, brothers in glory, fifteen years old. Dimitrios wondered, as they slipped across the crackling soil, whether death came all at once or slowly, and if it was hot or cold.

There was no handle on the outside of the wooden exit door, but a knifeblade easily lifted its catch, and a fortunate wind covered its creak.

"Swiftly now," Dimi whispered, and they ran to the door of Lucian's room; big Alain Rémy flung it open and Dimi and Robert charged through.

The room was crowded with Egyptian art, books, scrolls in wooden racks; the air was thick with incense. No one was there.

Dimitrios heard a voice from the hall: "Up here! Come on, upstairs!" It was not one of his men, and he knew that they were certainly betrayed. No one would be crying, "Give us a Ducas!" tonight.

Unless, he thought very clearly as he ran into the hall, unless he could make Lucian say it.

A guard stood at the top of the stairs, spear held out, keeping Charles and León at a distance. But he turned when Dimi came running, and little Michel Rémy dove to the floor, under the spear; he smashed the hilt of his knife on the guard's instep and stabbed up to the inside of the thigh. The man howled and fell backward, down the curving stairs, out of sight.

Michel stared at his arm, which was covered in blood not his own; he raised it to show the others, and they all had to look. Then Dimi's thoughts cleared a little. "On. On!"

The guard lay at the bottom of the stairs, his head thrown back crookedly. His mouth and eyes were wide open. The boys looked at him. So did the squad of soldiers at the other end of the hall.

"That changes matters," the serjeant of the guard told his men. "Take 'em for what they are."

There were two doors off the hall to the left, both leading to the library, both open. Dimi signaled, pushed, and the boys moved as a unit toward the nearer door. Long-legged

Robert and Jean-Luc got through; the rest met the guards' spearpoints and stopped.

"Rear rank turn," the serjeant said, "they'll get behind—"

Robert and Jean appeared at the far door. *"Keep going!"* Dimi shouted, but they came back instead, and as three guards tried to bring their spears around in the hallway, the two boys each got behind a man and slit a throat. The blood flowed incredibly red on gold and red.

The rest of Dimi's group tried to press the sudden advantage. Michel Rémy stepped like a dancer, until his toe skidded in blood; a guardsman thrust once, glancing off Michel's jacket, then drew back and thrust again with his whole weight. The spear went into Michel just below the ribs and came out his back, the eagle hilt pressed against his chest. Michel did not scream as he fell.

Alain did, and grasped the spear still sunk into his brother, pulling it from the guard's hands. Alain was half a head taller than the soldier, who stood paralyzed until Alain rammed his knife through the man's neck and spine, almost severing his head.

Spears were useless in the closeness and tangle. If the soldiers could have drawn their swords they might still have won the fight, but they did not. Charles killed a man, and Robert hacked off a sword hand, but as the man fell his spear caught León in the hip, and went deep. One soldier got a dagger out and punched it into Jean-Luc's chest; as he recoiled, the blade caught in Jean's ribs and leather jacket, and Jean-Luc fell on top of him, swearing and shouting for a few more moments until both of them were silent. Dimitrios threw the serjeant against the wall and cut his throat three times, realizing on the third stroke that he had learned bowshooting with the man, and that it did not matter at all.

León's leg was cut nearly off, and Jean-Luc was dead, and Michel. Alain stood over his brother, guarding him, with a knife in one hand and a soldier's sword in the other.

"We'll go on," Dimi said to Alain. "You cover our rear."

Alain nodded without speaking, his eyes fixed as a blind man's.

"The library's empty," Robert said. "Now we know where he is." He went quickly to the end of the hall, where it turned to the west gallery. His eyes widened, and his knife hand moved too fast for the eye to follow. There was a *thump* from the gallery, and a cry, and another *thump*. Robert whirled on the ball of his left foot to face Dimi and Charles.

His hand scrabbled at his chest, where the finned end of a crossbow bolt stuck out of his leather jacket. His fingers clamped on the bolt. He fell down.

There was silence.

Charles and Dimi looked at each other. Charles said, "We must go on." Dimi nodded, held Charles back with the edge of a borrowed sword, then went out into the open corner. Charles was instantly at his side.

Tertullian stood huge and black in the center of the gallery, just by the drape that hid the stairway panel. He wore black leather armor with plaques of white steel. He held a crossbow, loaded and cocked and absolutely steady. Next to him, on the floor, was a man with a crossbow on top of him; he was sprawled as Dimitrios now knew dead men to lie, though Dimi could not tell where Robert's knife had struck.

"Must I kill you good young men?" Tertullian said, in an iron voice to match the iron rest of him.

"You can only shoot one of us," Charles said, "and it should be me." He took a step.

"I'll kill you both. Shoot one, cut one. Or use my hands. It won't matter."

Charles took another step, and Dimitrios two to catch him. Tertullian did not even move his eyes.

Dimitrios looked at the wall hanging, at the arched ceiling, then at Tertullian again. "I know I cannot kill you," he said carefully, in the middle-class Greek he knew Charles did not understand. "But you must let me try. For the Lion's sake."

Everything was frozen for a moment more. Then Tertullian pointed his crossbow at the floor, and without even a shrug turned and walked away.

When he had gone, Dimi pulled the drapery aside, found the crack in the stone with his knifeblade and lifted the catch. The panel opened silently. Dimi gestured with his eyes; Charles nodded, and they went up the stairs, through the dark and the cold, stale air.

The upper door's latch made the faintest of clicks; the panel swung in.

Lucian stood less than ten steps away, on the other side of a cluttered table; he was looking out the bay window, at Alesia spread below. A heating-vent in the floor rippled his white gown.

The bald head turned, the sharp nose wrinkling. Lucian held a double-barrelled hand-gun against his chest; with startling speed he leveled it and twitched a trigger. Fire erupted.

Charles's head burst backward like a melon on pavement, splattering and streaking down the wall.

Dimitrios lunged; as his feet left the floor, he very distinctly saw Lucian take aim again, his finger move, the second striker fall. There was a little brassy click. No flash. No explosion.

Dimi skidded over the tabletop, sending papers and ink flying, and struck the Egyptian in the chest. Lucian's head slammed against the window and cracked the glass; he groaned, and groaned again as Dimi landed on top of him. Dimitrios thrust his knee to the man's crotch, then swore; he pressed his knife against Lucian's throat.

The ribbon holding Lucian's eyeglasses had broken, and the lenses lay against his cheek; his brown eyes crossed slightly, blinked. "Dimitrios, you're hurting me."

Dimi almost drew the knife back; then he pushed it closer, till a line of fresh blood showed along the stained edge. "Did you . . . kill my father?"

Lucian blinked again. "Extinguishing a family is not a simple problem," he said pedantically. "Massacres have survivors; or worse, create indelible rumors of survivors.

Exile is the training-camp of usurpers. Bribery is erratic; your father would not be bribed with the throne itself."

"Then why did you kill him?" Dimi did not care if a thousand soldiers came at the noise; he had only this one more throat to cut. "He . . . loved your Empire."

"He *obeyed* the Empire. He never loved it, as you do not. But men love you. It is a Ducas trait, the dangerous one. The reason the order was formulated to destroy the line."

"Whose order?" Now it seemed Dimi would have to escape, go on to kill someone more. He would do it, if it took forever.

"The particular experiment began in the reign of John the Fourth Lascaris."

That had been two centuries ago. *"I don't understand! What are you talking about? Who—killed—my—father?"*

"In a fashion, Dimitrios, you did. . . ."

Dimi's jaw clenched till it hurt.

Lucian said ". . . or I. Or a professional poisoner from Italy. Julius Caesar. The sun of Gaul. A weak blood vessel. Philip Ducas. The political science faculty of the University at Alexandria, to prove a theory of group behavior. Any of these. All."

He inhaled shallowly. "And I am killed by underestimating the intentness of boys, and the Ducas I knew to be most dangerous, because he was the most loved. And faulty gunsmithing . . . Dimitrios, were you ever fond of me, even a little?"

Dimi said nothing. The warm air from the hypocaust vent made a rushing sound.

"I do not want to be tortured, Dimitrios. I have seen it done, and you do not want it either. When you are done with me, cut the veins in your forearms. With their length, not across. A good old Roman fashion."

Dimitrios drew back, putting a knee on Lucian's chest. The Egyptian made no move to rise. Dimi looked at the edge of his knife, the point, the cudgel hilt.

Lucian said placidly, "It will not make you happy. I faint too readily."

Dimi made two deep, angled slashes across Lucian's

forearms. Lucian nodded once; then his eyes rolled up and his head turned aside. His blood was thin, but as red as any man's.

Dimi went across the room, to where Charles lay by the open panel.

They wore the same clothing. Their hair was the same black. Charles's face was a bloody hole.

Dimitrios pulled the rings from his fingers, let his knife drop. He felt the Raven medallion, a cold weight against his chest; he lifted it on its cord.

It was the first thing his mother would look for, if she was still alive; and if she were not, Tertullian would know it.

Yes, Tertullian, Dimi thought. *The Persian will know the Raven. Even if he thinks I was a traitor, he will not deny a brother his funeral.*

Patiently, deliberately, listening for the guards' approach, Dimi knelt to give Charles all he had to give: his own place in heaven.

When he was done, Dimi went to the bay window. Below him were the lights of Alesia, and the confluent rivers streaked with moon: obviously the valley had not risen in arms.

The basilisks are sleeping, then, he thought, *and will not see a King go by.* He opened the narrow window, muffling its creak with a drapery, vaulted through, and closed it again. He began to pick his way down the slope, toward the town.

He knew where there would be a horse that would not be missed until morning. He knew of a man in Troyes who hired soldiers for foreign wars, whether they had names or not.

Beyond that he knew nothing at all, except that he was cold.

Chapter 3
FIORENZA

CYNTHIA Ricci was not very drunk, but probably drunker than a doctor should be in her patient's presence. Especially when the patient is the most powerful *magnate* in Italy, whom the doctor and her doctor father have warned to stay away from red wine.

But then, Lorenzo de' Medici, *il Magnifico,* head of the Medici Bank and ruler-without-portfolio of the Florentine Republic, was probably past noticing. So was everyone else at the Medici summer villa at Careggi. For this was the last night of summer, and tomorrow Ser Lorenzo and the satellites in his orbit would move back to the Palazzo Medici in Florence city. And there would be a little more business in between the singing and the dancing and the poetry, philosophy, and wine. A little.

The hall was tiled black and white, chessboard fashion—Lorenzo loved chess—with fluted false columns around the walls and a frieze of Muses and bemused satyrs just below the ceiling vault. Midnight was made day by countless candles, on the table, in wall sconces, in chandeliers of faceted crystal. Arched doorways were open on Lorenzo's botanic gardens; fall flowers were blooming, summer's dying, and the mingled smell was astonishing.

The night air was unusually cool, and the houseguests had risen to the occasion by putting on the heaviest velvets and brocades they had thought to bring—completely upset-

ting the packing for tomorrow's journey, of course, to the
chill and silent dismay of the servants involved.

Messer Lorenzo knew the specific for that disorder, however. Another sheep went on the spit, more kegs were
knocked in, and very shortly no one cared if the clothes
were in their chests or on the floor (or on their backs or
anyplace soft, said Luîgi Pulci in a little extempore verse).

Messer Pulci was golden tonight: honey-colored velvet
for his doublet, yellow hose, golden wash on the lace of his
shirt and a gold necklace set with topazes. Next to him sat
Lucrezia de' Medici, Lorenzo's widowed mother, in dark
red and brown with fire opals in her blond hair, pretending
to be scandalized by the poem Pulci recited while she followed its text from the book in her lap. The first copies of
Pulci's new work to leave the printing-presses in Florence
had been rushed to Careggi by special messenger; a wildly
expensive journey for a little paper book that sold all over
Florence for a few *solidi*. Lorenzo had presented the books
to their author with great ceremony, pointing out that
Pulci's *condotta* of publication guaranteed him fifteen copies, and no Medici ever overlooked the fine points of a contract.

Lorenzo's brother Giuliano sat with Guidobaldo da
Montefeltro, discussing tournaments, mistresses, and fire-
arms, in no particular order. Giuliano wore a doublet quartered red and blue, with a lyon of England in gold on red
above his heart: a gift from King Edward IV of England,
who was king by right of arms and grace of Medici finan-
cial support.

Guidobaldo's father, Federigo the duke of Urbino, was
one of the finest mercenary leaders in Italy, one with
Francesco Sforza and the extraordinary Englishman John
Hawkwood. (Of course, it was not politic to make the comparison before the younger Montefeltro, just as Giuliano
never wore his jacket with its French blue quartering
when Louis, the perpetually exiled King of France, came
to visit.) Guidobaldo's doublet was of silk dyed *alessandro*,
a metallic blue with silver highlights, pleated horizontally

and studded with silver in a striking imitation of lamellar armor.

Cynthia felt a touch on her shoulder. Marsilio Ficino stood next to her, holding a pitcher of wine. Ficino wore a long white gown; he had translated Plato into Latin for Lorenzo's grandfather and into Tuscan for Lorenzo, and he liked to dress (he said) "a little like Ser Plato, a little like a priest"—which he had been, briefly—"and enough like a Florentine to walk the streets in peace." He was barely five feet tall in house shoes, very thin, with a huge beaked nose and eyes that were always happy and sparkling but distant—sometimes very distant, because Ficino had visions, of Plato, and the Graces, and odder things, and was convinced his soul left his body at times.

He poured wine for Cynthia, then himself. His fingers were long and very graceful. *"Salut',"* he said, and they touched cups and drank.

Ficino's eyes went wide and he plucked at the end of his nose, which had gotten into the wine and dripped red. Then he patted the top of his head, held the hand out as if gauging the distance to the floor, and said in a worried tone, "This cannot be my nose, *Dottorina* Ricci. This is the nose of a much larger man." He held her hand. "Tell me, Doctor . . . can a man be born with another man's nose?"

Cynthia tried to form an appropriately grave reply, but all that would come was laughter; and not even proper grown-up laughter, but giggling. She put both hands on her winecup, watched candles dance in the liquid; she was filled with giggles like bubbles, which must rise or burst.

Ficino took up a tragic pose. "Perhaps it is the telltale of bastardy," he said, and touched his nose again. It was really quite a big nose. "Not much of a telltale, though. Perhaps Mother was only unfaithful once or twice."

Cynthia thought she must giggle or die. She turned to the head of the table, in search of her host's mercy.

Lorenzo de' Medici wore a gown of intense, pure heraldic red, with the sleeves slit to show white silk. Flattened versions of the *palle*, the six red balls that were the Medici badge, were sewn on the breast. His chair was pushed back from the table, one of his feet braced against the table edge, and there was a silver-strung lyre in his lap.

He was not handsome, with a broad flat face and a large broken nose (though not so beaky as Ficino's) and coarse, straight, black hair. But his look was strong, as something made from Tuscan stone, and when he spoke his voice was as the voices of mountains.

Or when he sang, as he did now, working out the words for a new festival song. This one was about the planets in their courses around the sun . . . well, that was what it was supposed to be about; the lyrics concerned balls warmed by a central fire, and the tubes of telescopes thrust into darkness, and the white stream of the zodiacal light. Lorenzo's festival songs were all like that, hot bakeovens and tree grafting and casting bronzes, funny and delightful pretense of innocence.

And then he would take the same tune and give it new words, about his wife Clarice, or olive trees silver in the morning light, or his sons Piero and Giovanni, or Sandro Botticelli's latest painting—and the lust would become love, meanings not double but multiple, as the soul is multiple.

Cynthia loved him.

Lorenzo touched the lyre, striking candlelight from the strings. He looked up at Cynthia, tilted his head. *Oh, bloody flux,* she thought, wondering how she must look.

Cynthia's green velvet gown was conservatively slashed at the sleeves, showing a little silk lining dyed yellow with crocus. Her green cap and golden hairnet were almost uncomfortably tight. Cynthia was twenty-two, and her hair was pure white: a touch of the strange, that she had found either attracted men or repelled them. The gown's bodice was not quite low enough to show her breasts. Around her neck was a gift from Lorenzo: a thin cord of gold and pearls, holding a pendant crocus blossom in pure gold.

Not solid gold, but only Lorenzo and Cynthia knew that.

Lorenzo looked at her, and the pendant. He said, "Before the night dissolves, *Dottorina* . . . I have an offer to make you."

A number of things whirled through Cynthia's mind. None of the other conversations paused at all; only Marsilio Ficino might have heard—but Ficino was the arch-Platonist, always, in all things.

Lorenzo opened his mouth. A chime sounded. Lorenzo shut his mouth, blinked, started to speak again; another chime came out. With a sudden grin, he put hand to lyre, tossed his head back, and sang the next chime. Then he clenched a fist and declaimed the stroke of four.

By the sixth stroke of the clock, Cynthia's giggles had completely escaped control, and before midnight tolled everyone in the room was laughing, chorusing the chimes with Lorenzo.

"To the garden, everyone!" Lorenzo said as the last stroke died away. He got to his feet. "Outside, quickly!"

Laughing, awkward, the party disengaged themselves and their clothing from the table and went through the archways.

A full moon washed down the gardens with silver; pine and palm and cypress trees stood pale against sky and summer-soft stars. The gardens were laid out with a ruthlessly Aristotelian precision, radial paths of tessellated stone, golden sections of bushes and blossoms. At the center was a colonnade of white marble, with marble benches, around a bronze fountain showing Venus rising from the Aegean. Ficino had created the image, Donatello cast it in metal, and Botticelli reinterpreted it in paint with his inevitable layers of symbol and allegory added.

The poet Arturo Poliziano and Alessandra Scala, the designer and stage manager for the Florence Grand Theater, sat together on a bench in wildly animated conversation.

"Orpheus descends to the Underworld," said Poliziano. "*Descends.* All the poets use that word, descends."

Scala said "So we should cut a hole in the stage, and he can perform the act below the view of the audience?"

"Walking across a stage is not descending!"

"Or we could set up ladders . . . oh, just a minute. Have you spoken with Leonardo lately?"

"The Archimedian? Not since winter."

"He brought me sketches for a machine—a whole group of machines, really—to move sceneries and actors about. Make the gods fly, that sort of thing. Suppose, as Orpheus walks, the overworld begins to rise on Leonardo's wheels. . . ."

Poliziano wore violet, Scala absolutely black velvet set with hundreds of tiny silver buttons. "The god of night and goddess of the sky," Cynthia heard Ficino false-whisper behind her; then she heard the scrape of his foot. She turned quickly and took his arm; he looked up at her with a slight smile and a nod, and allowed her to assist his lameness.

The group began to take seats; Lorenzo insisted that all sit on one side of the circle of benches. Cynthia supposed that some presentation was coming, written by Lorenzo and staged by Alessandra; she well recalled the summer Lorenzo's *Life of Julian* had rehearsed here, going on to success in the city and, in translation, as far away as London and Byzantium. There, of course, the companies did not have Lorenzo himself as the Wise Emperor, and Cynthia could hardly imagine anyone else in the part.

There was a crack of thunder, though there had been no lightning and the sky was clear. Then a yellow-white streak of fire stabbed upward, hissing and crackling; it exploded in a shower of sparks and moon-bright smoke.

"From the Chinas," said Lorenzo. "Fire as an art form."

There were more eruptions, streaks, fireclusters, filling the sky with flowers of light in amazing colors. "The moon will be jealous," Luigi Pulci said, and composed a typically bawdy verse on the fruits of lunar envy.

"What are you thinking, *bella Luna?*" said a voice by Cynthia's ear. She turned and saw Lorenzo, seated on the bench next to her, facing outward with one knee drawn up and his fingers laced around his leg. His face was in shadow except when a firestar exploded, and even those left his deep-set eyes in darkness.

He was in his twenty-eighth year, wealthy beyond his ability to count, and thanks to Cynthia and Vittorio Ricci the gout that had destroyed his father did not trouble him at all. He was ruler of Florence in all but name. What Lorenzo wanted was Lorenzo's. Cynthia's gown was too tight, too warm; she could not breathe.

"I would like you to go to Pisa," Lorenzo said.

Many things were in Cynthia's mind. That was not one of them.

"Pier Leone wants to stop teaching for a while. He talks about going to Germany, and Alexandria; he wants to learn some new surgery while his hands are still clever, and I think write another book too. That, however, leaves the professorship open. Do you want it?"

"I—think my father might be a better choice."

"Vittorio's in the city, and you're here. But of course the decision's yours." He gave a small shrug, turned to look out over the half-dark gardens. "The crocuses will be blooming soon. Have you any difficulty in getting enough?"

"No. We are . . . discreet, of course."

"Of course." She saw the outline of his smile, wondered if a double meaning had passed her by. In the stuttering light from above, Lorenzo looked at his large, rough hands, flexed his fingers. There was a rattling chain of detonations overhead.

His eyes went again to the golden chain around her neck. He was still smiling, but now she saw that it was not a happy smile at all. His hands moved apart, and she wondered if he would touch the pendant, but he stood up, saying, *"Buona notte, Dottorina Luna,"* and went away as the sky burst red.

She put her own fingertips to her throat. Autumn crocus. Colchicum. Twice a day Lorenzo de' Medici took a measured spoonful of colchicum extract in brandy, an infusion prepared by the Riccis, and his gout did not afflict him; as simple as that. There were only two problems. . . .

Neither of Lorenzo's parents was able to tolerate the medication; it gave them vomiting and galloping diarrhea. Fortunately Lucrezia's disease was very mild, and diet kept her well.

Unfortunately, Piero de' Medici's was not mild. And so

Vittorio Ricci banned red wine and organ meats from the table, and consulted obscure books and distant physicians, and wrung his hands.

And his daughter collected the urine and blood that Vittorio would stare at like a mad soothsayer, and took notes on every possible variation of the prescription—and then took samples of vomitus and watery feces—and bathed and wrapped the patient's hot, purple-swollen joints, for days into years, until when she was fourteen Piero died, all twisted, and the last color faded from Cynthia's hair.

Lorenzo came to power at twenty-one. The infusion caused him no distress; that problem was over, and the second could come into its own. Colchicum extract, as every sophisticated poisoner knew, was deadly in marvelously small doses. The line between cure and kill was thinner than a knife's edge.

Thus the discretion. Thus the Riccis compounded their own medicine despite the apothecaries' guild, and killed two dogs and two piglets testing each batch. One gives poison to a prince with the utmost caution, even when it is with his consent.

The sky show was ending. Alessandra Scala was talking about showing Phoebus's chariot with wheels of genuine fire. Poliziano wanted to stage the burning of Rome. Lucrezia de' Medici suggested flame-breathing serpents, and Pulci, irreverent as always, proposed a war among the gods, held in the sky with weapons shooting fire.

Then the syncretist Ficino, sitting hunched with Lorenzo standing at his side, put all the ideas together, along with Lorenzo's new song: chariots blazing between the worlds as gods fought rebel gods, the destruction of a city—a planet?—by fire, beasts beyond imagining both to terrify and befriend the heroes.

"It needs a title," Signorina Scala said.

Pulci had his mouth open, but Ficino beat him to the pun.

"It shall be dedicated to Isis and Mars," he said, "and we will call it *Stella Martis.*"

A servant brought Lorenzo's lyre, and another for Ficino; pipes for Poliziano and tambourine for Lucrezia.

"Will you sing, Luna?" said the Magnificent.

"I only heard the words once—"

"Improvise," said Ficino, his eyes alive with joy. "What's life but an improvisation to the music?"

And Cynthia sang, words rising from within her like giggles to pop on the tip of her tongue, until as the eastern sky began to lighten she wondered if their horses knew the way to carry them home, and did not really care if they did.

Cynthia's feet knew the way from the Ricci house to the Palazzo Medici, and she did not care if they did not; crossing the Arno, she did not care if they carried her over the edge of the bridge to drown.

Vittorio Ricci walked, shoulders bent, a few steps ahead of his daughter. He wore a black cloak, and a mood to match. Cynthia looked up; the September sky was dull. The city was too quiet, the river too flat, the whole bloody world gone numb and tingling.

They were admitted at once to the Medici palace. Nothing was right there, either. She could hear the whispers of the servants behind her, feel their eyes on her back. She wondered, should she look outside, if the building stones would still meet fairly, columns stand straight; if the statue of Marcus Aurelius in the courtyard would be weeping bronze tears. No, that was wrong. The Philosopher Emperor was a Stoic; he would not weep for the death of all beauty in the world.

Lorenzo de' Medici was reclining on a couch, his head and feet supported by feather pillows. He wore a loose silk gown, a silk sheet over the lower half of his body. He was talking with his brother Giuliano, and Francesco Sassetti, general manager of the Medici Bank; the tightness in Lorenzo's voice was perceptible to Cynthia all the way across the room.

"I wish I knew why my good friend the Duke Sforza required so much gold on short notice. I only fear I do know.

What is the extent of the Duke's indebtedness now, Francesco?"

"According to Messer Portinari, some five hundred thousand Milanese pounds . . . one hundred twenty thousand florins, Magnificent." Cynthia almost gasped. The Ricci were not poor, and all their house and movables were worth less than a tenth of that.

"In fact," said Lorenzo, "I do not know what to make of any of Galeazzo Maria Sforza's actions of late—not since those noble young idealists tried to kill him. . . . Ah. *Dottore* Ricci, *Dottorina* Ricci. Please come in."

The doctors approached. Sassetti bowed to leave.

"Francesco."

"Magnificent?"

"Write to Portinari. Ask him the consequences of liquidating our branch in Milan."

"Magnificent, the consequences would be—"

"Disastrous. I know. But get Portinari's figures. Assure him that whatever happens, he will retain a position with us."

"And if the Duke Sforza should hear of this proposal?"

"Francesco," said Lorenzo very patiently, "unless the Duke's devious brother has dropped incontinently dead, I hold it as a fact that the Duke will hear of it. If I know Ludovico Sforza, the Duke will be reading your letter well before Portinari does. As for what Galeazzo Maria will make of it—well. He knows I once made a war over alum, which is worth much less in the pound than gold."

Sassetti nodded and went out, tucking his hands into his long, flapping sleeves.

Lorenzo shifted his legs slightly, grimaced. "Now, Giulian', too late I understand why Grandfather never lent to princes. Sforza, and then King Edward, and poor Louis, and now the younger Sforza . . . Father and I are both fools. Court fools."

Giuliano said "Handling money is an art and a science."

"But not one that Ficino can pry out of Plato. . . . Ah. Excuse me, Vittorio, Cynthia. Come here, take a look."

Giuliano stepped back. Vittorio Ricci swept the sheet

aside. Cynthia's scalp prickled. She could sense Giuliano's chill. The younger brother had been sixteen when Piero the Gouty died. He had seen. He knew.

Vittorio said evenly, "You have not missed the medication? Or, perhaps, used the stale infusion from the previous batch? Or overindulged in the dangerous foods?"

"No, no, and no. Shit, Vittorio, I've taken my spoonful of medicine like a good boy since I was seventeen. I thought about taking an extra swallow this morning, but . . ." He closed his eyes as Vittorio's fingers moved his knee.

"Well that you did not," Vittorio said. "It could have been very dangerous."

Yes, Cynthia thought, *very dangerous to the house of Ricci.*

"Nonetheless, we may try that course. Slight increases in your dosage, until . . . Have there been any of the— untoward symptoms?"

Lorenzo was briefly silent. "When I hurt my side, in the tournament—you remember, Giulian'—I had the nausea, and I know I vomited, because Bartolomeo Lanzi caught my spew in his good helmet. Do you recall?"

"I remember," Giuliano said, and looked at Cynthia, his pretty face distorted with fear.

"Oh, brother, I haven't any fever. Do I, Luna?"

"No," Cynthia said. "Pain alone can cause the upset, yes."

"Then you have had nausea," said Vittorio. "And your stools?"

He spoke so calmly, so impassively. Cynthia wanted to strike him. She wanted to scream, thought that if this went on much longer she would have to scream, bloody murder.

Vittorio went on with his examination. Cynthia waited for Lorenzo to ask the question she knew he must—but he did not. It was Giuliano who took her into the adjoining room and asked, "Can he be reacting . . . like Father? After all this time?"

"I don't know," she said. "Perhaps it's just"— and then she shut her mouth tight. She had consented to this thing, but not to compound the treachery with lies—and the lie had come so easily. Silence had almost become conspiracy, without any real effort at all.

Giuliano looked at the floor, ran his fingers through his already disarranged hair. He looked like a troubled young god in one of Botticelli's panels. All he needed was a little comforting. She had none to give.

They went back into the room. Vittorio Ricci was packing specimen vials into his black bag. "Destroy the supply of medication you have," he was saying. "I will prepare a new infusion and bring it tomorrow." He closed the bag. "Come, Cynthia."

"Would you stay a little longer, Cynthia?" Lorenzo said.

Vittorio put his hand to his face, stroking his cheeks, squeezing away whatever emotion had been there.

"If you're needed—"

"I'll stay," she said. "Go on, Father."

The elder Ricci picked up his bag, made a stiff little bow, and left.

Cynthia looked at Lorenzo, determined to tell him no lies, even if he asked for a confession of attempted murder.

"Have you considered Pisa?" he said, and she had to think of all the possible meanings before realizing that Lorenzo had meant no more than he had said.

"I . . . could not leave now." Which was the truth.

"Well, I suppose I'd rather you didn't. Especially if someone must bathe my legs every day . . . oh, smile, Luna. Please smile."

She did. It was not the truth.

"You're what—twenty-two?"

"Yes, Magnificent."

"That name never sounded any sillier. . . . We're headed for trouble in Florence, Cynthia. There are only three states left in the North free of Byzantium, and now Milan wants war with us. I can hear that Imperial puppet della Rovere laughing himself sick in Rome." He tightened a hand. The fingers would not quite close into a fist.

"Luna. Go to Pisa. Marry an intelligent pauper, or a clod rich enough to keep to his mistresses. I'd tell you to marry

Giulian', and he'd do it, but it wouldn't help; you must get out of this circle before something terrible happens. Go to Germany and practice your art—or to England; Edward has peace now. We bought it for him."

She could not move, or think.

Lorenzo sighed. He tried to pull a ring from his right hand, could not get it past the knuckle. "Ah, shit. Help me to the cabinet, will you?"

Giuliano and Cynthia took Lorenzo under the armpits and walked him to a dark wooden armoire set against the wall. Lorenzo pressed a thumb against his ring and a thick metal prong snapped out; he put the key into an inconspicuous hole in the carved wood and turned. A panel swung open.

Inside was a small, stoppered glass flask of dark amber liquid and a silver spoon. Lorenzo took the flask and handed it to Cynthia, who tried to control her trembling as she accepted it.

"Messer Lorenzo!"

The flask shattered on the tiles.

A page ran into the room, dropping to his knees, skidding to a stop. "Ser Lorenzo—a coach from Milan—Messer Reynardo. And another person, in a hood."

Cynthia felt Lorenzo's shoulders go hard. "Very well. *Dottorina* Ricci, I suppose we've followed your father's instructions; now pardon me. Giuliano, see Cynthia out, then meet me in the quiet chamber."

The page said "Magnificent, Messer Reynardo asked that a doctor be brought. A surgeon."

Lorenzo said "In that case, Cynthia, will you . . . ?"

"Of course, Magnificent."

Lorenzo told the page, "Have Reynard and his guest enter beneath the roses. And get someone to sweep this up."

Giuliano kicked off his leather pattens, knelt to slip them on his brother's bare feet, then with Cynthia half-carried him across the broken glass to the couch.

"Best get me some lower garments," Lorenzo said in a suddenly exhausted voice. "And . . . you know."

"The chair?" Giuliano said.

"Yes. Father's chair."

Giuliano and the page went out. Cynthia took a roll of linen gauze from her bag and began to pad Lorenzo's swollen feet.

"I hope, Cynthia, I am not involving you . . . in an unpleasant business."

Cynthia controlled herself. It was rapidly becoming easier. "Who is Messer Reynardo?"

"A Frenchman. He calls himself Reynard; what his real name is I don't know. He was a gift from Louis; the only value for money I ever got out of that old spider."

"But . . . what does he do?"

"Why, *Dottorina,* can't you guess? He spies for me, on my good friend the Duke of Milan."

The quiet chamber was a specially built room in the cellar of the Palazzo Medici, with double walls to stop sound and a heavy door that locked itself on closing. The walls were of plain stone, and there were no furnishings but an iron candelabrum and several thick iron rings set into ceiling and walls and floor, frighteningly full of possibilities.

Lorenzo de' Medici sat in a padded chair on wheels that had been used by his father Piero. Giuliano stood behind the chair, his hands on the pushing handles. Cynthia was a little further back and to the left, her cloak over her shoulders with the hood raised.

In the middle of the room stood two people. The taller of the two was Reynard, who wore a leather jacket over his doublet and hose, all very dusty, and a plain-hilted small sword. His face was very bland, smiling in a vague way.

The other person, who had been cloaked and hooded until the chamber door was closed, was a boy, dark-haired, droop-shouldered, bow-legged. He was very pale, and stared vacantly at the floor.

"A halfwit?" Lorenzo said.

"Hardly," said Reynard. There was no French accent in his voice, nor any other sort of accent. "He could read Plato in Greek. What you're seeing now is the side effect of the spell; I didn't have time or energy to be subtle." Reynard touched the boy's head. He did not react. "It also means he'll come up quickly when I lift the control. Watch, now."

Reynard made a complicated motion with the fingers of his right hand, then swept them along his left arm. It seemed that he had pushed back the sleeve, though the jack was too heavy and stiff for that to be possible; still, his arm looked bare, the basilic veins showing large and blue on white skin.

Reynard's right hand brushed the boy's head again, then touched his temples, pinched the bridge of his nose; Reynard flipped his wrist to one side and snapped his fingers.

The boy blinked at Reynard's bare arm. He inhaled, and his tongue flicked out. Then he seized the arm with both hands and sank his teeth into the inside of the wrist, biting like a wild animal, making wet sucking sounds. Saliva flowed freely.

Reynard pinched the back of the boy's neck, muttered something. The light went out of the boy's eyes; his face and jaw went slack, his look once again empty and mindless.

The leather sleeve reappeared. Reynard turned it in the candlelight, showing bite marks that went almost through the leather.

Lorenzo said in a flat voice, "You are sure it was the Duke who did this?"

"Absolutely, my lord."

"There have been many rumors about Duke Galeazzo. . . ."

"Most of them are true, my lord. The Duke Sforza believes, probably rightly, that as long as his cruelties were confined to a few of the nobility, the bulk of his subjects would tolerate them, but the vampire disease would be seen as a threat to all."

"How long?"

"I believe he was infected after those three young men attempted to kill him early last year; that he was not in fact wearing armor beneath his doublet, and was mortally wounded. There was a vampire in the dungeons—an experiment of the Duke's—and the Duchess Bona offered him his freedom if he would save the Duke's life."

Lorenzo said "Bona would. And it just may explain his turn of mind." Then, sharply, "It required twenty months for you to discover this?"

"I have known since last winter, my lord."

Lorenzo's eyes narrowed. "Then why—"

Reynard tugged at his collar. "Last winter, my lord, the Duke was hungry, and I was available. Ludovico Sforza watches his brother's . . . donors very carefully, for signs of infection. I had to be very circumspect." He displayed a set of small black scars above his collarbone.

"I am sorry, Reynard. And are you . . . infected?"

"No my lord. Those he passes the disease to the Duke has nailed into chests. He stores the chests in a room, and spends time there alone, listening. He calls it his House of Peers."

"Sweet Venus, Galeazzo . . ."

Cynthia could not take her eyes from the boy. He looked a little like her brother. Spittle was drying on his chin.

"This one escaped for a time," Reynard's bland voice went on. "I caught him with a kitten for bait—"

"Oh, enough!" Giuliano cried.

"Is this the surgeon?"

Cynthia was abruptly conscious of all the men looking at her. "Yes," she said. "Shall I do it now?"

Reynard said "It has to be done, and holding him still costs me. Are you familiar with the—"

"I know the technique," Cynthia said, suddenly very angry. "Do you think I'm frightened?"

"I apologize, madame," Reynard said gently. "I myself am rather frightened."

She looked at the spy, or tried to; his face would not focus. Magic, she thought, an illusion like his naked arm had been. She wondered what he really looked like; if he could see his own face in a glass.

"Take off his shirt," she said, and took a scalpel from her bag, swabbed it with alcohol in an automatic action before realizing that cleanliness was not going to matter this time.

Reynard took off his belt and lashed the boy's wrists. "Pain will break the control," he said. "My lord Julian . . ."

Giuliano took the boy's ankles. Reynard lowered him to the stone floor and pinned his shoulders. "Madame?"

Cynthia knelt, the knife in her right hand, and began counting ribs with her left. The chest was very thin. She would have to go through the inner edge of the lung, at the point of a triangle whose bases were superior and inferior venae cavae, cutting the little rope of nerves in the heart apex.

She heard Lorenzo praying, to Minerva Medica. That was probably a good idea. To Asclepius, too. After the nerves in the heart, the cervical spine must be severed. Would any of the medical gods still listen to a Ricci? The men could have done it themselves with a dagger in the heart and a sword to the neck. The boy's pupils were pinpoints. A little further up. Amateurs usually got the dagger in the wrong place, her anatomy teacher had said. "Hold him now." *Forgive me.*

"Not much blood."

"No. Turn him over."

The second stroke was easy.

"What did Ser Lorenzo want?" Vittorio Ricci asked.

"I did some surgery on a boy in the house." She was too tired and disgusted to invent any more; Vittorio did not ask for any more. He picked up a paper from the table where he sat and handed it to Cynthia. "Another," he said. "Pushed under the door."

She read:

Most learned physicians:

We are most pleased with Messer Lorenzo's progress, and with your admirable discretion in the matter.

Please do not neglect to prescribe a treatment for Messer Giuliano, as requested in our previous letter.

When this course of treatment is complete, your relatives may end their visit with us and return to comfort, light, and air.

Yours ever watchful.

"Now you see I am right," Vittorio said. "If we had shown the first letter to the Medici, your mother, your brother and sister, would all be dead now."

Cynthia had nothing to say.

"I have made the new infusion. It tastes precisely of the colchicum, and has twice the concentration of uric salts as the prior formula. I had not expected the salts to be so effective; we may not have to use the pure colchicum extract. . . ." Vittorio looked again at the letter. "I do not know what we will do for Giuliano. But there are poisons enough for all."

Cynthia felt hollowness in her chest. She turned and walked away.

"I did not wish to involve you," Vittorio Ricci said after his daughter. His voice was unsteady. "But they must watch us at all times. You heard what Ser Lorenzo said about spies. . . ."

She heard him begin to sob, and her step almost faltered, but she kept going: let him weep, she thought. Let him cry enough tears for the both of them.

She was indeed thinking about spies.

She went to the kitchen, got an egg, an orange, and a bit of lard in a bowl. Then she went up to her rooms, closed the door, and locked it.

Cynthia took off her cloak, then her gown, and sat down in her shift before her dressing mirror. Next to the mirror was a pencil drawing, careful renderings of her by the artist from Vinci. It was a gift, in exchange for being allowed to watch her at dissections. She looked at the sketch, and the glass, and traced lines of bone and sinew in her face and throat. She unfastened the gold-and-pearl necklace, put it on the table.

She cracked the egg into the bowl, setting the shell aside, then dipped a brush into the clear albumen and applied it to the corners of her eyes and mouth, and more lightly to the rest of her face. She fanned the skin, feeling the egg drying, tightening, crinkling.

Lard and a little ash made her hair gray and dull and stringy. When the egg white had dried, she peeled the orange and used a piece of the peel to stipple on brown pigment.

She picked up the necklace, put her fingers on the crocus-flower pendant, squeezed and twisted; the petals opened on tiny hinges, revealing a hollow space within. When Lorenzo gave her the charm, he had made a silly romantic joke about love-philtres, spilled in an unsuspecting young man's wine. She took a tiny vial of blue crystals from her medical kit, filled the golden flower with the cyanide of potassium, then closed the petals.

Using the forceps and scalpel from her kit, Cynthia removed the membrane from within the eggshell and cut out two circles with tiny holes in their centers. She leaned toward the mirror, tugged her eyelid open, carefully applied a white disc of membrane to the eyeball. A tiny spot of pupil showed in milkiness. She did the same to her other eye.

Moving mostly by touch, she went to the wardrobe and selected a long gray gown with a short hood and cape. She pulled on white stockings and brown sandals. A carved staff came from the back of the closet. She tucked the necklace into her sash.

She went out of the house through the rear. She hoped not too many people recalled the blind sibyl from Lorenzo's *Vita Juliani.*

She walked around in back streets for a while, getting used to her diminished vision and the use of her staff, trying to blink as little as possible.

She reached the river Arno, looked across at the high slim tower of the Palazzo Vecchio, and Brunelleschi's enor-

mous Pantheon dome, the wonder of Fiorenza; they were
bright in the afternoon light. There was no haze at all.

There was a bench nearby; from it she could see down
the street to the front of her house. There she sat down, her
staff held erect, and watched, and waited.

There was a continuous stream of people on the streets,
many of whom bowed or saluted to her as they passed. A
young man knelt before her and asked for a prophecy of
success; she recited an ambiguous little verse from Lorenzo's play and told him he wore too much gold on his doublet, which was quite true. He stared into her filmed eyes
with astonishment and sheer terror, then pressed a gold
florin into her palm and took off down the street.

She almost smiled. Then she went back to watching.

Shortly she saw him: a man in a drab green gown, who
appeared at the corner of the Ricci house one, two, three,
four times. She gave him one more orbit of the house, just
in case he was merely very lost; then another man appeared, talked for a moment to the one in green. The first
man started up the street toward Cynthia, while the second took up the circuit of observation.

She sat quite still as the man in green approached, wondering if she had been recognized despite her disguise—or
if she had been seen at the very beginning, and they were
coming to tell her that the game was over—

The man passed by far to her right, without even a
glance toward her; he started across the river.

She gave him thirty heartbeats, all she could stand to
wait, then started after him.

Once in the central city, he took a roundabout path
through alleys and crowds; she would have lost him if her
staff and blindness had not cleared a way for her.

Then, finally, he vanished, and she was certain she had
in fact lost him; she kept walking, hoping for a miracle—
and nearly collided with her target in the arch of a doorway.

The door opened as they were disengaging, and a small
man looked out. He had dark eyes and a hooked nose, and
wore a black robe of coarse stuff. He was physically young,

but his expression held an ancient bitterness. "Good day, holy mother," he said, and made a bizarre gesture.

Cynthia had to exert herself not to stare at him; there was an intensity about him, palpable as heat. "Blessed be," she said, then turned and walked on, sweeping her staff before her. She heard the door close.

Cynthia turned at the next corner, turned again, came to the back of the house. The windows were shuttered with iron. There was a rickety wooden stairway to the upper floor.

She reached to her eyes and pulled out the membranes, squinting hard against the suddenly dazzling light. She went up the stairs cautiously, freezing at the creak of every step.

The upper door was not locked. She slipped off her sandals and moved silently inside.

The upstairs hall was cool and pleasantly dim to her sore eyes. It was very quiet.

A voice filtered up from below. Cynthia stepped through an open door into a small and sparsely furnished room; within, the voice carried clearly through the vent from the hypocaust. She listened at the grille.

". . . stayed in. The young woman locked herself in her room. That's all they've done."

"You see, it takes little to frighten the guilty." It was the intense man's voice.

"My lord . . ."

"Brother."

"Brother," said the other voice, "are you certain the doctors conspire with the Medici tyrants? I did not see—"

"You did not see? Did not see? You are a spy in the gods' own cause of freedom; what did you not see? Is there something you do not tell me?"

"No, brother Savonarola," said the first voice, much subdued.

"You understand, brother," said the intense voice, gently now, "that only in the good Duke of Milan is the salvation of Italy; that once the Medicis have destroyed the valiant Sforza with their usurious practices, they will sell both Florence and Milan to the Eastern Empire, that Lorenzo Medici may rule as the detestable Francesco Rovere defiles Rome. . . ."

Cynthis drew back from the vent. So it was Milan. And—since the man downstairs had denounced them in the same lying breath—perhaps Byzantium as well.

She wondered how such treachery could exist in the world. Dangle the word "tyranny" in front of some young simpletons and they would bite at it, like a carrot on a stick. And the ass would pull the cart—whoever might be driving.

But now she had a name: Savonarola. And she could find this house again, blindfolded—but she would return with the Gonfalonier of Justice and an armed troop at her back.

Someone was coming up the stairs.

She held still, but the room was tiny; she would be seen through the door. There was a narrow closet door, which she opened, finding enough room for herself within. She closed the door.

The footsteps entered the room.

Cynthia's heart raced, swelling up into her throat; she thought it must sound clear as a drum. The closet was empty except for a heap of linens on the floor. They were stiff, entangling her feet, and they stank. She touched her sash, where the golden crocus was hidden.

There was a rustle of cloth outside the closet. Savonarola's voice came clearly through the door. "O Maximin Daia, divine Emperor, aid thy servant in this his midnight hour; let Milan, city of the unholy Edict, where the godless Julian usurped the crown of Rome, now be thine instrument of destruction, first upon this city of aliens, then upon Milan itself, that that Empire that once you ruled may come once more into holy light. . . ." There was a sound like a handclap. "For women are worshiped here, and Jews walk in the streets. . . ." Another clap. "Aid me, Daia. Aid me, Zeus Friend of Men. . . ." By the third strike Cynthia knew the sound: a leather whip on flesh.

"Forgive me—" *Crack.*

Soon there was only whimpering, and the steady fall of

the lash. The stifling air of the closet, the sour linens, filled Cynthia's head, and with every crack of leather she shivered uncontrollably. The pendant with the blue crystals was just beneath her hand.

After ten thousand years the last sound stopped. Holding her staff with both hands, she used it to push the closet door open.

Savonarola lay quite still, face-down in a naked heap on the floor. Blood still oozed from the freshest scars across his back; those were laid over older stripes, and still older ones. She moved around him, unable to look away. She had a vision of him rising suddenly to his feet, pointing the whip at her, pinning her to the wall with his eyes and voice. But he did not move.

Cynthia realized that there was still pity in her. Then, perhaps, there was still hope for her soul.

There was no one else on this floor, certainly no hostages. She went downstairs; that floor was empty as well, even of servants. There did not seem to be a cellar entrance.

There was a moan from upstairs. Cynthia put on her sandals and went out into the street.

It was nearly dark when she returned home. She slipped in quietly, went to her room, began washing off the disintegrating makeup.

There was a knock. "Cynthia?"

"A moment, Father." She brushed her hair back, tossed on a cloth robe, and opened the door.

Vittorio held a candle and a goblet of wine. "You went out. Where did you go? I thought . . . they might have taken you as well."

"I—" How much should she tell him? He had no head for intrigue; that was why they had been so vulnerable. "I just had to walk for a while. I won't be having dinner at home, either; I'm going to the Palazzo Medici."

"I heard no invitation."

"I was invited after you left. Besides, you know we're welcome. Do you want to go? You shouldn't sit around the house so much—"

"No. No." Vittorio looked distraught. The candle wobbled. "Must you go out tonight, daughter? If a spy should think you are informing . . ."

"Please, Father, stop it."

Vittorio closed his eyes. Cynthia could feel his pain. But there was no more time to waste. "I must dress now, or I'll miss the first course, and have to make up excuses."

"All right. Will you . . . at least have some wine, before you go, if I'm to dine alone?"

She smiled. For all his weaknesses, he was a good man, and the best doctor in Florence, and she loved him very, very much. She took the goblet. It was a warm, sweet red wine punch, one of her favorites, and she drank most of the cupful. "Thank you, Father."

Vittorio nodded, took the goblet, reached for the door.

"Father . . . Lorenzo will send guards home with me, if I want. Will that make you feel better?"

He nodded again. She could see the tears starting. Quickly he closed the door.

She turned back to the dressing mirror, lighting two more candles against the growing darkness. The flames jumped, wavered. Cynthia felt warm. She turned toward the window. Her chair felt wobbly. She stood; the chair toppled with a distant, echoing crash. She turned around, her robe sweeping out half a circle, looked at the closed door; it was bent out of shape. The room revolved on without her. She took a step; her foot went miles to the floor. The only thing clear in her mind was the formulary description of the hypnotic in the wine. It was too late now to vomit it up.

Too late, too late, too bloody late.

Darkness drowned her mind.

Cynthia dreamed of her family: they were in a vindictive Hell of the sort she had never believed in, on an island surrounded by a burning lake; when Cynthia reached toward them, the fire rose. She could only get so close; it would engulf them an instant before she could reach them. The fire did not seem to burn Cynthia, but she had no boat nor anything to bridge the flames with. Yet no sensible god, none worthy of intelligent worship, would create a punishment that never ended; there must be some solution to the puzzle, some way out.

And just as she thought she had reasoned it out, she woke up, with no memory but of faces in the fire.

She was wearing her nightdress. Vittorio stood by the bed, holding a tray of food. He was her father, and a doctor who saw female patients every day; yet she felt more invaded by his changing her clothing than his drugging her.

There was direct sunlight through her window, so it was afternoon. But afternoon of what day? The next, she supposed. He could have kept her asleep for any length of time, but he would not risk her starving, and to be fed she must be awake.

He said "I've brought you—"

"You know very well I won't touch it."

He looked at his hands on the tray. "I am sorry I . . . did what I did. There is nothing wrong with any of this meal."

"Then you eat it." She swung her legs out of bed, sat up. Her head was not at all clear. Vittorio put the tray down and put his hands on her shoulder and arm, then reached to the foot of the bed for a robe to drape around her.

She looked hard at him, and saw that the look hurt him, and did not care.

She stood, tearing away from him, went to the wardrobe, and took out the first gown her hand touched. Vittorio turned, trying to say something but not forming the words. Cynthia threw the robe on the bed. She grasped her nightdress with both hands and pulled it over her head, standing naked and defiant and shivering.

Her father stood up, walked past her out of the room. He turned only to pull the door shut behind him.

Cynthia began to dress. There was a flash of bright metal near her foot; the crocus pendant. She picked it up, held it until it was quite warm and the golden petals marked the skin of her palm.

* * *

The banquet hall of the Palazzo Medici was set for twenty. There was one person at the table: Marsilio Ficino sat picking at an appetizer and gulping wine.

He looked up at Cynthia. It seemed to take him a long time to recognize her. "Oh . . . *Dottorina.* Come in. Sit down. There's plenty." He stood up, still holding the wine pitcher, and sat down at the next place in line, filling its goblet, taking a spoonful of its fruit cup. "I know how to do it. You start on that side and work *that* way."

"Where is Messer Lorenzo?"

"Lorenzo is . . . indisposed. And Ser Giuliano is ridden off . . . excuse me, has ridden off . . . to Pisa, to bring back *Professore Dottore* Leone. Is ridden off? Off ridden is, in German."

"Is there no one in the house?"

"I am. You are. He is. Lorenzo's parties are no fun without Lorenzo."

Ficino was not just drunk, Cynthia realized; in fact, he was not particularly drunk at all. He had been left alone, which bred melancholy in him; and she knew that in one of Ficino's temperament a melancholy could kill.

She knocked the goblet from his hand, splashing red over yards of tablecloth and settings. She took him by the arm and lifted him from his seat; it took a moment for his bad leg to lock, but finally he stood looking up at her. The bleakness in his eyes threatened to draw her in as well. She asked the gods who sent his visions to leave his spirit in his body, just for now.

"All right, *Dottorina.* Your slave. What do you desire?"

"Have Lorenzo moved to the quiet chamber."

"He can't stand."

"Bed and all, then! We'll also need a brazier, and a kettle. And two bottles of brandy."

"Is that his problem, *Dottorina?* He's in labor?"

She almost slapped him, but saw his faint smile and realized that his fickle humor had returned. She could not smile at all, she found, but Ficino would be well.

Unless Lorenzo died, of course, in which case nothing mattered anyway.

* * *

Lorenzo de' Medici was dying.

His arms and legs were contorted, in pain at rest and red agony in motion. But that was not the worst of it. His skin was hot and very dry, and she knew he would be itching everywhere; his kidneys were beginning to fail, and if that went beyond a certain point there would be no way on earth to save him . . . except the treatment that had saved Galeazzo Maria Sforza. And she would kill Lorenzo first.

She slammed the door of the quiet chamber, heard its bolt fall. Lorenzo and Giuliano each had a key. One brother would open the door, or the other would.

Ficino was pouring the brandy into the kettle. Cynthia took the pendant from around her neck, opened it, emptied the yellow powder within into the liquid.

"And what is that?" Ficino said.

"Colchicum extract."

"Oh," the poet said, very softly. "I understand."

Dosage and time were crucial. Lorenzo was to receive two measured spoonfuls of the infusion every hour. Cynthia had taken a little German clock from its shelf upstairs; it took ten minutes to prove that just staring at the hands was intolerable. Then Ficino began reciting poetry to the tick of the clock; and he knew volumes. The first hour passed. Two more spoonfuls. The second hour. Two more. The third. Ficino's voice began to rasp, and he wished for an untainted bottle of brandy. Cynthia tried to sing, as she had improvised at summer's end, but that had been too long ago. She could not invent words. She could not even remember a song. There was no music in her.

By the seventh hour Lorenzo had visibly relaxed. He asked for and drank a little water. Cynthia sponged his forehead, then, at his nod, gently bathed his arms and legs. His fingers were nearly straight.

After Cynthia fed him the dose for the eighth hour, Lorenzo breathed in and out slowly and said, "Well, Luna . . . well, well." They were all silent for fifteen minutes by the clock; then Lorenzo began to recite a poem. It was Dante Alighieri, from the *Commedia dell'Uomo*, the part where the poet has finally reached the correct exit from the corridors and courts of Pluto's kingdom. He had always loved Dante's puns on Pluto's cave, and Plato's.

Ficino took the lines of Virgil Magus, and the two of them went into recitative; Cynthia had no spirit to join the play, but the time began to pass much more swiftly. When the poet reached the moon, she knew she was meant to smile at the lines about Luna, and so she did, whatever she felt.

At the twelfth hour Lorenzo sat up. He took the key to the chamber door from his pouch and gave it to Ficino. In the poet's face was a light of clear and absolute joy.

When he had gone, Lorenzo turned his head. He spoke coolly. "Now, *Dottorina*, it is time you told me the truth."

She did.

"Savonarola . . . it seems I recall him; one of those who come to Fiorenza in search of freedom and at once demand the abolition of all freedoms they do not like. And who was the divine emperor, to whom he was . . . praying?"

"Daia. Maximin Daia."

"I do not recall that one. There are so many deified rulers. Probably me too, someday. I suspect this Daia is no friend of Minerva's, though. You can tell the Gonfaloniere enough to let them find the house?"

"I can take them there."

"No."

"I . . . understand, Magnificent." She wondered if there was any point in asking him to spare Vittorio. Possibly they would only be exiled. But she thought of the *alberghetti*, the little cell at the top of the Vecchi tower. On an impulse, she knelt beside the couch.

"What in Hecate's name are you doing?"

She looked up.

"If we're to rescue your family, I'll have to stay sick for a little while longer. I may even have to die for a day or two. Now. The Milanese, or the Byzantines, or both of them, will be attacking us at any time now. There's only time for one campaign before winter; if the city falls, it will be a long time before the weather changes. We need troops, and rapidly. Do you know the Duke of Urbino, Federigo? His son was at Careggi last summer."

"I have met him, Magnificent."

"Good. Federigo is the only chivalrous man left in Italy—and also the best *condottiere*, gods know how that happened. You'll take him a mercenary contract, fast as you can—I hope we've got a blank one somewhere." Lorenzo smiled grimly. "Tell him it is Byzantium coming. They've been trying to annex his duchy to the Roman states for years now, and he hates their bloody guts."

"Magnificent, I—"

"Luna. *Dottorina* Ricci. Yes, I trust you." More distantly he said, "If nothing else . . . only I can save your family."

Ficino came in pushing a cart with bread, eggs, jam, and a pitcher of golden apple juice. "It's morning," he said, a huge happy grin on his unshaven, sunken-eyed face. "A beautiful morning."

"Marsilio," Lorenzo said, "Call the Gonfalonier of Justice. Tell him to come quickly and quietly; there is treason, and we must strike it swiftly."

Ficino looked at Cynthia, suddenly sad again. "Yes, Magnificent. Could we have breakfast first?"

Gently, Lorenzo said "Breakfast in a moment, Marsilio. And have the grooms ready a post-horse for Cynthia. Quickly, please."

With a faraway glance at Cynthia, Ficino bowed and went out.

"Poor Marsilio," Lorenzo said. "He never loses his wits around beauty alone . . . but for beauty and brains he is an utter fool." He looked at the tray. "I don't think I can eat just yet. Would the cider be good for me?"

"Very good, Magnificent."

"Which? Very good, or magnificent?" He looked at her, shook his head. "You should eat, though. It's two days' hard ride to Urbino."

"Lorenzo . . ."

"Well, that's an improvement."

"I would wait until . . . the soldiers have opened the traitors' house."

"I would rather you were away quickly, and gone before we act against them . . . but that is too much to ask.

"If you will not smile, Luna, will you drink a little cider with me?"

She poured two cupfuls. "To *virtú,*" Lorenzo said, raising his cup to her. *Virtú:* Ficino's word for the special strength of the spirit, the strength to act and to be, despite all the world around you.

"Virtue had nothing to do with it," Cynthia said, and Lorenzo laughed and laughed as they drank.

Cynthia was ready to drop from the saddle and die; on second thought she lacked the strength to fall down. She kept falling asleep without noticing; the landscape would seem to dissolve from one scene into another, Tuscan plains into foothills, hills into Apennines, one mountain pass into another. The post-horse knew the way, though, and the courier who rode escort with Cynthia knew when to stop their travel for a little rest and food and water. They did not come to a full stop until almost midnight, and then, the courier explained, it was only because of inadequate moonlight for traveling.

Cynthia had waited in the quiet room with Lorenzo until the Gonfaloniere returned: they had taken the house, two spies, and Savonarola—but the house was empty of hostages, the spies knew nothing of any kidnapping, and the flagellant would not talk and probably could not be made to.

They would keep searching. The city was large. Cynthia would ride for Urbino.

Dawn came the color of a skin rash, the air full of the cries of birds too stupid to learn a song. It was cold, too. She got off her horse to take a piss, and abruptly was riding again, the pressure relieved, her clothes quite dry; the courier had not the smallest gleam in his eye and Cynthia didn't want to know the details.

She began to notice, dimly, that the mountain villages they had passed had less wood and more stone in their construction; some of the places where they paused might have been castles. Then, gradually, she emerged from her fog, and saw that the country was indeed full of fortified houses, and gates across the road, and little forts high up the slopes, good for dropping things on travelers from. She asked the courier if Federigo da Montefeltro had so many enemies as that.

"None at all, my lady. The New Romans—the Byzantines—tried to take Urbino from the good Duke, tried four times. They never got one foot of it, and they finally quit trying."

"So all this is left over from old wars? The forts are empty?"

"No, my lady. The Duke says the Romans will come again, and they're welcome to try."

At nightfall they came around a last curve in the road, to a twin-towered gate overlooking a steep valley. There were lights down the slope.

"Urbino, my lady," said the courier, unease in his voice.

Cynthia was startled by the number of lights spread out on the hillside; she had always heard that Urbino was small.

Then she saw that the lights of buildings were only a part of the total. There was a camp spread out around Urbino. A military camp. The sounds of metal being pounded, the flare of forges, carried up to them.

A spearman stepped into the gateway. "Who's there?"

"Messenger," said the courier. "From the Medici of Florence."

Cynthia saw the spearpoint waver in the air. She was suddenly quite awake.

"Both of you are messengers?" said the sentry.

"We're together."

"Wait here," the sentry said, and signaled to the gate towers. He turned and started down the track to the camp.

"Messenger, I said!" The courier threw aside his cloak, showing the livery badge and wings of Mercury on his coat. There was no response. He reached to his belt and drew the Rienzi wand, the silver rod that assured his free passage anywhere in Italy. Nothing happened. He leaned over to Cynthia. "Something's very wrong, my lady. They can't stop us, though, not lawfully. Follow me."

They walked their horses to the gate. Two spearmen crossed their weapons across the path. "You were told to wait," one of the soldiers said, but his voice was uncertain, and he looked sidelong at the silver wand.

A party was riding up the road. "Now what in Zephyrus's name . . ." the courier said, then, bewildered, "Milanese soldiers?" Cynthia felt dizzy.

The armed and armored men were indeed wearing the flower badge of Milan. At the center of the group rode a slim man, with a crimson cloak thrown back from his shoulder, showing ermine lining and a doublet diapered with golden fleurs-de-lis. His left stocking was brown, his right white.

The hands on the reins were delicate and very pale. His nose was hooked, his lips small and pouting. His eyes were absolutely black. His cheeks were white, with a vivid red bloom; Cynthia knew the condition. This was Galeazzo Maria Sforza, who raped noblewomen and sent their husbands and fathers illuminated parchments detailing the act; the Duke of Milan; the vampire.

"I have a message for the Duke," the courier said, "from my lord Lorenzo de' Medici of Florence."

"I am a duke," Sforza said, mildly, pleasantly. "What is the message?"

"The message is for the Duke of Urbino, my lord."

Sforza stroked his chin. "The land is full of dukes. It's hard to say who is duke of where—or what tomorrow may bring."

The courier held out the Rienzi wand, pointed it at Galeazzo. "My lord, let me pass. You know the law of Italy."

"No," Sforza said offhandedly, "I *am* the law of Italy. Guards, take these assassins." The Duke's black eyes shifted to Cynthia. Her hood was down and her hair fell around her face. Sforza's eyes widened, and his lips parted.

Cynthia spurred her horse and charged past all of them, hearing shouts behind her. The courier cried out once.

She passed the town by, riding directly into the army camp; as she had hoped, the soldiers wore the Montefeltro badge, not the Milanese. There was a large pavilion ahead, with light spilling from its flap. She reined in before it. The horse was panting. So was she.

A man with a patch over his right eye and a horribly broken nose took the horse's reins from her before she could grab them back. "Who are you?"

"Is this the Duke Federigo's tent?"

"Tell me who wants to know," the ugly man said, not harshly.

"I have a message . . . from Lorenzo de' Medici . . . tell your lord there is treachery."

She tried to dismount, slipped and fell; the man caught her, put her on her feet. "Come on," he said, and led her into the tent. The one-eyed man put Cynthia in a chair, poured her a cup of brandy, and made her take a swallow. Warmth rose within her.

"I apologize, Duke Federigo. I didn't know you at first."

Federigo da Montefeltro rubbed his ruined nose. "Didn't know it was that dark," he said. "Now, *madonna,* what do you have to tell me?"

"Sforza—" She looked at the tent flap. "The Duke Sforza killed my companion. He's coming—"

Federigo moved like oiled machinery. "You, there," he called to a knot of men, "watch this door. No one enters, not even Duke Galeazzo." He closed the tent flap.

"Now," Federigo said, crossing his heavy arms, "tell me the news from Florence."

It did not take long. Federigo stood still as a bronze through the story, not even blinking.

"I have Lorenzo's contract here," Cynthia said, opening her doctor's pannier.

"My lady," the Duke said, as gently as his voice would allow, "I have a *condotta* already. With Milan. Against Florence."

"What does that mean?" she cried. "Sforza is a monster—"

"And I am a man of my word," Federigo said. "I have

been a contract warrior for forty years, and not once—*not once*—have I broken a contract." He held up a hand, lowered it, shook his head as if not expecting her to understand. She wondered if she did.

He said slowly, "I know Sforza is a bad man. You should have known his father, the great Francesco . . . but there is still honor to be served in a contract with a bad man."

"Is there honor in a contract made under false pretexts?"

"In what way false?"

She thought of the mountain forts, of Lorenzo's advice. *He hates their bloody guts.* "This isn't Galeazzo's war. He's a cat's-paw. For Byzantium, the Romans."

Federigo made two fists. "Can you prove that?"

"No. But perhaps Sforza can."

Federigo walked back and forth. Lanterns flickered as he passed. He paused at a camp table, stared at a map unrolled upon it. "Very well. I will ask him." He looked at her, his one eye piercing. "I cannot break the *condotta.* But if this is more of the Romans' doing . . . it is a long march over the mountains to Florence. It might take a long time, that march, with winter so near."

"Thank you, Duke Federigo."

"You thank a soldier after the battle. Or not, as it happens. Come here." He took her hand in his own callused one. "I remember you, at Lorenzo's summer court. My son thought you were a witch. Are you?"

"No, my lord."

"But you know the power of the crocus." He pointed at Cynthia's pendant. "Guidobaldo doesn't know it, but his grandmother was a witch. She healed me with the crocus. . . ." He indicated a screen near the tent wall. "Go back there and watch."

She hid, looking out through a gap between the panels. Federigo went to the door and called, "Antonio! Tell the Milanese he can come in now. Without his guards."

Sforza entered. "Where is she, Federigo?"

"Who?"

"*Who.* The Medici courier. What did she tell you?"

"What did you expect her to tell me, Galeazzo?"

Sforza said in an amused tone, "Don't play intriguer with me, Federigo; it isn't your game."

"No," Federigo said, "no, I'm just a stupid, half-blind warhorse. I thought there was some little bit of your father's blood in you, but if Francesco set out to kill a prince he'd do it and have done, not corrupt others—"

"There's a little of a lot of people's blood in me," said Galeazzo with an ugly grin, "but what *ever* are you talking about, Federigo?"

Montefeltro told him.

"Oh, that's delightful," Sforza said, chuckling. "The Medici doctors, poisoners to begin with—ah, the white-haired woman! That was Lorenzo's Diana, wasn't it? Now, that will be a thrilling virgin doe to run down.

"You're not laughing, Federigo. I like the people I'm with to laugh, or else scream."

"I don't see the joke."

"Oh, too bad. Here's a better one, then. I don't care if you attack Florence with me, or sit here and freeze your back-side. All I really wanted was your name on the paper; your word recorded. There are quite enough soldiers marching from Rome." Galeazzo took a long, thin dagger from his belt, scraped at a fingernail. "Consolidation, Federigo. Byzantium gets Florence, Milan gets Genoa and enough of Venice to make the borders straight. Urbino will be in the middle of things, but you're used to that, aren't you?"

Federigo made a spectacularly obscene gesture. "What makes you think they'll stop at Florence, you stupid child? Why should they share Italy with you?"

Sforza looked suddenly startled. "They . . . shared France with the English. . . ."

Federigo went to the table, threw the map aside, snatched up the paper beneath it. "I may be no intriguer, but I know the Romans very well. They sometimes wait to take the pile, but they *do not* share." He shook the *condotta* at Galeazzo. "Pah! An idiot's word means nothing!" He thrust the paper into a lantern flame.

"Oh, no," Sforza said quietly, and moved with startling

speed. He seemed to hug Federigo; Cynthia could just see
the flash of the dagger hilt between Galeazzo's thin fingers. The Duke of Milan let the Duke of Urbino fall, shaking, to the ground. Then Sforza's black eyes blazed, and he
drew another, very thin knife from his cuff. "Half-blind old
warhorse, indeed." Federigo stirred; Galeazzo kicked him
in the abdomen, the small of the back. "I don't like the
taste of horses' blood. But let's see how you taste." He
knelt by the fallen man, probed at his throat.

Cynthia shoved Sforza's head forward, pushed her long
scalpel into the back of his neck, and cut the spinal cord.
Galeazzo's arms flapped, and he shrilled and gurgled. Cynthia pulled out the knife, yanked the Duke's hair, throwing him on his back; cut his doublet open. He was not
wearing armor beneath it this time, either. It was too bad,
she thought, that those Milanese assassins had not known
more anatomy.

She attended to Federigo. The long dagger was hilt-deep
in his armpit. It must lie perilously close to his heart. She
had heard of blades actually entering the heart, the muscle wall seizing on them; the victim lived until the steel
was withdrawn.

"Doctor Ricci?"

"Please be quiet, Duke Federigo."

"Bring . . . Ercole da Siena. My scout."

"Duke Federigo—"

"Will you save anyone? Bring Ercole."

Da Siena came in, a small wiry man in brigandine armor covered with dark blue velvet, a part of the night coming out of the night. He put his ear close to Federigo's lips
and listened. He said "Of course, my lord." Then he stood,
said to Cynthia, "I will have the horses outside in three
minutes. The others will deal with Sforza's men." Without
waiting for a reply, he was gone, silent in his armor.

"Duke Federigo," she said for the third time, knowing it
was useless.

"Go with Ercole," he said. "I have a son . . . who signed
no contract."

Ercole da Siena's hand was on her shoulder. Numbly, she followed him.

Da Siena led her across the mountains, through high stony fields and ragged passes barely wide enough for their horses, on paths that only eagles knew; and in half the time of the outward trip, by late afternoon of the next day, they were at the gates of Florence.

Da Siena had not spoken twenty words to Cynthia during the journey; now he said two more—"my lady"—turned his horse and rode back toward the hills and his master, or his master's son.

The streets were strangely empty. The doors of the Palazzo Medici were closed; Cynthia leaned against them, pounding, until they opened. Cynthia pushed past the servant, seeing nothing to either side, and walked fast to the main hall—almost colliding with the spears that blocked her entry.

"Let her pass," she heard Lorenzo say, and the spears were withdrawn; Cynthia staggered through the door.

Lorenzo sat in Piero's wheelchair. Lucrezia stood behind her son; she turned and left the room. Lorenzo was wearing his red doublet with the round *palle* on the breast.

On the couches in the center of the room lay Giuliano de' Medici and Marsilio Ficino; she knew they were dead even before she saw the wounds. Lorenzo tapped his fingers on his knees.

"What happened?" she said. He looked up sharply, and she realized it had come out as a shriek.

"Your father . . ."

Oh, no, no, no, she thought.

"He believed you had been taken hostage, I suppose. I don't really know. Giulian' had just come back from Pisa, and met him in the foyer. Ficino was in the next room . . . he heard Giuliano cry out, and came in." Lorenzo's hands gripped his knees. There was sweat on his forehead. "My poor lame poet."

"And my father?"

"Ficino returned with the Gonfalonier's men," Lorenzo

said, as if he had not heard. "They found the house where the hostages had been. They found a limepit. . . . There never were any hostages, Cynthia."

"And my father?"

"The fast poison. The blue salt. Now I am done hurting you."

Cynthia's mind was empty; there was nothing to think, nothing to say or do or feel. The universe was a black bottomless funnel to nowhere, and there was no end to horror.

A sound like thunder rolled through the still, cold air.

One of the household troops came in. "My lord, the Ten of War require your presence. There are cannon, the light Byzantine guns, ranging on the walls."

"Please ask them to come here. It will save time." The guard bowed and went out.

"Is the Duke of Urbino coming to rescue us, Luna?"

Cynthia told him what had happened in the tent.

Lorenzo closed his eyes, in pain or prayer. "One stone is removed from the arch, and the arch falls; then the pillars buckle, the walls shake, the structure collapses. . . The Archimedian—what was his name?"

"Leonardo."

"Leonardo once told me he could bring down Brunelleschi's Pantheon with a single swing of the pick. It troubled him, that something so great and beautiful should be so vulnerable. Where will you flee, Luna?"

"I am a Florentine, Messer Lorenzo."

"No. No more. Go north, through Milan. Milan's troubles will begin soon enough—the brick is already out of their arch—but now it is the safest way. If there's anything you need, money, a coach . . ."

"Lorenzo, I would rather stay."

"Bella Luna—do you remember the English story, of Arthur? Sending the one away, at the end, to tell the story?" He rested his eyes on the carved ceiling. She hoped he would not cry. He said "Madonna Lucrezia used to say that the incubus who brought Arthur down, was Theodora of Byzantium, after she turned vampire to save herself from

death. But surely not . . . surely they would not succeed in ruining a king, and then fail to take his country."

Lorenzo pushed himself to a table, took two goblets. There was a keg of red wine open, for those paying their respects to the dead. Lorenzo dipped the goblets to fill them and gave one to Cynthia. The cups were of red quartz, engraved in gold with LAUR. MED.

"You shouldn't drink *trebbiano*," she said. "It's terrible for your gout."

He smiled, put a hand on the side of his chair, and stood up slowly. He held out his cup. "To *virtú*," he said, "however little rewarded."

She looked at the *palle* on his doublet, red on red, as the wine in the cups. "To balls," she said, and listened to the Magnificent's laughter for the last time. The cannon thundered again, not as far away. She felt the strong fumy wine, and the touch of Lorenzo's lips against her hand, and wondered what would happen when finally she felt the pain.

PART TWO

Companions of the Storm

Is there a murderer here?
    —ACT V, SCENE 3

Chapter 4
ARRIVALS

THE mercenary put a coin on the bartop, spun it, and rapped his knuckles on the wood as the silver danced. After a moment the innkeeper appeared, very formal in his dark green coat and starched white apron. The other two men in the taproom had not moved at all, or made any sound.

"More of the hippocras," said the mercenary, in loud, thick French. The coin toppled and rang to a stop. The innkeeper picked it up, went to a kettle over a small fire, and filled a wooden pitcher with the syrupy wine punch.

Across the room where the two men sat, the fire crackled in an updraft, and snow drove against the windows with a rattling sound.

"Bad night," the mercenary said, into the air. "Do you suppose the coach will get here at all?"

"It has happened," said the innkeeper, without inflection, "that coaches have been caught in the high pass by these sudden storms."

"That sounds very bad for the passengers."

"Usually they do not survive."

"And do they eat one another? I've heard that."

The innkeeper wiped spilled wine from the bar.

The mercenary said "You speak good French. Are you Italian?"

"My name is Jochen Kronig. I am Swiss."

"Ah, Swiss. Not too far for you to go then, when this damned Milan falls to pieces." The mercenary drank, wiped his black beard on his leather sleeve. "Will you go north, then? Back to Switzerland?"

"There will still be customers for my inn."

The mercenary laughed. "Right enough! There's always work for a man who's not particular, that's what I say. Pounds Milanese or gold bezants, who cares? Like your army, no? Swiss Army's always well employed, and they never put too fine a point on anything but their pikes." He laughed, drank. "Have some of this yourself. I'm paying. Come on, have some, against the chill. Never be too particular about who buys the wine, that's what I say."

The inkeeper glanced at the two other guests, who still kept to themselves. Then he stared straight at the mercenary. He raised a flat silver tasting cup on a chain, filled it, sipped. "Thank you, sir. Most gracious."

The mercenary burst out laughing. Then he picked up the pitcher and his cup and crossed the room to the two seated men. "Speak you French?" he said, in terrible Italian.

One of the men was young, dark. He wore a doublet of deep gold velvet, with metal plates riveted beneath the fabric, and high cavalry boots. On his sleeve was a band with the fleur-de-lis of Milan. He was staring at his muscular hands.

The other man was much older-looking, hair all gray. He wore a long gray gown with a plain white shirt showing at the throat, and a heavy black cloak was across his shoulders, though it was not cold in the taproom. He tilted his head up; his eyes were friendly, but penetrating. *"Je parle français,"* he said pleasantly.

"I am Charles," the mercenary said, with a sort of bow. "Charles de la Maison. Soldier in the service of Fortune. You?"

"Timaeus Plato," the old man said, then smiled. "Soldier in the service of Learning."

The other man continued to look at his hands. After a moment Timaeus Plato said "This is Captain Hector.

Please excuse him; he has no French. He is in the same line of work as yourself, and—"

"I can guess," Charles said. "Duke Sforza's dead, Ludovico's dithering, and his paymaster's Eris-knows-where. Hey, Captain!" he said, in his bad Italian. "Cheer up, we've all been there. Here, have some of this treacle, make you sick enough to forget anything."

Hector looked up slowly. He pushed a cup across the table, watched Charles fill it. *"Grazie,"* he said.

"If you excuse my Italian, I can talk that we all hear, no?" Charles said. "Why sit you here? From Milan going?"

Timaeus Plato said "Eventually."

"Ah, you meet somebody, from the coach off. Francer? Swiss?"

"I wonder if the coach will ever get here," Plato said absently. "Is it true that sometimes they eat one another?"

"Eat, yes, raw. Why meet man in nowhere inn, in country falling under Byzantium?"

"I can't imagine," Plato said, "unless to kill him."

Captain Hector's eyes flicked sidewise.

Charles laughed. "Yes, kill him. Good way to pass time, think about if enemy come through door. How kill him? How get away? Keeps mind busy. And who know? We all got enemies; maybe one come through door, and better you be ready, or dead." He drank from the pitcher, with loud slurps and gurgles. "Say, where did go that magician? Italian?"

"I suppose he's in the barn," Plato said. "That's where he's sleeping, and the earlier he goes out, the less snow there'll be to wade through."

"Ah. I think, that thing to speak on, two wizards in same inn."

Plato said "Who's the other?"

Charles said in French, "And if your friend didn't take his pay in advance he has goat's brains." He moved the pitcher to tap Hector's cup, smiled broadly. "And probably other parts too."

Hector looked blank, drank. Wind rattled the windows. There was a noise, a series of noises, from outside the taproom. Kronig the innkeeper came around the bar, a cloak over his arm.

"The coach?" Charles said. Kronig went on past. Plato stood to follow him; Charles and Hector looked at one another for a moment more, then went as well.

There was a coach in the innyard, snow piled a span deep on its roof, its lamps beating uselessly against the sheets of white. The horses stamped and snorted fog like dragon's breath.

The coach door was opened and the step kicked down before the coachman could reach them. A tall, slender man in glossy boots and a silk cloak stepped down, then reached up to assist another passenger: a woman wrapped tightly in yellow velvet. A gust pushed her hood aside, and gold hair blew out straight. The man's cloak flapped back as he steadied her on the steps, showing the courier's wings of Mercury on his jacket, the Rienzi wand in his belt. There was a large leather pouch slung across his chest.

Timaeus Plato spoke for a moment with the coachman. On returning he said, "Not the scheduled coach from the north. This is a special, from the south; just the courier and the gentlewoman."

"From Milan City?" Charles asked.

Plato did not seem to notice the question. "They've stopped for a meal, and to check the pass conditions with the southbound driver."

"They're not going any farther," Hector said, looking at the black and white sky.

Not a quarter of an hour later the regular coach arrived, the driver knocking inches of snow from his shoulders; confirmed that the pass into Switzerland was closed until further notice.

As the new and old guests entered the inn, the innkeeper bustled, calling for porters, issuing orders to kitchen and chamber staff. Warm wine and mulled ale and herb tea appeared.

"I had an officer like him," Charles said, "thank Eris only one. The Swiss Army must be a Hell with pikestaffs."

There had been two passengers on the coach from

Switzerland. One called himself Antonio della Robbia, a Medici banker. He wore a long gown of brown stuff, hose particolored brown and white, and he fairly dripped jewelry. Della Robbia's voice was thick, and he sneezed and apologized.

The other had on a severe, straight-lined gown of white linen with a loose cowl. His boots were practical, if unfashionable, and well worn. Perched on his large nose were eyeglasses with tinted lenses and fine silver frames. He introduced himself, in careful schoolbook Italian, as Gregory von Bayern, natural scientist.

Timaeus Plato spoke loudly in German. He took von Bayern aside, and the two of them spoke rapidly.

The courier's name was Claudio Falcone. Charles said "You are from the Sforza, yes?"

"Yes," Falcone said distantly.

"Maybe I then know your message."

Falcone turned sharply. There was a silence. Charles looked around for a moment, apparently enjoying the response, then tossed his head back and shouted "My dear Anybody: *Help!* Sforza." He laughed, alone. Then he said "And where is your companion? This is only an infantryman's sizing up, you know, but if I were on a journey, with threat of being snowed up, nothing else to eat—"

"The *lady*," Falcone said coldly, "has business to the north. Naturally I offered my coach . . . and my protection." He touched the silver wand.

"So, I am in the wrong business," Charles said.

Jochen Kronig said "The *signorina* is changing. There are hot baths upstairs, for all travelers; there will be dinner shortly."

The main inn hall was warm, and brilliant with lamps and candles, the windows shuttered against the piling snow. As the guests descended from their rooms upstairs, having changed from traveling clothes into clean brocades and velvets, Kronig met each one at the foot of the staircase, asking after the quality of each accommodation, the handling of each bag, the temperature of each bath. As the interrogation ended the guest was presented with a mazer of hippocras, hot and strong with ginger and cinnamon.

In the hall, table servers in linen tunics walked silently on leather pattens, with plates of hot parsnip soup. There was Brie cheese with honey and mustard, and dried pears plumped in sugar syrup. In the gallery above the kitchen doors a lyre and recorder played, and innkeeper Kronig apologized that more musicians were not available.

Kronig turned. His eyes widened and his round face flushed. *"You!"*

In a corner of the hall, a man stood next to one of the servers. He wore a voluminous gown of dark blue cloth, coarse and patched, and a cylindrical Turkish cap with a yellow tassel. His shoes were undyed leather nailed over wooden soles, his hose heavy wool. He was busily loading a trencher with slices of venison, beef, and fine white bread from the tray the servant patiently held.

The man froze, staring at the innkeeper; then he stuck the slice of beef he held into his mouth, made a finger gesture, and pointed at the fireplace; the fire blazed up, throwing colored sparks. All heads turned. The man used the moment to snatch a pitcher of wine from the sideboard and get a good head start to the door.

Kronig fumed. "Nottesignore the mighty wizard," he said tightly. "I thought he was in the stables. Well, we'll see how he enjoys it after—"

"Here, my good host," Timaeus Plato said, holding out a silver penny. "Men must eat. Even wizards."

Kronig was intantly mollified. "Of course, Professor Doctor."

Falcone the courier was wearing a sharply tailored black doublet and tight silk hose, his courier's heraldry prominent on his breast. The banker, della Robbia, had changed into a fur-trimmed gown of red and gold, with red hose. The hot bath had done wonders for his cold. Von Bayern still wore white linen, but had exchanged his boots for white leather house shoes. Around his neck was a light silver necklace, with a convex black disc pendant: a pellet, a heraldic cannonball.

"Where's the French . . . fellow?" Captain Hector said, taking a sip from the silver-footed mazer cradled in his hard hand.

"You're right," Plato said. "He's not here."

Falcone said "The lady is still upstairs," and looked suddenly murderous; he put a hand on the stair rail, looked up. Then he smiled, turned back. "Gentlemen . . . the Lady Caterina Ricardi."

She descended with an easy, precise step, expertly controlling her long skirt of *alessandro* silk, the color of sword steel fresh-blued. The gown's collar was quite low. Her yellow hair was bound up with gold rope and fixed with a long golden pin, in the Grecian style.

Even the wind fell briefly silent.

"Lady Caterina," Claudio Falcone said, "is of the theater in Milan, one of its foremost—"

"Please, Messer Falcone," she said in a dry-humored voice, "you will have the gentlemen thinking too much of me . . . in any of several wrong ways. I worked with costume and makeup. My acting was limited to the crowd scene and the chorus."

"The lady is too modest, of course," Falcone told the others. "I know she appeared on stage many times—"

"Really, Messer Falcone; for a courier you are not very closemouthed! Very well, yes, in Plautus I was a favored knockabout"—she smiled as the others tried to control their expressions—"and in the great production of the *Odyssey* I was Penelope's understudy, and for two hundred performances I had to be ready . . ." She glanced at Falcone. ". . . to put my suitors off."

There was laughter, and Falcone turned pink. Timaeus Plato said "Our host looks distressed. Perhaps we should sit down to this remarkable dinner, before it cools." Then Kronig laughed too.

The musicians played sweetly over the herbed beets and bacon, the gingered fish; it was, in fact, a remarkable dinner for a small inn in November, but mouths were not free to remark much. The Sforza courier made a few more at-

tempts to break through the lady's reserve, but her wit
was not as brittle as it had appeared at first.

Dessert was Damascus-plum funnel-cakes, fantastical
and delicate as lace and dusted with sugar; Jochen Kronig
insisted they must be eaten with black herb tea instead of
wine punch. As the diners relaxed, Timaeus Plato said *"Signorina* Ricardi, I am reminded of the cook's line, in
Pseudolus. Do you recall it?"

Her look might have been challenging, or merely amused.
"I do know Plautus, *Professore Dottore."* She raised a
spoon like a scepter, and declaimed, "I . . . am the savior of
mankind."

Antonio della Robbia, who had talked mostly of how bad
the exchange rates were at the Medici branch in Bern,
turned casually and said "Lady Caterina, were you involved in the production of *Vita Juliani,* written by my
late master Lorenzo de' Medici?"

"Yes," Caterina said. "Of course. I remember it very
well."

Falcone spilled sugar on the front of his black doublet.
He looked discontented.

"I am sorry," della Robbia said. "I was not thinking of
the late enmity between our cities. In Bern we were all far
removed from that. I was only remembering Ser Lorenzo."

"I knew him somewhat," she said, with a soft edge in
her voice, as near drunkenness produces.

"Would you like to drink to him?" della Robbia said
quietly.

"And to the Duke Sforza as well?" Falcone said.

"Of course." Della Robbia stood, raised his cup. The musicians paused. "To the Medici, and the Sforza. To the lords
of Italy." Cups were raised, emptied. The storm howled
through the shutters and the candles flickered.

Claudio Falcone stood, and the wine butler hurried to re-
fill the cups, but Falcone waved him away. *"Signorina, Si-
gnori,* I must confess that I am not used to such hours and
such fare, and I am quite done for today. I must say good
night."

"Your rooms are quite ready," Kronig said.

"That being the case," della Robbia said, "I shall retire also. I am one of those who must read an hour, make some business notes, before I may fall alseep. Good night to you."

"We have a small but choice library," the innkeeper said. "If anyone wishes for tea or wine before bed, or a little snack"—they all groaned—"please ask. There are bell-pulls, of course; ring at any hour."

Caterina Ricardi rose, the others following suit, spilling things. "The coach trip was very long. My compliments, Messer Kronig. And good night to you all."

Kronig beamed. *"Buona notte, Signorina."*

After Falcone, della Robbia, and Ricardi had gone up the stairs, Kronig said "And will you gentlemen require anything?"

"The use of your taproom," Timaeus Plato said. "Mulled ale for myself, and whatever these gentlemen wish to drink, in good supply. And complete privacy."

Captain Hector said, "You understand what 'complete' means—no tapsters, no scullery maids, not even you?"

"Captain," said Jochen Kronig, half hurt and half lordly, "I *am* Swiss."

The old man in gray settled into a chair before the taproom fire, hands on a leather blackjack of ale. The hearth and two candles made the only light. The old man reached up to the right side of his face, put fingertips around his eyesocket, leaned forward. He gave a small sigh. Candlelight sparkled from the eyeball that lay in his palm.

"Venetian glass?" Gregory von Bayern asked, examining the eye. Hywel Peredur nodded. Gregory said "I thought I saw it actually move, with the living one."

"You actually thought it did," Hywel said, slipping a leather eyepatch into place. "A sympathetic illusion. Necessary, I suppose, but it gives me an awful headache after a few hours."

"Then you are, in fact, a wizard."

"I suppose I must be."

Von Bayern looked puzzled for a moment, then gestured

toward Captain Hector, who stood against the wall, arms folded. "All right, *Herr Doktor* . . . Peredur. I have answered the Captain's request for an artillery scientist, somewhat too late, it seems. And you asked me *auf's Deutsch* to be quiet and trust you until we could have a discussion. What are we then discussing?"

"Artillery, possibly."

"Surely the Milanese do not still propose to have Captain Hector invade Switzerland."

"There is no longer a Milan to propose anything," Hywel said. "Now there is only Byzantium."

Gregory said quietly, "And does Byzantium propose . . ."

"The Empire proposes to expand. To annex the world, in careful, patient steps, exactly as it conducted affairs in this country that used to be Italy. Will you grant me that, as a hypothesis?"

"Yes. I will grant you that."

"I have some cause to know that they are planning to disrupt Britain; *are* disrupting it. You know that there was a dynastic war?"

"*Die Plantagenet,*" Gregory said. "Yorks and . . . and . . ."

"Lancasters," said the Captain.

"Yes, Lancasters. But the war is over, is it not?"

"The Lancasters are dead, mostly," Hywel said, "but the tensions are not. I believe the Empire is trying to start another civil war. Not tomorrow, but soon enough that the fabric of the nation would tear under the stress. Flourish of trumpets, alarums; enter Byzantium triumphant." He paused. "They're really very good at it."

"You mean to stop them?" Gregory said, cautiously. He rubbed the frames of his dark glasses with a fingertip. "Are you then a very powerful magician?"

"Oh, no one's that," Hywel said mildly. "I know some things about how the Empire works. And the Captain knows a very great deal about their military practice. He was an Imperial himself . . . be calm, *Herr Doktor.* The Captain's family was murdered by Imperial directive; he's not one of them anymore. While we're in private, his real name is Dimitrios Ducas."

Dimi looked up. "He knows these things. I don't know how he finds them out."

"And you, *Herr Doktor* von Bayern, are a German artillerist; and the Germanies are still in advance of Byzantium in the technology of guns. You also are a very fine mathematician, and your English is excellent."

Gregory's eyebrows rose. Dimi said "See what I mean?" Dimitrios pushed away from the wall, went to the fireplace. "You know well enough I'll go with you," he said to Hywel. "I've no more mercenaries, and no more war here. And if you could learn my name, it's time to move and change again. But why should the Doctor join an enterprise like this? Fighting the Empire is the nearest thing I know to an unarmed charge uphill."

Hywel looked at Gregory. He rolled the glass eye in his fingers. He spoke very softly. *"Seit wann ist die Blutnot bei Ihnen?"*

Gregory said "I am a vampire eight years now."

Dimitrios turned. Ale spattered into the fire.

Gregory said "I thought I hid it well."

"You do," Hywel said. "The white clothing to hide your paleness, the glasses . . ."

"What is this?" Dimi said, a dangerous edge in his voice.

"A disease," Hywel said, "like gout, or pissing sugar."

"Or leprosy, which spreads," Dimitrios said. "The enemy of my enemy is not my friend." He muttered rapidly in Greek.

"The blood of bulls tastes unpleasant," Gregory replied in the same language, "but indeed I have drunk it. Also the blood of snakes, which tastes foul."

Tension was visible in Dimi's whole body.

Hywel said "Please go ahead, *Herr Doktor.*"

Von Bayern sat down across the table from the two men. "I was an associate professor, working at the University at Alexandria. An Imperial official, a magistrate . . . well, she seduced me first. Or I allowed myself to be seduced. Or . . . There is not much blood involved, actually, not at one

time, unless the person is driven to gorge. And infection is
not inevitable. That is what a young man says to a young
woman he desires, is it not? There is not so much blood, not
so much pain, as she has heard, and no consequence is inevitable. Until one morning one wakes up, and is sick." He
smiled, absolutely without humor. "Hungering for strange
things . . .

"I saw my mistress only once again after that, at the
closed court session where I was asked to leave Alexandria."

"You were given no choice," Hywel said.

"I was, for Imperial justice is fair. They had the knives
on the table, ready."

Dimitrios said "And if you had any—honor, you
would have accepted them! But instead you came back, to
spread—disease—"

Gregory stood up, leaned across the table. "You will *not*
speak to me again like that," he said in a deadly tone.
"You do not, cannot, know, what I am or what I have done.
I have killed animals, yes, who cannot be infected. And I
have taken human blood, because without some little of it
I would go mad, gorging-mad, but always I have taken it
with the knife, or the hollow needle, and a cup, never with
nails or teeth. I am Gregory, Fachritter von Bayern, and I
have done what I must, but I have *never* infected another
man or woman!" He turned away from both other men.
"Aber's macht nichts, nicht wahr? You do not know. You
do not know what it is to hate what you must do to stay
alive. To hate yourself for what you cannot help but do."
He bent his head and stood quite still, his face hidden.

Dimitrios emptied his mug, put it on the table with a
bang. In a low voice, he said "I guess I do know that." He
pulled the Milanese badge from his sleeve, threw it on the
table. "I'm with you," he said. "Both of you."

Hywel poured some ale. "Then here's to the enterprise."

"Well begun," said Gregory, and knocked his mug
against Dimi's. The two of them stood like that for a long
moment, not moving or speaking or smiling, and then they
drank.

Dimitrios shortly went up to bed. Gregory stood by the window, looking out at nothing. Hywel faced the fireplace, watching the flames.

Suddenly Gregory said "Can you read minds?"

"I can, but I don't. Faces and bodies can be read as well, or better, and much more easily."

Gregory nodded.

Hywel spoke in German. "It was necessary that he be told. Especially so since you must feed soon. . . . I saw the signs, at dinner. I imagine . . . it is very painful, the hunger."

"Yes," Gregory said, and clenched a fist against his chest. "Yes."

By the time of full light the storm was over. Snow still fell, but gently. The windows of the main hall were unshuttered and bright. Sky and earth outside were the same luminous white, bits of trees and rocks visible between like penstrokes in a faded drawing; there were no shades of gray.

The guests came down to a table loaded with coddled eggs in silver cups, ham and sausage and brains, herring in crust and bread with honey; India tea was served in China-ware cups of an eggshell delicacy.

"It's as if we were visiting royalty," Caterina Ricardi said. "What is my bill going to look like?"

"I suspect there is a sound economic reason for our host's generosity," said Hywel-Timaeus Plato. "Wouldn't you say, Ser Antonio?"

Della Robbia chewed a piece of bacon, looked thoughtful, swallowed. "Why, of course. Thought *is* impeded by a full belly." He turned to Caterina. "You see, *Signorina*, this inn will certainly fall under Imperial authority, as a part of the Directorate of Highways."

Caterina looked blank.

"My lady has never traveled on Imperial roads?"

"Roman roads, but . . ."

"The roads are the world's finest," said Captain Dimitrios-Hector, "and the food served along them is the world's

worst. Worse than camp kitchens, and even more uniform.
Put simply, my lady, Ser Jochen may as well be generous,
for tomorrow he will be an Imperial service."

"And yet," said Hywel, "he begrudges that hedge-
wizard one decent meal."

"Why, Doctor," Dimitrios said formally, "he *is* Swiss."

Della Robbia laughed, turning it into a cough as Kronig
entered. "Sir, has your cold returned?" the innkeeper
asked, and the banker shook his head violently to cover his
expression. Kronig said "But where are my other guests?
Were their hours late?"

Dimitrios said "Where did that Frenchman go, anyway?"

"The unpleasant, drunken fellow?" said della Robbia.
"Perhaps he simply fell into a stupor."

"He was unpleasant and drunk," Dimi said, "but not
that drunk."

Hywel said "Messer Kronig, has Charles de la Maison
taken meals in his room?"

Kronig looked hesitant, as if about to betray a state secret, then said "No, sir. Not even wine."

Dimitrios said "That's very wrong. Men like that don't
miss meals like this—"

A scream, loud and high and long, cut him off.

Kronig went to the stairs and up them with astonishing
speed. The others put down their plates and disentangled
their napkins and followed.

"Which was the Frenchman's room?" Dimi said. "If he's
messing with a serving girl, I'll gladly give him a faceful of
goat's brains."

"That's not where the disturbance is," Hywel said
quietly, and pointed down the hall; at an open door stood
Jochen Kronig, his hands on a trembling chambermaid's
shoulders, interrogating her in a rapid stream of Swiss-
Italian dialect.

Dimitrios reached the door first. He looked past the
innkeeper and the maid, who kept on talking; then Dimi's
hands curled very tight, and he turned to face Hywel with
something close to fury.

Della Robbia reached the door. He said *"Signorina* Ricardi . . . do not look at this."

"Don't be ridiculous," she said, and walked on faster. Hywel was left alone as he slowly proceeded down the hall.

Kronig, suddenly conscious of what went on in the corridor, sputtered a protest and tried to close the door, but Caterina Ricardi pushed him aside. She stared. Her face set hard. She stepped back to let Hywel view the scene, but she did not turn away.

Claudio Falcone lay on his bed, staring at the ceiling, clearly and entirely dead. He wore only his black silk hose, and the sheets were knotted around his legs at knees and ankles. His wrists were tied to the bedposts with pieces of the bell-pull; a linen napkin had been stuffed into his mouth and tied there with another length of cord. Brown blood spotted the linen, and ran in a dry track from his right nostril. There were several cuts on Falcone's arms and upper body, but not much blood from any of them.

Hywel went into the room. Just above Falcone's left shoulder was a patch of congealed blood. A piece of hollow quill had been thrust into the neck, into the large artery. The open end was blocked with granular blood.

On the bedside table were a small knife and a wooden drinking mazer. There was blood on the knife, and in the cup.

Hywel turned his head, in a sudden cold draft: a pane of the window was slightly open. Snow had piled on the sill and the floor.

Hywel turned back to the dead man. The skin of the face was waxy pale, the eyes wide. There was a dark spot at the right temple. The cloth-choked expression might have been horror, or pain, or despair, or perhaps some feeling no one could know and survive. Hywel closed the eyelids and covered the body with a sheet.

Kronig said "I will have the room scoured—"

"Don't do that," Hywel said. "Don't do anything but lock the door."

When the group got downstairs, one man stood in the hall, placing slices of bacon on bread.

Gregory looked up, smiling below his dark glasses, flushes of red brilliant in his cheeks. "Good morning," he said. "Are you all late to breakfast, or am I early?"

"Lady Minerva," Caterina Ricardi almost shrieked, "he is a vampire!"

Chapter 5
DEPARTURES

GREGORY'S smile disappeared, but he did not otherwise react; he did not move as Antonio della Robbia rushed toward him. Della Robbia struck von Bayern across the face, grasped Gregory's left arm and twisted it behind his back. A little white roll tumbled across the floor. Gregory did not speak.

Hywel put a hand on Dimitrios's wrist, gripped it tightly. No one on the stairs took a step farther.

Della Robbia forced Gregory into a chair, still levering at his arm. He reached to von Bayern's face, pulled off the dark glasses, turned Gregory's face to the windows. Gregory spasmed, tried to cover his eyes, made a whimpering, gurgling sound.

"Enough of this," Hywel said. Della Robbia looked up, startled. Even with his leverage, he was having difficulty holding von Bayern.

The innkeeper said, "His bed was not slept in, the maid says."

"Nor was mine," Hywel said, his eyes fixed on della Robbia. "*Herr Doktor* von Bayern, for his condition, and I for my age do not require much sleep. We were up together the whole night, in the taproom, drinking . . . *wine*."

"Is that true?" della Robbia said. Hywel's look was withering. Della Robbia released Gregory, who turned away from the light and groped across the breakfast table for his glasses. He found them in the butter, put them on half-covered with it, and sat shaking.

"Was any one else not in his bed last night?" Hywel asked Kronig. "Messer Charles, for instance?"

They went back up the stairs, leaving Gregory. Kronig's passkey opened an empty room. "You're certain this was de la Maison's?" Hywel said, sniffing the air. It was apparent that no one had used the room for any of its usual functions since its last cleaning. Kronig affirmed that it was the right room, and opened the remaining unoccupied rooms on the floor. All were, and had been, empty.

"What about the wizard?" Dimitrios said. "The one in the barn?"

"He is the next one to ask," said Hywel, "since he was with the horses all night."

Cloaks were brought. Kronig, with Hywel, Dimitrios, and Antonio, stepped out onto the covered inn porch.

"Wait," Hywel said. "Look."

"Damnation," Dimitrios said.

All the way across the courtyard the snow was deep and smooth and unprinted. They crossed to the stables; not a single footprint led from the building.

Guido Tommasi, called Nottesignore, was washing his face in the horse trough when the men came in. "Ah! Good morning, good sirs. Innkeeper, about that dinner last night . . . fear not; I shall provide my own breakfast. Watch." He made a set of elaborate passes in the air, his patched blue sleeves flapping. "Abracadabra . . . abraca-vitti . . . dit! Dit! Dit!"

An egg appeared between his fingers; then there were two eggs, then three. Tommasi presented them to Kronig. "I should like those fried in butter, with the yolks whole . . . and, if you would, a little bacon . . . ."

Kronig looked bewildered. Antonio della Robbia said "Wizard, will you swear before myself and these gentlemen that you did not fly by magic to an inn window last night, and there do murder, for foul magical purpose?"

"What?" said Tommasi. An egg fell out of his sleeve.

"A man was killed last night," Hywel said calmly. "It's

quite simple; you cannot be responsible, unless you can fly through the air."

"In that case," Tommasi said, "I cannot fly." He looked around at the others, then said "I *especially* cannot fly when hurled from high windows to test my claim."

Dimitrios laughed sharply. Antonio gave Hywel a sidelong look. Kronig shook his head and turned to leave.

"Innkeeper . . ." Tommasi said.

They paused.

"While I deeply regret my inability to fly, perhaps certain other of my powers could be of assistance? If I were warm, and could concentrate?"

Kronig grimaced. His hand tightened, then froze on the eggs in his palm. "Come, then."

"And I wonder," said the wizard Nottesignore, "if the murdered man had a breakfast he will not be eating . . . ?"

Yolk and albumen dribbled from the innkeeper's fingers.

"I had not thought," della Robbia said as the servants took their cloaks, "but we left the lady alone, with the vampire."

In the main hall, the lady was applying a cool compress to the vampire's eyes, and offering him India tea with honey. "Can you begin to understand that?" Dimitrios said, aside, to Hywel.

"Perhaps begin to," Hywel said.

Tommasi launched himself into breakfast with an inspiring will, and though the others' appetites had been badly damaged by the scene upstairs, before long a sit-down, stand-up, and move-around meal for six was in progress. Innkeeper Kronig watched with a look of satisfaction that vanished whenever food got near Nottesignore's capacious sleeves.

"Suppose that it was this mercenary Charles," della Robbia said. "Where is he now? Surely he could not have escaped last night on foot. Or even this morning. Wizard, did a man take a horse last night?"

"No," Tommasi said. "And no, sir, I do not snore too loudly to know. My talents," he said with a flourish, "detect all such evil as it approaches."

"Even the woman's husband?" Caterina said, and smiled awkwardly; there was laughter, and Tommasi bowed.

Hywel said "How would you have gotten away, Nottesignore? If you had killed the man."

"Why, I would have cloaked myself in invisibility—"

"Assuming you could not do that. Or transpose yourself in space."

"Well," said Tommasi, not at all chastened, "I think I would have hid. Just as soon as I had done it."

"Where?" della Robbia said.

"There are more places to hide in an inn than a beehive has cells," Tommasi said, with a sly look at the innkeeper. "I'd hide, until the others had found the body, and gone out to the stable to check on the horses and invite Nottesignore to breakfast. *Then*, I'd go out to the barn—"

"In the tracks the others had made," Dimitrios said.

"—saddle the best one, and go, go, go."

Dimitrios della Robbia, and Kronig all started from their places. "Gently," Hywel said. "Might as well send a servant to get snow in his boots. If he's gone that way, he's gone now."

"Well, I'm going to look," della Robbia said. "And if he's not there, I'm going to take a horse and go looking afield. Anyone else who wants to come is welcome. Captain Hector?"

Dimitrios said "I love a ride in the snow."

Della Robbia said "Perhaps the lady would come? The air is fresh, and not cold while still."

"Yes," Caterina said. "I think so."

"And the wizard Nottesignore assist us?"

"Well, I . . . "

"After a heavy meal, one should take some exercise."

"Ah, of course. But I warn you, as my name suggests, my powers are not greatest in the day."

"Of course. And you, Doctors?"

"My joints are like glass in the cold," Hywel said, "and I

fear snow-glare would be quite hard on *Herr Doktor* von Bayern."

"As you say, then. Innkeeper, if you will have horses made ready?"

"At once. I do hope that you find him."

"If the man is on foot in the snow," Hywel said, "how can they fail?"

Hywel and Gregory sat in Hywel's inn room. The curtains were fully drawn, making the room quite dim; a decanter of brandy was between the two men.

"What did you feed on last night?" Hywel said bluntly.

"They keep rabbits in the kitchen. I took two."

"What did you do with the carcasses?"

"Buried them in the snow. I can find the spot if—"

"It doesn't matter to me, and it wouldn't make the others any happier. You're certain it was rabbits."

"Yes," Gregory said bitterly. "I washed up, threw the bloody water down the privy, came down to breakfast. . . . You see, kindness is deadly to vampires; it makes us less careless." Then, more softly, "Why did you lie for me?"

"Because I need you," Hywel said flatly, "and whole. This enterprise is already short one eye."

Gregory sipped brandy, gently touched the side of his head. "Well," he said, "now I suppose you have me."

Hywel said "Blood down the privy, eh. And if someone's bold enough to look there, you can always claim to have piles."

Gregory chuckled.

"How good a locksmith are you?" Hywel asked.

"Fair—how do you know about that?"

"Gunsmiths are usually good with locks. Could you open one of these room doors?"

Gregory looked at the lock. "I think so."

"Then let's look for a murderer."

Claudio Falcone's room was very cold. The scents of candlewax, lamp oil, wood, and linen were just being displaced by the heavy, acid smell of death. The courier's bound wrists stuck out from beneath the sheet, the fingers curled tight.

Gregory pulled the sheet down, stared at what was underneath. Hywel turned, said "Oh. You hadn't seen him."

"No," Gregory said. "Now I understand. It *was* a vampire . . . "

"No, it wasn't. It's an excellent imitation—"

Gregory said "I have seen things you have not."

"—except for this." Hywel put a hand on the window, pushed it shut. "No one went out this way; the snow is undisturbed, and you'd have to be an acrobatic circus dwarf anyway . . . or a bat."

Gregory said "You don't believe that bat-shape, wolf-shape nonsense! Or perhaps that I can turn into smoke and seep under doors?"

"No. And whoever did this doesn't, either. Look at the horrid *care* of it; the ropes, the quill, the cup—he imitates a real *gwaedwr*, not any imaginary one with hypnotic powers or snake fangs—and *then* he opens the window. Why?"

"I don't know. Why was he killed?"

"That we may find out. Start looking for his courier's pouch. A leather bag, size of a middling book."

Gregory covered the body again. During the search, he said, "Could there have been magic involved? That Italian wizard—"

"Is no more a genuine worker than you are, and there's not one within twenty miles."

"Suppose he concealed his powers behind the tricks."

"Can you become a bat? There are many things magic cannot do, and hiding itself is one of them."

They did not find the bag. Hywel noticed a small space between the bedside table and the wall. Taking care not to disturb the knife and cup, he pushed the table aside. There was a small clunk.

"Was ist's?"

"A ring," Hywel said. "Caught between the table and the wall. I wonder . . . " He tried to push it onto Falcone's finger, but the hands were too rigid.

Gregory looked at the enameled design on the ring. "I

know that pattern. Six red balls . . . the Medici." He looked up. "Antonio della Robbia, the Medici banker."

Hywel massaged the orbit of his glass eye. "Yes, the Medici. You rode from Switzerland with the banker, *Herr Doktor*; what did you talk about?"

"We did not talk . . . he was very quiet. And I was growing hungry."

Hywel nodded.

"But that is the Medici sign, I know."

Hywel said "I know it too. In truth, I cannot imagine any educated person west of the City who would not know it. And since it speaks in a voice like thunder, *who would leave it at the scene of a murder?*"

"There is the window business," Gregory said.

"Yes, the window. Maybe the killer is just careful and careless at once. We all make mistakes." Hywel rolled the ring over in his hand. "But some kinds of care and carelessness just do not go together." He sighed. "Let's go downstairs. The others must be back soon."

"Nothing out there," Dimitrios said, sitting before the fire in his riding clothes, his booted legs stretched out straight. "A lot of very bad cavalry country, covered with snow. More snow coming too, I think."

"What about the ravine you pointed out?" Caterina said. "Could he have gone down that?"

"Not and lived. Unless . . . have you ever seen Nordic snowshoes, schees? Long wood slats, and narrow. I knew a Varangian mountaineer who could go down slopes, faster than a horse sprints. But even so, that ravine was thick with trees."

"Still," Jochen Kronig said, with distinct hope, "The man could have gone down there?"

"There were no footprints," Dimitrios said, "or marks in the snow, so he didn't go this morning. And last night, in the dark, and the storm . . . "

"But he could be dead in the ravine?" Kronig persisted. "Not found until the spring?"

"Not until high summer," della Robbia said. "When it will be the Byzantines' problem."

"Let them dig for him," Caterina said.

Dimitrios said "could he still be hiding here?"

"That's a fine thought to sleep on," said della Robbia.

"No," Kronig said hurriedly. "We have searched everywhere. All the servants, the coachmen. Even the doctors helped to search."

"Oh?" della Robbia said. "What about all the places the wizard spoke of? Where is Tommasi, at that? Captain Hector, you came back with him, didn't you?"

"No, I didn't"

"Charles de la Maison," Hywel said, "has vanished, leaving no baggage but an unpleasant memory. It is as if he had no physical existence at all."

"A ghost, perhaps?" della Robbia said.

"We have *no* ghosts," said Kronig.

"Magic," Caterina said, suddenly intent. "An illusion of appearance; a glamour."

"That is the word, I believe," Hywel said pedantically. In the same tone, he went on: "Supposing that Charles de la Maison was another person in disguise, who then was he? We must determine who he was *not*. He spoke with Captain Hector, with Innkeeper Kronig, and with myself—will you gentlemen confirm that he spoke with me?"

As they did, a servant came in in a snow-fringed cloak and spoke in the innkeeper's ear.

Hywel went on: "And he spoke to, or in the presence of, all four coach passengers—not to mention that he could not very well have been present here and aboard a coach at the same time. That leaves only Nottesignore."

"Where *is* Tommasi?" della Robbia said. "He's escaped—ridden away from us while we were searching. He must be miles away by now."

"Lady and gentlemen," Kronig said, "the wizard Guido Tommasi is not miles away. He is in the barn. The mystery," he said with enormous relief, "is solved."

* * *

Nottesignore dangled from a beam, his toes two feet from the straw-covered floor. He had kicked off his wooden-soled shoes as he died. One lay next to an overturned barrel nearby; the other, and his yellow-tasseled fez, were much farther away, near the door.

And in the middle of the barn there was a pile of blackened straw and smoldering leather, the fire beaten out and doused with snow. Bending very gradually, Hywel crouched beside the mess. He smelled lamp spirit.

The leather was the courier's pouch Falcone had carried when he arrived, cut all apart in search of hidden pockets—not just slashed, but expertly dissected.

There were some bits of partly burned paper, really only ashes held together by the ink on them. *The English King's debts* . . . Hywel read from a scrap, and from another . . . *interests of the Bank abroad* . . . Then his first touch disintergrated them. He sighed, tapped his fingers on the still-warm straw.

A flash of color caught his eye. Hywel reached in, pulled out a small, soft lump, of a vivid red color: a wax seal, melted down. He rolled it over in his fingers, flicked it away up his sleeve as Tommasi had done with his eggs. He got to his feet as Jochen Kronig approached.

"This letter explains it all," the innkeeper said. "It was rolled up inside his belt."

Good people:

> *For the murder of Claudio Falcone, a courier under the wand, I make confession and the only atonement I can. I thought to find wealth in his purse, but found only worthless papers. For this terrible waste, I am not worthy to live. I am sorry.*

> *Guido Tommasi*

"He threw the rope over the beam, stood on the barrel, and kicked it over," Kronig said. He looked at Tommasi's congested face. "A bad way to die, I think."

"Terrible," Hywel said, "but ordinary enough." He grasped the hem of Tommasi's gown and lifted it as high as he could, exposing the dead man's lower body, the thick woolen hose stained front and back. The fecal smell was strong.

"What are you doing?" Kronig said, as everyone stared.

"Clever, but still careless," said Hywel, letting the gown fall. "Careless in the strangest ways."

"Doctor . . . "

Hywel took the ball of sealing wax from his sleeve. It was hard now, cold, red as blood. He put it away again. "Let us all go into the hall, Messer Kronig. And if you have a hand-gun in the house, I suggest that you load it."

The problem with Nottesignore's confession," Hywel said, "is that it makes no sense."

"Since when do men's motives have to make any sense?" Caterina said.

Caterina and Dimitrios sat in chairs near the fireplace. Della Robbia leaned on the mantel; Gregory stood with his back to the windows, which were dim now in the late afternoon. Hywel was at the table in the center of the room, Kronig a little behind him.

"I will grant you that they often do not," Hywel said. "But suppose that Charles de la Maison is Nottesignore disguised. What is his motive in ceasing to be Charles? Charles has food, drink, a warm room. Nottesignore has none of these."

"When he decided to rob the courier," said della Robbia, "he may have supposed the man in the barn would be less suspected."

Dimitrios said "The footprints—"

"Would have been blown away by the storm, if he left early enough," Hywel said, "a possibility I did not mention to Tommasi because I wanted him to be a little overconfident. Well, he was, and that is my contribution to his death.

"Messer della Robbia, you are a banker. You must have a great deal of money with you."

Della Robbia laughed. "On a journey alone? Traveling money only."

"And *Signorina* Ricardi? Surely you have, if not money, then jewels?"

"I . . . no. A few things, of mostly personal value."

"Ah? Then our robber is cleverer than I. I would have thought a banker or a court lady likelier targets than a government courier. But no matter. The thief strikes. He enters the courier's room"—Hywel spoke very slowly— "kills him, in a particularly slow and elaborately cruel fashion . . . and goes out to his safe and unsuspected barn with his prize. Opening the pouch, he finds not gold, not letters of credit, but only ducal papers. In a fit of remorse over his waste of time and effort, he hangs himself. End of tale."

"Except," Dimitrios said, "that Nottesignore was alive this morning."

"That is true," Hywel said. "So let us try to salvage the hypothesis: we assume that Tommasi kept the pouch, without opening it, all night and most of the day. . . . He did not strike me as such a patient man."

"Nor me as a murderer," Dimitrios said, with a glance at Gregory, "at least not a fancy torture-murderer. But we're still short a Frenchman. Charles couldn't have been anyone *but* Tommasi. . ."

Hywel said "No one expects a single inn guest to be in disguise. Why should one expect two?"

All present examined one another.

Hywel said "Suppose two men meet at a coach station. One is a wandering hedge-wizard, good at sleights and disguises as such people are, hungry as they usually are. Call him Guido. The other . . . call the Agent.

"The Agent offers Guido a chance to travel by coach instead of on foot, and a warm inn bed—which, since it is November and snowing, sounds better than money. All Guido has to do is pretend to be the Agent for a little while."

Della Robbia said "It sounds like a very shady arrangement."

"But Guido is a little shady. And cold. And he agrees.

The coach departs with Guido aboard; the Agent is left behind at the station with Guido's clothes. But he does not
put them on. He dresses up as a mercenary, in leather and
steel, gets on a fast horse such as mercenaries prefer to
ride, and follows the coach; and passes it.

"So he reaches the inn that will be the next coach stop.
He makes sure that the guests there see him, remember
him, but don't become too interested in him; some well-
placed coarseness and insult does that well. And when the
chance arises, he changes into the wizard's clothes, puts in
an appearance, changes again."

"But where does Charles *go?*" Dimi said.

"Both disguises, Guido and Charles, have faults. Guido
cannot stay in the inn, and Charles's makeup and language
have an ever-increasing chance of being penetrated."

"Or punched in," Dimitrios said.

Hywel said "My lady, how closely may a quick makeup
be examined? No, that's a poor question. How long before
it slips, or wears off?"

"It depends on the kind, and circumstances," Caterina
said very evenly. "Hours, perhaps."

"But if the wearer were to, say, eat an elaborate meal?"

"Meals on stage are the very bane of a makeup artist's
life."

"Or bathe?"

"Almost anything would have to be reapplied then, of
course."

"If the hair were colored with saffron, would pinning it
up in the Grecian style protect it through a bath?"

Ricardi said pleasantly, "Surely, *Professore* Plato, you
are not suggesting I am *that* good an actress." There was
general laughter.

"No, my lady. You would not have been interested in the
pouch that Falcone carried, not after he reached here. You
have traveled together; he liked you; he would have satisfied your casual curiosity, though of course never revealed
the bag's contents. But the Agent was not so fortunate. He
had to recover his own identity, in order to get close to that

pouch; and thus poor Guido must sleep in the barn after all.

"Surely Guido would ask for a little extra recompense for this change of quarters. But not money—he could not spend it without drawing suspicion. Something practical. Food? There was a groaning board on his way out, and for tomorrow he had a few eggs . . . picked up . . . at his last stopping place. But the Agent had something he did want; he had seen them in the Agent's baggage.

"How else would a man in a forever-mended gown and wooden shoes be wearing new woolen hose when he died?"

Antonio della Robbia said "You've already made alibi for the vampire, and the lady is removed from consideration. So it must be me that you are trying to hang by my hose."

"Nottesignore was the one hanged," Hywel said, "but in your noose. As it was your quill in the courier's neck." He paused. "All Medici bankers were agents . . . spies . . . to one extent or another."

"Well," della Robbia said, "guilty."

Without any surprise, Hywel said "You admit it."

"Freely. Why should I not? Do you recall what Falcone was? A courier from Ludovico Sforza—thus a courier for the Byzantine Empire. Is there anyone in this room, this inn, this poor ruined land that was Italy, who loves Byzantines?"

Hywel said calmly, "One of us hates them a very great deal." Closing his eyes tightly, Gregory took off his glasses, breathed on them, polished and replaced them. Dimitrios looked at his knuckles.

Hywel said "There were always limits to the protection of the wand. A courier would lock his door, and because locks can be picked, brace the door as well. But Claudio Falcone opened his door to someone. Surely not a Medici agent. Certainly no one else here. Except the lady."

"Yes," Caterina said. "He practically tore down the door for me."

"We can grant him that little bit of humanity then, even if he was Imperial," Hywel said philosophically. "And

once more we've forgotten about Guido the hedge-wizard.
Before we forget him forever, consider that there must
have been some reason to kill him. Why did you kill
Nottesignore, Agent della Robbia?"

"He knew I'd killed the Byzantine courier, and threatened to expose me to the Empire. I still have a mission to
perform."

"I don't believe either of those two things," Hywel said.
"Why should he threaten you with that, instead of simply
doing it? You couldn't pay him more than the Empire
would, and you could and would kill him. No. Tommasi
knew something, that much is true, but it was a threat
right here, right now."

Hywel got up, tapped his fingers idly on the stair rail,
went to stand near Caterina. "My lady, did you tell
Claudio Falcone you were *Dottorina* Cynthia Ricci, the
Medici physician?"

She smiled grimly. "Is she so famous as that?"

"The family is well known in the schools of medicine.
And your *alessandro* gown suits your natural hair color
much better."

Cynthia said "You're much more observant than the
Byzantine was. No, I didn't tell him, and he didn't guess."

"Is it suddenly all right to kill Byzantines and nameless
wizards, just because they *are* those things?" Hywel said
with sudden force. There was a silence. Then, in his former
tone, he said "I think he did guess, *Dottorina* Ricci. But too
late. If he had known it in the coach, he would be alive.
Now, this is very important: did you make the cuts in Falcone's body, or did you only instruct Messer Antonio?"

Cynthia looked at Hywel, at della Robbia, a confused
glance at Gregory. "I—"

Della Robbia said "I learned the cuts from a book. In the
inn library."

"There is no such book," Hywel said. "The only medical
book there is a treatise on the gout. By Doctors Vittorio
and Cynthia Ricci. Their portraits appear in the frontis-
piece."

Cynthia stared at della Robbia, who said gently, "There

is no reason to tell them anything. They cannot prove or prosecute. . . ."

Hywel put his fingers around Cynthia's wrist. His hand did not tighten, but the fingertips probed. Cynthia's head snapped up, her eyes wide. "No! *Stay out!*"

"She did nothing," della Robbia said angrily. Dimitrios was halfway out of his chair, and even the innkeeper took a step. Only Gregory remained still, his eyes invisible.

"I only told him what to do," Cynthia said brokenly, "and knocked on the bastard's door. Is that what you want? *Is that what you want?*"

Hywel stood wholly rigid, sweat dripping from his face. Then he staggered, took his hand from Cynthia's, sat down hard. His breath came shallowly and fast. Gregory poured a small glass of brandy and handed it to Hywel, who drank it down. Cynthia bent forward in her chair, hands cupped over her right eye.

Hywel reached into his belt pouch, took out the enameled ring with the six red *palle*. He held it out. "Have you ever seen this?"

Della Robbia said "Why, that's mine. Where did you—" He reached for the ring.

Hywel gave it to him. "Before you put that on, let me warn you that I put a small magic into it. If anyone but the owner puts it on—it will tighten and pinch off the finger."

Della Robbia looked at the ring. "Now who doesn't believe whom?"

Hywel mopped his face. "No one *always* bluffs."

"If it isn't mine, then whose is it?"

"Falcone's," Hywel said. "He had taken it out to show the *Dottorina* when she came to his room."

"What?" Cynthia cried.

"He recognized you, sometime during dinner," Hywel said gently, "and took the ring from his pouch as proof of his identity."

"Then why didn't he show it to me?" Della Robbia demanded, still holding the ring but making no move to put it on."

"Spies have signals to recognize one another; words, gestures. When you didn't respond to his, he knew you weren't what you were claiming. You said you still have a mission to perform, and I said I didn't believe you; your mission was to kill a disguised Medici courier, and you have. Using Nottesignore and Charles and *Signorina* Ricci as your stalking horses."

Della Robbia laughed out loud. "That's incredible! Then what am I—a Sforza agent?"

"Byzantine, I should think, but Ludovico the Moor probably thought you were his."

"Incredible. And of course beyond any proof."

"Nottesignore had proof. Remember, he'd carried your bags. He'd worn your clothes."

"Dottorina Ricci, do you see what this is? These men are all Imperials—"

Hywel drew out the red wax ball. "The last *palla,"* he said.

Cynthia held her gold hairpin as a stiletto. "I will kill the next man who steps near me."

A servant was carrying a leather traveling bag down the stairs.

"Dottorina Ricci," Hywel said, "do you know the significance of particolored hose, the left leg brown, the right white?"

The needle wavered in her grip. "Of course. In Milan, only the Sforza and their favorites could wear those colors."

The servant put the bag on the table near Hywel. Hywel reached inside. "Tommasi surely knew that. He must have felt very grand wearing these." Hywel pulled out the hose, brown and white, exactly like a conjuror producing silks.

"Those are *not* mine. They could have been put there at any time—"

Hywel felt along the hose. "There is a legend that a murdered wizard curses his killer. I think Nottesignore has left us one last trick." He reached into the stocking. His hand come out holding a large white egg.

Della Robbia kicked at the fireplace. Burning logs rolled out onto the floor. He grabbed at the window curtains, throw-

ing them across Gregory, and slammed his shoulder into the
window, crashing through it in a spray of wood and glass.

Gregory literally tore apart the curtains entangling
him, ripping the heavy fabric with his hands. He reached
inside his gown, produced a very small gun, all of metal;
moving like something with clockwork inside, he leveled
the gun at the broken window. *"No,"* Hywel shouted, and
Dimi's arm struck Gregory's; the shot went high and wild,
echoing. Snow fell from the trees outside.

Gregory faced Hywel. His expression was only curious.
"The message," Dimitrios said quickly. "Only he knows
what the message was."

"Then the next time I will shoot to wound," Gregory
said. "Which way will he go?"

"Where we can't follow," Dimi said at once. "Come on."
They went through the window, toward the stables.

The light was beginning to go red, a mass of clouds
heavy with snow in the western sky. There were no sensa-
tions at all but the cold and the sting of windblown snow;
no smells, no sound.

Gregory and Dimitrios rode on della Robbia's trail; as
Dimi's vision worsened Gregory's improved. Dimi wore a
long fur coat and carried a saber. Gregory had only a light
cloak fastened at the throat, and two handguns, all the inn
staff had loaded.

"You do not want a weapon?" he asked Dimi.

"I have one. I don't like hand-cannon."

Gregory nodded. "And I am a little afraid of knives. How
far to the ravine?"

"That mass of trees ahead."

A black horse, the kind mercenaries prefer to ride, stood
in the snow at the near edge of the defile. Enormous footprints led up and over the edge.

"You talked about snowshoes," Gregory said.

"Schees. Not ordinary snowshoes. He won't get halfway
down the slope with those."

They dismounted, walked carefully to the edge of the ravine. It was very steep, almost a gorge; still, it was

crowded with trees in black clumps. Water sounded from
somewhere far below.

"I see him," Gregory said.

Della Robbia was a few dozen yards away, his hands
braced on a tree, struggling to plant his snowshoe a little further down the slope. Gregory drew one of his guns, pulled the
striker back. Dimitrios shouted "Della Robbia!" It echoed
back and forth, and snow fell from loaded branches.

Della Robbia looked up. He reached to his belt, drew and
pointed a long horseman's gun. Dimi pushed Gregory
down as the shot exploded.

Snow shifted. Branches broke. A limb struck della
Robbia across the shoulders. He flailed, skidded, started to
tumble down, picking up snow as he fell, his shouts rising
and bouncing back. Very soon he was lost to sight, and to
hearing, and after a few more minutes the snowslide
ceased to rumble.

Dimitrios stood up. Gregory pushed himself up on an
arm, lying indifferent to the snow, and uncocked his gun.
He looked down the slope.

Dimi said "I wonder if we could even have gotten the
message out of him."

Gregory said "Perhaps not. But between you, and I, and
the wizard and the woman, were there any other kinds of
fear to offer him?"

Dimitrios held out his hand. Gregory took it, and got to
his feet.

Cynthia Ricci sat in the inn taproom with Hywel Peredur. Neither had spoken since the riders had gone, most of
an hour ago.

Finally, and a little drunkenly, Cynthia said "Why did
you have to . . . touch me?"

"Falcone's murder was confusing," Hywel said, not
looking at her, "because it was partly one person, partly
another. The precision of the cuts was yours. Opening the
window was della Robbia, thinking he was putting the cap
on the scene."

"And tying Falcone down . . . to bleed him while he was conscious . . . which one of us did you think that was?"

"But Tommasi's death," Hywel went on, "was all one person's doing. An ordinary faked suicide, except for the hose. Tommasi's hose were the only thing linking him to della Robbia—so why didn't he remove them?"

"I don't know."

"Because they were fouled, and he didn't want to. Would the *dottorina* have been as fastidious?"

"No," she said, with a half-smile. "I think . . . I could have killed Falcone, that way. For what I thought he was. Is that what you had to know?"

"No," Hywel said tonelessly. "I had to know if you killed Nottesignore."

She inhaled sharply. "Why him?"

"It could have been . . . that he *was* Charles de la Maison, a masquer's joke . . . and della Robbia a banker, wearing his Sforza hose because he had truly forgotten . . . and you an assassin.

"If this were so, you enlisted Antonio's help in killing Falcone, not the other way around, and opened the window either as a false clue or just because torture is hot work. But 'Charles' saw you, and you him, and he fled to the barn and his other identity for safety. You were certain that della Robbia would lie to protect the wronged and righteous lady—all you'd killed was a Byzantine, after all!— but the other witness must die; and so let him die in a way that would let Messer Antonio take credit as well."

At length Cynthia said, "And did you believe that? The whole other story was just—"

"There are two possibilities. This one was much simpler."

"But not true," Cynthia said, as if she were not certain.

"No. Not true."

They were quiet again. Then she said "Was there really a spell on the ring?"

He took her hand before she could react, slipped the Medici ring on her finger. "I don't know if della Robbia knocked it from the table . . . or if Falcone managed it, to keep della Robbia from finding and using it."

"And the egg—was it really Nottesignore's?"

Hywel said "He was a clever conjuror. I should think it would please him to know that his last trick exposed his killer."

Cynthia began to smile, but it crumpled. "But he'll never know, will he? Poor little man, who never hurt anyone. . . . Do they always win, Doctor . . . Peredur? Does the Empire always get what it wants, no matter what we do?" She put her hand on the table, near Hywel's arm but not quite in contact. "When we touched—I felt how much you hated them."

"That is a danger of the technique."

"Can we hurt them at all?" She stopped, drew her hand back, closed her eyes. She turned the ring on her finger. "Oh . . . what I've said. A doctor. How could I have said that?"

"People can be hurt," Hywel said. "I don't know if the Empire can. It is strong, and inhumanly patient in pursuing its goals." He watched her for a moment. There was the suggestion of a tremor at the corner of her eye. Her hair showed white at the roots above her high forehead. "But possibly . . . if we act in a single place, for a single goal . . . we can stop them."

Cynthia said "There is a place I know of, called Urbino. They can be stopped."

"I know a place called Britain. Would stopping them be enough, my Lady?"

She looked at her wrist, ran her fingertips over the pulse point, looked at Hywel with the question fully formed in her eyes. But she did not ask him what he knew. She said "No, not enough. There's never enough revenge, is there, Doctor? Once it starts, it just goes on, and on. . . . We have to act for those who aren't yet hurt." She smiled then, like a flower opening. "An ounce of prevention."

Hywel poured brandy from his own glass into hers. He put his hand over his left eye for a moment. Then he uncovered it, blinked, smiled. He picked up his glass. "To the enterprise."

From outside came the whinny and clop of horses. Snow was beginning to fall.

Chapter 6
PASSAGES

BYZANTINE France was quiet under snow on the first day of December, in the dull light of a winter morning. The Imperial road was clear to both horizons, empty except for one fast coach.

The hooves of four horses struck sparks, four wheels dusted up white powder. The coach rocked insistently, a worn leather spring squeaking time. One window was slightly open for air; the others were shut but not curtained. The light on the four passengers was very gray.

Hywel Peredur sat on the left side of the front seat, looking at nothing in particular. Dimitrios faced him; he wore a leather jack and woolen trews, and watched the white fields pass through narrowed eyes.

Gregory von Bayern had wedged himself tightly into the right rear corner, his head against the gathered window curtain, a dark cloth wound loosely across his eyes. His hands were inside his white sleeves. He seemed to be asleep despite the motion and the noise.

Cynthia sat in the remaining corner, staring out at the departing landscape. Her lips were slightly twisted, and a few white hairs stuck out crookedly from her black velvet hood. A book was open in her lap.

Hywel said "Doctor Ricci, if you'll tilt your head back, you'll—"

"I'm not sick," Cynthia said flatly. She closed the book.

It was Marsilio Ficino's *Harmonia Platonica*, a cheap Swiss edition purchased five days ago in Geneva.

Hywel, after a moment, began to hum in time with the screech of the spring. "Would you like to sing a bit? It does wonderful things to the time."

She said "I don't sing."

"Oh. A loss. Captain Ducas?"

Dimi said "I don't know any songs suitable for a lady to hear."

Cynthia smiled very faintly, said "You might be surprised at what we . . ." Then the smile went away, and she did not finish the sentence. "Forgive me, please. I like to travel . . . but lately there has been so much riding, and so far . . . before this, I was always needed near Fiorenza."

Hywel said "You are needed where you are going, Doctor."

She looked at him, weary-eyed. "Thank you, Doctor."

Gregory moved without waking. Dimitrios looked him up and down.

Very quietly, Hywel said "Does he make you uneasy?"

"No. I . . . don't know what I think about him."

Hywel nodded. So did Cynthia.

A little after noon they left the Imperial road, and after a few minutes on a side track the coach stopped at what looked like a farmhouse than a coaching inn. Rabbit pelts were stretched on frames in the front yard, and there was no signboard.

Cynthia touched Gregory as he stirred, said "Stay asleep. I'll bring you dinner, as before."

"No," Hywel said, "it's all right. All of you come in."

Gregory blinked in the semidarkness of the coach, then put on his dark glasses, raised his head, and went in with the others.

They were met by a very tall, muscular woman in an apron and cap. "Hywel!" She shouted, and gave the wizard a hug that nearly picked him off his feet.

"Juliette," Hywel said. "These are my friends." He introduced them. Juliette cocked her head at Gregory, who took a half-step back; then Juliette said something in a consonantal language, a question or an accusation.

"No, my dear," Hywel said. "He is German. And we are all very, very hungry indeed: we've been on the Empire's roads for a week."

"O-o-oh," Juliette said, shaking with mock horror. "Do you even recall what food looks like? But go inside, warm up." She smiled at Gregory. "There is new blood sausage. Now go in, all of you. Hywel, was Alain driving you?"

"Barré."

"That explains it. Barré won't take a piss until his horses are tended to. I'll send Claude with a platter for him." She paused on her way out of the hall, and said "Stefan has news for you, Hywel. He'll be down very soon." She bustled out.

Gregory looked after her. "I do not understand. She is not . . ."

"No. But her husband is. Come along; when Juliette says very soon she means it."

They went into a solar, which almost lived up to its name as the sun struggled with the clouds. On the inner walls, cavalry weapons were mounted, and there was a small portrait, tooled on leather in high relief, of a hawk-faced, helmeted man. The leather was somewhat worn, as if it had been rubbed for a long time. There was very little else on the walls.

After a moment, there were sounds of footsteps on stairs; a door opened and a man came into the room. He was broad-shouldered, his gown loose around his waist. His skin was quite pale and a little waxy, with a distinct high flush in his cheeks; there could be no doubt that he was a vampire. Below coarse, dark, curly hair and a lined forehead he wore spectacles with heavy steel frames and glass much darker than Gregory's eyeglasses; they had side panels of black glass, so the man's eyes were entirely covered.

"Good afternoon," he said, in a heavily accented voice. "I am Stefan Ionescu. Hywel I know is here. Will the rest of you introduce yourselves?" He went to the nearest

empty chair and sat down, facing straight ahead; as each
introduction was made, he turned to face the speaker directly, never nodding.

Hywel said "There are messages, Stefan?"

"One from Cherbourg. Your ship has arrived, and will
depart for England in twelve days. Another from Angers:
le Chaudronnier must see you. It is most urgent."

"No other details?"

"Hywel. Do I forget?"

"No, Stefan. You do not forget." Then Hywel spoke in
the language Juliette had used, and Stefan answered; they
both laughed.

"Dinner," said Juliette from the doorway.

Dinner was lentil soup, followed by hot pork in aspic,
with a potent red wine. Despite what the hostess had said,
there was no blood sausage on the table.

Late in the meat course, Juliette came out of the kitchen
with two shallow, covered mazers. One she set before Gregory, the other at Stefan's left hand. Then, without a pause,
she took a decanter and a tray of crystal glasses from the
sideboard and poured a dark liquid for all the others, then
herself.

Hywel lifted his glass. "To life," he said, "and every joy
in it." Stefan thumbed open the hinged lid of his cup and
held it toward the center of the table. Gregory uncovered
his mazer, his hand not quite steady. The others raised
their glasses. There was the sweet, strong aroma of plum
brandy.

All drank. Gregory took a small sip, then a larger one;
he closed his eyes and lowered his cup, licking his lips absolutely clean. Cynthia looked at him, then at Hywel, who
nodded slightly, then at Juliette Ionescu, who smiled back
warmly. She went to stand behind her husband, put her
long-fingered hand on the hollow below his collarbone.

Dimitrios lifted his brandy glass, said "To the horsemen
of Wallachia, who have fought the good fight for many generations . . . and won."

Stefan laughed aloud, banged his fist on the table, and

they toasted again. Gregory's eyes were still tightly shut. Stefan said "Any more salutes?"

Cynthia began to speak, and all except Stefan turned to her, but she shook her head instead.

"We must be going, alas," Hywel said.

Juliette shook her head. "Oh, no. There are beds enough."

Stefan said gently, "And they have business in Angers, and a ship waiting beyond. It was good having you here, Hywel. It was good having you all here." He pushed his mazer across the table; it clicked hollowly against Gregory's.

"Thank you," Gregory said distantly. "Thank you all, very much."

They boarded the coach and were away, Juliette waving from the yard, a movement at an upstairs window that might have been Stefan, snowshoe hares dashing for cover as the wheels went by.

When they had gone some distance on the Imperial road, Cynthia asked Dimitrios, "Where is Wallachia?"

"Two hundred miles as the eagle flies, northwest of the City itself," he said, in a satisfied voice. "Like a finger in the Empire's eye. But they've never been able to take it. The mountains are too hard, and the soldiers harder yet. The Empire won't—can't!—admit it, but there's more than one corner of the world like—"

"I know," Cynthia said. "How did you know Stefan was from there?"

"The sword and lance on the wall. No other pattern like that in the world."

"Wer zerstört ihn die Augen?" Gregory said.

"He met Juliette in Varna, on the Black Sea," Hywel said, not particularly to Gregory, "She'd been sent to the East as a wife for a Byzantine coronal, a present from the Auvergne *strategos.*"

"They can do that?" Cynthia said sharply.

"Some will not," Dimi said.

Hywel said "Stefan led a raid on the train of . . . presents from France. But his horse was shot, and he was taken."

Cynthia said "And the Byzantines infected him?"

Hywel ran a finger around his glass eye. "He was already a *gwaedwr*. So are all the lieutenants of the Wallachian warlord . . . so is the *voivode* himself, Vlad the Fourth. That was his portrait, in leather on the wall. No. The Byzantine coronal pinned Stefan's eyes open with bronze nails, then tied him facing the sunrise."

Cynthia tilted her head back, closed her eyes. Gregory looked down, a hand to his face.

There was silence; then Gregory said "I thank you, Doctor. I was . . . indeed hungry."

"Juliette does not have the disorder, as you saw. Nor do their two grown children. You see, when you told me that you had not passed the disease, I believed you."

"I supposed that. . . . How did the Ionescus come to France?"

"That was partly my doing," Hywel said plainly.

In a thoughtful tone, Dimitrios said "How long have you been at this enterprise of yours?"

"Magic is a building of many small efforts toward a final, greater end," Hywel said. "Magic is slow."

"We're coming to a border," Cynthia said. "Is this English France?"

"We're entering Touraine," Hywel said, without looking out. "French France. The Partition left two provinces, Anjou and Touraine, neither English nor Byzantine."

"I remember that, a little," Dimi said. "The buffer state."

"Of a sort," Hywel said. Gregory pulled the cloth from his eyes, replaced his glasses.

The coach halted, and there was a knock at the door. It was opened by a man holding a ceremonial spear; over his breastplate was a blue velvet tabard diapered with fleurs-de-lis. He bowed slightly, breathed fog. "Good day, gentlemen, lady. May I know your business?"

"I am Doctor Horace Peregrine," Hywel said, "and the

lady is Doctor Caterina Ricardi; we are physicians, on our way to Cherbourg. This gentleman is Gregory, Fachritter von Bayern, an academic associate who has chosen to travel with us. And Hector, there, is our personal guard."

"To all of you, sir?"

"To me, sir," Cynthia said. The border guard looked up, then bowed again. He said "Thank you, sirs, madame. Please enjoy your travel, and travel safely."

The door closed. The coach rolled on, past small but elaborate stone gatehouses to both sides of the road.

"Very nicely said, Doctor Ricardi," Hywel said. Dimi's eyebrows were raised.

"I know a little of what looks suspicious," Cynthia said. "One guard for three acquaintances?—And I know what men . . . understand."

Dimitrios shook his head, not quite laughing.

"Angers holds enough nobility to stock a good-sized nation," Hywel said, "or perhaps two. There is René, the Duke of Anjou, and his court. There is Louis, King of France, and *his* court."

Dimitrios said "They're persistent, at least. The Partition's over three hundred years old."

"In counting generations, the French heralds are as meticulous as Jews. From the day the Partition was signed, they have preserved every noble line on paper; they know every name of every rightful noble of the France that might be . . . that still is, in a hypothetical sort of way."

"But what do all those nobles do?" Cynthia said.

"What has there always been for the kings of little countries to do? They scheme. The eleventh and current Louis has a talent of it, too—more than a talent. A gift. He sends his envoys to the cities of the world, and they are received as if sent by a real king on a real throne—even the bankers did, and you would have thought them to have had more sense. . . . I am sorry, Lady Cynthia."

"It's all right," Cynthia said. "Ser Lorenzo and his father spoke often of 'poor Louis' and his bad debts. I don't

remember them ever calling him a king, though . . . just a
risk they chose to take."

"The same reason his ambassadors are received," Hywel said.

Dimitrios said "All children play at kings and queens,
but there's an English army to the west and a Byzantine
army to the east, and they aren't made of toy soldiers."

"Duke René had a daughter, Margaret," Hywel said,
"who married a man named Henry. The marriage had
some qualities of a game, but Henry the Sixth and Margaret of Anjou really were King and Queen of England."

"Shouldn't Anjou then have become an English property?"

"The English councillors who helped arrange the thing
must have had that in mind—you see, Anjou occupies an
awkward place on the map, thrusting into the midsection
of England's territories, a thorn in the flank."

Dimi said "That's Byzantine mapmaking."

"Yes. It certainly wasn't Henry the Second's idea. But
. . . Henry's most recent namesake didn't inherit many of
his ancestor's qualities. He was an . . . ineffectual person."

Cynthia said "Do you mean impotent?"

"No. Disinterested, possibly, but Margaret did have a
son, of undoubted parentage. No, I mean weak-willed,
which is only a fault in common men but a disaster in
kings. Margaret, however, had enough will for the both of
them and a kingdom besides."

Cynthia said "How much of a fault is that?"

Hywel laughed. "None at all. Especially if you are Louis
the Eleventh of Nowhere, and you would like an army of
Englishmen to fight an army of Byzantines over two countries you would like to rule yourself. The foreigners collide,
are disorganized, and the people rise in rebellion—"

"And it will not end in Paris, it will not end in Gaul,
blah, blah, blah," Dimitrios said dryly. "I know that prin-
ciple. But it did not happen."

"No. Because Richard Plantagenet, the English Duke of
York, started a civil war to prosecute his own claims to the

throne, and not incidentally against 'the foreign Queen.' Civil wars are very distracting."

Gregory said "And the Yorks won."

"It was more complicated than that. Richard of York was killed in the war, as was one of his sons. The other three sons kept fighting . . . and eventually, just over sixteen years ago, one of them became Edward the Fourth, long live the King."

Dimi said "The Sun Lord? I've heard he was a very great leader, a marvelous general."

"True enough, though Henry wasn't any sort of leader and Margaret scarcely had the chance. It was not a very grand war, militarily.

"The Royal House of Lancaster fled to Angers, and lived in the same mock pomp as everyone else there for nine years. Then they put together a force of disaffected English—who are always to be found in Brittany and the Côtentin—and came back to England, where they deposed Edward and ruled for a year."

"How?"

"Byzantium," Cynthia said.

"Edward's brother George," Hywel said.

Dimi said "One reason civil wars are so distracting is that the enemy so often names himself with his steel in your back. . . . For only a year, you said?"

"Edward assembled his own little army, with Italian money and some Danish ships, and crossed the Channel. And brother George turned his coat back. There were two very bad battles. Henry's son was killed, and Henry was taken to the Tower of London, where someone shortly murdered him. I've no idea who."

Gregory said "It is hard to rule a country with two kings."

Hywel said "And a little after that, René ransomed his daughter back home, where she has been ever since."

Cynthis said "I'm surprised Louis didn't try to marry her to Edward."

"He'd already tried that, with his daughter-in-law. It was all arranged, through Richard Neville, the Earl of

Warwick, one of nicest schemers in England: Edward
would take the crown and a French princess, all in a
week's time. *Then* Warwick was told that the King already had a Queen, a knight's widow he'd married in secret. A Lancastrian knight's widow, at that. Warwick
went purple and Bona of Savoy went elsewhere."

"Bona," Cynthia said unsteadily. "She went to Italy,
didn't she? She married Galeazzo Maria Sforza, the Duke
of Milan."

"Yes, she did."

Cynthia said "Does every marriage in the world have
troops behind it?"

"Above the rank of Baron, just about all. . . Look." Hywel pointed out the window.

To the right was a stone curtain wall, over forty feet
high, with more than a dozen cylindrical towers along its
length; the towers were banded, black and white. Spires
rose from within the wall, sharp against the red evening
sky. Just beyond the fortress, lanterns and watchfires
flickered from the dark surface of the river Loire.

"The Château d'Angers," Hywel said. "All a country's
royal palaces, in one place."

The street was narrow and dark, but fairly clean, and
the air was pleasant with kitchen smells and some strong,
spicy, unidentifiable aroma.

Hywel paused beneath a sign: a copper relief of a three—
legged cauldron, with painted leather steam rising from it.
Hywel knocked at the door, which opened a little.

"Peredur!" said the man within, then more quietly,
"Peredur. Come in. Come in, all of you."

The man who led them in was short, and extremely bent;
he walked with a scuttling motion and from any distance
seemed dwarfish. His nose was large and straight, his grin
crooked, his eyes receding below a heavy brow. Hywel introduced him as Quentin le Chaudronnier, "that rarity, a
genuine alchemiker."

Gregory said politely, "By which you mean he can turn
lead to gold?"

"By which I mean he does not claim to do so. Quentin, I heard you had news for me."

The twisted mouth turned down. "Yes, and not good news, either. Come back, all of you, where it's warm." The rear of the house was very warm and steamy, and the source of the exotic smell outside; indoors, it filled the nostrils and then the head. Half a dozen metal cauldrons boiled on red fires. Glass flasks by the hundreds, in every shape and color, were racked on the walls. There were bins and jars of dried plants, and bunches of leaves and stems were suspended from the ceiling.

Quentin paused by one of the vats, arching his shoulders even further. "This one needs a moment, Peredur. Take them up."

Hywel led the others through a tight-fitting door and up an enclosed flight of stone steps, to a pillared hall; intricate chemical apparatus covered tables and shelves.

"Don't sit on a table, whatever you do," Hywel said. "And be very careful of puddles."

Dimitrios leaned a hand against one of the pillars, then pulled away; he tested the surface with his fingertips. "Chimneys," he said, and rested a leather-covered shoulder comfortably against the stone. "What does he do in the summer?"

"Research," Quentin said, entering from the stairwell. "In the countryside, where there is no one to smell my mistakes." He held out a small spray of dried blooms to Cynthia. "Crocus, Miss Ricci, and fennel, and rosemary. I knew your father, just a little; there is plenty of gout in Angers. How is the Doctor?"

"Dead, Master Quentin," she said calmly.

"Oh." Le Chaudronnier looked down, his arms dipping, puppetlike. Cynthia reached out and took the plants. "Rosemary," she said, "for memory's sake." Quentin looked up, brightened a little.

Then he turned to Hywel. "Now my bad news, Peredur. The exemplification, Clarence's paper—it does exist. Queen Margaret has it, and she means to use it against him."

"Who is Clarence?" Dimi said.

"George Pantagenet, the Duke of Clarence, " Hywel said. "The King's untrustworthy brother." Then to Quentin, "Why now?"

"You haven't heard? Ah, you've been in the East again. Well. The Duke's been half out of his mind since his wife and son died a year ago. He talked about marrying a French heiress, someone from Burgundy—"

Dimitrios scowled.

"—and then he . . . arranged a judicial murder. Some poor woman, one of the Duchess's servants, was dragged from her bed, accused of poisoning the Lady, tried and hanged, all in a single morning. They did the same to a man, for killing the boy."

Quentin turned his face away. His shoulders tightened. "There was gossip everywhere, some of it very gleeful, but I know this is true. King Louis called me in and told me the story."

"Why you?" Cynthia said.

Without facing her, le Chaudronnier said "Because according to the testimony, the Duchess was given the poison more than nine weeks before she died of it. Louis wanted to know if there was such a slow poison, and if so, if I could make it for him."

"And is there?" Dimitrios said.

Cynthia said "Of course not!" No one spoke; the bubbling of the cauldrons below was faintly audible.

Awkwardly, le Chaudronnier said "I apologize, my lady; your father of course told me you were a doctor as well, but I had forgotten."

"No harm done, Master Quentin."

He nodded. "There was more gossip. Accusations of death by magic, the Duke interrupting a royal council, even a rebellion, I heard."

"Another one," Hywel said flatly.

"They are saying that the King of England is very angry, and perhaps his brother has lived too long."

"Done too much for one life, certainly. And the exemplification will not help Edward's temper." Hywel looked around at the others. "I've told you that Clarence supported Henry the Sixth during the year's Readeption. Since then there has been a rumor of a document, under Henry's seal, that gave Clarence the crown of England should Henry leave no male heirs—as he did not. It was his price, apparently, for helping the Lancastrians back to power." Hywel turned to Quentin. "Do you have the correspondences?"

"Yes."

"Get them."

Quentin gave Hywel a strange look, seemed about to protest, but scuttled off.

"Clear this table," Hywel said, indicating one with a square top of heavy dark glass. Dimitrios moved glassware and Gregory stacked and shifted papers.

"Surely the Duke couldn't depose his brother on the basis of one paper," Cynthia said.

"It has taken less," Gregory said.

"And Clarence is silly enough to try," Hywel said. "But that's not the intent. The document isn't for George's use anymore—as if Henry and Margaret ever intended he use it. It's for Edward, and the courts of law."

Quentin reappeared, carrying a roll of paper and several smaller items. He brought a little spirit lamp from another table, and handed a box and a small steel file to Dimitrios. "This is ink, the formula Louis uses for official papers. File it down to powder. Professor von Bayern, can you do a formal script?"

"Good enough," Gregory said, and was handed a pen and vial of liquid ink.

Hywel unrolled the paper, weighted it at the corners. "The date would be . . . the July or August before they sailed. August, I think. Less time for George to change his mind. And the year still counted from Henry's original crowning. August, 33 Henry VI. Inscribe that here, please, Gregory. And here: Henry VI Rex Britanni, Margaret Regina, George Clarencis. You're not trying to forge their signatures, understand, just establish points of correspondence."

"I understand. I saw this done at the Library, to restore a damaged manuscript."

"Except that this," Quentin said intently, "takes place over a distance, with poorer correspondence, and is considerably more costly to the worker. My Lady Doctor, will you watch Peredur, in case he—"

"Oh, stop it, Quentin," Hywel said mildly. "I'm not so old as that."

Quentin looked around. "Is that what you told them? Well, he lied to you: he's at least—"

"Chaudronnier," Hywel said, and Quentin stopped.

Quentin took a stick of sealing wax from one of the boxes. "Also Louis's own formula. As I ought to know." He held it in the lamp flame. There was a distinct scent of wild cherries.

"Where's the seal?" Dimitrios said.

Without answering, Quentin held the soft stick over the paper, letting heavy red drops fall.

Hywel put the fingertips of his right hand together and pushed them toward the hot wax.

Cynthia raised her arm to stop him; Gregory touched it, preventing her.

Hywel's fingers paused a fraction of an inch above the blob of wax. His eyes were shut tight and his forehead was creased.

Untouched physically, the wax began to deform.

A man's profile etched itself: an eye, a nose, a chin. Around the edge, little bits of wax sank down in the shapes of letters.

Hywel eyes opened. "The ink, now," he said, his voice slightly strained.

Quentin took the pan of powdered ink from Dimitrios. Tapping it with a finger, he began to dust the black powder onto the paper. The black specks leaped like ants on a hot plate, and they clung, in the hazy outlines of writing. The images darkened, sharpened.

Cynthia read " ' . . . and should the said Henry die without surviving issue male, the said George shall succeed him in . . . ' "

Quentin picked up a brass-nozzled flask, pumped a plunger with his thumb. A mist spattered the paper; it smelled of ammonia.

Hywel relaxed a little. Cynthia put her hand on his wrist, shoved back his sleeve and felt for his pulse.

Quentin sanded the paper, fanned it. "It's fixing fairly well."

The document was not sharp, but was readable enough. Dimitrios said "That's clear enough to hang a duke."

Gregory said "You are not a lawyer."

Hywel said "Neither is Edward. Hold it up."

Dimitrios took the right-hand corners, Quentin the left; they stretched the paper vertically.

Hywel read the document over, more than once. His breathing was slightly labored. Then, abruptly, he reached out and tore the seal from the vellum. The lettering instantly sagged and ran.

"Now," he said, "we go after the original."

Cynthia put two fingers against Hywel's throat, touched his forehead. "Tomorrow," she said firmly.

There was a moment's silence. Then Hywel said "Yes, you're right, tomorrow," and he turned away from them, took a step; all four of the others moved to catch him as he staggered, but he did not fall.

"The reactive glamour," Hywel said, "is the least exhausting to maintain for a long time, and for our purposes more useful than a straightforward disguise or a distractive glamour." He took his fingertips away from Gregory's cheekbones. "There."

"I don't see any difference," Cynthia said. There was a towel over her shoulders, and her hair was brushed up.

"No, you do not. You know us, and expect to see us where we are. If I look in a glass, I'll see myself. It's the people who don't know us—or expect us—whom the suggestion will affect."

"But how do you know it works at all?"

"It works. The disadvantage is that one can't know what the other person is seeing. And if a group of people compare what they saw, there can be trouble."

"I might want that sort of trouble," Dimitrios said, "if I didn't want the group to catch me.

"True . . . but then they'd be hunting a magician."

"Speaking of noticeable things, this stuff smells awful," Cynthia said, as Quentin le Chaudronnier sponged color into her hair, turning it from white to absolute black.

"The scent mostly fades," Quentin said, "and a little rose essence will take care of the rest."

"And the smell of dyed hair is hardly rare at this court," Hywel said. "Gregory, would you go behind that door for a moment?"

Gregory went into the stairwell. Hywel said "Now, Dimitrios, you leave the room, that way." Dimi went out.

Hywel opened the stairwell door, motioned for Gregory to come back into the room. As he did, Hywel stepped outside, called out, "All right, Dimi, come back, please," and shut the door behind himself.

Dimitrios came in, looked straight at Gregory and said "Now what?"

Hywel came back into the room, stood next to Gregory. Dimitrios blinked several times. "I guess I see," he said.

"It's all in what you expect to see," said Hywel. "Magic or no magic. Keep that in mind when you visit Louis.

Hywel and Gregory approached the gatehouse of the Château d'Angers, its striped flanking towers like two chesspieces drawn up in defense. The last daylight washed the black and white stone with gold.

"Louis the Good built the place just as Henry and Manuel Comnenus cut the world from around him. A few of his royal successors have professed to find something ironical in that." Hywel turned to Gregory. They both wore long formal gowns, black, and heavy winter cloaks with full hoods. "Have you ever been to Paris?"

"I have," Gregory said. "I am sure no amount of irony can compensate its loss."

Hywel looked over his shoulder at the salmon-colored sky. "You shouldn't have let me sleep so long."

"It was not my doing, as you know. The Doctor would not allow them to awaken me either."

"She thinks you're too frail and I'm too old." Hywel sighed. "Maybe I am too old."

"You have not said how old you are."

"How long have you been a vampire, Gregory? I asked that once."

"After a few years of this life, one ceases to count them as years. There becomes only the time between hungers."

"It is much the same for wizards."

The gatehouse guards wore silk tabards over armor of lapping steel plates, burnished bright. They seemed very uncomfortably cold. "What is your business?"

"We are here by request of Queen Margaret," Hywel said slowly.

The guardman hesitated. "Let me see your faces." Hywel and Gregory pushed back their hoods, opened their cloaks to show they wore no weapons. The guard blinked steadily as he examined them. "Very well," he said, and turned away. "You may pass."

A page met them within the entry hall. "Your cloaks, sirs?"

"There isn't time for that," Gregory said. He put a hand on the boy's forearm. "Take us to Margaret, quickly, and do not announce us. Is that understood?"

The page looked down at the hand on his arm, then up at the half-hooded face, and his eyes went wide and big-pupiled with fear. "Yes, Your Lordship," he said, "Th-this way."

Gregory let the boy go. As they followed him, Gregory looked at Hywel, whose shadowed face was smiling.

A small coach pulled up to the château gate, stopped with a clatter and scrape. A man vaulted down from the driver's box; he was powerfully built, a cavalryman by the way he patted the horse in passing. He opened the coach door and knocked down the step, took the hand of the woman who emerged. She wore boots with soft tops; the hem of a red velvet gown was visible below her cloak. Her hair was the color of the winter night sky overhead.

"Special courier," the man told the gate guard. "For the King."

The gatekeeper looked from the man to the woman. He said, "Courier from whom . . . and on whose authority?"

The woman held out her hand. Something lay in it that shone in the lanternlight. "Give this to Louis," she said, in French with a strong Italian accent.

The gatekeeper took the ring, held it so it caught the light, saw the six red balls enameled on the boss. He bowed slightly. "If you will wait inside, please?"

They crossed an open courtyard, over a hundred yards on a side, pale-bright with moonlight and yellow light spilling from innercourt windows. The gardens were black and white, barren and snow, with precise stands of evergreens trimmed to perfect cones. The skeleton of a hedge maze, iced, shone like filigree silver. From the maze center rose the marble arm of Diana, aiming her bow at the full moon. Sculpture chesspieces the size of human beings stood idle in a midgame.

They passed through a door flanked by a brooding Odin and imperious Jupiter; Nut arched her body above the portal. Light and warmth spilled out and swallowed them.

The château was full of tapestries and armors and banners and ornate old furnishings; too full, in fact, cluttered, the riot of shapes and heraldic colors clashing like noise. Floors creaked under the load and walls rattled as mice went about their affairs. Even the lights were too bright, too many cressets making too much flicker and smoke.

As the steward approached to take them in to the King of France As It Was, Dimitrios said quietly and casually, "I wonder how many palaces they stripped to fill this one?"

Cynthia said "If this is all that's left—" and then the steward appeared, and with two armed men to either side. The soldiers had a bored look, and did not seem ready to do anything to anybody. The party threaded through more overfull corridors; half the alcoves in the place seemed to house two or three courtiers conversing in mumbles and snickers.

A pair of doors, thick wood sheathed with figured bronze panels, opened on a beamed and bannered hall. The remnants of a meal were on a side table; a blue-gowned butler moved about the table with a silver-handled broom.

On the other side of the room was a huge fireplace, surrounded by courtiers and children; a little girl fed bits of meat to two sleek white hounds. An ornate chair, with an empty hawk perch and poles for an absent canopy, was half-turned toward the fire. In it sat a man dressed in blue velvet and cloth of gold, showing an elegant profile and imposing gray eyebrows. On his head, at a slight off angle, was a golden circlet with gold lilies.

He held out the Medici signet. "What does the Duke of Florence send to me?" he said, softly but resonantly.

In an absolutely level voice, Cynthia said, "The Medici of the Florentine Republic, who never called themselves dukes, have greetings for and a request of Louis, King of France." She paused; the man on the throne nodded slightly. "And where is he?"

A small clatter came from across the room. The butler had put down his tray and broom and was walking, hands outstretched, toward Dimitrios and Cynthia. He was sharp-eyed, long-fingered, with a strikingly long pointed nose. He applauded, then reached inside his gown and produced a crown like the first man had worn, but set with sapphires and topazes. Four hands from the crowd settled a gilt mantle on his shoulders, and the steward tossed a length of blue velvet over the canopy supports above the throne.

"Oh, go on, Villon, go on," said Louis XI, and the gray-browed man got out of the chair and doffed the crown. Louis sat down with a rattling sigh and crowned himself. "Milady appreciates my little joke? Villon is an appalling poet, but I think he makes a rather good king." He stroked his nose, peered forward. There were tiny red twinkles in his eyes, both merry and feral. "But we have not met, I think."

"Doctor Cynthia Ricci, my lord." Dimitrios stirred, and she shoved her boot against his, inconspicuously but hard. "This is my . . . traveling companion, Hector."

"Oh? Of course we have heard of you, Doctor. But I had thought . . . " Louis made a plucking motion at the hair of his temple. "Ah, well, *vanitas, vanitatem.* How is Ser Lorenzo? And his brother?"

"Dead, of course," Cynthia said, rather coldly. "And if my lord is done with his testing—"

"Not quite, Doctor," Louis said pleasantly. He tilted his head to one side. "What say you, fox?"

A man in a long leather coat, heavy trousers, and riding boots stepped from between two gaudy courtiers. His face was very plain, utterly unmemorable.

"I remember her, my lord. Though you are correct about her hair—it was white. And I do not know the man."

"Very well, Reynard. In what context do you remember her?"

"As a doctor of medicine," said Reynard the spy, late of the Milanese court. "But one that my lord Lorenzo trusted with most secret matters."

Louis held his head cocked, as if waiting for more details; but Reynard stepped back and could no longer be seen.

Louis smiled, which was not particularly attractive, twitched his nose. "So then, Doctor. If the Medici are dead, and the Florentine Republic is now . . . something else, who brings me greetings—and a request?"

Cynthia looked after Reynard a moment longer, then said "Not every Medici is dead, my lord, and many corporations of the Bank are still active."

Louis nodded. "Corporations, *mais oui.* If I were a corporation, I wonder, would my body live on after my soul had departed it? Pardon, Doctor. Proceed."

"It involves a document . . . concerning the brother of Edward of England, and this brother's accession to the English crown. The Bank—"

"Wait," Louis said. "This hall is too drafty for words that might start fires." He pitched his voice up a little. "Gérard." The steward appeared at the King's elbow. "See that there is diplomatic wine in my chambers. And attend to the gentleman's wishes."

"I stay with the Doctor," Dimitrios said, and was not kicked.

"My dear fellow," Louis said, levering himself from the throne, "I'm a fifty-four-year-old king, and I haven't taken a woman by force in a very long time." He made a sound half sigh, half groan. "But unlike Edward, I didn't stop too soon for my own good. Come ahead, then, both of you."

Large, dark eyes stared at Hywel, and a candle was held near his face.

"What in the Goddess's name," said Margaret of Anjou, "are *you* doing here, *tonight?*"

She stood in the doorway to her room, in a white gown of simple, vaguely Grecian style, her hair ornamented with scarlet cord. Her face was round, her features even, but there was a darkness around her eyes and her throat was corded and sagging.

"Madam?" Hywel said. "May we come in?"

She looked from Hywel to Gregory and back again. "If you've come this far, then one more doorway won't matter. Come in." Margaret turned to a tiring-maid, who stood by with a handful of silk. "You will go."

"My lady." The maid gave both men a look of sheer bafflement, then went out, still clutching the undergarment. The door closed behind her.

"Now," Margaret said, "what is this all about, and why are you here?"

"The document," Hywel said, "the exemplification of the Duke of Clarence. It is necessary that we take it to England at once."

"And you were to have it tonight. *In England.*"

Carefully, Hywel said, "The document is . . . in transit?"

She gestured toward the window. "Is this not the night of the full moon?"

"Yes, madam."

"Well, then. It was explained to me by my wise advisors that the full moon at its height would assist in the transfer . . . there was some analogy of mirrors." She paused, and her voice went icy. "Are you now telling me that I was wrongly advised?"

Hywel hesitated. Then Gregory, in accented but clear English, said, "Madam, were you told our presence was necessary for the operation?" Hywel passed him an eye-flick and a nod.

"I had thought that was why he insisted on it, rather than a simple and earthly mode of travel." She looked at Gregory. "But you're here as well . . . are you now necessary to him?" She stabbed a finger at Hywel, turned to him. "Is that so? It's not enough that you've survived every political death around you . . . you've decided to escape the physical one as well?"

Gregory was silent, expressionless. Hywel said "I suppose the half-latent novice has managed to completely reverse his explanations. You see, Your Grace, the moon indeed acts as a mirror—to reflect the sending. Surely this is how he explained it . . . that the moon would block us, so that I must come here for the document."

"No. That is *not* what he said. He was to send the paper, and you would take it to the usurper. . . ." She looked back to the window. "I saw the moon and thought of you, just before you entered."

"There is a ship waiting, madam. Where is the document?"

Margaret sat down, still looking at the wide, white moon, blurry through the windowpane. "I was thinking of Suffolk, too . . . the moon over the Channel, I suppose." She turned back to Hywel. "For a moment, when I saw you in the door, I thought you were William, you had his face. . . ."

"My lord the Duke of Suffolk is dead, Your Grace."

"Of course he is," she said firmly. "Dead on an English

beach with his poor head hacked off. We had York's head for that, and one of his four unclean sons'. . . . I was in Scotland then, when they killed York, but the news flew up to me. And I was happy. I had been Queen of England for a dozen years, and seen countless Englishmen die, but it was in that moment that I understood how much my enemies' deaths could make me happy."

She fixed Hywel with a stare. "Does this affect your thinking at all? Does it matter to your plot-raddled brain that I count all of you my enemies now, and my last joys on earth are your several deaths?"

"Only George Plantagenet's death is of interest to me now, madam."

"You're a perfect liar. Everything interests you that advances your interest. And where is that interest now? Do you think Byzantium will give you miserable, foul-spoken Wales as a payment?"

"*Wales*, Your Grace?" Hywel said loudly.

She ignored him. "I wonder if Wales, or Scotland, will have Edward when he falls, as my father houses Louis. I was the Scots' guest, and I know they would not stand mildly by and let Edward be their king, as my father does. Henry and I had a claim on the wealth of England, and doors were open; but Edward of March won't have that . . . usurper usurped . . . he'll sleep on rocks and thistles, and take out his lusts on sheep." She laughhed; it was a pleasant laugh, and quite merry.

Louis's outer chamber had high, narrow, leaded windows, and slightly less furnishing than the rooms before it. Cynthia and Dimitrios sat in low-backed chairs facing the fireplace an Louis, who was in silhouette, his face invisible.

Louis said "What, then, is the bankers' interest in the foolish Clarence's paper?"

"There are considerable loans outstanding from the Bank to Edward of England," Cynthia said. Her words were somewhat cadenced: a messenger, but one who knew what her message meant. "Some of these loans have been difficult in collection."

"That is a problem with loans to kings."

Cynthia said "Some of these debts were incurred in the name of the Duke of Clarence. It is the opinion of certain lawyers for the Bank that, if Edward proves the Duke to have conspired in treason, he might also declare these loans *ex parte* and void."

Louis examined refractions in his wineglass. "Even assuming that this document is . . . more than a rumor . . . why should I save the Duke of Clarence from his brother's righteous wrath?"

"The Bank is apolitical, as you know."

Louis laughed. "Of course; excuse me, Doctor. Continue."

"You have a document of no particular value to yourself, and of some value to the Bank. They wish to purchase it."

"And what price do they set upon it?"

Cynthia took a small sip of wine and said nothing. She was thinking about Falcone, the courier she had helped to kill; wondering if this had been his destination and his message. She had seen the bits of paper in the fire, when Hywel's mind was touched to hers. Perhaps they were expected here. Perhaps she was doing Lorenzo's last will.

She smothered all such thoughts.

Louis was chuckling again. "My debts are also the debts of a king." Then he looked at Dimitrios, head tilted, and his fingers drummed the arm of his chair. "Hector. *Hellene? Byzas?*"

"I am an advisor to the lady," Dimi said in crisp French, "on technical matters."

"Then you must excuse me. One must never assume too much or too little." Louis paused, then spoke rapidly: "The paper's worthless, of course . . . an idiot's bargain with two exiles over something none of them owned. It's not worth a foot of land or one gold . . . *bezant.*"

Cynthia said "Then any price for it is a profit."

"It belongs to the Queen of England."

"To the Duke of Anjou's daughter," Dimitrios said in a low voice. "And you are the King of France."

Louis sat back, turned so that his nose showed sharp in profile, stroked it; his smile was highlit.

There was a rapid knocking at the chamber door.

Louis's fingers stopped moving. "Enter," he said, irritated.

It was Reynard. He bowed, said, "Your pardon, lord, but there is an active magician in the castle. I sensed him a few minutes ago. It is not Flambeau or Wirtz."

"Where is he?"

"I cannot be certain, my lord; I was trying to avoid close contact."

Louis turned to face Dimitrios and Cynthia. "Reynard . . ."

"Majesty?"

"Wait here. See that no one disturbs our guests, especially not strange wizards."

"My lord."

Louis stood, walked out past Reynard, who closed the door and dropped its latch. He leaned against the doorframe in an attitude of confusion and tension, but his face was blank as always.

Cynthia sat quite still. Dimitrios filled three glasses with wine.

"We will go at once," Hywel said. "And I think I will give *Monsieur le Magicien* some practical instruction. . . . By Your Grace's leave?"

"Not yet," Margaret said, a little softly. "I never knew you to be so impatient. . . . You said it was contrary to the rules of magic. It's a long way to Calais; you can wait a little longer." Then, unkindly, "There are rooms in the château. Are you no longer interested in castles?"

"Your Grace does us a disservice."

"Oh, do I? The Queen of England does a disservice to two serpents in doctoral gowns?" She got out of her chair and went to where Hywel stood, looking him almost eye to eye. "You have a rare and unnatural talent for survival, and

that makes you a useful instrument, but never forget that
an instrument is all you are."

"Yes, madam."

" 'Yes, madam.' " She turned to Gregory. "And why do
you stand there, all righteous and satisfied? Do you think,
because you came late to this business, you are better than
this soulless husk? Your talent for survival is just as unnatural as his." She reached into the front of her gown,
produced a medallion on a chain; an eight-rayed star in
gold, with a central bloodstone. "Do you know what this
is?" She dangled the star in front of Gregory, who took two
halting steps back, then turned away.

Margaret paused then, as if surprised at the reaction;
the medallion jingled on its chain.

Her back was to Hywel. He looked up sharply, rotated
his head, touched his temple. "We understand, madam,"
he said. As Margaret turned toward him, he made an urgent gesture, just out of her sight, toward the door. Gregory nodded.

She said "As you understand that I am a ridiculous
woman, who would be naked in an English dungeon if the
promise of my father's lands were not worth a few bezants
to Louis . . . whom no one ever calls ridiculous . . . I want
to know you understand better than that."

"That is the sigil of beloved Ishtar, Your Grace."

" 'Beloved'! You'd call a toad beloved, and kiss it. But
yes, it is Her sign. And now that the Sun Defiled wears the
English lions, it is my sign." She looked at the star, at Hywel. "I am Ishtar. I am the door that lets in the storm. For
my sake, brothers will kill one another." She caught the
medallion in her left hand, squeezed it hard, turned to
Gregory. Her large eyes were intense, and every pretty or
pleasant thing was strained out of her voice. "And I am the
Lamia, who will have Hera's children dead, for my own."
She held out her fist with the star inside; a drop of bright
blood ran between the clenched fingers. *You.* Will steal.
The life. From the Woodville Hera's children."

Hywel's hand moved slowly toward the back of Margaret's neck.

"And from the Neville woman. Who gave my son *nothing*. And ran to sanctuary in Richard Plantagenet's bed."

Hywel's fingertips touched Margaret's hair.

Her stained hand fell. Without any fire, she said "Now, go; you are commanded to England. There kill, like the good men you are."

"Your Grace."

"Madam."

"Though I am dispossessed and naked on the floor of the house of the dead," Margaret said calmly, as the two men went out, "still I am the door that lets in the storm."

The starburst of Ishtar fell bloody to the floor.

Dimitrios stood at the windows of the audience chamber. In the courtyard beyond, lights moved. No sound penetrated in. Dimi looked at Cynthia, who looked at Reynard, who smiled back at them both. The spy sat comfortably in Louis's chair; the firelight was bent slightly around his cheeks.

Cynthia said "Do you trust me, Messer Reynard?"

"At the very least, *Dottorina*," Reynard said pleasantly, "the question is badly phrased."

"I withdraw it. . . . I have some reason to believe that the intruder is looking for me. If we left the castle, he would not find us."

"He would not find you here, that is certain."

Dimitrios took a step away from the window.

"*Signorina*," Reynard said, "I've seen you with a knife in your hand. We are not different. It's not the employer, it's the job." He stood up, went to face Dimitrios. "You were one of their soldiers, weren't you?" Reynard said to Dimi, in accentless Greek. "Before you got into this."

"Yes."

"Then you know the routine, I imagine." Reynard turned his head, said "Best of luck, *Dottorina*. Merry meet again."

Dimi drove his right fist into Reynard's flank; his left hand chopped behind the spy's ear. Dimi caught the collapsing figure across the chest and lowered it to the ground.

"My father's best spy once had himself whipped to the bone," Dimi said to Cynthia. "Now that we've saved him an explanation, let's go, before we have to explain our—" He pulled back from Reynard as the magical glamour cleared from the spy's face. Cynthia breathed in sharply.

"Hywel said that sort of spell was difficult to keep," Dimi said, very softly. "Now we know why she bothered."

"She said we weren't different," Cynthia said hollowly.

Crystal-cold air cut across the courtyard, and the full moon was sharp as a new-struck coin. There had been no time to recover their cloaks; Dimi's armored jacket glittered, and Cynthia's gown showed purplish in the moonlight. There were a hundred yards to cover to the gatehouse, all white and silver light. Yellow lanterns bobbed off to the left.

"Do we run?" Cynthia said, reaching to the hem of her gown.

"No." The word was a sharp puff of fog. "Walk fast, but lightly. Shadow to shadow."

They wove through the darkness of the trees, stopping and starting as the lanternlights swept by. Dimitrios was all a piece with the night, even his misty breath seeming part of the scenery; Cynthia pulled her sleeves tight, fought shivers, kept going.

Finally the gateway was in clear sight, across a stretch of open grounds; brightly lit, and guarded.

Dimi tapped Cynthia's shoulder, pointed; among a group of statues, almost the same distance from the gate, were two figures in cloaks. One pulled back a sleeve, gestured whitely.

Cynthia was pulling the pins from her hair, letting it fall. The pins slipped from her stiff fingers, tinkling on the pavement. "S-sing me an un-unsuitable song." She pulled her gown up along one leg, pinned the hem high.

"What?" Dimi said, almost too loudly.

"You s-said you knew some. In French, I hope." She took

his arm and draped it across her shoulders. "You're a French knight, and I'm a French lady. Now, act naturally, before I turn blue and crack."

The guards at the gate steadied their spears at the sound of voices; then they saw the staggering man and the woman in red with her hair unbound, roaring and giggling through "Forty-four Knights in the Lionheart's Tent."

The couple got halfway into the gateway before bumping into a line of armored men. "Hey, Jacques, where'd you get her?"

"And where you gonna put her after?"

"Some guys know how to stay warm."

A man in a plumed sallet said "We can't let 'em through here, not until the noise is over. Take 'em back to—"

Dimi's straight fingers went into the officer's throat. Cynthia's boot came down on an instep, the heel of her hand driving to the corner of the guard's jaw.

A black cloak fluttered around two men, and they sank down quietly, Hywel's hands on their necks. Gregory struck twice at the backs of skulls; there were awful crunches and the men fell, twitching wildly. Gregory's white face was set very hard in the torchlight.

Cynthia said "We didn't—"

"We did," Hywel said. "The coach, now."

Gregory tossed his cloak across Cynthia's shoulders and climbed to the driver's seat. The others got inside; it was a close fit. Gregory twitched the reins and they were off, without any fuss.

"Is it already gone from the castle?" Cynthia asked.

"It was never kept there," Hywel said, looking out the coach window. "Did Louis agree to sell it to you?"

"I think he would have."

"So did Margaret."

The coach stopped before a shuttered storefront; the signboard outside was black, speckled with silver stars and a moon with a contented smile. A. GUILLAUME, it read, ASTROLÓGE PHILOSOPHÉE, KARNACISTE.

Dimitrios tried the door. It would not move. "Shall I knock?"

"No," Hywel said, "He can't be disturbed in what he's doing yet, and we don't want to meet anyone else. Back door." He looked at the moon at the apex of the sky. "Quickly."

Dimi's knife lifted the latch of the back door, and he opened it with both hands for silence. They stepped into a small, untidy kitchen smelling of smoke, beer, and old cheese.

Beyond the doorway, light spilled down a flight of wooden stairs. Dimitrios took a step up, on the ball of his foot; the stair creaked only faintly, and there was no sound in reply.

At the top of the stairs was a candlestick, and beyond it was a room that glowed furnace-red, without heat.

The room was large, with a beamed and cupolaed ceiling. The light came from wall lanterns with blood-red glass; everything was red and black. Around the walls, supporting the ceiling beams, were figures of gods in the Egyptian style.

In the center of the room, a man sat at a table with a mirrored top; the table shone with milky moonlight from an open cupola above. On the surface, in the light, was a large sheet of heavy paper, with writing and a ribbon and a seal.

The magician held up a hand, tilted his head back, framing something overhead in his fingers; his other hand moved on the tabletop, trailing phosphenes after the fingertips. He was quite a young man. A clicking and whirr came from an orrery in the corner, little enameled worlds revolving in the darkness on wheels of red brass.

A fringe of rainbow light drew itself around the edges of the document, reflected in the tabletop; a double rainbow with darkness between. A draft rose from nowhere, rustling the draperies and the charts on the walls.

Dimitrios moved.

Yellow light sheeted down the doorway. Dimi bounced from it, dropped to one knee. Smoke rose from his leather sleeve.

.   The magician at the table turned his head.

Gregory took a step. *"Wait!"* Hywel said. Cynthia

reached for Dimi's burned arm. Hywel pushed back his left sleeve, knelt, then planted his right hand on the floor, fingers spread.

The wizard, Guillaume, stood up slowly. Hywel tensed, shut his eyes, thrust his bare left arm into the doorway. The sheet of light came down. Yellow-white lightnings danced across Hywel's shoulders, down his right arm. The floor beneath his hand cracked and blackened.

"Now," Hywel said, rasping.

Dimitrios stood up, pushed past Cynthia and Gregory, and went into the red room. A spark appeared above Guillaume's head, and white light descended in a cone around him.

Dimi stopped, knife half-raised; with a snap of the wrist, he threw it at the magician.

The blade hit the cone of light and hung there, the point a handspan from Guillaume's chest. Then a little knot of white-hot energy formed around the knifepoint, spinning down the blade, leaving nothing but glowing metal dust that blew away on the rising wind.

"*Guillaume,*" Hywel cried out. "Dimitrios—don't touch him."

Dimitrios looked at the table. The paper grew hazy, transparent; through it, its reflection was visible, still sharp in the mirror. Dimi reached down. His fingers went right through to the glass.

Guillaume moved inside his cone. Dimi stepped back, reaching for his short sword. The magician raised his fists. Gregory stepped into the room. Guillaume pounded the inside of the cone of light. Darkness pooled around his hands. He opened his mouth, stretched it in a scream. There was no sound. Something fell in flakes from Guillaume's hands, his face. It was his flesh. Dimitrios stared.

"It's too late for him," Hywel said. "The paper."

Dimi reached for the document, and touched only mirror. "It's gone. There's only—"

"*Correspondences,*" Hywel said, with the last of his breath.

Dimi grasped his sword hilt. Gregory had already drawn

his little steel gun. Flame spurted. The seal of Henry VI exploded in glass slivers and bits of bright red wax.

The cone of energy stuttered and vanished. Dimi drew his gladius. Guillaume fell down hard. A smoking paper, bearing formal black script and the fragments of a seal, fluttered down beside him, and the wind was still.

There was a sudden, gagging stench of rotten meat.

"What did you do?" Cynthia said dully, staring at the oozing, corrupt mess on the floor. Above it, a carved Egyptian held out the ankh of immortality. The orrery planets had stopped their motion.

Hywel leaned against the doorframe, not looking in or out. "All that light and noise had to draw power from something," he said. Anger rose in his voice. "He was already driving two works, costly, direct ones; and then, with anything but whole concentration, he set up a third to guard him from attack. But he didn't give it any point to *stop* guarding. *I* didn't do anything. There wasn't anything I could do. He must have been very young and strong, to last as long as he did."

Hywel swayed, turned to face the others. With a sudden startling bitterness he said "Only a madman would ever do genuine magic, when there are so many tricks to hand. But we're all mad. And we'll keep it up until we extinct ourselves."

Then he stopped, and sat very quietly.

From below came a pounding at Guillaume's front door.

Dimitrios and Cynthia helped Hywel stand. Gregory stuck the Exemplification of Clarence in a lantern flame, put it burning on the broken glass of the table.

"Out the back door," Dimi said, "before Louis's men think of it."

Hywel nodded and said very calmly, "We have a passage to England waiting. Let's see if any good at all was done tonight."

PART THREE

Directions of the Road

Plots have I laid, inductions dangerous,
By drunken prophecies, libels, and dreams.
—ACT I, SCENE I

Chapter 7
UP

ANY city the size of London must contain every sort of person and belief, and at the end of the year they all found something to celebrate: the lengthening of the day after the Solstice, the longest night itself (and the lost things found upon it), the birth of Mithras, Saturnal, year-change in all its social and numerological and astrological implications, the twelvemonth of city refuge that made serf or villein into townsman, transforming his life of rural toil into one of urban poverty.

And on this December day, everyone in London seemed to have taken their celebrations into the street, which was colorful and noisy and surpassing merry but made a traveler's progress just about impossible.

Hywel and Dimitrios, Cynthia and Gregory turned left and right and sometimes around, blocked at all turns by processional dancers, bear-baiters, staff-swingers looking for a keg or a skull to crack open, minnesingers weeping into their lutes. The gutters ran with mint water and foxed beer, a little blood when the Little Johns collided, and the more usual savories. There were green-sashed Gawaines and horned Hernes, Kyrils with crown and quill, and choristers singing recitatives to Anybody listening. Milk Street ran white: the Worshipful Company of the Art and Mystery of Dentistry was turned out in mass to cheer the passage of the Sun into Capricorn, auspicious for the pulling of teeth.

Another few zigzag blocks they rode, and there came a sound like gunfire. Dimi leaned forward, Gregory's hands tightened on the reins. Smoke drifted on the cold, still air, and footsteps clattered. A serpentine form emerged from a side street, waving and stamping, showing golden spines and the eyes the size of platters. The beast dipped and bobbed on two dozen human legs with wood-soled shoes. People around it cheered and tossed little burning sticks that cracked and flashed fire.

"A dragon of the Chinas," Hywel said. "The little thundercrackers are harmless, but mind your horses." He turned to Cynthia.

She sat a little forward on her sidesaddle, staring at the dragon and the explosions. Her face was set, showing no discernible feeling; her left hand emerged from her black cloak, clutching its edge, the knuckles in an arch of pain.

Dimitrios reached out to touch her; she turned, as if waking abruptly, and said, "Thank you, but I'm all right. I was just holding the animal still. . . . No sense getting one's neck broken over a few fire-flowers."

Dimi nodded. Hywel turned back to the street ahead. Gregory did absolutely nothing. When the dragon and its party had cleared the street, they rode on through the burnt and smoky air.

Wooden docks, well-frosted, thrust out before them into the half-frozen Thames. They turned at Hywel's direction, and shortly he called a halt. They were before the stone face of a riverfront house, at least a hundred feet long and three or four storeys high, with towers at the corners. The stone was not decorative, the windows were narrow against entry, and the door was heavily reinforced with iron.

"Impressive," Dimitrios said, looking up at the towers.

"Very warlike," Cynthia said flatly.

"The place is called Baynard's Castle," Hywel said, dismounting slowly and a little clumsily. "It's defensible enough. It hasn't been so long since that sort of construction was necessary." He went to the ironbound door, knocked hard. "And here we come bringing old times back," he said quietly.

The door was opened by a man in a cap and gown, both dark red; embroidered around his collar were white roses and stems, and a gold key hung on a chain around his neck. His face was long-jawed, and his square beard was gray.

"I regret, sir," he said, "the Duchess is not . . . *Magister Hywel?*"

"Will the Duchess see me and my friends, Hugh?" Hywel said. "We've been a long time in getting here."

The butler pulled the door wide. "Come in, Magister, please, and your company. I'll get the Irish lads for your horses, and tell the Lady; she'll be pleased, I know."

As they entered the high, dim hallway, Hugh said "It's been so terribly quiet here for so long . . . and now you're here, and young Duke Richard's expected from the North any time. Cook's going to be pleased; she hasn't made a really fine meal in such a time—"

"Hugh," Hywel said, almost offhand, "what about Duke George?"

Without breaking stride, the butler said levelly, "How much do you know, Magister?"

Hywel smiled. "Years don't dull your edge, Hugh Wetherby. We know there's trouble between George and Edward, real trouble this time, and it's a fair guess Richard isn't coming on a casual ride."

Wetherby said "The Duke of Clarence is in the Tower, on the King's orders."

"On what charge?"

"They took him from Warwick's Inn on a charge of interfering with the King's justice. An affair about his poor wife, and her maid—"

"We know."

"Well. But there's no one in London who believes that will be the charge when Parliament sits."

"Do they believe treason, Hugh?"

"Some say the King means only to give his brother a good scaring, but the Duke never has learned from his frights and the King has become very determined." Looking straight ahead, Wetherby said "Is that why you've come, Magister?"

"We have a little good news, Hugh."

"The Lady will be pleased to hear good news," Wetherby said, suddenly formal. "Your usual room is free, and for the lady and gentlemen . . . is the lady married?"

"Not at all, sir," Cynthia said.

"Well then. Would you all like to rest a bit, and I'll tell the Duchess you're here . . . and she'll see you at dinner."

"Or not, as she pleases," Hywel said gently.

"As she pleases," Wetherby said, and unlocked a door with an iron key from his belt. "The maids will be up soon. I'll send hot water."

When the butler had gone, Dimitrios said "Now what was *that* about—'if she pleases'? You said you were a friend of this family."

"I am," Hywel said, "and Hugh knows it . . . but the family's split, and he wonders whose friend I am now."

Cecily Neville, dowager Duchess of York, had been called the Rose of Raby in her youth, and she was still quite fair and smooth of face; seeing her, it was not easy to imagine that eleven children, the executions of a husband and son, and a long chain of battles and captivities had come between then and know. In her pose at the dinner table, however, relaxed yet elegant, one could clearly perceive the mother of a king.

"My daughter Margaret," she was saying to Cynthia, "considered becoming a priestess of Minerva, but there was a German alliance to cement. And Ursula, the youngest, seems determined on a career in one of the knightly orders. You should meet; you'd be an inspiration to one another." She smiled warmly. There was a silver owl pendant at her throat; its diamond eyes glittered in the light. "You're not eating, dear."

"I'm sorry, Your Grace . . . it must be the travel. I don't mean to be rude."

"You're not, of course. When they drove my Richard out of the country, I turned myself and the children over to King Henry; he didn't dare hurt me then, for fear of thunderbolts as an oathbreaker . . . but believe me, dear, in that year I learned what rudeness was."

The Duchess looked around the table. "I also learned about running a tight household; would anyone else care to eat the Doctor's dinner?"

Gregory covered his unused plate with his linen napkin. Hywel sipped his wine and shook his head. Dimitrios said awkwardly, "Uh—I shall."

Duchess Cecily motioned to a servant, and Cynthia's dish was set before Dimi. "Thank you," he said, forming the words carefully. "It is very good meat."

"I hope so, Captain," said the Duchess. "It's Royal venison; men have died for shooting those deer."

Dimi looked at her, eyes large; she had spoken in Greek nearly as clumsy as his own English. Behind his winecup, Hywel smiled slightly.

Cynthia seemed scarcely to have noticed. "If you would excuse me, Your Grace—"

"Of course, Doctor Ricci. Shall I have some tea and honey sent up to you?"

"That would be most kind." Cynthia stood, bowed, and went out of the dining hall.

Silence hung after her for a minute or two. The hound by the fireplace went to take a bone from the Duchess; she wiped her fingers and said "Which of you knows her best?"

Hywel said "She's lost her entire family, suddenly and not pleasantly. Then, just when we met, she was duped, by one of . . . their people." Cecily's lips compressed. Hywel said "No—not that. Not quite that. She betrayed a friend to death, not knowing he was a friend."

"Is that all?"

"That's all I can tell you." He paused, the Duchess's gaze not leaving him. "Because of how I learned it, Cecily."

Dimitrios looked up when Hywel used the Duchess's given name. She nodded, said briskly, "I must never forget what you are. Now, Hugh said you had good news."

"I doubt as good as I had hoped. We saw Margaret in Angers, about George's supposed agreement."

"I see. I suppose I should not ask how that was arranged. And is there such an agreement?"

"No such document exists, my lady."

"That is good news, then . . . to know there is one tiny bone of sense in George's body." She sighed. "But I do not think it will save him, not now. Edward has become so . . ." The dog licked her hand, and she tossed it another scrap. "Edward has become King, and that's all of it."

There was a commotion from the hallway outside, a sound of boots and dogs barking, shouts; the door opened and a man came in, stomping. He was dressed for the road, and clearly had been riding hard. There was dust on his leather coat, slush on his boots and gold spurs. He was not tall, but was powerfully built, with a warrior's big shoulders. Dark hair hung to his collar; his features were even, flat, not unattractive. He pulled off his cap with a ringed hand, shouted, "Good evening, Mother! Time for rejoicing: despite the roads and London, the younger son is—" He looked around the dinner table. "Oh, *shit.*"

The Duchess said calmly, "Welcome home, Richard. Didn't Hugh tell you we had guests?"

"He said, er, something. There was a lot of . . . noise." One of the dogs that had come in behind Richard was yapping at his heel. *"Shut up,"* he hissed, and swiped his foot at the animal.

Cecily shook her head, started to say something, then burst out laughing instead. "Come here, son of autumn."

They embraced. "Enough, now," she said. "Is there any soil left in Nottinghamshire, or did you bring it all on your clothes? Now say hello to the guests."

Richard turned, bowed formally, then stared. "Peredur!" He took Hywel's hand in both of his own. "But I didn't expect you here!"

"Things worked out differently. I'm glad to see you here,

though; I've brought these gentlemen to meet you. This is Dimitrios Ducas, Captain-at-arms, and Gregory, Fachritter von Bayern, artillerist. Gentlemen, Richard Plantagenet, Duke of Gloucester, Constable of England, and Warden of the Northern Marches."

"What Peredur means," Richard said, "is that I chase Scotsmen around Robin Hood's barn."

"I've told them something of the situation," Hywel said, "and they're willing to serve with you. If you're interested in having them, of course."

"Of course," Richard said lightly. Then, more seriously, he said to Hywel "Who else is in this bag of tricks?"

"Albany is in Denmark."

"What's he doing in Denmark?"

"Wavering, I imagine."

"But you think he'll go through with it?"

"The chance to be a king, even king in your brother's place, is a very strong magnet. But to be drawn by a magnet, one must contain some metal."

"When I was a boy, he talked like that," Richard said to Dimi and Gregory, who looked back, puzzled. "I don't understand it any better now." He touched Hywel's sleeve. "But I trust him. And I need trustworthy men, especially now. The pay isn't bad, either; I know—I'm the paymaster." He leaned over Cynthia's abandoned place, picked up the full winecup. "The gods won't mind," he said, and drank.

Richard put the cup down. "It's been a long day, for the middle of winter." He patted Hywel's shoulder, gave his mother a kiss. "I'd better go wash Nottingham off. Tell Cook the burglar in the kitchen tonight is only a starving duke. Good night, all." He clomped out, spurs rattling, pursued by the barking dog.

Gregory said "Does he know that his brother is imprisoned?"

The Duchess said "He knows. It is why he came to London, without his wife and son. I only wish . . . " She paused, looked around, seemed about to wave a hand and dismiss the others without further conversation;

then in a level voice she said, "I wish I knew what he's come to *do.*"

The morning sky was low and dark and threatening, the streets below very quiet. Hywel turned away from the narrow window. Around the breakfast table, Duchess Cecily was eating boiled eggs and reading from a book on a stand, the new Caxton printing of Malory's Arthuriad; a maid turned the pages to keep them clean. Richard and Dimitrios were eating bread and herring from their hands, talking between bites, not seeming to care how much grease and beer got onto the map of Northumbria spread between them. Gregory stood at a far window, looking out through his dark glasses on the dim cityscape, nibbling disinterestedly at a piece of white bread with comb honey.

Cynthia came in. Her hair was pulled back severely, tied with black ribbon; her face was drawn, and the spots below her eyes looked like bruises. She walked with an unnatural, forced steadiness, as if at every step she feared to fall.

Richard and Dimi did not look up at first. When they did, Richard practically leaped to his feet. "My lady! Peredur didn't tell me—"

"Doctor of Medicine Cynthia Ricci, late of Florence," Hywel said. "Cynthia, this is Duke Richard, the King's brother."

Cynthia stood silent for a moment, her eyes showing no comprehension; then she said "A great pleasure, Your Grace. I'm sorry I did not make your acquaintance last night . . . but I retired early. Impolitely, I fear—"

"There was nothing impolite about it," the Duchess said firmly, looking over her reading spectacles. "As I told you. My word is followed in my house, milady."

"Of course, Your Grace. I'm . . . sorry I forgot."

Cecily smiled, nodded, went back to her book. Richard said "If anyone was rude, I was; I think I drank your wine. But . . . you're a doctor? A doctor I need very much. Hywel, you're a wiz—you're splendid."

"I hadn't intended that Doctor Ricci accompany you," Hywel said. "I meant for her to come with me, to Wales."

Richard tilted his head. "That's something other than splendid, Peredur. I didn't think you were that sort," he said with a polite leer.

"Naturally," Hywel said at once, "Cynthia is free to do as she wishes." He looked at her. She was rather pale, and seemed to wince at the wan light through the windows. Hywel stared at Gregory, who looked back, impassive.

Cynthia said "I hadn't realized we were to part company at all. I'll have to think . . . I'm afraid I'm not thinking well, just now. Do we have some time?"

"Certainly there's time," Hywel said. "There's rarely a good cause to hurry things."

Richard said "I'm here for a Parliamentary court, and I won't be leaving until it's over. . . . A month, at least."

"You're here for more than that," said the Duchess in an ominous tone, and they all turned. "A note came this morning from Windsor. Your eldest brother's decided to carry through his son's marriage, and since he's called everyone to London anyway, it might as well be done at once."

Richard said "Which son?"

"Richard of Salisbury. The"—an instant's hesitation—"Duke of York."

· "He's three years old, Mother," said Richard Gloucester, amused.

"Four, as if that had anything to do with it. The bride's just turned five."

Cynthia said clearly, "How many troops does she come with?"

Cecily looked up, startled. "Why, no soldiers as such, dear, but most of Norfolk duchy. I see you know how this is done."

"Only above the rank of Baron," Cynthia said. "My lord Richard, I should be glad to serve as a doctor again; I have not done so in too long a time." She bowed and walked out.

"Well, she isn't *too* polite, is she?" Richard said, awed. "I like her, Peredur. She knows what idiocy is."

The Duchess dismissed the girl who had turned the

pages. Then she said, in a high voice, "What did you marry, Richard, youngest?"

Richard winced at the last word. "Annie Neville, of course, Mother."

"Not whom, what. You married half the Neville lands, which were gotten by Percy and Neville tracts marrying Beauchamp and Despenser properties. If this was not made clear to you, we shall have some lawyers whipped. Do you understand, youngest son?"

"Yes," Richard said, grating, " . . . Your Grace."

Cecily nodded. Then, in a much softer voice, she said, "And, in the year since, have you come to love your half of the Neville estates?"

"I—" The rest of the words seemed to stick in his throat. He looked at his mother, who regarded him steadily; he looked in the direction Cynthia had gone; he put up a hand to partly hide his eyes. Then he swallowed, said "Oh, *blast,* yes," and sat down heavily.

Richard looked at Dimitrios, who looked back, confused. The Duke said "Annie and I grew up together, in her father's house at Middleham. Runts of the litter, both of us— hush, Mother, I've seen those verses about 'Richard liveth yet'—and we used to knock each other down, because, you see, we were the only ones who could.

"And then we got big enough to matter in the war, and Annie's father changed sides, and I didn't think ever to see her again. And we killed her father."

"The footmen killed Warwick," said the Duchess, not loudly.

"Their knives," said Richard, not quite shouting, "but our war. Then Henry the Idiot and the bitch-goddess pushed Anne over the sword with their weasel son, who wasn't old enough to know what he had to put in, let alone where, and *that's* what I give for marrying children to improve the breed of kings!" His fist cracked into his palm.

After a little while Dimi said "If I might change the subject . . ."

"There are no objections," the Duchess said.

"I . . . don't know your faiths, and I am sorry if this is a wrong question, but tomorrow is an . . . important day. Is there—"

Richard held up his hand, put a finger to his lips, said "The finest one in the West, ever since the Legions were here. But that's not for Mother to hear." He pushed back his cuff, just revealing the Mithraic brand on his wrist. He and Dimi stood, bowed to Duchess Cecily, and went out.

Hywel said "Cynthia must go with me, of course. I'd thought the rage might have gone out of Richard, but I can't say I expected it." He rubbed his seeing eye, adjusted the other. Gregory touched his glasses.

The Duchess said "I have a brave son, who became a gluttonous king, and a pretty son, who has become a treacherous fool. Richard is angry, but he is the most constant of my boys still living."

Hywel said "It's her pain, of course . . . all her senses are cut off, as an ache turns to numbness; she can function, walk, talk, but she's a shell. I think I know someone in Wales who can help . . . but until then, we have to keep something else from filling that shell."

Suddenly, Hywel said to Gregory, "Have you fed recently?"

Gregory put down his piece of bread, still unfinished. Without inflection, he said "Not on anyone you know."

"Hugh Wetherby will see that you're saved the blood from the kitchen, Doctor," the Duchess said. "No one else will know."

"Thank you, *geehrte Frau*. It is difficult in cities . . . there are no large wild animals, and many people. That is . . . it is difficult to take the hard path." He looked at Hywel. "Did you think I would go to her?" His tone was merely curious. "She would kill me."

Cecily said "Her pain, you said, Hywel . . . what are you not telling us?"

"Nothing that I may say."

"But something you could say."

Hywel spoke quite coolly. "What I learn in certain ways I do not repeat. It is an essential rule. Wizards who will not keep rules . . . Gregory, you saw the Frenchman die. And, Cecily, I think you recall, at Wakefield, in the snow. . . ."

The Duchess's lip trembled. Then she said "And what of Doctor Ricci? How far does the rule extend?"

"I can do things I may not do," Hywel said sharply. "I didn't say I'd let her die."

"Where I am," Gregory said, "there is no death. What are we going to do?"

When the young man who would become Edward IV fought his first great battle, a strange thing happened in the sky overhead: three suns shone together. Edward's advisors were still divided as to whether this was a sign from the gods or a refraction phenomenon of the "sundog" variety. Edward himself played no favorites: he went from no particular faith to the earnest worship of Phoebus Apollo, in time constructing a new hall in the London Pantheon, and endowed a school of opticks at Minerva College, Oxford.

The London Apollonium was triangular, with a solar disc displayed at each corner, and a lavish use of gold leaf on virtually every surface, including the seats; it was said to be the only place on earth where wearing out one's clothes increased their value.

The centerpiece of the hall was a paneled dome of clear glass, designed by the Oxonian scientists. It projected a shaft of milk-white light downward, casting glory upon the central altar, and now, as the sun reached the meridian, beams were thrown to the corner discs, and thence reflected again, creating a three-sided halo of pure radiance.

The little Duke of York and his bride Anne Mowbray were standing in the downward light; the sword on the golden marble floor before them shone like a sunray. Thomas Bourchier, Edward's high priest, intoned the verses of the ceremony, standing like a pillar in white samite and several pounds of gold. Next to him stood Edward, with the Lyons of England and a rayed sun on his broad chest; as Sun Lord he was fully as important to the ceremony as Bourchier, not considering the power temporal he represented, or that they were anyway brothers-in-law.

A little behind Edward was the Queen, Elizabeth Woodville. Gold ropes on her gown emphasized her striking figure, and her yellow hair was combed high, set with tiny gold mirrors. She looked out at the audience, not at the bride and groom, and quite unlike the King's there was no interest in her look.

The bride's parents were not on the dais. Her father, the Duke of Norfolk, Earl of Nottingham and Warenne, Earl Marshal of England, was dead two years almost to the day, her mother a little less. There was a great-grandmother in Norwich, but she was not present; rheumatism or something. Not that there was any shortage of nobility. The temple was packed with lords assembled for Parliament. Little Anne's father's dukedom and earldoms had been transferred over the past eighteen months, and the recipient was very much in evidence. Anne was marrying him.

Thomas Bourchier lowered his arms, linked the couple's hands. A pair of pages moved up silently to help them hop over the sword. The high priest whispered to Anne Mowbray Plantagenet, and she turned and planted a kiss on Richard of Salisbury's lips. He goggled back in utter bewilderment.

The audience stood and cheered. Some of the great ladies were crying, as always at weddings.

Three sets of footsteps echoed through the twisting halls of the White Tower, coming to a stop at an iron cell door. A key was put into the lock, turned.

"Leave us alone now, Simon," said Richard of Gloucester to the turnkey. "What you don't hear no one can ask you to tell."

"O'course, Your Grace," the man said, and with a nod to the Duke and Hywel Peredur, he went off down the hall.

The room was fairly well appointed, for a prison cell. There was a small fire with a scuttle of sea-coal nearby, an honest bed, a small pile of books. A wooden platter held some bits of drying cheese and apple cores.

George, Duke of Clarence, turned away from the barred window. He wore a plain brown gown belted with cord, leather slippers. His brown hair was to his shoulders, and his beard had grown, but his face was unlined and his eyes were bright. "Hello, Dick. Come all this way to watch them hang me? And you've brought a friendly ghost along. Hello, Magister."

Hywel closed the door. Richard said "George . . . it's serious this time."

"With you it's always serious, Richard. Games, and tilting at the ring, and making bastard babies were all very serious with you. And putting Edward on the throne, that was seriousest of all. What's he sent you in here to do, Dick? Kill me quick? That certainly makes sense. If Parliament should vote wrong, you'd be years in killing all of them."

"George . . . why do you try to make me angry?"

"That's like the seriousness, Dick; everything makes you angry, nobody has to try. All right, I fought you; I helped Warwick throw you out of the country. I did it, and I lost, and I know what that sort of loser gets. Just like Henry. . . . Tell me something, Dick, about old Henry—was it you then, too?"

Richard threw a punch at his brother. George put up his arm to block; Richard swept his other fist down and caught George on the side of the head, knocking him to the floor.

George got to his hands and knees. Both brothers were breathing very hard. Richard held out his hand, helped George up. George sat down again, still panting.

"George," Richard said, "Peredur . . . has a question . . . for you. About the paper . . . with Henry and Margaret."

"Oh . . . that. If you want to know why a man signs his own death warrant, I don't know. Stupidity, I suppose, but it seemed like a wonderful idea at the time."

"The document was destroyed," Hywel said. "Margaret was trying to send it to England."

"Destroyed?" George said, looking up. "Edward doesn't have it? The court won't see it?"

"She was sending it by magic," Hywel went on. "We stopped it. But we need to know whom she was sending it to, who would have taken it to the court."

"You stopped . . . oh, gods, Dick. I didn't . . . I mean, I'm sorry."

Richard started to speak. Hywel touched his shoulder; Gloucester said nothing.

Clarence was looking around the room with a wondering expression. "Sent it to . . . you mean a wizard?"

"Very likely. Perhaps a wizard-astrologer."

Clarence stopped still. *"Stacy."* He shook his head. "But Stacy's dead."

"John Stacy of Oxford?" Hywel said. Clarence nodded. "He's dead?" Another nod.

"You *have* been away," Richard said. "Last May, Doctor Stacy, and the Thoth-priest at his college, and George's man Tom Burdett were all arrested for plotting to kill Edward by magics. Edward put together a high commission especially to try them; there were a dozen barons on it, and five earls. Talk about the majesty of the law."

"Tom was innocent," George said. "I had his oath."

Richard said dryly, "And of all the men in England to read his statement to the Lords, you chose the same loudmouth who read all London Henry's case for usurping us."

"He was . . . a philosopher," Clarence said blankly. "He only said what he thought was right."

Hywel said quietly, "Did Edward order a guilty verdict?"

"Yes," Richard said roughly, "I suppose he did. Of course, this was a month after George had the Twynho woman dragged out of her bed and hanged, in the speed record for legal process."

Clarence reached out with both hands, caught both Hywel and Gloucester by the sleeves. "You weren't there when Isabel died," he said, on the edge of a sob. "She just lay there, couldn't move, couldn't lift her hands . . . and when I kissed her, I could taste the poison on her breath. It tasted of fruit, and she hadn't had fruit. She was so long dying . . . in such pain. . . . Maybe I went mad; I won't deny it if you say so." He closed his eyes, and the tears ran. "Now I'm scared, Dick. I've lost a kingdom, and Bel, and everything. Sweet Venus, I'm scared." He looked at his brother, tightened his grip on Richard's sleeve, smiled crookedly. "Edward will get his verdict even without the silly paper, you know. But . . . thanks, Dick."

Gloucester did not speak, move, blink. Then he turned to Hywel and said "I'll get Simon." He pulled free of George's grip and went out of the cell.

Hywel and Richard emerged from the Tower into a bright, cold January day. From across the city, the sounds of music and cheering were drifting on the air, from the revels at young York's wedding.

"Do you think Doctor Stacy is your man?" Richard asked.

"I don't know. Surely Louis must have known about the trial, but that hardly means Margaret did."

"Could they have sent the paper to a dead man?"

"To any correctly prepared location, whether or not anyone was there." Hywel shook his head. "I'm really looking for the man Margaret thought I was. The moon was full over all of Britain that night; this seemed as good a place as any to start."

Richard was not looking at him. "Maybe he did go mad, when he lost Bel," the Duke said intently. "She was my Annie's sister, you know . . . maybe he went mad. But too late for it to save him. What do you think, Peredur, wizard? What might Edward and George and I have done? If we'd hung together, I mean?"

Hywel said "I didn't mean to make you lie, just then."

"It was my doing," Richard said. "I've always wondered what it would be like . . . if my brother loved me."

Cynthia Ricci could just see the London Pantheon from her upper-floor room in Baynard's Castle. Unlike the other Pantheons she had seen, it was not a single building sacred to all gods; it was a hundred or more individual temples run together. Every few years, Duchess Cecily said, a noble or wealthy merchant built a new hall to his or her favorite deity, even if that faith already had a temple in an outdated or rundown style. The result was a riot of materials and architectures, a great holy maze that rambled and arched and cloistered and thrust towers at the heavens. According to Dimi, the Mithraists had their cavern elsewhere in the city, but its exact location was a Mystery.

Cynthia watched the wedding party spilling out from the Apollonium with its shining dome. Horns and drums and whistles were aduible from here. She put down her hairbrush, sipped at cold tea with honey. There was an untouched chunk of bread near the cup, its butter going rancid.

Behind her, the door clicked. She turned, still holding the tea.

Gregory came in. He was lightly dressed as always, in an unfastened gown and a white linen shirt open at the neck.

"If you would draw the curtain," he said softly, "I could remove my glasses."

She pulled the heavy drape across the window. He lifted the wire frames from his nose and ears, massaged the spots where they had rested. *"Danke sehr.* They are a burden." He sat down, sighed. "Everything is a burden, not so? Life is a burden."

"Is something the matter?" Cynthia said, without feeling.

Gregory squinted, looked at the bedside table, the buttered bread. "I see you know what it means when food loses its flavor. I know that, well. Chickens' blood. Pigs' blood. A diet of kitchen offal does not sharpen one's taste."

Cynthia looked down, at the blackred tea in her cup. She set it aside. "You told me that you—"

"I say many things. Most of them are true. This one is true: it is good to survive. *Das Leben ist lieblich.* You are a healer, a good one, *Fräulein Doktor;* do you not think life is not better than death?"

She stood up. "Gregory, are you well?"

"Well? *Ja, 'bin ganz wohl* There is no disease that can

afflict me, no drug poison me. I will live for a long
time. . . . Who knows how long. But you tell me, *Fräulein
Doktor,* what good is a long life when all taste for life is
gone? Who would live forever on a diet of pigs' blood?"

Her head turned sharply, toward her medical bag across
the room. Gregory followed the glance, smiled. He stood,
walked toward her. She sidestepped unsteadily. Gregory
reached to the nightstand, picked up the knife that lay
next to the bread. He held it loosely in one hand, squeezed.
The steel blade bent into waves between his thumb and
fingers. *"Ach."* A line of blood, pale pink, showed on his in-
dex finger. He put the finger into the teacup, stirred, drew
it out and licked it clean.

Cynthia said "I'll—"

"Will you? You have said that you know how, but can
you?"

"—scream. I do . . . know how . . . to scream." She stood
absolutely rigid, save for a tiny tremor at the tips of her
fingers.

"But who will hear? They are at the wedding, or the
prison. We are alone." His voice became very gentle. "Is
that not the problem? We are both alone."

She relaxed just a little, and said slowly, "There are . . .
quills . . . in my kit. I can help, Gregory. I'm a doctor.
You're ill, that's all."

"That is anything but all. Even supposing it is a quill
you mean to offer me, not the scalpel"—her eyes flicked
sidewise—"do you think that is all I need? Hunger is only
put off a while, I know that. I have not always drunk from
chickens and pigs."

He looked at the darkened window, stroked the drape.
"A city is an impossible place for one like me. Too many
walls, too many lights, too many people close together.
Like being smothered by food." He shook his head. "Have
you heard of this country to the north, Scotland? They say
the people live far apart. A traveler vanishes in the mountains, and a thousand things may have happened. It is
cold, I hear, but cold is nothing to me. And they admire
strength." He picked up the wavy knife, squeezed again. It

broke with a sharp sound. Cynthia shuddered briefly, then controlled herself.

She said "I've known many people with chronic diseases." Her voice was quite steady. "They all have bad days, doubtful days. Why don't you—"

"A fascinating word, *chronic*. It means *of time*. A disease of time, that is the truth." He spoke intensely: "The only problem, the *only* one, is that one is such a long time lonely." He reached out, touched his white hand to her white cheek, tenderly.

"You had better go to your own room, Gregory," she said, with barely restrained anger. "You had better rest quietly for a while. That's medical advice."

He let his hand fall. "Perhaps not the only problem. . . . When one is strong, nothing taken by force has any value. The blood of dumb beasts. Do not think what you are thinking; I would not do that. I am patient. I can afford to be."

He put on his glasses, closed his gown, and went out.

She stood there until she began to tremble; then she sank down to the floor and sat. She did not scream, or cry, or do anything but breathe deeply and evenly. Then she kicked the broken pieces of the knife under the bed, and cursed in Latin.

Duchess Cecily was drinking tea and reading from Malory's Arthur when Gregory came downstairs. She looked up from her book without speaking.

"I cannot promise she will go to Wales," Gregory said, "but I do not think she will go to Scotland."

The Duchess nodded. "Are you all right, Doctor von Bayern?"

"I am all right. Though while I spoke to her . . ." He laughed once, ash-dry. "In fact, I am well. I told you, I have given this . . . performance . . . before. It is not all play-act, of course; I am the hungry animal, I know. But this time, the reason was better than hunger. . . . Yes, I think I am well."

The Duchess smiled and turned a page in her book.

Gregory said "My Lady . . . why did you think the Doctor would reject me? Others . . . have not."

Cecily said "You are not so unattractive. And Hywel is a wise man in more than the conventional sense, but there are things he does not always see. A time back, you said that Cynthia would kill you if you attacked her; that is right. She's not a hollow vessel needing someone to fill her; she a knight needing a quest. For her soul's sake." She paused, looking at the illustration on the book page, of jousters riding one another down. "That's why she must go with Hywel: there are better quests than war."

King Edward IV showed a darker splendor in Parliament than he had displayed in the temple the day before. He wore the lyons and the shining sun on blood-red velvet, and he did not sit in a shaft of light, and he did not smile at all as he read the Bill.

"The said duke nevertheless, for all this no love increasing but growing daily in more and more malice . . . "

"I'll agree with that part," Richard said to Hywel.

" . . . intended and purposed firmly the extreme destruction and disheriting of the King . . . "

"Extremely destroyed. How destroyed *is* that?"

" . . . upon the falsest and most unnatural-colored pretense that man might imagine, falsely and untruly noised, published and said, that the King our sovereign lord was a bastard . . . "

Duchess Cecily murmured "Is that a sop to me, Edward? Your father and I used to compare those stories . . . in bed." Cecily turned, patted Cynthia's hand. Cynthia smiled faintly, from somewhere far away.

"And over this, the said duke obtained and got an exemplification under the great seal of King Harry the Sixth . . ."

Hywel closed his eyes. Dimitrios stared. Richard smiled.

"For which premises and causes the King, by the advice and assent of his Lords spiritual and temporal . . . "

Richard said "Never kill a brother without the gods' approval."

". . . and the Commons . . . "

"And especially not theirs."

". . . ordaineth, enacteth, and establisheth, that the said George, duke of Clarence, be convicted and attainted of high treason, and shall forfeit from him and his heirs for ever the honor, estates, dignity, and name of duke . . . "

Richard muttered "And one more thing. *Say* something, George, blast it; call him a fat booby, say anything. What can he do to you now?"

George stood entirely silent before the court.

". . . and all his properties and possessions."

A hammer came down, and it was law.

Dimitrios said "How do the English put a royal duke to death?"

"My father had his head hacked off," Richard said. "But I don't think Edward will want anything so spectacular." He looked across the hall at George, still motionless. "Perhaps we should ask George."

Cynthia gave the Irish stableboy her medical bag, and he lashed it into place on her horse's pack; it was the last thing to be loaded.

Dimitrios said "I hear Wales is beautiful. I hope you find it so." He held out his hand; she took it, then said "Fare you well, Dimi. Minerva watch you," and put her arm around his shoulder, touched his cheek to his.

"Take care, dear," Cecily said. "And take care of Peredur; he's older than he claims." They hugged. The Duchess said "Careful, dear, so am I," and pressed something into Cynthia's hand. It was the silver owl. Cynthia looked up, starting to shake her head, but the Duchess folded her fingers closed on the pendant. "Call it a loan. Till you visit again."

"I wish you were all coming with me," Richard told Hywel. "We'll need healing, and magic couldn't hurt."

"I hope you don't need too much healing," Hywel said, "and magic always hurts."

Richard turned to Dimitrios, "You see? He's still talking

like that. Good roads and company, Peredur. Good days
and dreams, Doctor Ricci."

Dimi helped Cynthia onto her horse, while Hywel slowly
got into his own saddle.

A hand thrust toward Cynthia. Gregory stood there, in
cloak over tight-belted gown, the sun reflecting from his
glasses. He held his hand steady, within her reach, but
made no effort to touch her. For a few moments the wind
made all sounds and motions.

Cynthia put her hand in Gregory's. He kissed the knuckle, let go.

She said "I'll see you, won't I, Gregory . . . when you
come back from Scotland?"

"And you come back from Wales."

The boys handed the reins to the riders, and Hywel and
Cynthia rode away from the house, up Thames Street to
Old Dean's Lane, and there turned out of sight.

Dimi said "I guess you had to do that. Before she went
away."

Gregory looked up the street and said nothing.

"These last few days, I've been afraid we'd find you with
her knife in your heart."

Gregory said "I haven't had any fear of that at all."

There were no windows in the little room under the
Bloody Tower, and the candles within did little to brighten
it. The air was thick with closeness, and sweat, and the
fumes of wine.

It was crowded. Richard Plantagenet, Duke of Gloucester, was in the room, and with him Dimitrios Ducas and
Gregory von Bayern, and Sir James Tyrell, a man of Richard's household just arrived to accompany his master back
to the North.

There were two other men, in leather aprons and coarse
linen shirts; the shirts were soaked with red wine. They
had carried in the last man in the room, who lay on his
back on a rough trestle table: George Plantagenet, attainted traitor, condemned, dead.

George's body was sodden with the strong red wine

called malmsey; he lay in a puddle of it, it ran from his ears and nostrils, it matted his hair and beard. His brown gown was saturated. One of his slippers was missing.

Richard touched George's cheek, moved his head. The open eyes stared, red-filmed.

"'E didn't 'ardly struggle none, sor," said one of the aproned men. "Said 'e'd got wot few men 'as 'ad, enough wine t'sate 'im."

"Course, we wasn't gon'ter larf," the other man said, "but 'is Grice wanted us to. 'Is former Grice, 'at is."

"Very well," Richard said. He took a sack from his belt; it clanked when he set it next to George's head.

The first man said " 'E'd a word for you, Yer Grace, an it please you."

Richard did not look up from his brother's face. "Well?"

" 'E said 'e didn' blame Yer Grace."

Richard turned to Tyrell and said, "All right, that's the end of it," and went out of the room, followed by all the living.

Just outside the door was a pile of stone blocks and a tub of mortar. The aproned men stripped off their wine-soaked shirts, tossed them into the room, and began to stir the mortar.

"An it please Yor Grice . . . "

Richard said "You've two jobs to do and be paid for. You weren't hired as messengers."

Richard and Tyrell, Dimi and Gregory walked on down the corridor. From behind, they could hear the sounds of the workmen stealing the candles from the little room.

When they were out of the halls, under a black sky without moon or stars, Richard began to chuckle softly.

"Are you well, sir?" Tyrell said, reaching for the Duke's arm.

Richard pushed him away. "Fine, James. Go ahead and laugh, James; he wanted us to. I've only just thought. George had his last joke on Edward tonight, and like all the best nasty jokes, the butt of this one won't understand it. 'Enough wine to sate him,' indeed. When King Edward puts a finger down his throat at dinner, for the joy of gorging double."

Shortly his solitary laughter died away. As they passed out of the courtyard, Richard suddenly pounded his fist on the stone wall and shouted, "Do any of you read stories?"

Dimi said "Stories, Your Grace?"

"You know. Storybooks. My mother has every one ever made, I think And . . . in every story I ever read with brothers in it, one of them kills the other. Well. Here's George dead. But in the stories there's alway some *reason.*"

Richard shook his head, as if trying to clear it of wine vapors. Still angrily but less loudly, he said "There's nothing left to do in bloody London. I'm ready to go." He faced Dimi and Gregory. "Will you come with me, and chase Scotsmen? There's no glory in it, and it's terrible for your soul, but by the Dog it's the only war we've got. And the pay is good." He smiled, with the blackest of humor. "I know, I'm the paymaster."

Dimi gave a brief glance to Tyrell, who stood quietly by; then, with his mouth open as if he had just understood a mysterious thing, he looked at Gregory. Gregory had removed his glasses, and his eyes were very white in the night.

The men marched on up the street, singing in four languages songs about blood and fire.

Chapter 8
DOWN

THEY had a boar, in the Yorkshire snow.

An old beast, someone had said, gray-bristled, surprised while it rooted in the iron earth. Now they had three dogs dead, a horse down and its rider hurt, a beater maybe worse than hurt. And the brachets were yelping, racing each other through the brake, throwing up snow; the archers nocked arrows, and spears pricked the colorless sky. The horn wound long, for no useful reason.

Dimitrios supposed the ninny with the horn must not be of Richard's cavalry; a glimpse of Sir James Tyrell grimacing confirmed it. No matter who or where, a man's household always had a few like that; this Dimi knew without quite allowing himself to think it.

But gods, the hunting had been good.

The barking ahead increased. The riders pricked and whispered. Richard appeared then, suddenly on the right, dark cloak afloat, spear of white ashwood held like a standard, or a thunderbolt. He rode a strong white mare named Surrey. He looked at Dimi and Tyrell, gestured with the hand that held the reins, then rode on. The two men followed.

Tyrell called his horse Palomides; it was a dark brown gelding of terrifying aspect and worse manners in its owner's absence, the grooms' dread. Richard had given Dimi a white mare much like the Duke's own—though given was

the wrong word, Dimi well knew. Olwen was loaned to
him, as he was allowed a room in Gloucester's house and
meals at his table. A mercenary was entitled to those
things, and gave service in return. No more was implied,
or expected.

The three men had pulled clear of the main body of the
hunt; they passed a startled beater, who waved his cap.
The ride was very silent, snow muffling hooves, no leaves
to rustle in their passing.

There was a little hump of ground ahead, maybe a dozen
yards long and two or three high; beyond it, snow was flying. There were barks, and snaps, and grunts. A signal
from Richard, and Tyrell broke right, Richard and Dimi
passing to the left; all cutting corners, jumping the ends of
the rise.

The dogs had the boar outside its nest. There were
bushes and branches and rocks all around; the winter had
stripped the bushes and picked the stones out dark on
snow, and still it was a good bit of concealment. Then they
were right, Dimi thought; it was an old boar, clever, dangerous. He could see the baying hounds now, but not the
quarry.

Then he saw it, as the gray head thrust up and a long
steely tusk ripped a dog open. Blood went everywhere. The
hound made a noise more surprised than hurt.

It was a big beast, nearly white, as if stones and
branches and dirty snow had grown tusks and a temper.
Dimi glanced at Richard, at the White Boar badge on the
Duke's breast. Richard's face was set hard, flushed in the
cold.

The hounds were still in the fight, biting at hide that
was like studded leather; there was more dark blood, impossible to tell what animal's. Another hound was gored,
in the throat. It gave a gurgling whimper.

Richard showed his teeth. Without speaking or sig-
naling, he pointed his spear and brought White Surrey to
the trot.

Tyrell looked concerned, but calm. He nodded to Dimi,
and they pursued.

Richard called to the hounds, and they scattered as the horse bore down. The boar tossed a carcass after them, as if in contempt. Richard dipped his spear and drove for the throat.

The gray head swung, and the spear grazed it, cut into the flank, skidded out. The boar growled, snorted, aimed for Surrey's forelegs.

Richard wheeled and struck the boar with the side of his spear, barely cutting it but spoiling its charge. Man and beast recoiled. The Duke stabbed, and this time the point bit in. Richard leaned on the shaft as the boar turned, tried to pull itself free.

Tyrell struck from the other flank, his spear sinking to its crossguard. He levered upward; the tusks tipped back, the snout pointing at the sky. A bit of throatskin showed pale.

Dimi's point found the spot. Blood ran, steaming. The pig shrieked. The three of them held it like that, struggling on their spearpoints, until at last it closed its eyes and was still.

The rest of the mounted party was reaching them now. A squire, perched on the hump of earth above the nest, started to raise a cheer. "Hush," Dimi said, without thinking. Everyone was silent.

The boar rose again, fighting. The spears still held it. The squire stared. Archers and spearmen held their poses. Richard said "Shamming won't save you, Sir Hog," not gloating.

At length the beast went down for good, and the squire got to lead his cheer.

Richard leaned on his spear, as if suddenly exhausted. He said to Dimitrios, "The head's yours, if you want it, Captain." The Duke had a vague smile; Tyrell, a more definite one.

"Thank you, Your Grace." Dimi dismounted, drew his long sword. There was a good bit of slicing before the head came free, rolling half over in the brown snow. Dimi wiped his blade, noting the nicks the good Eastern edge had taken on neckbones and spines; he sheathed the sword. Finally he picked up the ugly trophy—it weighed a good thirty pounds—and hoisted it onto the forepart of his saddle. Olwen gave a disconsolate whinny.

Richard said "Now there's a soldier for you—who else would volunteer to ride home with that thing in his lap?" As the party laughed and clapped, Dimi saw the Duke's small nod toward him, heard him say, much more softly, *"Chairé, miles."*

Hail, soldier: not an improper, or even rare, thing for one brother in the Mysteries to say to another. They were both of *Miles* rank, for different causes but the same reason—too much else to do.

But it was an unexpected thing for the Duke to say just now, and as they rode back to Middleham, Dimi looked from one White Boar's head to the other, and remembered what Duchess Cecily had said about her son: she wondered what he intended to do.

After the Duke of Clarence was dead, they had gone from London to Nottingham, a town overlooked by a castle on a stark thrusting rock. The castle had a high, solitary tower; Richard admitted to a "barely healthy" fondness for the tower room, its view of the fortress, the town, and the Forest of Sherwood that spread over two hundred square miles.

For two weeks Richard heard reports of bailiffs and tax collectors, oversaw trials, hanged poachers of his brother's venison. There was a strange, messy case of a poacher taken wearing green clothing, with robin feathers in his cap and a robin's eggshell hung around his neck with ribbon—or, the foresters said he was a poacher; the man would say nothing.

Richard explained to Dimitrios that, not long after Edward had become king, a man called Robin Mend-All led an uprising against him in the North. "You know of Robin Hood, of course. . . ."

"No, Your Grace."

"No? Well, he's a sturdy yeoman who springs up to shoot at bad Plantagenet kings when their good relatives are away. If he can't shoot us personally, he takes out his grievance on our deer."

"Is this man a rebel, then, Your Grace?"

Richard looked thoughtful. "Mend-All was a respectable gentleman named Conyers, hired by my infinitely ambitious father-in-law Warwick to raise the countryside. But they're both years dead." He fingered the hilt of his dagger. "As is Henry the Idiot, and Coeur-de-Lion. So I don't know what this man is."

So they put the poacher to the question, burned him a little and scourged him and finally racked him apart, and they found out nothing.

"I don't understand," Richard said, turning the little blue eggshell over in his fingers. "We'd only have hanged him for the deer. Why would an ordinary robber want to be taken for anything more?" He made to crush the hollow shell, then stopped, and placed it carefully on a table. That afternoon, they set out northward.

Middleham Castle was an enormous cluster of buildings, old enough to be defensible and new enough to provide some comforts. Its two central buildings measured over fifty yards wide by nearly a hundred long, and rose four storeys; the walls were rectilinear, pleasing to the eye (though Gregory expressed professional doubts), the lead roofs slanting this way and gabled that way, black as void in the sunless afternoon.

It had been the centerpiece of the Neville estates; it was part of what Richard had married, and now he and his wife and son lived there by choice.

As the hunting party trooped through the gates, horses snuffling, people coughing, hounds yapping with that limitless mindless energy peculiar to dogs and small children, there was a deep, loud, rumbling *boom* from the outer court, and smoke rose.

Dimitrios looked up. Gregory von Bayern was standing next to a bronze canister set upon a stone block. The smoking cylinder seemed quite small to have produced so much noise. Gregory was drawing with chalk on slate, and that too made a surprising amount of very irritating noise. He wore a heavy cloak, a broad-brimmed hat, and doeskin gloves. He had been dressing warmly of late. Dimi wondered how much of the castle population knew that Ahriman's Serpent was among them. He was no longer surprised by what could be hidden in the midst of men.

The boar's head was displayed on a platter, carried three times around the high-ceilinged great hall; a minstrel with a good voice and indifferent lute-picking sang the boar-hunting verses from *Gawaine.* Someone suggested that, in the spirit of the poem, the head ought to be presented to one who had stayed in the castle, in exchange for whatever he had won that day.

Gregory stared at the platter set before him. *Wasn't that a dainty dish,* Dimi thought, and tried to recall who had suggested the game, and what reason someone might have had for baiting vampires at dinner.

Gregory stood up slowly. In his densest German accent, he said "Today I was conducting *Zersprungsdrückprüfungs . . . ach, das bedeutet* bursting-pressure tests, on a simulated breech. . . ." He produced some notes from the sleeves of his gown.

There were shouts of "You win the trade, you win!" and "What were you expecting, a kiss?" Gregory sat down. Dimi relaxed.

The boar, unfortunately, made better spectacle than dinner. The meat was tough and dense, coarse on the tongue. A great deal of beer and wine were called for, and the meal ended early and awash.

Dimi went out to the stables by the light of a half moon through broken clouds. James Tyrell was there, tending Palomides; he nodded to Dimi and went out. The grooms looked at Tyrell's horse, and at Dimitrios, and seemed at once to think of important tasks elsewhere. Dimi stroked Olwen's mane. She whickered softly. Palomides was quiet. Surrey seemed to be asleep.

"You're fond of her, aren't you." It was Richard, standing in the doorway, holding a tin lantern. "I knew it when you first saw her."

"I had a white mare when I was young," Dimi said.

"Oh? Lucky Raven. I wanted one. All the great knights I read about—storybooks, you know—they all had white horses. White stallions, in the stories, but I wasn't *that* stupid even then. Gods, I wanted a snow-white horse."

Dimitrios was puzzled. Luna had been his as soon as his father was convinced he was ready to care for her; what were the sons of English lords denied? Finally he said "Couldn't you have one?" It was not a polite question, but he had discovered that mercenaries could often get away with an honest rudeness.

Richard looked across the stables, to White Surrey's stall, and smiled. "I'm sure I could have, for the asking. I was a duke's son, after all. And that was the problem. I had this idea, quite as much gotten from books as the original notion of a white horse, that as a duke's son I was obligated not to ask for the things I wanted. Does that make any sense to you?"

Dimi thought about telling Richard some of his history . . . who and what his father had been. But all he said was "It makes sense to me, Your Grace."

Richard laughed. "I forget, you know Peredur too. Tell me, someday, how you met him." Then he stopped laughing. "Do you want her, brother *miles?*"

Dimi knew he was not being offered a horse—or, rather, the horse was not a gift, and it was the least part of the bargain. Richard was asking for the oath of fealty, nothing less. If given, Dimitrios would be Richard Gloucester's man, no longer free to sell himself elsewhere, expected to come, and go, and obey at his master's word until one of them died, or committed some hardly thinkable treachery. And in turn Duke Richard would stand behind him, feed and clothe and arm him and take his part in law—which law Richard himself was, in the North.

Dimi wanted to ask why. The Duke was forward, even headstrong: Dimi had seen that in London, in Nottingham Castle dungeon, on the boar hunt. Dimi had the sudden feeling that if he asked the Duke for a reason, the offer

would vanish, never to appear again; he would remain as
he was, with nothing more implied or expected.

He could have any choice, as long as it was final, and as
long as it was now.

For the second time in his life Dimitrios Ducas knew
how utterly weak he was; how fatherless.

"She is a beautiful mount," he said, "and I would be
honored to have her."

"Well," Richard said, looking at the stable floor, "that's
settled."

Dimi waited. He did not feel anything; no surge of regret
for lost freedom, but neither any sudden warm rush of be-
longing. Nothing at all might have happened.

Richard said "Well," again, and hesitated, as if he too
had expected something that had not come. He looked at
Olwen, said "Did your white horse have a name?"

"I called her Luna."

"You could call this one that, if you wished. . . . I don't
think horses are vain of their names."

"That was a long time ago, Your Grace."

"Hm? Oh, of course. As you wish." He walked to Surrey's stall, looked in for a long moment, then said "Well.
Annie will be waiting. Vows, you know." He smiled. "Good
night, brother." No title; just the word.

"Good night, my lord."

Again the hesitation, the abstracted nod. The Duke
went out.

Dimitrios patted Olwen, stroked her mane, then snuffed
the lantern and went out of the stable. The clouds had split
open, and the half moon was very bright on stone walls
and snow, the roof lead showing ghostly highlights. Dimi
nodded to a bored door guard and went inside, up the
stairs.

In the hall above, he nearly collided with Gregory. The
engineer wore cloak and hood. He had papers in his gloved
hands, and something that looked like a weapon—but it
was only a brass quadrant, the cord of its plumb weight
wound around it.

"*Ach,* Dimi, pardon," Gregory said. "I wanted to thank you for dinner."

"What?" Dimitrios was not sure if he would know sarcasm in Gregory's quiet voice.

"It was not beef. It did not bleed."

"*Oh* . . . Where are you going?"

"To check a measurement from one of the *Halbkulverins.*" He adjusted the stack of papers. "We had a student saying, that if you doubted your results at night suddenly, you must test them at once, or the *Heinzelmännchen*—the little ones—would by morning have changed them."

"You didn't believe that. . . ."

"No. But sometimes it happened so. So we check. Is it very cold, outside?"

"Rather. . . . Why do you care about that?" He spoke accusingly, without meaning to.

Undisturbed, Gregory said "I do not feel it, true enough. But the cold does injure my flesh. And sometimes I am in a mood to care. A doctor told me—" He tilted his head, examining Dimi's face. "No, my friend. Not the *Fräulein Doktor.* Excuse me now. Good night."

Gregory brushed by and was gone, silently, down the steps.

Dimitrios looked at the wall. There was a tapestry there, of Saxons and Normans, another damned tapestry of people killing people, and this one did not even show a clear victor. He wondered what had passed between von Bayern and the Italian woman, knowing that it was wrong for him to wonder.

He had been talking with her, idly and with no intentions, and had tried to turn the talk to better times past; he was suddenly aware that he had never seen her happy. He'd spoken of his old circle of friends, his *cohors equitata,* their adventures, his pretty white Luna.

And she had struck him across the face and gone out storming.

He did not understand. And he had still not seen her smile.

Dimi turned away from the tapestry and went to his

room, thinking that the vampire had his cannons now, and the Duke had his household, but it would still be weeks before there was any fighting.

Dimitrios and Tyrell had led their squadrons half the length of Annandale, across the Scottish border on the track of some cattle thieves. It was a slow pursuit, through the rugged Border country and a September fog, outriders posted against an all-too-possible ambush, but the quarry were slowed by their four-legged loot, and the trail was clear where the ground was soft. A few times Dimi thought he heard mooing, a thin noise on the air like something unnatural. Only his imagination, he supposed, and tricks of the wind. Only the fog and the cold were real. Those, and the men ahead.

There was a light in the fog: a fire. Dimi whistled low, and his men pulled in around him; he could hear Tyrell's answering owlhoot. The companies angled apart, to pinch the waiting Scots between them. There would be a mounted scuffle, nothing worth calling a battle; some men would get hurt, and the raiders would scatter. The English would return home with their cattle and some wounded Scotsmen for the gallows. Then the Scots would burn an English village for revenge, unless the English borderers burnt a Scottish one first, and on and on: that was Border warfare.

It was, Dimi kept forcing himself to think, the only war they had.

He and his company had come alongside the fire; it glowed weirdly in the mist, with the dawn behind it. As Dimitrios expected, it was a line of burning bracken across the trail, meant to stop them in disorder and give the rearguards some light to kill by.

What he had not expected were all the dead men on the ground.

"Do you . . . do you think they're shamming, sir?" It was Bennett, the squire who had cheered for Richard's boar hunt, half a year and a war ago. Dimi's first thought was to hush him, but he just said "No," and walked his horse forward. There was motion ahead, across the firelit space; Tyrell doing the same.

They set out pickets and began looking over the scene. There were eighteen men lying dead, and seven horses, and a cow. Some had been hit by crossbow bolts, but most were gunshot. Limbs were off, and a head. Tyrell brought a brand from the fire, held it to light a corpse's face. Dimi heard Bennett gasp and move away, to be sick out of the officers' sight.

The skin of each man's face had been slashed to the bone beneath, two cuts at right angles. Most had not bled, the dead do not, but some had.

Dimi could not recall seeing the particular mutilation before. He knelt by one of the bodies, supposing it might be an English prisoner left here for them to find; he said as much to Tyrell.

"No, sir. They're Scots, just as much as them that did this to'm." He nudged the body with his boot. "These are the ones we've been after all night. They'd'a not rode so fast, an they knew what they do now."

"You mean *they* were ambushed?"

"Easier work than riding to England for your beef and horses."

"Who, in the Dog's name?"

"Maccabees," Tyrell said, and spat. "Outlaws. They live in the hills, and now and again they come down and burn a temple of a god they don't like—and they hate 'em all, save their own."

"They're Jews, then?"

"No. Nazarenes. Jeshites."

Suddenly Dimitrios understood the significance of the cuts: the crosses. "The Doctrine of Julian is that *no* faith—" He broke off, aware that Tyrell and several of the others were looking hard at him, aware that he was doubly foreign here. He was not even certain what he had been about to say next.

Tyrell tossed his burning stick aside. "Wasn't us who made 'em outlaw," he said, then more loudly, "Come on, lads, it's none of our worry now, cows or dead."

As they mounted, the sun was trying to burn away the fog, and only partly succeeding.

Dimitrios was out at dusk by lanternlight, killing a stick of wood. In shirt and hose, he circled the post, watching it, shifting his guard, then moving smoothly forward to slice off a bit of wood. Mostly he hit the spots he aimed for; he could less and less decide whether he cared. His favorite practice had been to cut cross-strokes squarely on a mark, but he had no taste for that tonight.

"You use the point well," Richard said from behind him. "Is that Italian style?"

"A little . . . my lord," Dimi said, winded.

"But you're using a German sword."

Dimi held the blade across both hands; light flashed along the broad curve. "I practice with it, because of the greater mass."

"Ah. That makes sense. I've never seen a style quite like yours; I can tell the German power cuts in it, and the Italian surgery—"

"It's just a bastard style, my lord, picked up here and there."

"No insult meant," Richard said, surprise in his voice. "Surgery's just a word; I didn't mean you were a bone-cutter. . . . There's a story about old John Talbot, when he was doing down rebels in Ireland: King Harry the Fifth said, 'John, have you heard? They call you a butcher.' And Talbot said, 'I've heard, sir; an they who says it had ever dressed a hog themselves, they'd speak with more respect.'. . .

"Ah, brother. The Duke of Gloucester has a big mouth tonight. First I call you names and then I talk on rebellions."

"You've done nothing to offend me, Your Grace."

"No, done nothing, but said a surfeit . . ." He looked at the house they were quartered in for a week; it was now brightly lit. "I came out because I wanted to talk to someone who didn't sound like home or Scotland. . . . I was missing Annie, you see."

"Of course, my lord."

"Of course what? Of course I miss Annie, after three months? Yes, of course I miss Annie. I suppose that's what it's all about, isn't it, missing her when I can't see or touch her? Leaving her is . . . like marching off to a battle, knowing I might be killed; but if I live, there she'll be again. . . . I tell you, brother, the best Persian whore isn't like a woman you've missed."

To have something to say, Dimi said "I believe you love the lady, Your Grace."

"I suppose I've said so, haven't I. Well. It's true. Not just true—it's exclusively true." He folded his powerful arms, shook his head. "I had my occupations . . . had children by two of them . . . but never since. You don't believe that, do you?"

It was not an accusation, but Dimi said "Of course I do, my lord."

"Annie wouldn't either, so I've never told her, but it . . . is . . . true. I said it was like going to battle . . . if there were anyone else, I think it would be like knowing I couldn't die in that battle. You understand: if you couldn't be killed, only kill other men until your arm got tired, it wouldn't be battle at all. Just a job of work. I think you, of anyone, understand that."

"Yes, I do," Dimi said, relieved to finally understand something.

"Brother Edward has a wife, and three mistresses all at once, and Father knows what temporary help . . . that's not war, it's the silk trade."

"Are you suggesting I should marry, my lord?" Dimi said, thinking of a kitchen maid at Middleham, thinking bitterly of how his liver had pinched at the mention of Italian surgery.

Richard turned sharply to face Dimitrios, mouth open. *"What?* Oh, no, no. I wouldn't suggest a thing like that; you'd do it." He turned away again, and the lantern threw his face into deep shadow. "I was suggesting that we were both very lucky men, that we should both have been able to be faithful." He turned back. "Dog's teeth, Captain Ducas, you're bleeding."

Dimitrios looked at his hand, saw the streak across his left palm where he had gripped the blade without feeling it at all.

Olwen was panting in the November air when Dimi rode through the gates of Middleham Castle. He left her in the stables with barely a pat for goodbye, walked across the courtyard seeing very little. A young woman caught his eye as she ducked out of his sight: it was one of the kitchen girls . . . he'd forgotten her name. She had been willing, when he got back from the North, and he hadn't been able. Now she had some notion that he would murder her if the word got out.

Dimitrios wondered if he had really given her that idea, and he supposed he really had; his step slowed down as he realized that he might even have meant it.

There was a peculiar quiet in the house. Windows were heavily draped, the fires burned high; scented oils in the lamps kept the air smelling good if not fresh. Cook kept the boards full of hot spiced wines and sotelties—meat shaped into peacocks and elephants to disguise that it was salt beef or pork again. The manor was really very snug. But there was no riding to hounds.

Dimitrios felt as if smoke and pressure were collecting in his head, and he must shortly burst from it. He had seen hard winters enough in the Alps, harder by far than this; but then there had been places to go, work to do. He had never been a whole cold winter in one house, and he hated it.

But this was his lord's house, and he could not hate it.

"Dimitrios." It was Richard, with Gregory and two of the household captains. Tyrell was not with them. "Come along. There's a man in from Edinburgh, on foot the whole way, and we'd better hear his news before he freezes to death."

They went into one of the smaller halls. Tyrell was pouring brandy; he gave the glass to a little man seated before the fire, dressed in not quite rags. A spy, of course, Dimi thought. No one would have traveled from the heart of Scotland in this weather with ordinary news.

"Are you thawed, Colin?" Richard said.

"Enough, thank you, your lordship." The man's voice had a heavy Scots accent, but he spoke clearly, rapidly, precisely. "The Duke of Albany is in Edinburgh Castle, sir. Imprisoned by the King."

"Heimdall couldn't keep watch on that man," Richard said, then "How did Albany come to return?"

"An offer from the Danish King, Your Grace. King James would marry Denmark's sister, and the Scots would have the Orkney Islands for dowry. Albany would be governor of the Islands, and possibly Admiral of the North Sea."

"And possibly more, and English ships possibly fewer. But you said he was imprisoned—James didn't like his brother's proposal?"

Not smiling, Colin said "Say rather he disliked Milady Denmark's. But for safety's sake he locked both his brothers up. Albany's still there, but John Mar's dead."

Richard twisted a ring on his finger, said quietly, "How?"

"He'd a fever, and they bled him, and a drop too much. That's widely said, and I think it's true. Jamie hasn't the bent for secret murder."

There was nothing in Colin's tone, but Dimi saw Richard's shoulders arch. Gloucester said, "And are there still lairds of Scotland who would rather see Albany king than James?"

"I'd say more of them than ever, sir, as James neglects 'em for his new-made men. But they're quieter than ever, of course."

"Still as the grave, I shouldn't wonder." Richard took a glass of brandy. "How old is this news, Colin?"

"The Duke's boat landed twenty days ago, and he's fifteen in his cell. Mar's dead twelve. I were a corbie, would'a been quicker."

"You must have wings already. I withdraw the 'old,'
Colin."

Dimitrios saw the spy smile faintly. He knew then, as
something long forgotten, the fierce pride behind such a
smile.

Dimi counted five before he spoke, so as not to blurt or
stumble on the words. He said calmly, "I'll bring him out
for you, Your Grace."

Richard turned around. "A company couldn't breach
Edinburgh, and we aren't going to war for Alexander Stuart." He said the last quite flatly.

"Not a company. Just I. And Colin, if he'll show me the
way." The plan, the actions, were falling together in his
mind as he spoke.

"You've done this sort of thing?" Richard was intent, his
fingers stroking his dagger hilt.

"I've done it." *Since I was a child,* he thought. "The
Scots are not the only raiders in the world."

That got an appreciative chuckle from the captains, a
nod from Richard. Colin the spy had a crooked grin: in a
very light voice he said "And what comes when you're
taken, and I can't recall ever having met you?"

This was his moment, Dimi knew. He wondered if the
old Welsh wizard had known this was coming, all along.
"How is to you know me?" he said, in atrocious English
with the accents of a Greek fisherman. "I are come out of
the Eastern Empire, and everything I say is the biggest
lies."

Colin laughed out loud. Richard said, very softly, "Oh,
well said, brother, oh, well said."

The first thing Dimitrios saw was the mountain, a bare
bulk with snow on its spine, streaking down its flanks. At
one end of the rise a cylinder of rock thrust up, the head of
the crouching beast.

It was sometime in midafternoon; the sun was hidden
above lumpy, steel-colored clouds. The snow was not dazzling nor the bare rock stark. There were only white spots
and black spots on gray.

"Some call it the Lion," Colin said, following Dimi's look, "and the Mithras-men have their cave in it somewhere. And the spire, the head, that's Arthur's Seat."

"King Arthur ruled here?"

"Why, didn't you know, man? Arthur was a Scot." Colin did not seem to be telling tales, but then he was a spy by trade. "This is the lane to Castle Rock."

Edinburgh Castle was a set of unadorned stone boxes with one high tower, slopes falling away almost vertically from them; down the one manageable approach were lines of spiked walls, one of them mounting a row of brass cannon. The shot from one of those culverins would split a man into his component limbs; Dimi had seen that happen, quite close up.

His siege eye picked out patches of dull ice, loose snow, and he tried to gauge the movements of the guardsmen on their paths. They seemed to be alert in the middle of the quiet afternoon, which was not good for the current enterprise. The guards were heavily dressed, in leather and metal and furs, and that might tell against them in a chase. Not that he had any wish that it should come to a chase.

Colin said "It's a strong house, no mistake. Th'lairds 'ud burnt anything gentler, long ago." He pointed at the main gate. "Shall we go in, and be falsely welcome?"

The guard said "Who's there?" as he and his partner crossed their spears across the path. The men wore chest armor of lapped steel plates riveted over leather, that Dimi supposed might turn a glancing bullet. They had large bucket helmets with face shields blinkering their vision. Around the first guard's neck was a silver charm that Dimi at first thought was a Jeshite's Latin cross hung inverted; but it was only a hammer of Thor.

"It's Inver Drum, that's who," Colin shouted, "and you'd better let him in, 'cause he's cold an' wants his whisky."

"And you?" the man asked Dimi, with a remarkable lack of deference.

"My name is Hector. I am a captain of . . ." The guards were both staring at him.

" 'E's no' English," Colin put in. "Can you wooden'eads no' fathom a man by his speech? The Captain's an Eetalian, late of th' money wars. More's not for two such oafs t'know. Let us through."

The guards seemed to take this as perfectly normal behavior. They cleared the path.

Colin and Dimitrios stabled their horses at the base of the slope. Dimi rode a chestnut gelding; he had left Olwen at Middleham. A white horse was too memorable, not to mention the risk that they might have to leave Edinburgh by any means to chance.

A covered stairway led up the hill. It was wide enough for two men to walk comfortably—or to defend against any number attacking from below. The door at its head was sheathed with iron, with the figure of a lion worked into the metal.

The halls were plain, dark, smoky, and loud. There were banners and racked weapons and plenty of black iron, but no gilt and little glass, and none of the manor-house pleasantries like clocks or mirrors or dwarves. The furniture was angular, hard.

The great hall they entered was familiar enough. There was a crowd, variously eating and drinking and talking and threatening each other's chastity. The air was very thick, because of the tiny windows, and the darkness in the upper corners hung like something waiting to pounce. There were dogs as always, little wiry terriers, and a pair of falcons struggling with their hoods and jesses.

"Inver Droo-m!" A red-bearded man pushed toward Colin. He was a head and a half taller than the small man, and twice as broad; a huge basket-hilted sword swung dangerously wide from his hip. He began a conversation with Colin, in Scots that Dimitrios could not understand a single word of.

He felt very odd, in his Italian gold velvet and slender Damascus blade, among all these people in wool with broadswords; odd, pretending to be . . . whatever. He recalled Colin's appearance at Middleham, supposed the spy was every bit as convincing a peasant as he was a laird right now.

Colin returned. "Good luck of sorts. Everyone wants to talk about Albany, an' King Jamie's awa' so they're makin' free to do so. And that gives us an excuse to leave any good time. Can you take care of yoursel' a while longer?"

"Yes," Dimitrios said, not irritated and wondering if he should have been.

"That's good then." Colin left Dimi in a corner and vanished among men and women all taller than himself.

Dimi stayed to the walls of the room. He had learned some words of Scots in his months on the border, and a number of people were speaking English. Someone handed him a pewter mug, which reduced the need to converse. The mug was full of whisky, burning raw stuff. Dimi sipped slowly and was glad he had made its acquaintance before: they did not have a day to spend on hangovers.

He was unique in the crowd, and could not go unnoticed—but Colin was that. The trick, of course, was not to *keep* anyone's notice. He thought about the dissemblers he had come to know lately: von Bayern hiding his disease, Peredur hiding his eye and his magic; even Doctor Ricci had the talent. While Dimitrios Ducas, when all the power of Byzantium might have borne down on him, had just gone soldiering and been unseen. Suddenly he felt rather secure. He took a swallow of the whisky, tasting smoke and fire.

"Hector!"

Dimitrios almost did not turn, but he remembered himself in time.

"Hector, *frére lupin!* How in death's name do you come here?"

"Georges. Well met," Dimi lied, thinking that it was not impossible, after all, just highly unlikely, and even more unfortunate.

Georges des Martz was an Alsatian mercenary Dimi had worked with some five years ago. Now he was wearing a steel-mesh vest over leather, a woolen cloak, a gold thunderbolt on a chain around his neck. Georges had always been one for death gods, Dimi recalled, though a good fellow in a fight; he would have taken well to Odin.

Georges said "Last I heard of you, you were going to Milan. But that's over now, isn't it?"

"Yes, it's over." Dimi tried to tell if their French conversation was attracting unwelcome notice.

"And now you're up here. Don't have to hear a raven tell what that means. How soon, Hector?"

"What?" He looked for Colin.

"War with England. It's what I came here for . . . but of course you'd know that, you heard enough of my papa's old grudge with Hawkwood. Stupid, yes, but family tradition. And when I go through damnation, not to mention England, to get here, what happens but these people deny there is any war to be. I tell you: they do it to drive the price down. *Seigneur le Mort,* these people are cheap. Do you know there is not one palatable wine in this privy of a castle? Cheaper than Swiss."

Someone touched Dimi's sleeve. He turned his head much too quickly. "Come along then, Captain," Colin said, "I've a much better offer than this man."

"You see?" Georges called as Dimi let himself be led away. "They've got the money, but you've got to scare them into spending it."

Dimitrios followed Colin through a series of dark, empty corridors, a not great but confusing distance, to the threshold of a room lit only by its fireplace. Two armored men were playing chess before the fire; a third sat, possibly dozing, in a straight-backed chair next to an ironbound door. Light spilled from beneath the door. Colin gestured, and he and Dimi moved silently away, back through the halls; avoiding the main hall, they were shortly outside without attracting any more notice.

It was nearly dark, without moon or stars. Colin pointed at the castle's high central tower, a slender square column pierced by windows at six storeys. The lowest window was

lit, as was the highest. "That's David's Tower," he said.
"I've shown you one end of it. Albany's at the other."

"The door is only opened from within that lighted
room."

"That's so."

Dimi stared at the tower for whole minutes, ignoring
Colin's impatience. Suddenly there was a bit of brick-red
light on the stones, as the clouds moved up from the western horizon. And in the light, there was a flash like crimson lightning up the tower.

"What in death's name . . ." Dimi said softly, half conscious he was swearing in French.

"Well," Colin said, "it is a possibility."

"It's more than a possibility," Dimitrios said, "it's practically a law of siege warfare: later architects are always
adding things to fortresses that compromise their defense.
Big windows, drainpipes, privies, permanent bridges to re-
place the draws . . ."

They were in Colin's small house in Edinburgh town. Its
upstairs bedroom had a plain view of the castle, and they
had spent the whole night there, alternately arguing
plans, pacing, and looking out the window. On a table lay
the equipment that Gregory von Bayern had prepared for
them on extremely short notice.

"Are you certain that the Frenchman is no danger?"
Colin said, for the first time in at least an hour.

"What does he know that no one else knows? He even
had the right name for me."

"I don't know what's inside other men's heads. I'm a
spy, not a wizard. And spies know that anything in a
man's head can be gotten out."

Dimi thought about disagreeing, thinking of the Nottingham poacher, but he said, "Georges is nothing to do
with this."

"As you say." Colin looked outside. "It's nearly daylight. Time we slept." He pulled a cloth across the window.

Dimitrios packed von Bayern's equipment into a rucksack, putting it far away from the fireplace. He snuffed the

lamp and went to sleep, and dreamt of raiding castles, and woke up twice during the dream. At least he did not wake crying out in French, for Colin would surely have misunderstood.

Colin said "I think it's going to snow."

"I hope you're saying that for luck," Dimi said, but he could smell the weather changing too. "You're not suggesting we wait—if there's a storm, it'll cover the whole place with ice."

"I wasn't suggesting a thing. Snow on our track could be lucky. Never turn away from luck, that's a Danish faith. When you see Albany, ask him if he brought any Dane luck with him."

Dimitrios was silent for a moment. "Do you know . . . if the Duke knows French?"

Colin looked up. "It's a minor court disgrace that he doesn't. Why?"

"I thought . . . I might avoid speaking English to him, until we're well away. So if we don't get that far, he can suppose I was from . . . well, you know. Would he know Greek?"

"Alexander's not the learned brother. Sorry. Not a bad idea, though, Captain."

Dimi was not certain he agreed. He was starting to dissemble again, or pretend he was a dissembler.

They passed through the castle gate without trouble. The challenge and response were the same as the previous day, except that a guard asked why Inver Drum had not brought some Italian women along as well. Dimi smiled: garrison troopers, believing in the mysteries of women from far away. Mercenaries learned differently. Dimi's smile faded.

They put their horses up, examining the stalls for another saddled mount; there was a fine-looking dun, and a bay with a sidesaddle. "He'll ride what's to ride," Colin muttered, and they started up the way to the castle; but Dimi slipped out a door in the side.

He sidled along the slope, toward the base of the tower.

A fresh breeze made his cloak snap; he took it off and spread it on the ground, ramming the brooch pin into the hard earth to hold it. Beneath the cloak he wore a black leather vest, black woolen shirt and trousers, soft-soled boots, and the rucksack. He opened the pack, took out a pair of heavy leather gloves with metal-scaled palms, the kind a swordsman wore to grasp the enemy's point. He tugged them on, pulled the wrist laces tight with his teeth.

He looked up: on the towertop nearly thirty yards above was a bright reflection. It was a metal Thor's hammer almost as high as a man, of iron covered with silver, mounted there to draw lightning according to a physickal theory. A braid of copper wires led from the silver hammer down the wall, held every few feet by an iron spike driven into the masonry; the cable was anchored in the earth just at Dimi's feet.

He thought about water barrels on roofs and unsecured exits for fire, and determined that, in the unlikely event he ever built a house, he would not let a natural philosopher within sight of the plans.

He grasped the copper cable in a metal-palmed glove and pulled, lifting himself from the ground; there was a little slack, as he had hoped, but only a little, also as hoped. He put a knee and bootsole against the stone and reached up with his other hand.

The iron cable anchors were not thick, and showed rust. The cable itself was fused together in spots; Dimi thought at first that it was ice, but realized the metal had been melted. There must be something to the drawing down of lightning.

He began to breathe hard, and his hands hurt. He had supposed the cable would be like a wire-wrapped sword hilt, but it was the wrong shape for a comfortable grip. He looked only up, not down at all, saw four more storeys above him. Three dark windows, then the bright one. Thirty feet to fall. It was no less painful to rest on the wire than to climb it. He reached, grasped, pulled.

His lungs hurt, and his throat. The air was very cold, though the tower blocked the wind. He thought he heard a

human shout, but it was only blood complaining in his
ears. Two dark windows, one light.

Hand over hand, watch the slip of the boot, knees entirely in the way. Ball of the foot on a wire anchor, cutting
like a caltrop even as it gave leverage. No possibility of
resting now. Shift of balance, the rucksack trying to tug
him off the wall (it felt like an actual tug, a hand pulling
him). One dark window.

Let the glove scales do the work, don't worry if a wire
strand breaks (and now one does), ease down a
handsbreadth as the copper tries to snag a pack strap,
push the wire back, step up again.

Bright window just a step away.

As he turned, the wind shifted, and snow blew into his
face, a light snow but driven and stinging.

There was a flutter of darkness at the bright window.

Dimi reached faster than he thought, grabbing for a bar
of the window before the drape should darken it.

And he lost the wire.

Elbow, chin, chest struck cold wall; his left fingers, not
the whole hand, curled around the iron bar. Other hand
up—loose, its fingers nearly insensible—bring up the arm
and lock the hand on the bar *and* pull—

It was not a large window, but the tower walls were very
thick, and there was plenty of room for half a man's back-
side to rest outside the black iron bars, while his left arm
hooked through them and his head dropped onto his heaving chest, and the snow spattered down.

The drape fluttered aside. "Who in Hel's name are you?"
said the Duke—but he did not say it loudly.

Dimitrios turned, still trying to decide what to say. Then
he saw the brand on Albany's forehead, and in an instant
he knew. Taking a deep breath, he said in good classical
Latin, "A fiery chariot shall bear you to Olympus, tossing
in a whirlwind; you shall be free." And he showed the
brand on his wrist.

Alexander Stuart stared, then nodded. Dimi nodded
back, reached over his shoulder, and produced the end of a
thin woven rope from his pack. He handed it through the

window, pointed at the ceiling beams. Albany smiled, took the rope, climbed a chair, and began anchoring it.

Dimi reached into the pack again and produced a metal cylinder, a few inches thick and a span long, and a longer, thinner steel bar. He closed the drape partway, leaving him some light but masking his silhouette. Then he put the cylinder between two of the window bars, inserted the thin bar into a socket in its side, and began a twirling motion. The cylinder lengthened. Shortly it was wedged firmly between the window bars. Then the bars began to bend outward. After a few minutes, they slipped from their sockets with a small grating sound.

Dimitrios handed the rest of the rope coil to Albany. He began to make gestures, but Alexander just nodded once, wrapped the rope around his upper body. Dimi nodded, slid into the tower room.

He took a glance around, noting only that he had seen worse prisons. Albany boosted himself to the window and went out backside first. Dimitrios watched him descend, swaying in the wind but graceful, and better still swift. He touched ground and unwound the rope from himself.

Dimitrios wound it on and went out the window. He kicked off from the wall, feeling the heat of the rope through his hands and around his body. In a single motion he glided by the windows he had crawled past earlier; dark, dark, dark, dark—

Light with a man standing in it.

Dimi fell flat, eye on the window. There was a knife in his boot, weighted for throwing, but he would have to make the one throw final, and it was an upward throw against a man in armor. Better chance was to wait, hope he had not been seen.

The shadow moved away from the window. Drapes blocked the light. Dimi got up, drew the boot knife, and cut the rope away from his shoulder. They were still safe; men on their way to give the alarm didn't bother drawing curtains.

Albany stood in a shadow. Dimi wondered if the Scotsman had raided a castle in his time, if the sons of Scots warriors played knights-and-wizards in the castle halls. He picked his black cloak from the ground, shook snow-flakes from it, and handed it to the Duke, who put it on with a slight courtly bow. They moved off together.

The stableboy was playing with a puzzle of twisted horseshoe nails. He looked up, looked down. Then he stared up again at the two men who had come in. *"My lord—"*

As Dimitrios reached into his saddlebags, Albany tossed back his hood and looked the boy in the eyes. "Aye, lad, its masel'," he said, and then spoke briefly in Scots. The stable lad nodded very solemnly, bowed his head, and folded his hands.

Dimi struck him just behind the ear with his knife hilt, hating himself, praying to the Raven he had not hit too hard.

"Was that necessary?" Albany said angrily. Dimi ignored him, opened the cloth bag he had taken from the saddlebag. The Duke repeated himself in Latin. Dimi took a wooden box from the bag. All sides of the box were drilled with holes. On one side was a small brass mechanism, with a mainspring and a friction wheel: a gunlock, without a trigger but with a length of thin cord attached.

"Machina infernalis," he said flatly.

Albany looked around at the stables, the horses calm in their stalls, the lad unconscious on the straw-littered floor; he looked deadly grim, and he nodded.

They carried the boy out to the covered stairway, just as Colin came down the steps. Albany started, but Dimi touched his arm. Then Dimitrios saw the blood on Colin's cuff.

Colin glanced at himself. "It's the other fellow's; he won't be following," he said casually. "Evenin', Your Grace."

When they returned to the stable, Dimi put the box on the floor and piled straw around it. He stretched the string from the lock to the exit door; then he wound the spring.

Albany mounted the dun horse. It stamped a little, jangled the bit, but the Duke stroked it and it was calm. He draped the black cloak around himself, put up his hood. The three men rode out.

"Leavin' so early again?" the guard said, shouting to be heard above the wind. The men at the gate seemed more concerned with the snow than the people passing.

"Other work tonight," Colin said, and spoke some words of Scots that Dimitrios knew, and any soldier would have understood anyway.

And then they were past the gate, and the glittering muzzles of the guns, and cantering lightly down the hill, wind rushing like a full sea casting icy spray.

The orange flare was extraordinarily brilliant; Dimi imagined he felt its heat three hundred yards away. Gregory had spoken of Greek fire compounds when he made the device, but Tertullian had never shown Dimi anything so potent and compact.

In his mind, again, Tertullian walked away from him, leaving him to duty. Now was the time to ride away, before any more old ghosts came back.

Fire shot up, and smoke, and orange light sparkled in falling snow. "Now, Your Grace," Colin was saying, "for Berwick, as if Hel rode after us, for assuredly he does."

They covered half the sixty miles to Berwick and England, and were sheltered in a barn; the farmer knew Colin, though he called the spy Mister Blair, and he did not ask the other travelers' names or business. There was whisky and cold water, and cold hare pie, and all of them were delicious.

There was a small door in the corner of the barn loft, that seemed to lead nowhere; after the Duke was asleep, Dimi took a hooded lantern and opened the door. Just as quickly he closed it again on the moonstruck gleam of the altar cross.

"Are you surprised, Captain?" Colin said. He took a sip of whisky, tore off another bit of pie. "As Inver Drum may be a laird, though he owns damn few sheep, so Mister Blair may be a Maccabee."

Dimitrios nodded, sat down in the hay.

Colin looked across at the sleeping Duke. He poured himself a little more whisky. "An' none of them any damn use once we're over that border. Have you ne'er burnt bridges behind yoursel', Captain?"

Dimi nodded.

"Well. Better to burn 'em yoursel' than have another do't."

Dimi nodded again, and then he was asleep.

The air was still, with a fog in from the sea, as the three men rode into Berwick. The castle windows were all alight, shafts of yellow in all directions, and the Duke of Gloucester's banner flew in the wet air. Dimi was reminded, not pleasantly, of von Bayern's fire machine.

"Well, Alexander. Welcome to England again. You'll excuse me for insisting that Berwick is England?"

"Richard . . . I thought it must be you at the back of all this. No, I can't contest your being here . . . not tonight, surely, even if I wanted to." He smiled. "And Berwick's an expensive mistress, isn't she?"

With a sudden bad humor, Richard said "That's true enough." He looked Albany in the eye. "That's something we're going to talk over."

"Just you and I . . . and Edward?"

"And Edward," Richard said evenly. "But just now there are fresh clothes for you, and hot food."

Albany sighed. "But before that, Richard . . ." He nodded toward Dimitrios. "Who is this brother, who will not speak to me?"

Richard looked puzzled for a moment. Then he grinned, and said "This, brother *leo*, is the *miles* Dimitrios, a man of my house. If he would not speak, then duty kept him silent. I am quite certain of that."

Dimi said "Thank you, my lord," and not just for the praise, though it was the sun in his heart; it was that the sun had at last driven the Alesian ghosts away.

Albany was led into the castle. Richard said "What about the lairds, Colin? If Albany returned with an English army, which way would they leap?"

Dimitrios was startled, but he seemed to be the only one who was. Colin said "King James has exalted too many tradesmen at the lairds' expense. They speak already of finding a place high enough to hang the King's advisors from; they lack only someone to bell the cat. And someone to sit on the throne."

"Even if the English put him there?"

"Men who make and unmake kings see all armies in the same color."

Richard laughed dryly. "I deserve that, I suppose. Go and change, now; we're not having horse for dinner." Colin bowed and departed.

Richard said to Dimitrios "He got that line from my father-in-law. Just as I got Colin. The man's been a spy his whole life, I gather."

"What will he do now, my lord?"

"Eh? Oh . . . blast, you're right." Richard looked in the direction Colin had gone. "I suppose he knew it must end some day. Better an English pension than a Scottish rack, don't you think? Well, what are you waiting for? You're as salty as Colin, and it's your feast too."

Dimitrios was the first one changed and down to the dining hall. He waited, as did the others, for Albany and Colin; the soup went cold. Finally Dimi rose, said "My lord . . ." Richard nodded. Dimi climbed the stairs three at a time.

He knocked at Albany's door. It swung open. The Duke was sitting before the fire, dressed in clean clothes. His eyes were open and did not blink.

Dimi went in, touched him. Albany gave a small, whimpering gasp and fell, twisting, from the chair, a hand clawing at his abdomen. Blood spilled black in the firelight. The Duke's lips moved silently.

"Get your doctors!" Dimi shouted at an astonished servant, and ran a little distance down the hall and kicked in a door.

Colin, or Inver Drum, or Blair, or whoever, was seated almost exactly as the Duke had been, and for a moment Dimi thought he had guessed wrongly, that an unknown

murderer was still loose in the house—but then the spy
turned his head and looked bleakly at Dimitrios, and
turned the bloody knife over in his hands.

"Why?" Dimi said. "Why *now?*"

"Because now we're in England," Colin said. "The Scots
will think their brave bloody Albany escaped to you, only
t'be murdered in search of Jamie's favor. You may still get
your war wi' Scotland, an' maybe not, but alliance you'll
hae none. Och, it feels good t'tell absolute truth, just
once." He looked at the knife again. "Too bad your French
friend wouldn'a told the truth about you." He picked at his
cuff. "He'd'a lived."

Dimitrios lunged forward, pushing Colin's knife aside.
Colin tried to trip him; they both fell. The ghosts were
back again, Lucian instructing Dimitrios in how to kill
him. As he drew his own dagger, Dimi realized that Colin
was waiting to be killed—and he did not strike. "Who did
you do it for?" he shouted.

The spy smiled, in absolute triumph. "That you'll ne'er
know, will you?" He moved his fingers, a stroke and a
crossing stroke: the Jeshite sign. Dimi turned his head.
Colin closed his fingers around his knife.

Dimi stabbed him through the heart, a faultless stroke.
He was good at killing, he knew. It was why he would
never own anything but a horse and a knife, why a woman
like Cynthia Ricci would always turn away from him, because all he was good for was killing, killing, killing, and
he was so extremely good at that that he would never lack
employment.

Dimitrios pushed himself off the dead man and sat in the
heat of the fire.

When he finally looked up, Richard was standing in the
doorway. He wore a breastplate over his clothes, and a
sword hastily buckled on; there was a gun in his hands.

"Dead?" he said.

"Yes, my lord." There was no room for apology, as Richard must know.

Perhaps he did. "No blame of yours. He'd have known
what would happen if we took him alive."

"And Duke Alexander, my lord?"

"Dying, as the doctor's honest enough to admit. I daresay you've seen gut wounds."

Dimi thought that there was one more spirit of his memory that had not appeared, but he could not speak the thought even to be rid of it.

Then, again, Richard did it for him. "The Doctor von Bayern. If we could bring him here, would he . . . give of himself?"

"I don't know, Your Grace. But . . ." Richard had said he was faithful to duty. He was trying to be. But the path was not clear. ". . . would the brother lion want the gift?"

Richard seemed to flinch, as if it were a factor he had not even considered. "Of course you're right. What would we be saving him for? The wildest of the lairds wouldn't see him king in such a state. No. Let the serpent go hungry." He smiled. "And think of the lives saved, now that we're out of the war." Richard turned and went away, down the hall.

Dimi felt his hands shaking, beyond his power to control. He had seen his duty; he had found himself; and then, more swiftly than any man ever had, he had failed the one and lost the other.

Chapter 9
ACROSS

"WHAT an odd little excuse for a castle," Cynthia said, pointing as they rode past.

Hywel said, "That's just the juliet tower. There was a Norman keep around it, but that's down now. . . ."

"Who destroyed it?" she asked, in a dull and morbid tone.

"A man named Owain Glyn Dẃr," Hywel said. She did not press him for a reason; he was glad of that.

They rode on north, up a stream valley. Mynydd Troed stood white and sharp to the right; to the left was countryside laid out like a giant's fortification. The stream, just cracking with spring, was the moat; the edges of Fforest Talybont, still crystalline, made a fantastical palisade around the hills called the Brecon Beacons, keeps half a mile high. "That one is Gwaun-rhudd. And the saddle mountain, high afar off, is Pen-y-fan."

Cynthia said "And the name of the place we're going?"

"Llangorse. I think we'll stay there a few days."

"Whatever." She looked up; it was just past noon, and the thin clouds were brilliant. She turned back to Hywel. "What did you say it was called?" He could see the haze in her eyes.

"Llan-gorse."

"Perhaps in a few days I'll have learned to say that," she said, but her voice was mechanical and she did not smile.

Llangorse was bustling; people carried lumber and tent-cloth through the streets, and they were not dressed for a working day. Hywel watched Cynthia, but she paid no attention.

They stopped at an inn whose sign showed a castle half sunk in water. Hywel paid for two of the five guestrooms, and gave a boy an entire penny to carry a message.

"Not that it is my business, sir," the innkeeper said in singsong English, "but why would yourselves want to stop here with the sun still high, and Brecon not five miles yon?"

Hywel said, in Cymric, "Aberhonddu has not what Llangorse has." He used his northern, Gwynedd accent. A local inflection would only have further confused the man. "The smaller festivals are of the most interest to us . . . we are professors, you see."

"Oh, I do see, sir." The innkeeper smiled. Scholars might do anything.

Hywel went up the narrow, noisy stairs, knocked on Cynthia's door.

"Entrare."

She was looking out the window, still wearing her headscarf, dusty cloak, riding boots. Her bags were untouched where the porter had dropped them. "They are setting up a fair . . . is that why we're here? To go to a fair?"

"It's one reason."

She said "I haven't been to a fair in a long, long time. It sounds . . . very nice." She turned her head, looked at her baggage. "I only brought traveling clothes. Do you think I'll be dressed well enough?"

"I'm sure you will." Hywel's throat felt tight. "Excuse me now, Doctor." He closed the door, feeling a drop of cold sweat slide down his flank. She had cared about something—something minor, but something.

Feeling better than in days, he went to his room, to change, and to wait for the messenger boy's return.

* * *

Cynthia came down the stairs. Hywel stood to meet her, hearing all conversation stop in the inn hall, feeling a small joy at the sight of her.

She wore a sleeveless gown of felted wool, forest green and without ornaments, smooth and straight of line nearly to severity. Her blouse sleeves were of rust-colored linen, puffed slightly, cuffed tightly with pearl buttons. A scarf of absolutely white sendal wrapped her throat, trailing long ends down her back. A green lace caul held her hair back from her forehead, shaped it into smooth white curves around her face. Her belt was silver cord, and Cecily of York's silver owl glittered on the green cloth above her bosom.

Then Hywel looked into her eyes, and his spirit died again. He took her hand, which was cold.

As they left the inn, Hywel picked up a crooked oak staff that rested against the wall. He wore a brown robe tied with braided leather, and a leather patch over his missing eye.

They fell in with a stream of people moving southward from town. The townsfolk were wearing clean linen gowns, cheesecloth wimples, the quilted jacks of bowmen, felt doublets, brightly dyed hose. Some of the men carried shields made of sticks and paper, painted with colorful devices. A woman rode by on a dappled palfrey, garlanded with woven pine needles; after her came a man cap-a-pie in whitewashed canvas, couching a wobbly lance striped red and white.

Cynthia looked around at the procession. "Sometimes, at the summer parties, we would improvise costumes. But that was forever ago. . . . Hywel, what is this fair?"

"Arthur's Court. Tonight and tomorrow, everyone here is a lord or a lady."

"Or a wizard?" She looked at his robe and staff. "When I first met you, you called yourself Plato. Are you a Platonist? Your nose is sharp."

Hywel had seen the long-nosed man in her memories, wondered who he was. He was aware that memories were struggling within her for release; they must be careful now, lest something rupture. "Look," he said. "There's Arthur's pavilion, and within it the Round Table. Beyond is the lake, Llyn Safaddan. Just at dark, the Lady will appear bearing Caliburn, and there'll be a splendid first court. Then tomorrow, the Triumph, and the joining of the Kingdom. In the afternoon, the Cauldron Quest, and finally the Evening Court. . . ."

"Do all your people worship this dead king?" she said, voice dull again.

He knew she was fighting the pressure of memory; knew she was trying not to be afraid. "Not worship," he said, and took her hand again. It was quite damp. "Believe in Arthur, yes, I think so. Actually they believe in a hundred individual things: noble knighthood, justice, repelling the invader, the leader who will return . . . the love that forgives anything . . . all of which are Arthur."

"But he was an English king, wasn't he?" she said, with a sort of numb determination, staring at the knights in trumpery armor. "Isn't this . . . another country?"

"Oh," Hywel said lightly, "Arthur was born a Welshman. Ask anyone here; it was England he joined to the Kingdom, not the other way around."

The sun began to set, and the lake turned red; torches were lit, and lanterns with reflectors of tin. A small boat appeared, with a woman standing in it; there was only a small stiff sail, and no one seemed to steer the craft (though there was a heavily draped couch in the stern that might have concealed marvels, or an engineer).

The Lady's boat parted the reeds at the lakeshore; Arthur, in flowing robes of purple and gold, waded into the shallows to meet her. A duck, disturbed, quacked furiously after the King. There were appreciative shouts from the audience.

"There's a legend," Hywell said, laughing, "that the birds on Llyn Safaddan will sing at the command of the rightful King of Wales. The fellow hardly needs to take the sword now."

But he took it anyway, and held it up so it caught the

light from a focused lantern and blazed like pure fire. Arthur strode ashore. The Lady's boat shuffled itself off the
stones and away. There were the sounds of kegs being
knocked in, the smells of bacon and mince pie.

Cynthia turned at another, stranger sound. She walked
toward it; Hywel followed her, to a small pavilion near the
King's huge one.

In the tent, a young man was singing, while next to him
a lady stroked a bow across a psaltery. The words of the
song were not matched to the music, but rather a counter-
point, the man's voice playing free with the rhythms.
Singer and musician shot each other glances all through
the tune; they seemed to be competing, the woman playing
now quicker, now slower, the man always just holding his
own. Finally they reached the same note, held it for a full
breath and stroke of the bow, and stopped. There was ap-
plause.

Hywel looked at Cynthia. She seemed to be trying to
smile, or cry, and failing at either. He said "It's called
penillion singing. The musician must play a common song,
one everyone knows; the singer must improvise. You
heard how it's done; the singer can do as he pleases with
rhythm, so long as it somehow suits the music—and they
finish together."

She nodded, not looking at him. A man with a long bass
recorder was taking the musician's chair, while another
singer cleared her throat. They played and sang less in
competition, more complexly, and finished on a short,
plangent, almost painful note. Hywel said "Would you
care to sing? There are always instruments looking for a
singer, and there's sure to be a song you both know."

"But I don't know your language."

"No one will mind."

"I can't—how can people make up words to music as it
plays?" She turned and walked out of the pavilion.

Hywel waited. There was a high-pitched cry from the
dark outside. He lifted his robe just enough to walk fast.

He saw a clump of figures, in one of the areas set off for
tomorrow's mock battles. All of them were small. As Hy-

wel drew close he saw that they were all children; all except one, who was Cynthia, kneeling. On the ground before her lay a boy, seven or eight years old; his left arm was covered with dark shiny blood. He was crying with vigor.

"What happened?" Hywel said, in Welsh.

There was silence. Cynthia was stripping away the boy's tunic with precise cuts of a dagger. *"Lume di qua,"* she said. After a moment, she snapped in English, *"Light!"*

The children milled and murmured. Hywel looked back; people were coming, but not rapidly. He held up his left hand, cupped his fingers, gathered the thought. A white spark appeared in his palm, then a downward shaft of bluish light. There were gasps. Cynthia did not look up or speak. The wounded boy kept whimpering.

"What happened?" Hywel said again.

"Please, sir, we were playing," one of the boys said, sheer terror in his look. "Playing Cei and Bedwyr, sir. We just had tin swords, sir, William's father's the tinsmith—"

"And didn't he tell you tin has edges?" Hywel said gently.

Cynthia said, in Italian, "Hywel? Get me some wine to wash this. Not pond water."

Hywel let his witchlight fade. Cynthia looked up sharply, said "I need—"

Hywel turned to the adults who were arriving. "Would you get that lantern over here, please? The doctor needs some light. And does one of you have a cup of wine?"

"Here's strong soap in rainwater, and a boiled sponge. Will those do?"

The speaker was a small, stocky woman in a gray wool gown and white linen cap. She was flat-featured, forty or a little more, with bright eyes. She produced a bottle and sponge from an enormous shoulder bag. Softly, she said to Hywel "Is this your friend?"

"Ie." Hywel turned, said in English, "Cynthia, this is Mary Setright; she's a healer. She speaks English."

Cynthia looked up, took the soap and sponge. "You are a doctor, my lady?"

"I'm a witch," Mary said, and smiled. "Boo." She took a

roll of linen gauze from her bag. "Tell me when you're ready for this."

Cynthia nodded, bent to work again, began washing the cut. The boy yelled. Startled, Cynthia drew back her hand, raised it to slap him.

Mary smacked the roll of gauze into Cynthia's open palm, held it there. Cynthia turned, looked up, eyes very wide; then she shook her head slowly and closed her fingers on the roll. She picked up her dagger again with her left hand, looked at it. Hywel felt himself tense. Mary let Cynthia's hand go.

Cynthia cut a length of gauze and wrapped the wound, tucking the ends of the bandage in neatly.

The boy was helped to stand, and was taken into custody by his parents; Hywel could hear the first words of the tin-smith's lecture to his son.

Rapidly the crowd, and then the children, dispersed, until only Hywel and Mary were left standing in the field, and Cynthia still kneeling. Her scarf was half unwound from her neck and trailed on the ground.

Mary Setright touched Cynthia's arm. "You did that marvelous well, sister. Come, now, don't you want some dandelion tea?"

"I'm supposed to do it well," Cynthia said raggedly. "I have a doctorate in medicine from the University of Pisa. My father is the best doctor in Florence. That is, he was." She looked up. Her head wavered. "If I had ever struck a patient, my father would have turned me into the street, to beg copper florins like a blind woman." She stared at her hands; they trembled. "I might as well be blind . . . do you see? How can I hold a knife now?"

Cynthia pressed her palms together, as in supplication, and turned to Hywel and Mary. "Madonna . . . Messer Ficino . . . forgive me: I am the only Ricci left." Her voice was remarkably even.

Hywel said quietly, "Mary . . . please, you mustn't ask me . . ."

Mary put her arm around Cynthia, got her standing.

"Sweet heaven, Peredur, do you think I can't see? Now help me."

They moved away from the lake, two supporting one, until the light and noise of the festival were entirely lost behind them.

Hywel leaned against the hearth in Mary Setright's cottage, staring at a medallion. He had picked it up at Arthur's Court, when it caught a flicker on the ground.

It was wide as two fingers, cast in white metal, with a hole for a cord or chain. The face showed two dragons, one incised dark, one bright in relief. The dragons were fighting, and the dark one was clearly winning the combat.

He knew the symbolism well enough; anyone born in Britain would have. The Red Dragon and the White, that Merlin had prophesied Uther should find.

The Red Dragon was the kingdom of Wales. The White . . .

Hywel turned the disc over. Stamped on the back in Roman capitals was the legend REXQUE FUTURIS. And everyone in Britain knew that much Latin: the second half of Arthur's epitaph. THE FUTURE KING.

He closed his fingers around the medallion, shut his eye, and reached into the metal.

His mind recoiled from the contact. The medallion felt red-hot in his hand, for just a moment; he opened his eye, but the thing lay cool in his unmarked palm.

There were minds at work here, he knew, who did not have his fear of the energies of magic: people playing with wildfire.

He put the medallion away as Mary came in from the other room. He said "Is she all right?"

"Of course she isn't," Mary said, not sharply. "And she'll be worse before she's better. . . . Will you fetch some water, Hywel? In the kettle."

"Surely." He took the black iron kettle from its firehook and went outside.

The cottage was set in a tiny clearing, invisible from

twenty yards away. A clean, singing creek passed near the
porch; Hywel submerged the kettle.

The walls of the cottage were clear pine, and the roof
was thatch, all tight and warm. The thatching was still
faintly green, and moist, and it would not burn; Hywel had
seen to that. And insects did not infest Mary's roof, as they
did every other thatched roof in the country, but that was
not Hywel's doing. Mary told the vermin to go, all but the
spiders whose webs she harvested for wound dressings,
and they all but the spiders went away.

When he came back from the creek, she was standing on
the porch. "I've sung her asleep," she said, "but she's still
not resting; she talks, in her native speech—Italian, is it?
She talks of poison, and a man with a scourge, and quick-
lime. She said she is a *gwaedwr,* though I can see she does
not need blood. What has my sister seen?"

Hywel carried the kettle, heavy as his thoughts, into the
cottage and set it on its hook. He had seen the image of the
little blackeyed man, the flagellant, when they touched:
he had no idea who he was, and there was no one to ask.

But he had seen the vampire murder with ordinary
sight, and told Mary about it. She said nothing in response, but sat in her chair and rocked, and hummed.

Hywel felt his eyelids drooping. "No, Mary. Not me.
Stop it."

"I'm doing nothing, brother. You must sleep, as all the
Lord's children."

He was suddenly enormously tired. Mary was singing
again, but perhaps it was really only himself. He usually
slept only every three or four nights, but lately he had
missed even that, because Cynthia was so terribly vulnerable at night. . . .

"Sleep now, brother Hywel. I'll watch our sister tonight."

He sank down onto a cot by the fire, not even feeling the
bump; she pulled off his boots and put a folded cloak under
his head, and he had no power to resist.

The last thing he saw, far away through a golden haze,

was Mary's shrine on the wall, the twinkling candles and the Latin cross.

And then he was awake fully, a coldness around his good eye. Mary drew her finger back, still dripping clear water. "Get up, Hywel. I can't make her rest; we must try to do something. I need you to hold her."

Hywel looked at her as he stood, not really understanding; then he heard Cynthia cry out from the other room. "You mean . . . hold her down."

"That's so."

He followed Mary into the bedroom. The bed was a large one, of oak spindles; afternoon light slanted across it, and Hywel realized how long he had slept without stirring. Through her screaming? he wondered. He looked, not willingly, at Cynthia.

She lay with her knees drawn up, her hands above her head clutching the bedstead; her woolen nightgown was pulled up crookedly, exposing a pale shin and kneecap, bony as a child's. A nightcap held her hair. Her face was a bloodless mask, eyes closed, mouth open, flesh drawn tight, an ink sketch of despair. She made a sound like a kitten drowning.

He was afraid, then, to touch her. His empty eyehole ached. "Must we . . ."

"All right, then, get me her silk scarf," Mary said calmly. "You can wait outside, and I'll tie her hands."

"Oh, no . . . no. I'll do it." He sat on the corner of the bed. Cynthia's eyes snapped open, and she stared. Hywel reached out, gently unwound the fingers of her right hand from the bed spindle. The pattern of the turned oak was printed on her palm.

"I will not eat," she said suddenly. "I'll starve, or swallow poison, but none of your food or wine."

Hywel loosened the other hand. Cynthia looked down at herself; she grasped her gown in both hands, tugged at the fabric. A bone button shot away, struck the wall.

Hywel, startled, caught her wrists, syllables rolling unsummoned through his mind; he felt muscle and tendon

warming, relaxing. Her grip went soft. At once Hywel let
go. "Mary—" He slipped an arm under Cynthia, lifted her
to a half-sitting position, let her lean against him. Her
back muscles were like sheet iron. He put his arms around
her waist. Her fingers brushed his forearms; he felt pins
and needles. *"Mary."*

Mary had a web of string stretched between her fingers;
a cat's cradle. "Tell us now what happened, sister." Her
voice was soft and warm as autumn sunlight. "Tell us now,
and let it into the light, for the evil cannot stand the light."

"No," Cynthia said, and pulled at Hywel. "Let me go."

"There is no redemption without love, no love without
contact," Mary said. "Our Lord knew this, and became
flesh, so that there could be contact, and love, and forgiveness. Tell us now, what happened at the inn in the snow?"

Cynthia shrieked *"Hywel?"* and writhed in his hold. He
hugged her, feeling her muscles strain, joints creak. And
despite himself he used the power, and she relaxed. "Hywel . . ." Cynthia said, slurring the words, ". . . wha' did
you tell her . . . ?"

"What do you fear said?" Mary said, and worked her fingers in the figure of string. "Say a thing and the pain is
past with the echo, but fear goes on without an end. Tell us
now, about the messenger." In the cat's cradle, a knot dissolved.

"I did not cut him," Cynthia said. "I taught the spy the
points . . . I took the quill from my bag. But I . . . I . . ."

"And why did you wish to help the spy? In understanding there is peace. Tell me now, sister, what was the thing
that set your soul on such a course?" Another knot melted
from the cord.

Another spasm. "The Sforza Duke . . ."

They drove backward in time and deeper into hurt: psy-
chic pus oozed out, and black blood, and a stink of corrup-
tion.

Hywel sensed it as well; having looked upon the memories, they were partly his now, and now he understood
what he had seen. He was trapped in a foul closet while
Savonarola tore his flesh, and he wanted to vomit.

At once he erased the nausea. Too quick, too easy, he thought; he was already doing enough damage to himself, and to Cynthia. Mary had trapped him, with the best of intentions. She did not understand, and never would.

Of all the wizards he had known since first Kallian Ptolemy opened his mind, he had known only five who were not corrupted by the power. Five, in hundreds.

They did not form any sort of union, those five. One was a Chinese priest, fat and bald and sensual, strange jolly humor echoing in the silence of the Tao. The Russian hermit was hairy and louseridden, living his whole life in a smoky cave full of crooked idols, some of them perhaps older than Man. Here was an ordinary village wisewoman, in an ordinary little house that was the same size inside and out and did not stand on chicken legs, whose god had required a comically absurd passion and the whole mechanism of Roman justice to conditionally redeem his creations. The fourth held that all gods were lies, that the cosmos was a machine, like a clockwork or a watermill— but a *perfect* clockwork or watermill. The fifth . . . he did not want to think about her, and anyway she was dead.

"I was always taught that the scalpel was not just a knife, it was a tool of the Art, it was *sacred* . . . and I took a sacred thing and cut into a little boy's heart. *And I did it very, very well.* . . ." She rocked back and forth, shaking her head miserably. Hywel stroked her hair, feeling sweat start on her forehead.

He knew what kept those five alone from devouring themselves. It was not the sorts of spells they worked, nor the names they worked in, nor magic circles or eye of newt or the phases of the moon. He knew what it was, but knowing could not save him, because the parts of him that could sustain faith were all burned out.

The string hung loose and untangled from Mary's fingers. Cynthia was quiet, apparently calm. Hywel could feel her inaudible sobbing through his fingertips. He took his hands away, afraid of touching something not physical.

It was very dim in the room, and the small fire made moving shadows. Mary said "Sister, are you there?"

"Yes, Donna Maria. How long have I . . . is the fair over?"

"You need to rest now," Mary said, and began to hum softly.

"No. Please don't make me sleep." She was not pleading. "Hywel? Is there still a fair? Please take me to it."

Hywel stood up, took her hand in his. She slid her feet to the floor and stood, smoothing her nightgown with complete dignity. "Well, I shall need my clothes. I'm only suited now for a mad scene." There was an abrupt small silence. Then Mary opened a wardrobe and took out Cynthia's clothing; it was all quite clean, and smelled of spring rain.

Hywel and Mary went into the kitchen, which seemed cold to Hywel; his sweat drying, he realized.

Mary said "You're taking her, aren't you?"

"She wants to go. You could have interfered more easily than I."

"I don't mean down hill to a fair. She has some need for that; I felt it when she asked. No, Peredur. You want her for a crafting, don't you?"

"I have no intention of hurting her," Hywel said, aware of how he already had.

"If I thought you did, I would never let you out the door," Mary said very certainly. Hywel did not doubt her.

Mary stepped close to him, looked up at him with an expression of infinite sadness. "I have said to you before, this work of yours will not make you happy. When will you believe this, and rest?"

"Never," he said finally. It was only half an answer, because he did believe her. He had believed it before he knew she existed; he had known for over half a century, since his first departure from the Beautiful City Byzantium, that he was not on the road to any heaven.

She had helped to prove it to him, though he would never tell her so.

Cynthia appeared, tucking up her hair; she walked unsteadily, and her face was gray and drawn, but Hywel could see a life in her step, a calm in her eyes, that he had not seen in her before. "Shall we go?" she said.

"You'll visit again, before you travel on?" Mary said.

Hywel said "Of course."

Cynthia said "Are we leaving so soon, then. . . ? I would like . . . to learn to say the name of this place."

Mary hugged them both, and Hywel just heard her whispered prayer.

He led Cynthia out of the house and through the forest, to the sounds of Arthur's Evening Court, which were audible afar off.

The King's battle with his bastard son was beautifully staged, spear and sword glittering in red sunset: as Mordred pierced his father's body, and Arthur crawled up the shaft to swing Caliburn for the last time, Llyn Safaddan seemed all blood.

As stars came out, hard as the points of spears, the Lady's boat appeared across the water. Bedwyr departed with Caliburn, returned twice to lie about casting it away, and was sent out twice again. The boat touched shore, and three queens debarked to bear the King aboard; they sailed away without steersman or oar.

Bedwyr appeared again, stumbling and convincingly awestruck; someone in the audience shouted "Found beer, did you?" There was a loud thump from that direction, and no more comments *ad libidem.*

The lone knight on the strand dropped to his knees, his muslin armor creaking. "My lord," he said, "where have you gone? I have done as you commanded me. I cast the sword—truly, my lord, I did it—Arthur, where are you?

"There was a boat, Arthur, a little boat, with three ladies in't, great ladies they must have been. And Caliburn was turning over and over in the air like a wheel, and the lady at the prow of the boat put out her hand, and she caught the sword, by the hilt.

"There was another thing in the boat, I could not see what it was for the setting sun . . . but I think it was a treasure, for it shone like red gold.

"Oh, Arthur, it was a wonder; I wish you had seen it."

Gwenhwyfar appeared then, dressed all in white mourning, with a veiled maiden to either side of her, and behind her two bowmen in green. She came to within a few paces of where Bedwyr knelt, and stopped.

The knight looked up. A moment passed, as if both were thinking that *now* it would be only love, and no adultery, but too late, too late. Then, in silence, Bedwyr stood, moved next to Gwenhwyfar—but did not touch her—and they walked side by side out of sight, maids and archers in their train.

Hywel turned; Cynthia was gone. He knew how to follow her.

When he reached the pavilion, a harp and recorder had begun to play; a moment later Cynthia's voice joined them, rich and clear, and Hywel pushed his way through the crowd.

She was singing *penillion*, working words to meet the meter as the melody spun on: she sang in Italian, of course, but as Hywel had known, it did not matter at all.

He slipped between the last few people and saw her, and saw that she was crying freely. Her voice remained absolutely clear: she would skip a beat to swallow a sob, then catch the tune in the next measure.

Hywel understood, without knowing or wanting to know the particulars, that the song was somehow at the center of the web of agony Mary had unraveled knot by knot; the tears had been sealed inside layers of scar tissue. He half-wondered that they did not boil in the open air.

And he genuinely wondered if Mary's unspoken accusation was true: had he brought her to be healed only because he wanted her for his real work . . . his dragon-hunt? He touched his pouch, seemed to feel the medallion warming through the leather.

She would be a good hunting-partner, he thought, brave and intelligent and skilful.

"She healed the tinsmith's boy last night," someone whispered, "and two witches came at her call, and obeyed her."

"She spoke to them in an unknown tongue; I heard it."

Hywel heard the mutterings in the crowd; he said nothing. There was nothing to say. They did not, perhaps could not, understand magic, because their dreams of power and the facts of the craft were so very different.

"Rhiannon," someone murmured.

"Rhiannon . . ." said more voices.

They believed that just reading a person's mind gave the reader total communion with that person's soul. They were wrong, so cruelly wrong.

"What is life," Cynthia Ricci sang, eyes flooded and glowing, "but an improvisation to the music?"

Cynthia and Hywel were descending from the mountains at Cader Idris. It was a brilliant high summer day, with a fresh and delicious breeze up the estuary from Cardigan Bay. Hywel sat down on a rock, put his feet up on another, exhaled. Cynthia untied the scarf covering her head and let the wind lift her hair.

She saw Hywel turn away, as if he were embarrassed. She wondered if he might actually be so, or want her to believe he was; small possibility of either. The wizard had too many secrets, she thought. He had bound himself tight with rules he would never consider imposing on another human being.

Lately he seemed to have taken a rule of silence as well. "You said the old Romans had a camp near here, Hywel. . . . Did they use this pass?"

"Never twice," he said, looking at the ground.

She waited.

Eventually he said "They were never allowed to find their way deeply into the mountains. If a party found this pass . . . remember those tall rocks we passed between? There would be someone there, waiting."

She nodded, thinking of Urbino's hill fortresses, where there had always been someone waiting for Byzantium . . . and, since Duke Federigo had a son, perhaps there still was. She hoped so. Then, not quite seriously, she said "And do skeletons in legionary armor walk this trail by night?" This country seemed to have an overwhelming fondness for spirits, of both varieties.

"They dumped the bodies away, below. So those that came after—and with the Old Empire as the New there was always someone to come after—were led farther and farther from what they sought." He looked at the toes of his boots.

It was one of his rules, she knew, that no one should ever know when he was sad; so she gave no sign of knowing, and changed the subject. "Who is Rhiannon, Hywel?"

He turned toward the estuary, put his feet on the ground and his hands in his lap. There was one of those white medals in his fingers; he seemed to find them everywhere they went. He turned the disc over in his fingers.

She said "You've heard people call me that. I must guess it's not insulting."

Hywel put his medallion away. "She was a healer. According to some."

"Like Mary Setright?"

"Something like her. You could say that Mary is to Rhiannon as you are to Minerva."

Startled, Cynthia caught at her owl pendant. "I didn't know—"

Hywel looked at her, finally, at her eyes, then her hair. "Some say she was the moon. Often she's a lady on a white horse swifter than wind. . . . Why are you laughing?"

"Because if I didn't I'd cry," she said, and tied her scarf on again. "You know, don't you, that Lorenzo de' Medici called me 'Luna,' for the color of my hair? Dimitrios spoke to me once, or tried to . . . he talked about riding a white mare called Luna. But his English was not very good . . . and I was not well . . . and I struck him, poor man. When all he wanted to do was tell me a story."

She looked northward. "I wonder how they are, Dimi and Gregory."

"I am sure they are with Richard," Hywel said, starting down the road again, "and I think they are alive."

It was a few days past Iambolc, the February festival of

light, and the town of Conwy had finally fallen still; half a foot of snow had helped to hush it.

Cynthia paced across the inn room. It was not a large room, but there was not much in it to interfere with pacing. "I think we should go south for a while," she said.

"In a while it'll be spring; that happens even in North Wales," Hywel said. "And besides, we've just come up the coast . . . do you want to visit all those little towns and drafty castles again so soon?" He smiled.

She almost giggled. He was better today, and she was certain it was because they had spent the last few days quietly, not drifting across the country in search of plots and legends and planchets of white metal.

Wherever the things came from, they had spread far and wide. In every village they entered, they found the medallions, worn or carried close to the body and out of sight. Hywel would ask to see them, showing one of those he carried, and words would pass in Welsh dialects she could not understand.

He would not let her touch the discs; she offered to carry his sack of them, and he snapped refusal at her, stuffing the metal into his pack like a miser caught counting his gold.

Cynthia did not know if it was magic, or madness, or some commoner evil. She did know that she had no cure for it. She wanted to take him back to Brycheiniog, to Llangorse, to Mary Setright, before the red worm of the medallions ate any deeper into his brain.

"South means the coast, you know," he said, "or all the way across Gwynedd to England; the Romans gave us roads that all run crosswise, and the English liked the idea too well to change matters. Hard for us to communicate, easy for them to come in." There was a distance, a wistfulness, in his voice.

"There's a road straight south from here to Harlech," she said, "down the Dyffryn Conwy." Her Cymric was spotty but workable now, and when she'd asked about the road the innkeeper had seemed to appreciate her efforts and meet her halfway.

"Oh, no," Hywell said quickly, "we can't take that road. There's no purpose in it."

"Purpose?"

"A dozen years ago, Harlech was holding out for Henry against Edward, and my lord Herbert was told to take the place. He decided to make an example as he went up the Vale of Conwy, and he assuredly did. You could follow the army by the smoke of its burning, and crows would starve on what they left. I could show you an inn, where still the sooty bones—" He stopped, shook his head. "I don't need to cross the water at Caerhun, my dear. I know what its current is."

He turned up his left palm. One of the medallions was in it, caged by his fingers. He made a slight gesture and the disc disappeared, leaving only a red circle and two livid arcs, ghosts of the struggling dragons. Hywel said "It isn't gone, of course, but only hidden. This isn't magic, but only what passes for it." He shook his sleeve, and the disc slid out, striking the floor with a dull clink. As it fell, Hywel shivered, just faintly; he put his marked hand to his face, stroked both his eyes.

After a long silent while Hywel said "I am sorry, Cynthia. I've dragged you a very long way through a strange country, for a cause you never meant to be part of."

"I asked to be part of it," she said firmly. "And I am sure that Fiorenza, now, would seem just as strange." She saw him brighten, just for an instant; then he hid it, and looked down. Poor man, she thought, trying not to touch the world for fear he would hurt it. She realized that they had been over most of Wales, and she still did not know what part of it he came from.

She thought suddenly and intensely that he had touched her, and had not hurt but healed her; there must be some way of using that to help him.

"You should be careful what you say to me," she said, trying to sound playful but not mocking. "I've heard another legend of your Llyn Safaddan, about the witch who gives a man everything, then leaves him forever when first he scolds her. . . ."

Hywel's face tilted up very slowly. There was no readable expression there; not amusement, nor anger, nor even
active disinterest. "And you should be careful where you
go, and what you ask," he said, in a voice like wind
through a pipe. "Rhiannon once went into a strange house,
and found a fountain within; but when she touched it she
was held there, unable to move hand or foot, lips sealed
fast. It took Gwydion son of Don all his wit and the threat
of murder to free the lady." He paused, looked past her, out
the window. "And I, whatever you may hear, am not
Gwydion son of Don."

He held very still then, and she watched him very
closely, but his body told her nothing.

Then he stood up, and in a kindly voice said "But I do
have a taste for rabbit this evening. Shall we find some
dinner?"

Poor man was not the word for him, she thought; she did
not know what the word could be.

The carriage slammed and jolted, racing up the road to
Ludlow Castle; the first red leaves of autumn blew out of
the darkness, past the windows, and vanished again behind them.

Inside, Cynthia held to her armrests and looked across
at Hywel, and wondered how he could be so calm. She did
not like at all being gotten from her bed by armed men, polite as they were: their deference only made them more
frightening. She had several colorfully sickening ideas of
what might be happening, but no notion at all of *why*.

They were taken through heavily guarded gates and a
badly lit hall. From somewhere above came a high-pitched
wail, as of an animal, or a child.

They were led into a library . . . on second look, an office
lined with books. There was a large, littered desk, an as-
sortment of weapons and musical instruments on the bits
of wall not covered by bookshelves, a brass telescope on an
elaborate stand.

A man stood near the desk, leafing rapidly through a
book. He was blond, tall, with a warrior's build. He wore a

black velvet gown of scholar's pattern, but the collar was
white silk instead of linen, and there were more silver ornaments than most professors she knew would have any
notion of acquiring. The book, on the other hand, she recognized instantly; it was the most standard of medical ref-
erences, the *Liber Mercurius*.

He looked up from the book. He had an open, intelligent
look she found attractive at once; he also looked worried.
"Are you the persons . . ." His expression dissolved into
surprise. "Doctor Peredur? Is that you?"

"Yes, my lord Earl," Hywel said. "You did not know
who you were sending for?"

"Actually I didn't." The blond man shook his head,
closed the book with a thump, and put it back on the shelf.
"We heard there were a sorcerer and a healer passing
through—you are a healer, madam?"

Hywel said "May I present Cynthia Ricci, Doctor of Medicine and Surgery. Doctor, this is Anthony Woodville, Earl
Rivers; the Queen's brother."

"The Queen's abductor of innocent people, tonight,"
Rivers said. "I'm sorry you were brought here so rudely,
Doctor, truly sorry. As I say, we'd only heard of some healer's presence, passing through; and if I'd sent a man down
in the morning and found you gone, my royal sister would
. . . well. Elizabeth isn't a woman to make angry."

"No queen is," Hywel said mildly. "Elizabeth is ill,
then?"

"Much worse. The Prince of Wales is ill."

The child's cry came again, faintly. Rivers put his hand
on his chin.

"I think I had better see the patient," Cynthia said.

"Yes," said the Earl, "I think you better had."

As they climbed the stairs, Cynthia said "Surely you
have your own physicians here. What do they say?"

"They say they do not know, Doctor Ricci. The boy
seemed to have fever of the milder sort, but now . . . the
Prince is in great pain."

"In the abdomen?"

Rivers shot her a surprised glance. "Yes."

"With flux?"

"Yes. Bloody. . . . Pardon, madam . . . you are a Ricci of Florence, then?"

"I am the last Ricci of Florence," she said, needing to know if she could indeed say it.

"Oh . . . I understand, I think. Lorenzo de' Medici was my friend."

"He was my patient." It still hurt. She supposed it always would. It was better, surely, then an atrophied soul. "I remember him speaking of an Anthony Woodville of England . . . but, your pardon, sir, I believed you were a poet."

Rivers laughed, and his eyes were sparkling. "Madam, if you knew what it means to me, to hear that someone believed that!" He wiped his eyes on his loose velvet sleeve. "And of course your reputation precedes you here. Our physicians were rather upset when the Queen insisted a 'country healer' be brought in. I'm sure they will feel much better now."

That leaves only the patient to cure, Cynthia thought.

Suddenly Hywel said "Morton's here." He stopped on the stairs. "How long has he been here?"

"My lord wizard Morton has been traveling with Her Grace for some time now." Rivers gave a tight smile. "In fact, the old deceiver's got her liking him. I must say, he's talented."

"Indeed he has a talent, for . . ." Hywel did not finish the sentence. A door was opened for them.

Cynthia took in the familiar elements of the Sick Child's Bedroom Scene: the worried mother, the dithering cousins, the calm old nurse (who had probably lost all her own children in scenes much ruder than this), the child himself at the center of attention, often enjoying it—

But not this child. The boy on the ornate bed was genuinely suffering, skin flushed and dry, body rigid. Suddenly everyone else in the room faded into the furnishings; her bag was off her shoulder and she was at work. She had the subliminal awareness that she was being introduced to the

worried mother, who happened to be Queen of England;
she hoped her subliminal reply was appropriate.

She probed and tapped and listened and stared for over
an hour. The boy made more noises; eventually the Queen
went out on someone's arm. Cynthia had no complaint.
She knew, a little sadly and a little proudly, that she was
being her father's daughter: Vittorio Ricci insisted that
the patient was first, the patient's family a distant second.
The family became primary only if the patient died, and if
that happened the punishment was appropriate.

"Earl Rivers."

"Doctor?"

"I noticed that your library contains some medical
texts."

"I have books on all the sciences, madam."

"If you own a copy of Doctor Pier Leone's *On the Systems
of Muscles and Bones,* I would like to see it."

The Earl went downstairs himself. One of the others
present muttered "Any of us could have read a book." Cynthia opened her mouth to explain, but Hywel, who had
been silent and apparently disinterested until now, said
"Naturally . . . if you had thought of it."

Rivers reappeared, out of breath from the stairs, carrying the book. It was not thick, but of a large page size; each
page of Leone's commentary was faced by a meticulous diagram of anatomy or surgical technique. She noticed that
the book seemed almost new; the illustrations were probably more demonstrative than the Earl cared to look at.

She found herself examining the text for its own sake,
looking over the drawings as if they were views of home,
which after a fashion they were; Leone had presented her
with a copy on her ninth birthday. She colored all its plates
by hand. She wondered where it was now; unread in some
Byzantine satrap's library, or ashes.

A moan from her patient brought her back to England.
He must be only nine, she thought, or ten. "My lord Earl,"
she said carefully, turning to the pages she wanted, "you
said it was dangerous to anger your sister. What if the
truth is not what she wants to hear: will she be angry?"

"You sound as if you are passing a judgment." Rivers was grave, but in no way sarcastic.

"Perhaps, my lord. Hywel . . . may we talk, alone?"

Rivers said "We'll have rooms ready for you at once, of course, and your property brought from the inn."

"Thank you," she said; it came out wrong, too dry. "Then . . . we need another room, for a surgery; a stone room, so the walls can be scrubbed down with lye. A prison cell will do, if you can clean it, light it very brightly, and stop out any sewer vapors. Linen to drape everything—tell the maids fresh linen, not silk unless it's boiled; it's not the richness of the fabric but how clean it is." She turned to the little group of muttering men, certain now they must be the household physicians. "Are any of you gentlemen surgeons?"

The man who had spoken earlier now turned purple. With exaggerated politeness, he said "Is this what the Italians of such repute do? Drill for demons, and draw out evil with iron? I fear such methods are too . . . *new*, for England."

"You may go, Hixson," Rivers said, in a frightening tone, and the man went. Another of the doctors said quietly, "I will be pleased to help, madam. I have incised for abcesses, and cancer." He paused, looking very awkward. "Do you then propose to open the abdomen?"

"Sweet Lady, no!" But she understood: they thought, as had she at first, that the Prince had an intestinal abscess. Cutting through the peritoneum was never less than a desperate measure; in such a case it would be insanity.

Yet she found herself wishing it were only a case of acute abdomen. Calmly, she said "I intend to explore these nodules with a superficial incision." She watched the reaction. Apparently they had completely missed the nodules. She hardly felt triumphant.

"I have some experience in battlefield surgery," Rivers said. "I should like to be present."

"Of course, sir." She could scarcely refuse him, not with an heir apparent under the knife. "Please have me called

when our bags arrive . . . there are necessary medications.
Now . . . Hywel, may we talk?"

They were met in the hall by a servant, who led them to
their rooms. Just outside Cynthia's door, Hywel stopped
still, dismissed the page. "Good evening," Hywel said, not
to Cynthia but someone farther up the hall, "my lord wizard."

A man was at the end of the hall, descending narrow
stairs from what must have been a tower or attic room; he
had a roll of papers in his arm, with a brass instrument of
some sort. He was of middle age, with heavy black eyebrows and a beard slightly longer than the fashion; stur-
dily built, but not athletic. He wore a cap of red leather
lined with fur, and his gown was a heavy velvet, vivid red
and diapered with gold flecks. To Cynthia, he looked oddly
like a huge strawberry.

"And to you, my lord wizard," the man said, "and you,
my lady." He must, she supposed, be the man called Morton. Hywel confirmed it with a short, almost curt, introduction.

"You did not reply when I sent to you," Hywel said. Cynthia had to think for an instant before understanding that
he did not refer to human messengers. He was always able
to tell when there was another sorcerer nearby.

"I was busy, I fear. Naturally I did not know it was
you—"

"Nevertheless, I did not expect to find you in."

Morton smiled. "In Britain, you mean. Well. A man
must remain supple, Doctor. Do you feel no stiffness of
age? Oh—your pardon, my lady. Now, if you will excuse
me, good night to you both." He swept past them and down
a staircase.

Hywel opened the door to Cynthia's room, followed her
inside.

After almost two years of Welsh inns and cottages, the
bedroom of a royal castle seemed almost unreasonably
lush. Cynthia sat on the edge of the bed, felt herself sinking into feathers, wondered how she would ever sleep on
such a thing.

Hywel closed the heavy door, tripped the iron latch. "I might as well tell you now," he said with a deadly calm, "I can do nothing for the boy."

Perhaps he was too tired to be anything but blunt: certainly she was. "Then he'll die, in a year or two. Maybe he'll live as long as five—but it wouldn't be a blessing."

"Your surgery—"

"Is only to examine those nodules, be sure of what I suspect. I might be wrong; it would not hurt me at all to be. I've only seen the disease once in my life: Pier's book mentions only three cases."

"And he could not treat these?"

"No, he couldn't. But there's a footnote to one case: 'Referred to a sorcerer. Apparent remission.' So you see—"

"Cynthia . . . do you ever feel an aching in your muscles and sinews? A great aching, more than you would expect from exercise?"

"Don't change the subject." What had Earl Rivers called the wizard Morton? *Old deceiver.* She was not going to be deceived or distracted, not with her patient dying down the hall. "I have an oath to Minerva Medica," she said, and thought *Which I will not break again.*

"I do not." He lifted the latch. "You should rest now, Doctor."

"If you won't do anything, let me take him to Mary!" Was she shouting? The air was ringing. "Or anyone who will help—Doctor Morton—"

"How old do you think Morton is?"

"What? Thirty-five, perhaps forty, I suppose."

"He will be sixty in the next year."

"What does that have to do with this?" She caught her breath. "I don't know *your* age, Hywel."

"Before you choose to trust my lord wizard with Edward's life, not to mention his soul, I would remind you that Guillaume of Anjou probably had a similar trust in him as well." He went out, closing the door hard.

She realized, long delayed, that she had succeeded in hurting him, and he had not been able to deal with it.

Maybe he should be hurt, she thought suddenly; better than an atrophied soul.

She let her wooden pattens drop loudly to the floor, then lay back still dressed, sinking into the feathers for what seemed forever. The arches of the canopy above her were carved with images of a man-faced moon drifting through its phases, the full moon smiling down from the apex.

She wondered if he really believed that Morton was his unknown English wizard, or if he had only said it to frighten her.

Her arm and back muscles began to hurt, exactly as Hywel had said. It was the bed, she thought, and the suggestion; like a student who felt the symptoms of every disease she read about. Did Anthony Woodville, reading his books—

She knew it was not the bed. The pain had come before, and it was indeed much more than a common night cramp. It struck her worst while she slept, because then she dreamed, of straining to escape from a box nailed shut. Or a bed, with snow blowing through the window, and her blood draining out.

Hywel had seen her awaken, sweating cold, she thought. Perhaps he had watched her nightmares, despite his supposed rules for himself. He had done it once before.

She lay wide awake, paralyzed, less by the pain than the knowledge that just for an instant it had pleased her to have hurt him.

Cynthia took off her white cotton mask and hood, pulled the pin that held her hair, and shook it out. She was aware of Anthony watching her as she stripped off her silk gloves and linen apron. A servant took the apron, and the Earl's as well; she looked dolefully at the blood drying on Cynthia's.

"That was amazing," he said.

What kind of medicine did they practice in this country, she wondered; then Rivers said "I've seen battlefield cutting, as I said, but never anything so delicate as this. Then,

I admit, I haven't visited a school of medicine in a long time."

"You were a great help, my lord Earl."

"I like to be flattered, as long as I know that's all it is," he said easily. "I held a sponge and a hook—"

"Retractor," she said automatically; then, "You had Doctor Leone's book in your library. You didn't faint when I excised the nodules."

"All right! Pax!" They entered the solar, where a late breakfast was being set out. "Now I wonder if I can put a knife into a kipper." The sun shone through a window, over-gilding his hair; she thought he must surely be an Apollonian.

They sat down. Rivers stared at a platter of cut bacon and said quietly, "Is there really no hope for the Prince?"

"What I have said, I would not say lightly—but I would never say 'no hope.' " She had not mentioned magic to him. Her feelings this morning were too confused.

Rivers nodded, tapping his fingers on the table, making ripples in the pitcher of wine. "I should like . . . to have you available, Doctor."

She chuckled, not meaning to; he looked up and grinned foolishly. "I trust you take my meaning. Must you travel so soon?"

She did not answer, because she did not know; only that Hywel must do so. And now . . .

"Perhaps you would like a position . . . a teaching chair at the University at Oxford?"

Oh, White Lady, she thought. It might have been Lorenzo speaking: *I would like you to go to Pisa, bella Luna.* Her throat was quite tight, and she sipped some wine. Surely, she thought confusedly, losing her home did not mean that all places on earth must be alien. Even the half of the world that was not Byzantine was a very large country.

"We spend ten thousand pounds a year to hold Berwick under the Scots' noses; I think we can spend a little to endow a place for your better services."

As he spoke of the Scots, she thought of Dimitrios and

Gregory, and causes she had asked to be part of. "It is a most generous offer, Ser Antonio," she said, half aware her tongue had slipped, "but I . . . cannot accept it now. I am . . . sorry," and she knew she would be. "The Prince's acute illness will pass soon. He will feel much better."

"I am glad of that." He sighed. "But he will not *be* any better. . . ?"

"No, my lord. I doubt he will ever be that. . . . If I might be allowed to consider your offer again, sometime in the future?"

Rivers nodded as if he had not heard her at all.

Her bags were carried down to the castle courtyard a little after noon. Hywel was already there, mounted on a dark chestnut horse, a gift from the Earl; a white palfrey waited for Cynthia. She laughed when she mounted it, so that she would not cry. They rode out into a gentle October breeze.

After the castle was well up the south road, Cynthia said "Thank you for the light; their lanterns were all very smoky. Did it . . ." She worked not to sound snide. ". . . cost you greatly to cast it?"

"There is always some cost. But it's common light. It will not harm those cast upon, or darken the eye."

"I thought—" she let the statement drop: she had thought it was Morton in the mask and hood, throwing light from his palm onto her work. But Anthony told her later that Morton had departed the castle before dawn.

Finally she said "Where do we go next?"

"I cannot believe in impossibilities," Hywel said, "but some can, and do. We are going to Llyn Safaddan, to see Mary."

Hywel looked up past Talgarth Tower at the Mynydd Du, saw rippled gray clouds scraping the mountaintops. People were out on the road in numbers, headed for the circles of the old faith, to be safe against the spirits that would have the freedom of earth tonight—and if a wind that blew your roof off wasn't an evil spirit, what was? Cynthia had drawn up her hood, and Hywel dropped his staff by the way, and now fewer people made signs at them as they passed.

Hywel could see the circle fires, hear chants borne on the wind; but to his mind they were invisible, silent. His mind saw and heard the wizard who was working, miles ahead.

It was John Morton, he knew, at Aberhonddu—Brecon Castle drifted in and out of his witchsight—and Morton was crafting tonight as if he were a novice, just woken to the possibility of power.

But novices lacked control; the damage they could do was limited. Morton was not by any means a novice.

There was a little stone shed, all dark inside, just off the road. "Stop here," Hywel shouted. They tied the horses on the lee side of the shed, carried lanterns inside, and struck them alight; the place was bare, except for rags hung across the windows and door. There were smells of peat and manure.

Cynthia said "Mary's cottage isn't much farther—"

"It's warded against some things," Hywel said. "Her presence itself makes . . . just a moment." There was something more, now, in the air with Morton. It was not another sorcerer. That left only a few things it could be.

Hywel eased his Venetian eye from the socket. He held it cupped in his palm, shadowed. He caught one of the streaks of energy in the air, pulled it down and tied it. The glass began to sparkle, faintly, from within. He waited for it to come fully alight; then he scryed the pupil—

"What's the matter?" Cynthia was trying to get him on his feet. His knees hurt where he had fallen on them. He thought he might have lost the eye, but his fingers were painfully tight on it.

He had seen Morton with absolute clarity, as he worked in the tower chamber at Brecon. "Edward . . ." he said raggedly.

"The Prince?"

Hywel had also seen what was lying before Morton, and what Morton had done to him. "No. The King." He stood up, pulled one of the window rags aside to look at the sky. The moon was invisible; he knew it was in dying quarter.

That was good for the crafting but bad for the sending of it.
Even this atrocity, this outrage, was bound by the laws of
matter and energy. "We have a little time," he said, trying
to think how best to do what they must.

"Time for what? What's happening to the King?"

Carefully, he said "What can be done for a man who has
suffered a massive apoplexy?"

"Very little. Wait, work . . . love."

"Not good enough," Hywel said through his teeth. He
sat down on the dirt floor. "There are some candles, and a
piece of white Dover chalk, in my left-hand pack. Will you
please get them for me?"

"What are you going to do?"

"I'm taking you to Windsor," he said, working at his
bootlaces. "A short road, but a hard one."

"And this point of the Road is Windsor," Hywel said.

"And this point of the Road is Windsor," Cynthia said
after him. Hywel lit a short candle and put it into the triangle he had chalked on the ground, near the apex.

"And this is Windsor Castle, where the Road shall end,"
Cynthia echoed him. He lit the last candle, placed it upon
the acute point of the triangle; he dropped the bit of gunner's matchcord he had used to light the candles.

He stood slowly, feeling the wind through his light
woolen robe, the chill of the earth against his bare feet.
The candles gave no warmth, and almost no light.

Because it was his nature, he wondered just what it was
he was doing, what levers of the universe he pushed at, naked with candles. Certainly he could not transport two people a hundred and fifty miles simply by commanding it.
Nothing would happen outside, and something inside him
might snap and kill him; he'd seen it.

Yet there were rules, and rules. Strip, to carry less
weight—that made sense; fix the route with a map of chalk
and candles—he could understand that. But he did not
know why the Road must be walked barefoot, and without
lanterns.

And up in Brecon Tower a man was torturing and kill-

ing another, so that a third would suffer and die. It did not
seem to follow; it was just wishing, with a knife. And still
Hywel knew it would work. He'd seen it.

The last of Hywel's five sorcerers who never felt the
power gnaw their vitals was a Hungarian noblewoman,
who did no magic without an accompanying human sacrifice. She was powerful enough to get quite a lot of work
done.

She had faith absolute that as long as she had someone
to kill, she need never herself decline; and there was no evidence that it was not true. When she died, she did not
even curse the mob that tore her apart.

Hywel had been there to see the end.

John Morton had visited her some years before that.

Hywel stepped next to Cynthia, who stood, wrapped in
her cloak, at the base of the triangle. Candles flickering in
the darkness, the figure did faintly resemble a road, lanterns to either side, converging in the infinite distance.

"Are you ready?" Hywel said.

She nodded, let her cloak fall, stepped out of her shoes.
She wore a satin shift, silver-gray, and a silver ribbon tied
her hair. Later, Hywel thought, he would tell her about
Arianrhod.

"Hope we don't arrive in sight of King Edward," she
said, shivering a bit. "Might be ap-apoplexy on the s-spot."

Hywel said, "And, Cynthia . . ."

"Yes?"

"A large enough magic has . . . side effects. Corona, it's
called, or just spillage. Something like this . . ."

"You m-mean," she said, "that you were influenced, at
L-ludlow."

"I suspect I was. It doesn't change the substance of what
I said . . . but I'm sorry for the way I said it."

"Do you have to be a wizard to feel that? I mean, to be
affected?"

"No." When we destroy ourselves, he thought, we may
take the rest of humankind with us.

"Th-then don't apologize. Not to me. Just get us s-some-
where warm."

Hywel began to pave the Road. He could see Britain unfolding before his mind, candle-bright points of reference: Hereford, Gloucester, Oxford, Maidenhead. The Road stretched, a journey in a single step—

He was struck across the lower back, and fell hard, hearing himself groan. One of the candles rolled past his face and went out. He put up an arm by instinct, to stop the next blow; a hand grabbed his, a thick hand, not Cynthia's. Lanternlight flashed around. Something cold struck Hywel's wrist, something metal, greasy. Then a gloved hand caught his ankle, and there was the same coldness; if they were cutting him apart the knives were unearthly sharp.

Then his wrists were pulled together, and he knew what the cold metal was: lead rods, cast in the shape of snakes. Not as powerful as cold iron, but by the time he could gather his strength again they'd have cold iron on him.

He wondered, unable to help it, why the damned snakes worked.

Finally the lanterns stopped bobbing, and he could see the intruders: there were five or six men, ordinary men-at-arms, in the Duke of Buckingham's livery. Of course, he thought; Morton could hardly do his grisly business in Brecon Castle without the master's knowledge. One soldier carried a little pendulum of corroded silver cupped in his hand, and Hywel knew how they had been found.

He knew better than to try to speak, but he would have liked to ask them what cause they thought they were serving.

One of the troopers was kicking at the floor figure. As each candle went out, Hywel felt a little of the strength he had bound up in the construct return to him. He might, in a moment, even be able to—

Where was Cynthia?

He turned, as much as he could, and saw her. One man held her wrists behind her back; he had his spear propped against his elbow, and was fumbling with a leather strap, trying to pinion her.

Another trooper had his hand in her hair; the ribbon dangled against her throat. The man had set his long gun against the wall; on his baldric, a dozen wooden powder bottles clunked like muffled, dissonant chimes.

He started to push Cynthia to her knees. They were not leering or taunting; just doing the thing as if it were part of their job. Even beasts would grunt, Hywel thought.

The spearman snarled at his companion, "A-ah, let yo'r wick smolder a-an a bit." He got the leather belt around Cynthia's left wrist, pulled the loop tight; as he did, his spear began to topple over. He cursed and grabbed for it.

Cynthia smashed her right elbow squarely into his throat. He made a choked noise and staggered back, losing his grip on her. She swung her bound wrist forward; the gunner let go her hair and dodged the leather, dropping into a fighting crouch. The end of the belt whistled around and cracked like a whip into the spearman's face. He gurgled and clutched at his eyes. The gunner took another step back, drawing a long knife. His heel crushed out the last candle, then came down on the discarded bit of matchcord.

Hywel breathed a word of nine syllables, and stroked his forefingers together. The powder vials across the man's chest went off in a single long flash. He fell down, his heart and lights spilling on the ground.

"*Cynthia—*" Hywel said, and felt a knobby lead bit shoved into his mouth.

But she alone of all of them had not hesitated. She was already at the door, running into the night. Hywel could see her very clearly, a silver ghost on the wind.

The man with the pendulum snapped out a name. Another gunner, with a side glance at Hywel, blew on his match and braced his gun against the doorframe.

Hywel strained for a little more power, tasting blood in his mouth, not minding if he died for this.

But someone kicked him and broke the construct, and he fell down, thinking, Kill me, kill me and I'll curse you all blind; but they just held his head down with a boot to his temple. And he could not blind himself, but had to watch after Cynthia running, silver in the darkness, until the soldier shot her down.

PART FOUR

Turnings of the Wheel

Conscience is but a word that cowards use,
Devised at first to keep the strong in awe.
　　　　—ACT V, SCENE 3

Chapter 10
TRANSITIONS

THE King was dead, long live the King, as the saying went; but no thing is ever so simple.

Gregory von Bayern watched from the side of the hall as Richard Duke of Gloucester conferred with his captains. The news of King Edward's death had arrived at Middleham two days ago, and the house was upside down with shock and gossip and travel preparations. Then, this morning, a letter had arrived by fast post from London, and Richard had added a full mobilization of the household troops to the confusion.

"Lord Hastings states," Richard said, holding the letter with its heavy seals dangling, "that he has sent word to Earl Rivers, with Prince Edward in the marches of Wales, persuading him to show good faith in the public peace by accompanying the Prince to London with no more than a thousand men . . . a force which Hastings further says he is confident we can match or exceed." Richard looked up from the paper. "I trust we can, Dick?"

Richard Ratcliffe, one of the bannerets, said "We should have twelve hundred, Your Grace." He hesitated. "It's well known that the King meant you as his son's protector, my lord. . . . Does Lord Hastings propose—"

"Hastings doesn't propose anything, beyond that I can raise a thousand men, which is fairly common knowledge too." The men chuckled, "But his implication is plain

enough. The Queen's family has had the Prince's gover-
nance his whole life; would it surprise anyone if they tried
to keep it?" Richard put the letter down, tapped his fingers
against his dagger hilt.

Gregory looked around at the officers in the room. They
were, he knew, all Richard's liegemen. According to law,
their first allegiance was to the King of England, but their
oath was to Richard, and it was not the King's grace that
kept the rain off their heads.

Individual fealty versus collective loyalty: Gregory had
seen them in tension wherever he had gone. It was a way of
life in Germany, and Byzantium, and perhaps it was most
viciously played out in the University at Alexandria.
Wherever the field, Gregory had never known fealty to
take second place.

Gregory went silently from the room, climbed the stairs.
If Richard wanted the wheeled guns for his march to
London, they were ready; Dimitrios could answer tactical
questions better than he.

He entered his outer apartment, his workroom. Wood-
fiber boards were fitted over the windows, and diagrams
pinned to them. Richard's only complaint about Gregory's
working budget had been a joking one over his pin ex-
penses. They did have to be silver: iron would rust and
stain the papers, and an order to Germany for nickel pins
had never been filled.

Suddenly pleased he had thought of it, he pulled half a
dozen pins and stuck them inside his baggy sleeve. They
tended to disappear in his absence. The chambermaids
took them, but not for their own use; they went to the stable lads and pages, who had young ladies to impress.
Which girls might have been less taken with their gifts,
had they known how they were bought. But then, he
thought, the boys might not like to know what the pins
went on to buy. Some of them no doubt returned to his
drawing-boards, repurchased in coined silver.

He turned down his sleeve and patted the gray cloth. He
was at the center of a whole little economy of pins.

He went into the farther room, which was dark but for

the fireplace, and saw a figure sitting on the bed. She turned her head quickly. "Elayne?" he said, for her benefit; he could see her clearly. She was wearing a clean apron and cap over her gown and kirtle, cloth slippers on her rather large feet.

"They says you're leaving, Professor," she said, not hesitantly; Elayne was not a hesitant woman. "With the Duke an' comp'ny, to Lunnon."

"Yes."

"Why must you go?" No, not hesitant at all. "You haven't seen Midlum when the Duke's gone of winter. It's so quiet, an' the big house empty as anything."

"I've been asked to go."

"But not ordered? An' you anyway aren't the Duke's close man." She seemed to sense a triumph coming.

"I must go," he said, because it was only the truth and he would not see her falsely hoping, if hope was the name for her feeling toward him. A royal duke might for reasons keep a pet vampire, but he would keep its chain short, and he would not leave it winterbound in a castle where his wife was. Gregory supposed that Elayne understood this, but feared to insult him by saying it.

"I ha'ant been to the City," she said. "Is it a long way?"

For an instant he was startled, but of course she meant London, not Byzantium. "A few days, if the roads remain clear."

"You'll want not to be hungry, then."

He sat very still as she stood, removed her apron, and opened her gown. She knelt at his feet; he untied the laces of her kirtle. His hands did not tremble; he wondered if that pleased or disappointed her. Her fingers sought out the hooks that held his gown. She shivered.

He felt the flow of saliva, and a heavy sensation in his chest near his heart. He must feed first, to dull the edge of hunger, and then she could take her pleasure at length. He reached to the bedside table, closed his hand on a shallow wooden cup.

She sat down on the bed, cradled against his arm, pale in the firelight; alabaster and porphyry. He stroked her with

his fingertips, watching her smile and the curve of her
spine, to distract himself. The tension was growing much
too rapidly, as if he had been starving, which he had not.

He had found her at the worst possible time for both of
them. He had been in the kitchen, looking for the crock of
warm blood discreetly put out for him (as one might feed a
biting dog), when he heard an odd sound from the pantry.
Elayne stood all alone, in kirtle and apron but no gown,
hair loose, making a whimpering noise as she throttled
back tears. She had chewed a thumbnail until it was bleeding freely.

First he meant to turn and go; but it had been months
since he had even tasted human blood, and he supposed he
would kiss the wound, keeping his teeth together, taking
only a little on his lips. Then he took her hand and she
bowed awkwardly, tried to explain herself, and he thought
he must be polite and listen. . . .

The fire flickered high. Elayne was gasping, just slightly; Gregory shifted his fingers and she made a soft, de-
lighted sound. She would notice no pain when he opened
the vessel. He had been told, more than once, that pain and
fear made the blood taste even richer and better; they said
it about arousal, too. Gregory admitted the possibility of
unusual humors being released into the bloodflow, but he
did not really believe it.

He hoped that his taste would never become so jaded
that he would need to believe such things.

The thought made him hesitate. It was less than four
weeks since he had drunk from her. There was no threat
—he knew the safe times and quantities as well as any so-
ciety patient knew the Latin names of his diseases—but
how else would his tastes grow tired except through over-
indulgence?

And yet he was leaving soon, and might not be back in
months, if at all.

He wondered again which of Richard's horsemen had
cast her off, left her crying in the kitchen; she would not
give his name, fearing one man's wrath, or the other's.

Doubtless Dimitrios would know, but since the Scottish disaster Dimi had been too busy for conversation.

He saw that she was pleased, but that did not surprise him; he had earned his board that way before. He wanted to know if she was happy.

The *Minnesänger* whined that love was a hunger, and men perished for its want. That was shit, Gregory thought. Blood was his hunger, and if he wanted for it long enough he would not pine away but lose his reason, probably kill, until he was fed. Or was shot down in the street like any frothing dog. And so he must drink, from sweet trusting maids, while he was able to stop drinking.

He felt her calf with his thumb, finding the strong femoral pulse, positioning the wooden mazer. He took a pin from the sleeve of his coat, thinking, Here are two commodities whose markets I control.

At the scent of it, he felt a fire in his head, and he drank the cupful quickly, trying not to taste it at all, afraid that it might be much too delicious, and that it might not be delicious enough.

Gregory was wandering over the walls of York in the midmorning sun, dressed in a full-skirted white gown and a flat hat with a broad, floppy brim, gloves of white pigskin. He looked somewhat priestly, all dazzling on a bright cold day, and most people only nodded as they passed. If they did more, his story was that he was an engineer inspecting the city defenses for Duke Richard.

While it was strictly true, Gregory thought it was a ridiculous excuse: York was the largest city in the North of England, and one of the most elaborately defended. It would take a month, not to mention a team of surveyors with instruments, to cover all the ramparts and ditches, gun-angles and palisades.

But if the people who heard the explanation thought it was silly or suspicious, they did not say so. One offered blessings on Richard in the name of the divine Hadrian, saying "And tell him that York loves His Grace as he loves us, no matter who is king." Another required three repeti-

tions of the message before saying "Well, fancy that of the
Duke of York, an' un so young. . . . So wise so young da'n't
live long, they say."

Gregory sat on a rampart, put his hand up on a swivel-
mounted bronze saker. The metal of the gun was heavily
verdigrised, and there were white streaks in the green:
names and initials carved with the points of knives. A
string of crooked characters spelled out TAKE THAT SKOT-
LANDERS!

Pulling the brim of his hat to shade his eyes, he looked
toward the center of the city, at the dome of the Pantheon.
It was not a spherical dome, such as that of the Eastern
City's Kyklos Sophia, but a cone of twelve triangular panels. Where the base of each panel met its supporting wall
there was a plate, pierced with holes in the pattern of a
constellation. The plates were all black, but of four different materials: lacquered oak for the earth signs, obsidian
for the water, black marble with a wispy figure for the air,
and iron for fire.

The roof beams were of oak, the triangular panels a
wooden lattice of ashwood and thornwood, white and black
intertwined.

Richard and all his company were beneath the dome just
now, swearing oaths to faithfully serve the new King Edward the Fifth. That was why Gregory was out here alone
with his sore eyes and lame excuses: the oath, it was
specified, was to be taken in blood.

A man was riding up. Gregory heard him long before he
could see him. A dark horse, dark rider: Richard's man
James Tyrell.

"Good morning, Sir Gregory."

"Good day to you, Sir James. Do you come to call me
back? I had thought to hear bells, or something, when the
ceremony was over."

Tyrell swung out of the saddle. Palomides gave Gregory
an unfriendly look. Tyrell said "It isn't over, but by your
return it will be." He hesitated. "My reasons for . . . ab-
staining . . . are my own."

"I don't believe I asked them. I'll be coming, then."

"Sir Gregory, I would like to ask you something."

Gregory nodded.

"I was not ordered to ask this. It is a confidence, between knights."

"As you say," Gregory said, coolly curious. Tyrell was the only person in more than twenty years to call him knight. He wondered if the Englishman was aware of the differences between *Fachritterschaft* and the sort of knighthood he knew; if he would even call von Bayern "sir" if he were. Then, of course, in England it was not necessary that an engineer have formal rank before a baron would take his advice.

"The pantry girl at Mid'lam, Elayne . . ."

Gregory's curiosity peaked, though he did not display it. Was Tyrell going to confess to having abandoned the woman?

"May she acquire your . . . disease, sir?" It was politely said, but no less a demand.

Gregory thought that he had been very careless, very stupid. He considered how he might disable Tyrell without killing him; he had no dislike for Tyrell, and certainly none for Richard, and the man was only protecting his master.

But Gregory was not carrying his small gun—more stupid carelessness. Tyrell's sword was on the far side of his saddle. They would both have knives. . . . Tyrell was a soldier, but Gregory knew the line of every blood vessel in the body.

"No, Sir James," he said, watching Tyrell's eyes for the first motion of attack. "You have my word as a Fachritter von Bayern that she cannot become diseased." Supposing he simply offered to leave England—but no, he would have as much chance of persuading this man as of riding away on his horse if he did kill him. He wondered if Tyrell knew that vampires' strength was one of the true bits of the legend. "I have had women before. . . . I have passed the disease to none of them."

He was angry with himself, but his anger was entirely cold. Whores were better, he thought. They never spoke,

never offered when you did not want to pay, and most of all
never lied about where their pleasures came from.

"I thank you, sir," Tyrell was saying, and turning to
mount his horse again.

Gregory waited.

"An she were sick, t'would be Tyrell's job of surgery," he
said, with his more usual roughness; then, just a little
more softly, "Not a task I wanted, Sir Knight, but there it
is. Thanks again, sir, and since I can't wish you good
health, then merry meet again."

Gregory watched him ride away, then stood up from the
gun mount, adjusted his clothes, and began walking toward the Pantheon.

There was a sound from the southeast, probably still two
miles distant. He knew, even before he saw the riders and
the spearpoints, that it was a troop of soldiers on the move;
several hundred at least. They were coming from the direction of Wales, where Rivers, the King's governor, had
been.

Gregory steered his gown around a patch of slush and
took the straight way to the Pantheon. It would be the
safest place, whoever won the fight. He had decided long
ago never to lie to save himself, but to claim that he desired divine protection was no lie at all. It was not his fault
that other people chose to believe in gods.

As Richard emerged from the Pantheon, Ratcliffe and
Dimitrios a step behind him, linen bandages stained
bright on their forearms, the dusty new force of men
around them raised arms in salute, and their leader
walked forward with his hands wide.

"Harry!" Richard said. "Oh, well met, Harry!" Then he
squinted against the sun, at all the lances in array. "Well.
You're not out for your health, either. What does it all
mean, Harry?"

Harry was a handsome man, hazel-eyed and clean-
shaven, running to stoutness but not fat. He was wearing a
coat of steel plates covered in wine-colored velvet embroidered with heraldic knots, and red leather riding trews.

His swagger was as natural to see as a duck swimming. Dimi knew his type quite well: the cavalry coronal, of whatever army, who had outgrown his rashness but never his dash, and would now be settling down toward a long career of charges led and charges remembered, finally to die charging death on his favorite mount, four-legged or otherwise. Even the Swiss coronals were like that. For such men, powder and shot might never have been invented.

If this man was his master's friend, Dimi thought, there must be some good order in the world.

"You're here with twice my numbers, Dickon; I'd thought you knew twice as well what it means—and at that, this ride may be for our health. Didn't Hastings write to you?"

"He did. But he was very cautious."

"Cautious!" Harry slapped dust from his knee. "Yes, I can't fault that. Hastings is in London, in the midst of Woodvilles. . . . In a forest of Woodvilles, eh, Richard? A very thicket of 'em." He laughed, not dryly. "And now? Rivers brings in the royal roebuck, Anthony the great warrior—"

"Enough, Harry," Richard said, suddenly sharp. Then, quietly, he said "We need to talk, but not out here bleeding in the cold. Dick, Dimi, come along."

As they walked from the Pantheon court, Harry said "I haven't met your new man, Dickon. Foreign, isn't he? From the Middle Sea?"

"This is Dimitrios Ducas, Captain of Cavalry. Say he's not a good Englishman and you'll answer to me. Dimi, this is Sir Henry Stafford, the Duke of Buckingham, up from Brecon in Wales."

Richard Duke of Gloucester sat beneath a painting of his father, Richard Duke of York. The father's features were stronger than the son's, and he had been a physically larger man; but York had been painted at ease, and Richard burned with intensity.

Buckingham sat facing Richard. Ratcliffe and Dimitrios flanked the fire. Tyrell leaned against the wall, in a

shadow; Dimi wondered where he had been this morning.
They were gathered in a small town house, built by Richard of York just within the outer walls of York city. It was
designed after the new style, large-windowed and thin-
walled, built for comfort rather than massiveness, ac-
knowledging that guns were now and forever dividing
forts from houses.

Buckingham poured another cup of Armagnac brandy.
"It was Edward's will that you be Protector of England;
the lords know it, and the commons too—old women in
Wales know it, Dickon, so why do you pretend you don't?"

"Because I don't think Edward had any serious plan for
a Protectorate at all," Richard said. "I certainly don't
think he meant to die before he was forty."

Buckingham said "All plans are made in the dark. I
can't tell you Edward was the wisest of men, but he did
have a care for his sons. And for England."

"Hear, hear, for England," Richard said.

"Surely Hastings's letter said that the Queen's faction
is proposing a Council of Regency."

"If he'd written it in the tone you say it, the paper would
have burned."

"You know what you would do on a Council, Richard:
you'd count Woodville votes against you." He took a swallow of brandy, leaned forward in his chair. "There's the
other possibility. It's been said—never in the open, mind,
but how much is open about this?—that the Prince already
has a Protector, in whom King Edward must surely have
been well satisfied, else how would his son's knightly upbringing be—"

Richard stood up. "Either stop bringing Anthony into
this, or accuse him, Harry. Hastings implies, you suggest
—will someone bloody *say* something?"

"Very well, Dickon, facts. Anthony Woodville has possession of the next King of England, body and very possibly soul. Rivers is moving to London with armed men, to
hand the King over to his sister. Right now, if my Lord
Hastings's letters have been successful, we have Rivers
outnumbered." He stood then, to face Richard eye to eye,

and spoke without haste. "If you do not take possession of the King *now*, before he enters London . . . you will never possess him."

"We are talking about my brother's son." Richard's hand was tight on the hilt of his knife. Then he turned it. "But we're not, are we. He's not just a boy any longer."

"Nor a king, yet," Ratcliffe said quietly. Richard looked at him, surprised.

Buckingham said "As a puppet on Woodville strings, he could be the ruination of many good men." Then he folded his arms, looked at the floor. The fire cracked and threw up sparks.

Richard tapped some more brandy, tossed it back. "Where were Rivers and the King when the news reached them?"

"Ludlow," Buckingham said. "They were ten days leaving, for some reason."

Richard said "Tyrell?"

After only a moment's pause, Sir James said "With quick marches, we could be ready for them at Northampton."

"I don't . . . like that," Buckingham said nervously.

"What, Harry, faint of heart so soon?" Richard said, with a determined expression.

"My father died at Northampton."

"I know. I also know what he was trying to do there." Richard stared into Buckingham's eyes. "He was trying to keep a king from being taken by force. Well, blast, Stafford, my father died not a year after, trying to make a king. And when they killed your sire, they didn't cut off his head and stick it on a pike, with a paper crown to suit the bitch-goddess's fancy. Nor was your brother's head on another spike beside it . . . so don't you tell me what places are ill-omened.

"Tyrell."

"My lord?"

"We'll go to Northampton. But we will not set an ambuscade, not for the rightful King of England. We'll hear what Anthony Woodville has to say for himself. At least he'll be well-spoken; maybe poetical." He paused; when he spoke again, his anger had faded. "Any objection to that, my lord of Buckingham?"

"None at all, my lord of Gloucester," Buckingham said, relieved.

The Dukes retired, leaving the three captains alone with the Armagnac. Over a large cupful each, Dimitrios said "I have heard of this Sir Anthony Woodville on the Continent, as a scholar and a good knight."

"The best knight in England?" Tyrell asked.

"Yes," Dimi said, a little embarrassed. "That was said. But it cannot be true, then. . . ? If he is . . . at odds."

Tyrell said "It probably is true. That's the trouble." He finished his brandy, rapped on the keg. "An you two finish this off, do your puking tomorrow out of my sight?" He grinned. "I can't abide bein' the only sensible man in a crowd." He went out.

Ratcliffe topped off his cup and Dimi's. "This much for me, and then it's your problem."

"About Sir Anthony Woodville—"

"Do you mean that after two years in Richard's service, no one's told you about Francis Lovell?"

Dimi shook his head.

"He was the Earl of Warwick's ward, at the same time Richard was in Warwick's household. A little younger than Richard, not much."

"The Duke told me he and Duchess Anne were the youngest."

Ratcliffe started to rise. "I think I've drunk enough and said too much."

Dimitrios caught Ratcliffe's sleeve. "I'll believe he had a reason not to tell me, if you'll give me some grounds to puzzle it out."

Ratcliffe sat down again. "You understand, I wasn't there when any of this happened. But the hell with it—in for a penny, in for a pound.

"Richard and Lovell were close, very, like two boys get sometimes when they're about to be men together—have you ever seen that? I have, though it never happened to me."

"I've seen it," Dimitrios said, trying to think of nothing at all but what Ratcliffe was saying.

"They even went into his . . . your religion together. I don't know any more about that, of course. But a year or so after that, there was a tournament, one of those Marvel things where everyone comes as a hero of the stories. Richard and Lovell were Balin and Balan, the brothers. And Anthony Woodville was the Warrior with the Gilded Spear—do you know of him?"

"No," Dimi said, but he was beginning to understand.

"He's one of the sons of Morgaine the witch, you see. And Anthony's mother Jacquetta was a witch—really she was; everyone knew it. So it was a strange sort of joke, but at tournaments strange jokes do well."

"I think I see now," Dimi said. "Woodville killed Lovell."

"Tilting. Everyone said it was an accident, and I mean everyone; Lovell's shield and head were so badly held that when Woodville's spear struck . . . away both of them went.

"After that was when he started mixing books with his war. Of course, later the talk started about black magic, tricked equipment, the usual nonsense."

Dimi nodded. "But if Richard's forgiven him, I suppose that's what matters. No matter what other people say."

"You still don't see it, then. The Middleham boys were Balin and Balan. Twins, in identical armor. And they decided to play the usual twins' trick: when Lovell ran the tilt, he was carrying Richard's shield and wearing his helm, with the crest, No way anyone could tell, till they fished the head out of the pot, that Woodville hadn't ridden at Richard."

"Rivers!" Richard said. "Anthony, good evening. Come in, it's cold. Though I daresay not so cold as Wales. . . . If I may insult Wales in your presence?"

Buckingham came into the entry, wineglass and meat

pie in hand. "You may even insult it in mine, Dickon. Good evening, Rivers. Did you come hungry?"

"I admit I came curious," Rivers said slowly. "You said that you wanted to discuss the King, over dinner. I didn't expect an Irish wake."

"There's no corpse at this feast," Buckingham said.

Rivers said "There's Edward's."

"Yes. Well," said Richard, pressing his palms together. His tone became serious, but not angry. "Yes, I'm wearing black; I'm not done mourning Edward. But if you want tears, tread on my foot; I ran out of tears before brothers."

Rivers was impassive for several heartbeats. Then he said "I'm being a very bad guest."

"Let's call it false dawn, then, and begin over." With exaggerated cheer Richard said "Well met, Anthony Woodville, Lord Scales, Earl Rivers. Are you cold and tired and hungry?"

Rivers was smiling now. "Anthony's hungry, Scales is tired, and the Rivers all run cold."

Richard laughed. "Well, all right then. Let's not let Harry get a lead on us in there, or we'll both stay hungry."

Dimitrios followed, at a discreet distance, as the lords went into the hall.

Dimi leaned against the wall, a few steps behind Richard's chair. He had an excellent sight of all the doors and windows in the room. His light Damascene sword was buckled on, and a billhook was in the shadow of the hearth chimney. He had paced out the room earlier today: he could kill the first man through any door, and hold the rest with the polearm.

He was not sure how to count the odds in the room itself, with eating knives to hand, and furniture in the way. In such conditions no three elegant fighters were worth one good brawler; Richard was not, Buckingham did not have the look, but Rivers might be. But Ratcliffe would be here two breaths after the alarm, while Tyrell made sure Rivers was not reinforced further from his camp.

And if it came down to knives over the soup, Dimi supposed that one blow from behind would not be counted foul, even against the best knight in England.

Richard was saying "If you believe I'm condemning your stewardship of the Prince, you're wrong, Anthony. I'd rather have had you teaching him than a collegeful of dusty men who never smelled a horse. But all at once the student is out of the schoolroom."

Rivers said "The schoolroom has no walls, and the pupil is always in it."

Buckingham said "And what does that mean, Woodville? Are you preparing to keep—"

"Henry, shut up," Richard said agreeably. "Just my meaning, Anthony; a king can't live in a library, or a temple. Henry the Idiot left us overproof of that. But now Edward's on the throne, with all the powers and duties, armies and coinages, and what's England to do while he learns what to do with them?" He leaned toward Rivers, said "He's just at the age when power and duty aren't connected at all. Don't we remember that time?"

Dimi watched Rivers carefully. The Earl tapped a hand on the table without rhythm. It could not be seen, certainly not heard, as a signal to men outside . . . unless one of the earl's rings was magicked to do that. Dimi had worked for an Austrian prince who had such a thing.

Rivers said "What is it you want, Richard? Kindly name something in my power to grant: I cannot raise the dead." Dimitrios was startled; the Earl's voice had been very nearly a cry of pain.

Richard sat slowly back in his chair, mouth a little open; Buckingham's lips were compressed, it might have been with fright.

After a long, long pause, Richard said "I want . . . the custody of my brother's son, for the trip into London."

"All right," Rivers said, calm again. "Your claims are as strong as mine, after all; they're both rooted in what we think Edward wanted."

Richard nodded, picked up his cup. "Then I think I would like to drink . . . to the health of the King, and of England's Galahad—"

"Not yet, Richard," Rivers said. "Now I have to tell you the rest. The boy's health, Richard—"

Buckingham said quickly "What's the matter with his health? Is he ill?"

Rivers did not acknowledge the interruption. "We have a doctor's opinion that he's . . . dying, Richard."

"You have *what*? *One* doctor's opinion? Whose? And dying of what?"

"It's a disease of the blood system, a rare one. None of the house physicians knew of it at all, though you know how little that means around Elizabeth's doctors. This was an Italian physician, of the best reputation. She was traveling with that Welsh sorcerer you know: Peredur."

"A woman doctor? White-haired, good-looking?"

"I daresay."

Richard said "Dimitrios," and Dimi took a step forward to stand at Richard's right. "My man knows them both. Go ahead, tell me what they said."

"The sorcerer had nothing to do with it. The doctor said that Edward might live some months, or a few years, but—"

"Enough of what the doctor said," said Buckingham. "What did he do?"

"She," Rivers said, in an irritated tone. "And there was nothing she could do. There was an examination, and a surgery—"

"A *surgery?*" Buckingham said, astounded.

Rivers turned to Buckingham, mouth open to speak; but he shook his head instead and turned back to Richard. "Elizabeth never told your brother. And the Prince doesn't know—we didn't have any courage to tell him before his father died, and we're not notably braver now.

"The Queen insisted that a new physician be brought, another Italian, and he should be in London by now. I hope he will be some comfort for the boy." In a faraway voice he said "So you see, gentlemen, all the countermarching has been for nothing. When it becomes known that Edward will never reach his majority, how much will his Protectorate be worth?"

Richard said "Peredur was with her. What did he do?"

"As I said, not much. He was present at the examination and the surgery."

"And he did *nothing?*"

"He gave the doctor some light," Rivers said tiredly.

"And the two of them just walked on, after this."

"Rode, actually. I gave the lady a white horse."

Richard seemed to be struggling with a thought. Dimi's own mind was clouded. Of course there were things that doctors could not cure—he needed no more proof of that. But this man seemed to be saying that Hywel and Cynthia had not even tried.

More than that: he was saying she had *cut* a child, for nothing. Dimi knew Cynthia had been disturbed, hurt—but Hywel had said he was going to Wales to help her, and he had also said there were things he would not let her do.

And Dimi would not believe she had gone so cruelly mad; not if there was anything like a god in the cosmos. He found himself not even believing the story about the white horse. Rivers did not look like a man who had been slapped.

Richard said "Why did you wait to tell us this, Anthony?"

"I told you, Elizabeth didn't tell the King himself—"

"I'm not interested in what your sister didn't say. Why didn't *you* tell my brother?"

"It might have killed him sooner," Rivers said, without feeling.

"Or kept him alive," Buckingham said. "Edward did have a care for his sons. And for England."

Rivers said "Damn England. The boy was in my care."

"Oh, too late for that, Anthony," Richard said, anger finally surfacing. "You've played your trumps for tonight. So, Richard's going to press his claim as Protector? Well then, let him be Protector of dust. It's not just treason, Anthony, it's vomitous. Even Scotsmen let us drive back the cattle they fail to steal; they don't kill them in the road for spite."

"Burning God, Richard!" Rivers was halfway out of his

seat. "Do you want to know why I waited, tonight? I
wanted to hear what you were going to say. Three thousand armed men out there, and you ask me to dinner."

"We'd have given you a battle," Buckingham said
clearly, "but we thought you'd prefer the tiltyard."

Rivers's chair went over backward, with a crash that
rattled the draperies. He took a step toward the door.

Richard said "Captain."

Dimi caught the Earl's arm. Rivers turned; Dimi twisted
the arm into a wrestler's lock. He pulled, and pushed, and
took Rivers down to the floor. The Earl's mouth was open,
twisted. Dimi was surprised; the hold should not be *that*
painful. His armlock slipped a bit.

"Don't let him cry out!" Buckingham said, coming
around the table very rapidly. There was a brandy bottle
in his hand; he smashed it over Rivers's head, spraying
brandy and potsherds all over and thickening the air with
fumes.

Rivers was still conscious, but badly dazed. Dimi pulled
off the Earl's rings and tossed them aside, pushed a linen
cloth into his mouth. Another napkin tied his hands. Dimitrios made certain that Rivers was not choking on the gag,
then said "He's a strong man, Richard. These won't hold
him long."

"We have rooms for that," Richard said. "You did that
very well, brother."

Dimi saw the turn of Buckingham's head. "Thank you,
my lord." He was still puzzled: Rivers had hardly given
him a fight, nor was he struggling now. He wondered if the
man could be a coward, despite his fame; wondered what
other sort of man threatened children for his ends.

Ratcliffe had appeared, with men behind him, backing
him. "Dick," Gloucester said, "take the Woodville lord to a
room with no windows, and lock him in. Take that whole
squad with you; if he leaves this house, or even signals
from it, the King may be murdered. If he pauses before a
window, cut him down." They led the staggering Earl
away. Richard said "Dimitrios, you stay."

"Sir?"

"The King's at Stony Stratford. We're riding there now,
to fetch him out before anything can be done to him. I suppose they've got some black sorcerer . . . we must hope
that they're not ordered to hurt the boy if we appear without Rivers."

A link formed in Dimi's mind. "When we passed through
France, Your Grace . . . Hywel spoke to your King Henry's
widow. There was a sorcerer involved, and Queen Elizabeth's children. . . ."

"Margaret's in this?"

"I can't remember anything more of it now . . . it's been
a long while. But Professor von Bayern was with Hywel;
he might know."

"We'll ask him when the King's safe," Richard said, and
started down the hall. Without looking back, he said
"Bitch-goddess of Anjou! I told Edward, when he sold her
back to the French spider: some people are just too dangerous to leave alive."

"No, Uncle," said the King of England, "I do not understand why you have taken away my counselors, and I do
not know why I should not have them back. They were
given me by my father, whom I loved and trusted, and
were favored by the peers and my mother—"

"The peers and your mother," Buckingham said sharply, "are all of the same enormous and conspiratorial family. Their entire wish is to control your person, Sire, and
through you England; and if they could not control you
they meant to kill you."

The King shook his head. His gold hair was long and
loose; he had been in his nightshirt when Richard, Dimitrios, and Buckingham arrived, but insisted that they wait
until he had put on a white silk doublet bearing the Rising
Sun in gold. He wore sword and dagger as well, sized to a
ten-year-old boy.

"You ask me to believe that my mother would kill me,
like the queen in the story. *Really,* Sir Henry."

Dimitrios felt himself smiling. Edward was doing his
best to be kingly, as his father would want, and succeeding

very well. But then, Dimi thought, Edward's father had died suddenly and far away. And his father's brother was a brave, intelligent lord. And Edward was really a king.

"We do not blame the Queen," Richard said, "except as she may have trusted too much in her brother."

Buckingham said "It's a womanly habit, to trust for flimsy causes."

There was a moment's startled silence. Dimi thought that Henry Stafford was indeed the model noble cavalryman: only a soldier could be so tactless and only a nobleman could get away with it so often.

Edward said "I trust my Uncle Anthony with my life, and I do not think the cause is weak. Why, when I was lately sick, so sick I thought I would die, it was Anthony who brought the lady doctor."

Richard glanced at Dimitrios. "You were sick, then?" he asked the boy. "But a lady came?"

"Yes."

"What did she look like? What did she do?"

"She had really white hair, but she wasn't an old woman. She was very pretty, I think. . . ." The formality began to slip out of Edward's voice. "She looked at . . . *examined* me, and it hurt some but not as much as when Doctor Hixson does it.

"Then the next day she gave me some medicine, and a thing to breathe into that made me sleep. And while I was asleep she did a surgery. On my side, here. I had to wear bandages for a while, and underneath it's sewn up with silk thread. Do you think common people are sewn up with cotton thread?"

Richard said "Do you know what the surgery was for?"

"Uh huh. Lumps."

Richard said *"Lumps?"*

"Uncle Anthony had a little jar of alcohol, on the shelf with his medical books. There were some lumps in it, that he said the doctor took out of me. They looked like fish guts."

Dimi saw Richard's lips form a word, did not need to hear it. Richard said "And after the surgery . . . you felt better?"

"Not right away. But later. I'm not sick now."

"No, of course," Richard said. "And the doctor? Did she go away? Before you started to feel better?"

Edward looked thoughtful. "I think I saw her right after I started to wake up. But I was sleepy for a long time. Anth—Earl Rivers told me she left on the same day, with her companion the wizard. . . ."

If he has hurt her at all, Dimitrios thought, if he has hurt Hywel, we'll see how good Rivers is with a knife in a locked room. Then he saw the King staring, realized he had spoken the thought aloud. "Your pardons, Your Graces, please. . . ."

"I like your humor, Captain," Buckingham said.

Tyrell came into the room, which had been already crowded with four. "My lords Vaughan, Grey, and Haute are accounted for," he said to Richard, as if no one else were present. "If there was a wizard, or a black doctor, they've slithered off."

Edward said "What are you going to do with my counselors?" Fear cracked his dignity, and Dimi felt sorry for him; but at least now he would live and be King.

"Tell the Ludlow men," Richard told Tyrell, "they have the Protector's dismissal with thanks. And that they'll be paid as if they'd marched to London, in advance celebration of the new King's accession."

"Sir."

"Those men are my guards," Edward said, quite frightened now.

"We have two thousand men to guard you," Richard said, in a soothing tone. "And more importantly, we have removed the present danger."

Dimitrios said "My lord Richard—"

"Yes?"

"About Doctor Peredur and Doctor Ricci, my lord—the danger to them may be very great now."

"Of course you're right. Harry, I think this is a matter for you. You must have them found: start with Ludlow."

"Under the Protector's authority, Richard?"

"For now. Rivers can't be deprived of the Justiciar's office without proper process."

"Surely . . . you're aware, Captain Ducas, that there is a chance—"

"I know it, my lord Duke," Dimitrios said. His eyes hurt. He kept thinking: Peredur promised he would not let her die. And Hywel can't be dead; I'd have seen the sky split.

"I meant to say that Wales is a very good place to hide."

"I'll hunt them myself," Dimi said, too quickly, thinking of the last time he had made such an offer.

"I can't spare you, brother," Richard said. "Tyrell and Ratcliffe will be taking our friends somewhere for safekeeping . . . Pontefract, I think, James; it's rather above the woods line. No questioning, but not too much comfort, either. Dimitrios, you'll come with us to London."

"Is there no one," Edward said bravely, "who will come and go at the King's command?"

Richard knelt before his nephew, putting himself a little lower than eye to eye. The others went on their knees as well.

"I was no older than you when my father was killed," Richard said. "I didn't understand then what was going on over my head, either, and I was hurt a lot of times before I did. I do not ask you to love us for what we do; but I do ask you not to hate us, not until you have learned a little more about the world."

Edward said "Very well, Uncle Gloucester . . . you may rise."

The King's pony was brought. Richard said quietly to Tyrell, "Ride ahead, and get Rivers out of the house before we arrive."

"Yes, sir. Do I take him to Pontefract?"

Dimi saw Richard darken. "Yes, you do, and healthy, blast it."

The King said "My lord Protector." They all turned.

In a voice as hard and cold and clear as something carved from ice, Edward said "Once I have learned properly to hate, Uncle, then will I truly be King?"

Chapter 11
TRANSGRESSIONS

YEARS ago, during one of the German-Danish wars, Gregory von Bayern rode as *Gunner-und-Sprengsfachritter* in a minor court's minor army. The Count fancied black livery for all his men (and women, because he also maintained a company from the Rheintal order of Valkyries). Fortunately, the garb was comfortable and sturdy, not usually the case with vanity uniforms. And the Count's army was recognized where it went.

One clear winter day the *Schwarzheer* was winding in column through a village in Saxony, the population turning out to cheer and wave banners or clothing or towels or anything they had that was black.

When Gregory rode by, at the rear leading his guns jacketed in black leather, the waving and the shouting stopped. Suddenly. If there had been any direction to run, he would have spurred his horse and gone; he began to hope that the village had someone who knew how properly to kill vampires. There were towns that had become fascinated by a victim who could be displayed in agony for so long, in so many unique ways.

But nothing of the kind happened; the column simply marched on, trailing dust and silence.

"Look at yourself in the glass," the Count said that evening, and Gregory did. He saw a bone-white face looking out from a black hood, with two dark circles of glass instead of eyes. The Count was greatly amused, and asked Gregory thereafter to ride up front. Gregory did so a few times, until one night he shot a villager who had entered his room, intending to kill Death and save the world. Then he left the Count's service.

Eventually, he heard, the expense of black horses ruined the Count, but it was widely said that he had failed as a true artist, and also that he now sought someone to infect him with vampirism.

Now it was another blue December day, and Gregory was riding among five hundred soldiers all in black: the entourage of King Edward V, at the gates of London. They were, said Richard of Gloucester, in mourning still for Edward IV, whose funeral they had missed. The King was dead, as the saying went, long live the King.

In a meadow outside the city, they were met by a group of men in scarlet: the Mayor and his aldermen. After them came a party of bailiffs, with scarlet pennons on their spears, leading four wagons covered with cloth. Then another tide of color flowed from the gates: citizens, tradesmen, and guildsmen, dressed in deep violet that still seemed bright against the black the King's party wore.

Surrounding them all were the commons, come to look and cheer the King and the Protector of the Realm and days of celebration in general. Gregory saw a footman mobbed: he escaped half-stripped but apparently unhurt, and then the crowd ripped up his black clothing for keepsakes.

Gregory moved toward the center of the procession. It was all as bad as Saxony; worse.

Much worse. The sun made his head ache, the crowd-within-the-mob confined him doubly, and he was hungry, too soon and much too fiercely.

Another man was riding toward them now, and the scarlet and violet parted for blue and gold. He was wearing a half-armor, and a large sword with an elaborate hilt; he was quite a splendid figure.

"The King's Chamberlain," Gregory heard one of the serjeants say. "Lord Hastings."

The writer of letters, Gregory thought, and moved nearer.

"See what we have found," Hastings said, to the Dukes and the King but pitched for the crowd. He gestured, and the bailiffs pulled the coverings from the wagons.

There was the dull gleam of browned steel: pikes and bills, swords and axes and maces, heaped up like bones outside a butcher's. Hastings walked his horse to the nearest wagon, reached in with a gauntleted hand, pulled out a long-bladed sword. He carried it back to the King.

"Do you see, Your Grace," Hastings said, presumably addressing Edward, "the device upon the hilt? *It is a Woodville badge,*" he said, loud enough to be heard in Windsor.

He was certainly heard across the meadow. Murmurs rose like a wind. Gregory could hear the beginnings of a chant: "Down Woodville! Up Edward! Down Woodville!" Mostly it was distant, fragmented, from small knots of the commons, but shortly some of the men in black and violet took it up, and Gregory could see a red-gowned alderman nodding in time.

Richard said, "We thank you, Hastings, for your vigilance. And we assure you—we assure you *all*—the King's person is safe." He raised his hand, and the chanting fell. "And now, by our brother's authority as Protector of his heir and this realm, we request all lords of England now in the city to gather with us at the Pantheon, to take or reaffirm oaths of his surety."

They entered the gates in triumph.

Dimitrios went first into the Tower apartment; he checked behind the draperies and the arras, took a sip of the wine on the sideboard, opened the cabinet of a floor clock, and held a light within, knowing how small an infernal device could be made.

Then Hastings and Gloucester came in. Buckingham had gone to attend to the King's settlement in his rooms.

Richard said "What in the Dog's name was that business of the arms, Will? I couldn't think where you might have gotten all that old junk, until I remembered the stockpiles everyone built up for fear of Scotsmen."

There are people who call you a Scotsman, Richard," Hastings said. "In truth, that's a compliment beside some of the things said in council. They were looking at the country as ravens see a carcass. It was necessary that they be disarmed . . . in one fashion, or another."

Richard nodded slowly. "Well. After seeing what Rivers had in his mind, I can't say you were wrong. . . . Surely you didn't know—"

"Of course not. Rivers still grudges my holding the Captaincy of Calais over him, but a man can be ambitious without being a regicide.

"I knew something was wrong when the council proposed he bring all the men he could muster: there would have been six thousand—ten, possibly." Hastings scowled. "I had to threaten to go to Calais, taking every ship and document I could find. I'm not certain I could have done it, with Edward Woodville still Admiral; Dorset had a secret look, and I think wanted me to go and be sunk." He went to the sideboard, poured two cups of wine. "It has not been easy, Richard."

"That's the last thing I'd have supposed it would be." Richard took a cup. "How did Edward die, Will?"

Hastings chewed his lower lip. "Very quick, Richard. He didn't suffer, thanks be."

"But he died naturally?"

"I'm certain of it. The doctors . . . it was just so damnably quick."

"I need you to be certain, Will. Edward made you, and he made you very well. Of all the men and women in London, you stand to lose most by his loss, so it's you I'm asking. Was Edward murdered?"

"No, Richard. It was a sudden apoplexy, and natural, as I have cause to know. But—don't ask how I'm certain, please, Richard." His voice was level.

"Of course I'll ask," Richard said, sounding puzzled and a little irritated. "And I expect that you'll tell me."

"Very well, Richard." Hastings had ten years and a

handsbreadth of height over Richard, and now he took the
full effect of both. "It happens that Edward and I were together in chambers that night, with Elizabeth—"

"*With the Queen?*"

"With Mistress Shore," Hastings said, unshaken. " 'Jane,'
as some call her."

"I see," Richard said. His face was set in an odd expression, but he did not seem taken aback or chastened. He
turned a ring on his left hand. "Well. I suppose it is as
kingly a death as any, and one couldn't ask for one more
natural. . . . Where is my brother's concubine now, Will?"

"In my house."

Richard nodded. "I suppose that's safe. And warm, too."
He drank his wine. "Well. Shall we speak with the
Queen?"

"The Queen sends her regrets . . . but offers that if Your
Grace wishes to send any message by myself, she will give
it her earliest attention."

The messenger was an Italian diplomat, Dominic Mancini. He wore a fawn-colored gown with restrained gold
embroidery, and half-eyeglasses. His English was extremely precise, his manner one of courtly embarrass-
ment.

"Where is she?" Richard said.

"I am instructed not to reveal that."

"And why is that?"

"I am to offer the example of the Earl Rivers."

"Does the Queen know that Rivers has planned murderous treason against the persons of the King and his Protector?"

"She states that Parliament has not created a Protector,
so there can be no such treason, and she puts no belief in
tales of treason against the King . . . committed by Earl
Rivers."

"Do you come equipped with an answer for everything?"

"No, Your Grace."

"Well," Richard said, slightly amused. "You may tender
Elizabeth our respects, and all honor due her station, and

tell her that we hope to give the same in person upon our confirmation as Protector. Do you note that word, Mister Mancini—*confirmation?*"

"I note it well, Your Grace."

"Tell her that until such time, I have no requests. Has she any?"

"She does, my lord of Gloucester. She asks that the doctor brought for the King be allowed to see him."

Richard turned to Lord Hastings. "Rivers mentioned a doctor. An Italian. Who is he?"

"The Queen insisted the King's special physician be an Italian," Hastings said. "But Rivers did not bring him, nor the Queen select him. I did. He arrived a few days ago; his name is Argentine, John Argentine."

Richard looked relieved. He said to Mancini, "Tell the Queen that the King's health is of as much concern to us as to Her Grace. The King shall of course have his physician.

"That will be all today, Mister Mancini."

Mancini bowed to leave.

Richard said to Hastings, "Why *that* little whistling bird?"

"Why? As you said to me, it's a matter of what's to gain and what's to lose: Mancini can hardly have his eye on a peerage, let alone the throne; there are cheaper men to bribe, and he'd have a hard time hiding himself in Kent. Besides, we read all his mail back to Genova."

Dimitrios said "Your pardon, lord, but you say he is from Genova?"

"Yes, the University there. That's where Doctor Argentine is from as well."

Richard said "Is something wrong, Dimitrios?"

"No, sir. Just the opposite. Genova is not a Byzantine province."

"Well, that's one less worry," Richard said. "Not that it was ever too large, eh?"

"I suppose not," Dimi said.

"It is the vote and ordinance of this council, therefore, that the Duke of Gloucester shall be called Protector of the

Realm, and have in his charge the safety and education of King Edward the Fifth, until the same King Edward shall enter into his majority and become King in his own right. . . ."

As the meeting dissolved, Buckingham said to Richard "It's pleasant to know that the Lords can do *something* with alacrity."

Hastings said impatiently, "Do you think this was casually done, or lightly won? You've been here for a few days, and invisible for half that time. I've called in twenty years' worth of favors, and made such concessions—We're sworn not to prosecute Rivers and his company for treason, real *or* discovered, before this moment, and not to make any attempt, by act or decree, to violate the Queen's sanctuary. Richard is Protector as long as he doesn't protect against Woodvilles. Which brings to mind, have you seen your wife lately, Harry?"

"I won't take that from you, Hastings," Buckingham said, rather pleasantly. "The Queen's family didn't force *you* to marry their leavings. Bring my wife into this and I'll bring in your mistress: isn't Jane Shore the spiciest of scraps from a royal table?"

Richard said "Stop it, both of you. Rivers is still well out of mischief, and we never did mean to force Elizabeth out of hiding . . . though that little Italian is starting to make my teeth hurt. As for your women, I can't say much for either of your tastes, but that's something only fists can settle."

A man was approaching. He was bearded, with heavy black eyebrows, and he wore a padded red doublet embroidered with straight gold wire. There was an elaborate silver collar around his neck, and he carried a stoneware crock closed with lead seals and wire.

"My lord wizard," Richard said, manner cool.

"My lord Protector. I have a gift for the King . . . by your leave, of course?" He held out the jar. "Strawberries from my garden. Picked this morning. The King's physician suggested that fruit would be healthy for him."

Dimitrios looked out a window, at the leaden clouds of early January.

"That's . . . kind, sir," Richard said. He motioned, and Dimitrios took the jar. "Do you, then, know Doctor Argentine?"

"We have a friend in common. Messer Mancini."

Richard said "Well. . . . Thank you, my lord wizard. I'm sure the King will enjoy them."

The wizard laughed. "My berries have a better reputation than that! I only hope he does not develop a rash."

"If he does," Buckingham said sardonically, "you can expect an arrest for black sorcery."

The man in red and gold laughed again. "Oh, not after all this time, surely," he said, bowed slightly, and departed.

Dimitrios said "Can these actually be . . . strawberries? In January?"

Hastings said "Doctor Morton's gardens are most remarkable." Richard said "Doctor Morton's most remarkable. He's been on councils since Henry the Idiot's time; doesn't look over sixty, does he? Talk about strawberries in January, there's a hardy perennial for you. No matter the climate at court, he springs up, like a weed."

"You do not like him, my lord," Dimitrios said.

"I don't like anyone who had the confidence of—well." He eyed the jar. "Wouldn't surprise me if he watered them with blood. Well. Let's take Edward his treat."

An ancient Tower porter, wearing a gown and tabard that looked three or four reigns out of date, brought Richard and Dimitrios to the King's apartments in the White Tower, announced them in a voice that could hardly have carried across the room.

The King said "Thank you, Master Giles; do admit them," with singular gravity. The porter stood there, stubbly chin moving. Edward repeated himself, with less dignity and more volume, and Giles turned and gestured Richard and Dimi within. He closed the door behind them.

"Uncle; Captain Ducas. What do you have there?"

"First some news, Your Grace; the council has seen fit to

confirm your father's wish that I be your Protector and guardian."

"This must be a great honor for you, Uncle," Edward said. Dimitrios saw an extraordinary weariness in Edward's look, fear in his eyes. "You will be pleased to hear that we do not hate you."

Richard bowed slightly. "Now, Sire, a gift, from Doctor Morton of Holborn."

"The strawberries he promised?" Doctor Argentine entered from a side chamber. He was tall and slender and quick, with delicate features and hands. Dimitrios felt a shudder go through his arms, and tightened his grip on the pottery jar. He was thinking of Cynthia, of course, though the resemblance was only one of circumstances.

There was another peculiar circumstance, here, now, and he thought about speaking—but it was the Duke of Buckingham's habit to state the painfully obvious, and he merely put the jar on a table and took out his knife to cut the seals.

"I'll do—" Argentine began to say, and Richard said over him, "Morton said something about rashes."

"I don't get a rash from strawberries," Edward said, ten years old again. "I *love* strawberries."

"We'll begin with a few, to be certain," Argentine said, "and gradually increase the dose. That's always good practice with any item of diet; nothing to excess."

Dimitrios felt a small relief to hear him say that.

Richard seemed about to say something, but did not. Dimi thought the Duke must have been reminded of his late brother's dining habits.

Dimi cut the last seal and lifted the lid; inside were scarlet strawberries as big across as two thumbs, moist and shining and so fresh they had only the faintest sweet scent.

"Please tell the Queen that the King is well," Richard said to Mancini, "but he expresses a loneliness approaching melancholy. I therefore respectfully . . . I *humbly* request that Her Grace send the King's brother the Duke of York to join him."

"In response to such a request—" Mancini began.

Richard chopped his hand through the air. "I'll have her actual response, sir. Further make clear that the Duke will not be in a *secret sanctuary,* but in the Royal apartments, available to view. And tell the Queen that Doctor Argentine approves strongly of the idea."

"Your Grace."

Mancini went out. Richard signaled, without a word, to Dimitrios. They knew how Mancini would leave the Tower; Dimi moved faster, by a longer route. On the way he stopped in a small arms closet and changed his outer clothing; he was out on Thomas Street just ten ticks of the Tower clocks after Mancini, and in perfect sight of the messenger.

Richard said that an attempt to merely discover Elizabeth Woodville's sanctuary was no breach of an oath against entering it. That distinction did not concern Dimitrios; another did. But he told himself that he was not spying, not committing frauds of himself. He was hunting a human's nest, through a winter forest of building.

And since Richard would not give him leave to go to Wales—or to question Rivers in Pontefract—this was the only way he had of searching for Hywel and Cynthia.

A coach rattled up Budge Row, crowding pedestrians to either side. Dimi watched it; it could stop in an instant to pick up Mancini, but it passed him by. " 'Ware, sir!" Dimi heard, and nearly got his feet rinsed with slops. He crossed the street, his boots quiet on the paving stones, his breathing under complete control. All the people around him faded, except for one, and Mancini stood out like a figure on a shield. Dimi was faintly aware of the smell of acid and leather as he crossed Cordwainer Street, as a brachet may know there is a hare in the woods without abandoning the problem of the hart.

And then suddenly the whole shape of the forest changed.

Mancini was crossing the huge plaza surrounding the London Pantheon, making for the artless complex itself. Damn you, Dimi thought, and at the same time, How clever.

He did not stop, though he knew what would happen. He
thought of closing in on Mancini, but that would not lead
him anywhere not of his quarry's choosing. And, Richard's
distinctions or not, he dared not be caught pursuing the
Queen's intermediary.

Dimi actually succeeded in following Mancini through
three floors and dozens of turns of the Pantheon. Then
Mancini made a sharp turn; then there were two men in
fawn suits of clothing; and then there were none.

Dimitrios found himself in an empty cubicle, not more
than three yards on a side. On the front wall was a relief of
two-faced Janus, a few dried sprigs of fir twined around it.
The left and right walls had at one time been mirrored, to
create endless reflections of the worshipers; but panels of
mirror were missing and broken, and only one white stone
bench was left. Dimitrios sat down, between imperfect
doubles of himself.

Richard forgave him, of course; Dimi supposed his master knew that forgiveness was not what he wanted.

"Parliament has set the Coronation for three weeks
from now; there'll be a week's celebrating with the Iambolc feast to finish it off. Elizabeth *has* to come out for the
Coronation, after all." He shook his head. "Dimitrios, you
know more of the law of Byzantium than I, and unlike the
lawyers you'll tell it in English. Does the Empire have a
law of temple sanctuary?"

Dimi said "The state may make no law that favors a
faith. Since not all faiths have a rule of inviolability, such
a law would favor those that do. In the end . . . it was de-
creed by Justinian, after the last Tarsite riots, that if the
gods wished to keep sanctuary they would themselves punish its violators. He said, 'Let those who would be safe in
their gods pray, and keep a spear sharp.' "

Richard looked thoughtful. "And keep Mysteries hidden, eh, brother?"

"Yes, brother. The caves have always been a strength to
us."

Richard nodded. "You see, my father broke sanctuaries,

and asked Thor to strike him if he did wrong. Edward did the same. No doubt Elizabeth thinks no better of me."

Dimitrios did not reply. Richard looked out a window, said "It would be so much easier if the gods would stop us doing what we should not." He sighed. "As well ask that we not want to do it. . . . I have another task for you, brother, and this one won't please you, either."

It was, Dimi supposed, what he wanted: punishment. "Of course, Richard."

Richard's eyebrows rose, and the corners of his mouth. He turned the ring on his little finger. "Well, it's not so horrible as that. You know Hastings has been intercepting Mancini's letters?"

"I heard him say it."

"Well, for an old councillor he's shown a remarkable lack of guile. He's had the letters opened, copied, and resealed—without examining the originals. The Bull knows what he expected to find that way. You were a mercenary; you know sieges and secret messages. I want you to get one of those letters itself, and look it over."

Dimi thought it was the perfect punishment detail: making him spy again.

"Ask your German friend to help; he must know chemicals, and cipher mathematics. . . . How is Professor von Bayern, by the way?"

"He was well when last I saw him," Dimitrios said, and thought that it was a bad sort of truth; better truth was that he had not seen Gregory in weeks, and did not even know if he was finding his food.

Surely, though, he must be. The Tower must have an old-established system for feeding them.

Gregory lay very still in the dark, on his narrow bed, dressed in only a pair of hose. A little light seeped in around the draperies; he did not have a pin-board to block off the window. There was no fire. He was not cold, not able to be, and in the gray haze of light he could see as clearly as an ordinary man at noonday.

He was aware his little clock was no longer ticking. It

had a superlative Swiss spring, which could drive it for
sixty to seventy hours; so he had been on the bed for at
least that long. It was possible that he had been asleep for
some of the time, but he doubted it.

When the light failed, he thought, he would dress, and
cross London to Baynard's Castle. Wetherby would let him
in, and see that he had some blood from the kitchen. Some
animal's blood. He was just hungry enough, now, so that
he would not mind its taste, would not be reminded of what
tasted so much better.

He had been three days in this room. It had been eleven
days since he had taken a capon from the Tower kitchens.
After feeding, he cooked the bird in his room and ate it.

He passed all the flesh in lumpy pale flux. His body was
refusing to accept food. Not strictly true: all foods save one.

One of his kind had called it "the perfection." "Why on
earth would you resist it? You fill your body with garbage,
but the body knows its own. Men don't eat grass, but the
cattle that graze on it; *vrykolaka* do not drink from cattle—"

He had wound the clock, loaded his gun—not the smallest one—and gotten into bed. Now the clock was unwound,
the gun unused. He was done with the bed as well.

There was a knock. "Gregory?" It was Dimitrios's voice.

"A moment," he called; it hurt his throat. He put on a
robe, wound his spark lighter and struck a lamp to life; the
brilliance was excruciating, and he put on his darkest
glasses before opening the door.

"Gregory, I—*are you all right?* I mean . . . were you
asleep?"

"Resting, yes. I am fine, only a little tired."

"Well. I'm . . . glad you've got work to do.

"A man must keep busy."

"Are you busy now?"

"No. Come in. Forgive the light."

"Of course." Dimi reached inside his jacket, produced a
thick envelope with a seal. "This is a letter from . . . someone the Duke suspects of spying. I'm supposed to examine
it for secret writing, and I thought you could help."

"Well, I . . ." He looked at the window. It was not yet dark. And he had not used the skills in so long. "I'd be glad to help as I can." He took the envelope. "Let me get some things from my bag."

The hot blade of a knife slipped under the seal, freeing it intact from the heavy paper. Wearing his white silk gloves, Gregory eased the sheets out. He wrote notes on their order and orientation in the envelope. "The Alexandrine Library," he told Dimi, "requires a course in the handling of precious manuscripts. Hm . . . do you read Italian?"

"Enough to read orders and broadsheets."

"I can read technical works. Between that and your vernacular, let us see what is here."

The answer, after an hour or so of reading word-and-phrase and arguing over idioms, was Nothing. "He seems to have a great interest in English court costume," Gregory said. "You are certain he is not a social philosopher making a study?"

"We didn't really expect a message in the plain text."

"I cannot swear there is none. Word lengths may encrypt, or perhaps we should read every twelfth word . . . but let us try something else." He pulled the table lamp close, swung its lenses aside, held a page of the letter near the flame. Almost no light showed through.

Gregory took the warm sheet away. It seemed unchanged. He rubbed it between thumb and forefinger. It was a very thick vellum, and there was something about its feel. "How often does Herr Mancini write his letters?"

"Every two or three weeks."

"And does he expect them to be collected into a library volume?"

"What?"

"This is book paper, an expensive book paper. Feel it." He handed a page to Dimi, rubbed his fingers again on the one he held.

He felt a minute slippage.

"Now, what is this?" He held the paper to the lamp

again; touched the knife to the very edge of the sheet, rocked the blade.

The paper split in two.

On the inside surfaces of the separated sheets were characters in a faint brown ink, written along the weave of the paper.

"A heat-developing ink," Gregory said, "but where we could not see it develop. Here, let us open the rest of these surprise packages."

Shortly they had almost twenty pages of brown script, none of it readable through encipherment.

Gregory looked to the window; no light came in.

"Do you think you can break it?"

"I hope . . . *was meinst du?*" He looked at Dimitrios, at the letter. "I know some of the methods. But it could take time . . . I was going to leave here, tonight."

"Leave? Where for?"

"To . . . the Duchess Cecily's house. I was offered . . . her hospitality, as we all were. And it is so much quieter than the Tower. Especially with the preparations for Coronation."

Dimi let out a breath. "Across London? I'd thought you meant Scotland, or worse. Look . . . do you have the time to work on this? Really?"

"Yes, I do." He wondered if Dimitrios had caught him in his lie.

"Then take the letter with you. Lord Hastings is Captain of Calais; letters get lost at sea. Send word when you've done it."

"Thank you for your confidence."

Dimitrios looked surprised. "I . . . of course, Gregory. Do you need help moving your things?"

"No, thank you. I was almost ready to go."

Dimi looked him up and down, at his bare chest showing through the loose robe. Ah, you have caught me, Gregory thought, but that was not a lie.

"Well. Good night, then, Gregory."

"Good night, Dimitrios."

Gregory put on his gray gown, put the silent clock and

the gun and the letter into a shoulder bag with some more clothing. He tossed on his green cloak, was about to blow out the lamp, when he thought: Pliny's Transposition.

If he had to encipher a long letter every few weeks, transmitted long distances so that keywords could not be readily exchanged, it would be the system of choice. . . .

It will keep across town, he thought, and cupped his hand around the lamp flame.

No. It would not. By the time he reached the gates, the *Heinzelmännchen* would have begun kicking holes in the word-lattice building up in his mind.

He took off the cloak, spread the pages of the letter out on the table, found a sheet of drawing paper for constructions and calculations.

At the back of his mind, where he forced it to stay, lest thinking too much spoil it, was the thought that he was not hungry now.

The cipher began to break down. He had been worried that the clear text would be in colloquial Italian, as unintelligible to him as the cipher, but it proved to be in a workhorse Latin.

By the second page, Gregory knew that its author was not an Italian. His Latin and his cipher proved it. That is, he was not an Italian by loyalty.

By the time Gregory was finished, and dawn was lighting the window, he knew a great deal about the loyalties of a great many persons. And one for whom loyalty was not the issue at all. And he knew whom Margaret of Anjou had seen in his face.

He turned toward the window again, eyes closed, feeling the sunlight burning him. People would not be bustling yet, and that was necessary for what he intended.

He stood. There was no more time to waste. He could not wait until the sun was higher; he had to make the most of their natural disadvantages.

Giles the Tower porter was in the hall, leaning on a rack of poleaxes, asleep standing up by appearances. Gregory walked past him without a sound, keeping his shoulder

bag close to his body. He reached to Giles's belt and in a
fluid motion slipped a key from the porter's belt. Giles snif-
fled and twitched, but did not wake.

Gregory put the key into its lock, turned it; it was a
springless mechanism and it did not click. He pushed the
door open the width of three fingers, looked in.

The room beyond was very dim, with a fire too small for
heat or warmth. A tall, thin man stood at a table near the
wall opposite the window. He wore a light silk robe. On the
table before him was an earthenware jar, metal-sealed. He
was clipping the wires that held the lid in place.

Gregory pushed the door open, stepped inside, closed the
door. The man was slowly turning to face him, putting
down his wire shears. "Good morning, sir," he said, smiling. "I do not believe we have met."

Gregory said "I think you know why we have not, Doctor. I am the Fachritter von Bayern."

"Eccelente! I have wanted to meet you, Professor, very
much," John Argentine said. He took a step forward.

Gregory reached into his bag. "Please stop moving." He
rested the twin barrels of the gun on his left palm, his right
thumb on the split trigger.

Argentine stopped. He was still smiling. "I have had
guns pointed at me, Professor von Bayern. In fact, I have
been shot with them."

"I also," Gregory said. "However, this gun was built by
me. It uses fulminate locks, which are touchy but never
miss fire. It fires two cylindrical bullets, three-quarters of
an inch in diameter; the bullets are sawn radially to expand and splinter. You are a doctor; think about that. And
think also that I know better than most where to aim."

"I've been thinking that." He gestured toward the jar on
the table. "Do you mind if I finish opening that? I think
it'll interest you." He picked up the shears. "This has to be
done properly: break the lead and it'll be full of strawberries. Ah. *Ecco esso, Professore!*"

Gregory could smell it as soon as Argentine lifted the
lid: warm, fresh, human blood.

"There is quite enough for both of us, Professor." He

looked sharply at Gregory. "In fact, you may have all of this; I can see you need it more than I, today. How ever have you been living? London is a big city, I know, and suspects foreigners, but—"

"Be quiet." Gregory felt hollow. His head was full of sweet, blood-scented air. He did not have to be hollow, he knew; there was more than a quart in the jar, more than he had ever taken at one time.

His mouth full of water, he said "The King?"

"He'll be all right now," Argentine said. "They said a Ricci of Fiorenza treated him, and I can believe it—rare disease, beautiful surgery. But it could not cure him, of course. I know the disease . . . I am a specialist in diseases of the blood and vessels, you see·. . . and for this one only I am the cure. Forgive me, Professor. Only we." He looked at the jar. "Would you let me take a little of this for him? He's impatient. You know." Argentine put his finger into the blood—which still showed no sign of thickening or cooling—tasted it. "Can you imagine what it is like for him? He has never —will never—taste anything less than human food. Pleasures of kingship—"

Gregory's gun kicked and roared. The jar of blood exploded, sending a red wave over the table and the wall and Doctor Argentine, who clutched at his arm, dropped to his knees. There was a smell of burning and a sizzling sound, and Argentine whimpered like a kicked dog.

Gregory said "I did not mention the phosphorous filling, because I was not certain it would work." He tilted the unfired tube down to point at the shaking doctor. On the floor, little pools of blood were boiling.

The door was opened, and soldiers came in with a nobleman leading them. All stopped and stared, weapons half out; they looked unwell.

Gregory took his thumb off the gun trigger. "Your Grace," He reached into his bag, produced the translation of Mancini's letter. "We have a great deal of trouble. I hope that these are men you can trust."

Cautiously, the Duke reached for the papers, glanced at them.

"Yes, Professor, they are absolutely loyal to me," Buckingham said, and signaled for his men to close the door.

* * *

Dimitrios looked from the window of the tiny council antechamber, across to Tower Hill: some carpenters were hammering and sawing, raising a scaffolding for the Coronation ten days away. The noise irritated him. Not that anything would have been soothing this morning, he supposed. Richard had ordered him to arm and wait here, with two of his troopers from the Border fighting and a number of household men.

What they were waiting for, the Duke of Gloucester said, was a cry of *Treason.* It was not a thing to put men at their ease.

"All right, Bennett?" Dimi asked. The young man was leaning back, one boot planted against the wall, hands crossed on his raised thigh. His fingers drummed on his armored thigh, inches from his saber hilt.

"Sure, Captain." Bennett stopped tapping. *"Do* you know what this is, sir?"

"No. And if I did, I probably couldn't tell you."

Bennett managed a smile.

They could hear chairs being shifted in the chamber behind the door, and voices being raised; Dimi thought he heard Lord Hastings, but could not make out anything being said.

Then he heard a word he was certain was "Treason!" Bennett was already drawing his sword; Dimi motioned for him to be patient just one second longer, and then the door swung open with Richard pushing it. "I say it is the basest sort of treason!"

Dimi signaled, and the force moved into the chamber at quick march.

Hastings was there, and Lord Stanley, and the wizard Morton, with perhaps a dozen others. Buckingham stood near the windows, holding some large sheets of paper.

Hastings said "Richard, if you do not consider this—"

Buckingham stabbed a finger at Hastings. "We have *considered* you very long, sir, and it is that *consideration* that has allowed you to carry out your *considerable* crimes." He swung his finger on Dimi and the troopers. "Take this traitor out and *consider* him properly!"

Dimitrios looked at Richard. Gloucester had both fists clenched, seemed taut enough to snap and fly apart.

Bennett was the only one moving then. He laid both hands on Hastings's blue velvet sleeve, pulled him off balance, and shoved him toward two of the Tower troops. In another moment they were out of the chamber and down the hall.

Dimi was struggling to think. Something seemed to be preventing him, like a hand closed on his mind. He wanted to draw his sword, use it. Surely there must be another traitor here. "Richard," he said, and it did not seem to be his own voice.

Lord Stanley was moving toward the windows. When he reached them, he was holding his left arm, and blood ran between his fingers. Dimi looked down, saw that his saber was out, and its blade was stained.

"Hel take them, they're doing it," Stanley said, "on the raw lumber—" The sound of steel into wood cut him off. He turned his head; it wobbled like a doll's.

"Morton," Richard said. "You're doing this."

"I? Good my lord, I prune my gardens with different tools than this."

"We should take your eyes and your tongue," Richard said, "but you'd smell your way to favor again." He turned to Buckingham. "Harry, once you said Wales was a good hiding place. Take this . . . thing to Brecknock, and hide it away."

Lord Stanley sat down hard on the floor. He was not bleeding badly, but was pale. Dimi said "Tend the man, Robert," and his other serjeant went to Stanley's side. Then Dimi went to Richard.

"I'm all right, brother," Gloucester said quietly, brokenly. "Hastings and Morton . . ." He stared out the window. "Hastings and Morton killed Edward. I just learned it last night."

"The King is—"

"My brother Edward," Richard said. "No, no, the young King's safe—though Harry says someone tried to kill Doctor Argentine last night."

Richard took a step to the window, looked down. "Hastings was the last man I should have supposed it of . . . which I suppose he knew, didn't he?" He turned away from the scene outside. "I was thinking of titles and properties. I thought it was over bloody *Calais*. And it was just my brother's merry harlot. Well, we'll bring her in as well, and if she's a witch we'll have it out of her."

Morton said calmly, "Mistress Shore isn't a witch, you know. Questioning her would be most unnecessary . . . unless it is necessary for my lord's faith that he injure a woman?"

"If you speak one more word, wizard," Richard said, boiling over, "my men will cut off your left hand and give your magic something to occupy itself doing." He pointed at Dimi's bloody sword.

"Don't be troubled," Morton said. "There is always something that needs doing." He stepped toward Dimitrios, reaching toward the drawn saber. No one moved to stop him.

Morton swept his hand along the sword. There was a sparkling light as it passed, and then the blade was clean. Morton knelt, rubbed the same hand down Stanley's wounded arm. Then there was no blood there either, nor tear in the fabric of Stanley's sleeve.

"Take them out. Take them all away," Richard said tiredly. Dimitrios waved to his serjeant, who was staring, bewildered, at Lord Stanley's arm. The man nodded finally and snapped orders to the troops, who responded as men being awakened from sleep. Buckingham called after, "Keep a tight rein on the wizard, damn it!"

Richard said "Stay here, Dimitrios."

When the room was empty but for Gloucester, Buckingham, and Dimi, Richard said "There's news of Peredur, and the Doctor."

"What news? Are they alive?" If they were not, he knew the favor he would be asking next.

"We've read Mancini's letters," Buckingham said. "They've unmasked this whole conspiracy: Hastings, Morton, their supporters . . . even the Queen is involved." He fanned the papers he was holding.

"But Cynthia? And Hywel?"

Buckingham said "Your Professor has not deciphered the entire message yet. But they are definitely mentioned, in connection with Wales."

Dimi said "My lord Richard—"

"If you hadn't volunteered I'd have ordered you. Come back quickly, brother, and well accompanied." Richard turned to Buckingham. "And by the time you reach Brecon, you'll be confirmed as Justiciar of Wales. And I mean you *will* be confirmed."

"And the rest of Rivers's offices?" Buckingham said, bluff as always.

"Rivers won't be needing them," Richard said. "There'll be a rider to Tyrell this afternoon."

Buckingham nodded, with a broad flat smile that had no humor in it. "Then, Captain Ducas, shall we be gone?"

"Gladly, Your Grace."

As Dimi and Buckingham reached the door, leaving Richard alone in the Council chamber, Dimitrios paused and said to Gloucester, "I hope you will send my thanks to your mother, for the quiet of her house?"

Richard nodded absently, then looked up, with a puzzled expression; he shook his head dismissively and waved farewell, then went again to the window. There was much shouting from Tower Hill.

Dimitrios followed Buckingham around the Tower courtyard, to a small side door in the White Tower.

Dimi said "Mancini was reporting to the Eastern Empire, wasn't he?"

Buckingham nearly dropped the ring of keys in his hand. "How did you know that?"

"I should have known it sooner, much sooner." And maybe I did, he thought, but I didn't want to be a spy. "We knew they were planning against the English crown, as far back as . . . *Morton.*"

"What's that, then?" Buckingham opened a door, motioned for Dimitrios to enter. A few of the Duke's men were inside, in attitudes of boredom.

"Morton was at court when the French woman was Queen, wasn't he? He knew her?"

"Very well."

"Then he must have been the one she thought she saw, when . . ." He was trying to remember what Hywel had said. And Gregory had been there too. "You said Doctor Argentine was not one of them," he said, feeling suddenly very cold, "but I'm certain he must be. Some remaining part of Mancini's letter must mention him—"

"One should be careful, reading other people's mail," the Duke said, and raised a finger.

Instantly four guardsmen were on Dimitrios. He pivoted, gave one his elbow and another his knee, swung a gloved fist and felt bone crunch. Another pair of men came in. Dimi threw off a groaning man and turned.

Buckingham had a double-barreled gun aimed at his head from barely two yards away. Dimi was about to jump for him anyway, but then he recognized the weapon, knew he could not hope its firelocks would fail. He let his arms be held back.

"Yesterday," Buckingham said pleasantly, "I saw what a close miss from this arm—I see you know it—could do to a man, one who heals very quickly, fortunately for him. This isn't at all knightly, I know, but then I've always been a boor, like Sir Cei, who ran Arthur's house while Arthur was busy being knightly. And remember, Captain—I saw you tackle the best knight in the realm."

The Duke nodded slightly, and a white-hot flash consumed Dimi's world.

Dimitrios was not certain if he was awake, or even alive. His vision was entirely black, and he could not move. Then his head began hurting, and he supposed he must not be dead; there was too much pain for a limbo and not enough for a hell.

He might be blinded and crippled. That didn't bear

thinking on. Then he felt something cold against his throat: a human hand, quite cold. They had put him into a grave, then, alive, and not alone. He opened his mouth to breathe, knew that if he tasted earth he would have to scream.

The corpse hand moved to touch his forehead. "Dimitrios." Gregory's voice. Not a grave, then; no one would expect it to hold a vampire. But still there was the darkness. So perhaps a tomb. And he still could not move. "Gregory? Can you see? Where are we?"

"In a cell, somewhere in the London Tower. The one they call Bloody, I believe. I cannot see: there is no light at all, no window."

They had put Clarence in the Bloody Tower. *And then bricked it up.* "How big . . . is the cell?"

"Precisely nine feet six inches by nine feet two inches, English measure."

Dimi laughed. It helped his spirit, if not his headache. "All right, how do you know?"

"The last joint of my little finger is exactly one inch long. And there has been little else to do."

"You must be free to move, then. I don't seem to be."

"Your wrists are chained to the wall, above your head. Can you feel the wall behind you?"

"Now I can."

"Can you feel this?"

"What?" Something stuck his left hand. "Yes. Ouch." A weight bore down on his foot. "That too."

"Good."

Dimitrios said "How did they come to take you?"

Gregory explained his encounter with Doctor Argentine. "Do you know if he was badly hurt, by my shot fragments?"

"I don't think so."

"*Schade.* I was hoping for more even spread . . . Dimitrios, you had seen the doctor, had you not? Did you not notice he was one of my kind?"

"Yes. But I . . . I suppose I knew you too well, and I thought . . ."

"I see." Gregory said something in German. After a moment, he said "And your story?"

Dimi told him.

"Hastings did not kill anyone," Gregory said, "nor the Shore woman. Hastings was treating secretly with the Queen Elizabeth, not trusting Mancini entirely. Mancini was outliving his usefulness, I think; that is why he wrote such a long and detailed letter."

"Which Buckingham is using only selected parts of."

"I helped in that," Gregory said, and there was a silence; then he said "I organized my deciphered text in a manner that would have made such use easy. German scholar at work."

"Then Hywel and Cynthia—"

"There was no mention of them. If they did happen across the plans in Wales . . . and recall, Hywel was looking for such things . . . then I cannot hope they are alive."

"I can hope."

"I did not deny that," Gregory said, from some distance away in the darkness.

"At least, if they are alive, Buckingham doesn't know where to find them. . . . Wait a moment. You said you walked into Buckingham's men just as I did. *But you'd read the letter.*" Please, he thought, if any of them is to be a traitor, let it be the vampire.

"His name did not appear in Mancini's letter."

"What? What does that mean?"

"Perhaps that there was only no news. But Mancini was writing to the Byzantine spymaster in Genova—his name is Angelo Cato, if we are ever able to make use of that—about master plans. Suppose that Buckingham is not part of that plan."

"But we *know* he's allied with them."

"Perhaps they have not told him he is not a part." Gregory's voice was close again. Dimi felt the cold fingers on his hands, on the metal around his wrists. Gregory said *"I' dacht', i' hört die Schlüssel."*

"What?"

"These shackles are locked, not riveted. Excuse me now, but give me some quiet, and I will try to pick the locks."

"How do you expect to do that?"

"I have some pins. Up my sleeve, like a conjuror. Now quiet, please; very soon the cramp will enter your limbs."

"Gregory . . ."

Von Bayern's voice was very close in Dimi's ear. *"Ach, Mensch,* why do you think you are bound and I am free? When they brought you in, they poured a cup from one of Morton's jars down my throat, and what it has done to my hunger I cannot describe to you.

"Now let me open these bands, so that they may keep me from you. . . ."

Chapter 12
TRANSFORMATIONS

IF a holiday in London was like a disorganized melee, then a Coronation was a full-scale war. The aldermen were drumming up spirit and decoration, trying to outshow the rival precinct next door; the bailiffs were closing down the petty gamblers and unlicensed whores who were no longer worth the penny bribes they paid; city engineers marshaled carpenters and stonemasons for the big tasks of repair and debtor gangs for the little offal-carting ones, consulting their maps like grand strategists and occasionally dismantling part of a building that had grown to intrude on the legal street clearances. Ordinary citizens who would not know a glaive from a falchion were wearing swords in the streets, and addressing one another as "Noble Citizen!" whether either word applied; a few ran themselves or one another through, but that was expected. You could even call it prophesied, if you were licensed by the appropriate guild.

For two months there had been no crowned King of England; there was a Queen, but until a week ago she had been missing somewhere, and anyway dowager queens were stale fish on the market. The Return of the King was imminent, and in the dazzling light of that promise the memory that swords were first worn in the streets after Lord Hastings's sudden death bleached away.

Certainly the boys who threw stones at the old witch on

the street were not thinking of politics, and their chant of *Cundrie, Cundrie, pass me by! Loathly Damsel, prophesy!* referred to nothing found on the Parliament Rolls.

A stone hit the limping witch, and she turned her beaked and warty face toward them, and wrote a sign in the air. The urchins ran, whispering charms of protection; baiting the bear was no fun if the bear could bite.

The old woman resumed her foot-dragging walk. It was awkward, but not too slow, and her determination seemed to have no limits. She wore a brown wool cloak over layers of linen skirts, and round-toed leather shoes; stringy gray hair stuck out of her hood all around her ugly coarse-fleshed face.

She walked straight up to the great house on the river, hardly looking left or right, and pounded at the door.

The porter appeared, in cylindrical cap and cloak with rose embroidery, key around his neck. His surprise was hidden in an instant. "Madam?"

"Is Duchess Cecily of York in the house?" said the hag, in a voice that was tired but not at all old.

"I am afraid—"

"Oh . . . what is your name? Hugh." She put a hand to her face, dug the nails deep into the flesh; Hugh Wetherby paled.

And then the warts and wrinkles came away in a handful of charcoal and lard. "Tell the Duchess . . . I'm afraid I've lost her loan to me, and more besides. May I please come in?"

Wetherby took her by the arm and led her in, seeing the tears come to her eyes, wondering whatever could have happened that Madam Cynthia should return in such a state, and without Master Hywel.

Cynthia stepped from the coach into the Tower court-yard just as clouds were gathering; the sudden shadows did not dim her. The Duchess had given her a gown of pale green satin brocaded with white roses, threaded pearl-seeded ribbons in her hair, scented her with Cathay oil. Cecily brought out a walking stick of white ash with a green jade handle, "a gift against my old age I'm far too

vain to use. Now, don't argue. Do you think I'd have sent
my youngest girl to her tournaments without armor? Well,
then."

And indeed she was admitted past the Lion Tower, and
then the Bell, without incident. At the Bloody Tower, the
door was opened by a doddering man in a pop-seamed,
thread-picked surcoat, carrying a partizan that seemed an
impossible load, let alone a useful weapon. He listened patiently to her; listened twice. Then he wandered away,
closing the door on her.

It was opened again by a somewhat more coherent
young man, who was not much more help.

"I fear the Protector is occupied just now. You're a rela-
tive . . . ?"

"No." She wasn't in the spirit to construct worthwhile
lies. "There are two men in his service, Captain Dimitrios
Ducas and Professor Gregory von Bayern. If I might see
one of them?"

The guardsman thought a moment. "Why, yes, I know of
them. But they aren't here. They've gone to Wales."

"Wales . . . ?" she said, wondering if they could have
passed one another, on the road, in the night.

"With the Duke of Buckingham's company. The Duke is
to follow—"

The faint did not begin as a fake. Her legs had really
gone strengthless, and she decided it might as well be
played for useful effect.

"Madam?" The porter was terrified. She wondered why
syncope did that to everyone but the victim. Fear of sudden
death, perhaps, and fear of suddenly having a body at your
feet with everyone staring and no simple explanation.

"Come in, madam. Here—come in here."

Good thing it wasn't a real faint, she thought, as the porter half-led, half-dragged her to a little anteroom, got her
to sit, and then lie, on a trestle table. "I'll fetch a doctor, I
won't be a moment; you just lie there—" and he was gone.

Well, now she was through the gates.

She was tireder than she had thought (though of course
she could never have slept at Baynard's Castle, with Dimi-

trios and Gregory a mile away unmet) and even the wooden table was luring her to sleep. She shifted slightly to one side, and pain lanced up her leg: so much for sleep, she thought, but in a moment she was drifting again.

You can't sleep now. One wink now and you never will wake.

She went on hands and knees along the ditch, wet soil sucking at her, slipping now and then into the cold, muddy water; but the road was infinitely more dangerous.

Soon it was hands and one knee. Her right leg trailed behind her, useless, or at least too painful to be of much use. She tried to assess the damage by the twinges and stabs as she dragged along, knowing that if the ball were still in the wound she might be destroying herself with every movement.

Closing her eyes, she saw Hywel, boots hitting him, and it drove her on, as the rain began to fall hard.

Then she dropped, just on the edge of another rain-swollen ditch, and her arms would not lift her again. She saw them lying in front of her face, but they did nothing. She could not remember how to make them move.

There was light on the water before her, like moonlight. Were the clouds finally breaking, to let the moon through? Wizards sent things in moonlight, she remembered, and sometimes died in the sendings.

She had lost Cecily's owl, she realized. Her eyes hurt, as if she were crying, but any tears would be lost in the rain. Lost the silver owl and gained an ugly blob of lead, an alchemical miracle.

Then she lifted her head a little, and saw what creek it was that washed her fingertips, and the source of the light, and who was hurrying from the thatched cottage, singing the rain off her shoulders; and in a fleeting moment of absolute clarity Cynthia understood the difference between magic and miracles.

"Here are the forceps, sister. Can you feel them?"

"I—" Cold metal. A linkage to pain.

"They're on it now, Cynthia. Pull now, slow and smooth."

A pull on the metal. At the other end of the link, pain flaring. What in the White Lady's name was she *doing?*

And then she knew, and relaxed; she steadied her grip, and drew the bullet from herself.

Mary Setright had called it a providence: if the shot had been a fraction higher, less than recoil would have done in a less adept gunner's hands, or if there had been a pinch more powder behind it, the ball would have shattered the socket of Cynthia's hip. She might still have reached Mary's cottage, but she would never have walked again.

Of these things are legends made, she said finally to Mary, thank all the Gods our Lady Cynthia was shot in the rump . . . and Mary went, very quickly, from the room.

Later, Cynthia said, "Why did you do that . . . run away?"

"Why, sister, I didn't want you to see me crying."

"But it was a joke, Mary, that's all," and she reached up from the bed to pull Mary close, afraid suddenly that she had insulted the healer's strange quiet god.

"I know, sister, of course I know that; and I couldn't but cry, because I knew then you were going to be well."

Eventually they had to talk about Hywel. "I cannot find him," Mary said, simply as fact. "I have faith he is still alive. . . ." Cynthia knew she must be frowning; Mary took her hand and smiled. "Yes, just faith. Peredur is so torn, between his wish to go light on the earth and his need to *do.* . . . When he leaves us, I think something will happen, but I think it will be quiet."

"Did you love him?"

"Why, I do love him, sister." Mary began to rock her chair. "And yes, I loved him, and would again if he asked me. Someday we will be only spirit, and all one; but here on earth we're made of earth, and sometimes flesh must touch." She got up, poured hot water from the kettle into a pot of dried dandelions.

"When I first knew Hywel, he had two eyes, you know; and they were of different colors. He had made the one. I don't know how he lost the eye he was born with, or if he never had one there. But this eye troubled him. What it saw was . . . different from what his natural eye could see."

"Different?" Cynthia took a cup of tea.

"As you may look at a forest one day, and see this tree and that, and some day other trees, and another day just a mass of woods. Sometimes it hurt Hywel to look with both eyes at once, 'like a hot knife splitting my brain,' he said. And, being Hywel, he began to worry that he should prefer the made eye to the born one." Mary looked into her teacup.

Cynthia said, "You . . . put out his magic eye." She could see it being done, in her mind: she had done it, with the small curved knife and the hot cautery, before the healthy eyeball could sag and die in sympathy.

"Oh, no, sister. There are things one's own hand must do. But I cared for his wound."

And in her thoughts, then, Cynthia was not cutting out an eye, but pulling a bullet from a wound; she hurt beneath her dressings.

"You see, sister," Mary said, sweet analgesia in her voice, "why I could not have restored your leg entire. Hywel does not know he taught me this, but he taught it me with the eye from his own head. How could I not love him?"

"Here she is, Doctor."

"I can see that, porter."

Cynthia heard the Italian accent. She kept her eyes closed, trying to place it: Genovese, she thought. Thank Minerva, a free state. Perhaps it was even someone she knew.

"Will she be all right, Doctor Argentine?"

"I am certain she will be fine. But there is scarcely any air in this room with three; would you leave us?"

"Of course, Doctor. Shall I tell—"

"There isn't anyone with any time to spare." Was that impatience in the doctor's voice? "Besides, I'm certain she'll be on her way in a very short time."

She opened her eyes as the door closed. The doctor stood

looking after it, a thin man in a light gray gown. He turned toward her.

She did not suppose at all that the flush in his cheeks was from the cold.

"Are you awake, *Signorina?*"

"*Sì, Dottore.*"

Argentine tilted his head, leaned over her with a curious expression. Then suddenly his left hand came down on her throat, his whole weight behind it. The crook of his thumb pinched her without quite strangling, but she could get no leverage, certainly not with her bad hip, and his fingertips might have been iron spikes driven into the tabletop.

"*Per ché, Dottore . . . ?*"

"Because I'm hungry, *uccellina.* That old simpleton Giles caused me to have strawberries for breakfast. . . . Wait a moment." Argentine's thumb scissored on her throat, and his face swam in grayness. "I know who you must be," he said. "You're the Greek's woman."

Dimitrios, she thought.

"*Magnifico!* You may join him, then. There's plenty of room for you."

Where did he mean? In the grave?

"Very little light, I admit—"

Her right hand brushed her cane, on the table beside her.

"But he'll be pleased to hear your voice."

All right, she thought, so coolly she surprised herself; I will allow you your lust, and then when you have taken me to where Dimitrios is, then we shall see.

Gregory said he needed no more than a cupful. That would not weaken her too much, if Argentine did not spill much. There was the possibility he would batter her. And there was the chance that he would give her the disease, but it was small in a single feeding. One in eleven, she recalled. She started to catalogue every article on hematophagic anaemia she had ever read, titles and authors, sending her mind away; even lost Fiorenza was a better place than this.

Argentine said "The Greek captain's probably almost

dry by now . . . but you and the German can quarrel over his dregs." He brought his face to within inches of hers, bit his lip. Thin blood welled. Contaminated blood; certain inoculation if it entered her system.

No, she thought, not that, not for anyone's sake.

She grasped the jade handle of Cecily's cane, squeezed the ferrule. The handle and a six-inch stiletto blade parted from the wood with no sound at all.

Argentine showed his teeth, and she slipped the knife into the back of his neck, pushing at his chin with her left hand to keep the teeth away.

He cried out, lost his grip on her and then his balance, fell on the floor as his brain sought to recover his muscles. She dragged herself off the table, crouched, slashed across his gown, his shirt, his chest, his pulsing heart.

It was terrible surgery, and she began to weep for the profanity of the act. But as the tears ran, she searched his body, and found a ring of keys.

She stood, draped her cloak to hide the pale bloodstains on her dress, and went to find the locks to Argentine's keys.

She had no great trouble moving about the Tower; there were too many people too intent on their business. She simply acted as if she knew where she was going, and would make trouble for anyone preventing her. Someone had left a pile of gowns upon a hall table; she lifted one near enough to her size and changed in a convenient closet, using a wall hook to pull the back lacings tight.

One of the keys opened a suite of rooms, Argentine's by the equipment scattered around it; others unlocked the apartment closets. Another appeared to be for a similar suite elsewhere, but she could not find it. It seemed doubtful that Dimi and Gregory would be confined in these rooms.

That left one key, of black iron and oversized. And it left a great deal of the Tower to search—assuming it was even to a Tower door. They might as easily be prisoners in any cellar in London.

Cynthia started for the door, then paused and slipped Argentine's medical pannier over her shoulder. Feeling more whole than in months, she went into the corridor.

The old porter was standing there, holding his partizan at an alarming angle.

Cynthia paused before him. He did not seem to see her. She took the iron key from the ring and held it out to him.

He took it, shouldered his spear, and without a word started down the corridor. She followed, through a hall, and a gallery lined with dusty armors, and down a staircase five full turns; she realized they must be well below ground level.

Very little light, Argentine had said.

The porter struck fire to a wall lantern; Cynthia saw a short corridor with two doors to either side. The porter put the key in a door, turned it.

She could not wait any longer. She pushed past the old man as the door opened, stepped into the darkness beyond. "Dimitrios? Gregory?" Her foot struck something soft, and she knew what it was: a man, dead. It was too dark to tell any more.

"Cynthia?" said a weak voice.

"Yes, Dimitrios. Is this . . . is Gregory—"

"Gregory's sleeping," the voice said. As her eyes adjusted, she could just make out the figures at the back of the cell, faint gray shapes in the lanternlight from the door.

"Then . . . who is this?"

"A man named Dominic Mancini . . . a Byzantine spy at the end of his usefulness. Cynthia . . . are you all right?"

"Fine," she said. There would be time later for details. "We must get you out of here. Wake Gregory."

The only response was a long, shuddering sigh. Pneumonia, she thought. Doubtless it had killed Mancini.

Dimitrios said "How did you find . . . this place?"

"A Doctor Argentine—"

"Run," Dimi said, grating. "Run, Cynthia, now."

"The vampire is dead," she said, and at once hoped

Gregory had not heard. "He told me you were here, and Gregory. But he did not mention this man."

"He wouldn't have known. Buckingham brought him, only . . . well. Not long ago."

Buckingham, she thought; we will find him next, and he will tell us where Hywel is. Then Dimi's statement penetrated. "But then . . . what did this man die of, so quickly?"

There was a pause.

"Dimi?"

"He lost too much blood," Dimitrios said weakly.

And Gregory is sleeping, she thought, and wondered that she could at once feel so revolted, and so sad.

Dimitrios said "And then I stuck a pin in his heart, and broke his neck, and cut the cord with half of one of his eyeglasses. Then, just before he went to sleep, Gregory made me promise to do the same to him, before he woke . . . but I couldn't, I just couldn't. . . .

"Buckingham brought us another present, along with Mancini, you see. I used it on Mancini's neck. It's still there."

She reached to the dead man's collar. Silver flashed, and diamonds. The owl pendant looked up from Cynthia's palm, shadows making it look mournful.

Dimi's voice fell to a whisper. "After I saw that, I thought . . . just what he wanted me to think. And I couldn't lose all three of you."

Richard Gloucester, Protector of England, sat in the Council Chamber with his head on his folded hands. "The Duke of York is with the King," he said, supremely bitter. "The Protector, in his wisdom and power, succeeded in withdrawing the King's brother from sanctuary." He brought down his hands hard on the arms of his chair.

Dimitrios said "The Duke of Buckingham, Richard, and the wizard—"

"We'll get them. Oh, yes, we'll get them." He stood up suddenly, walked behind his chair. "But in two days' time we're to crown King of England a boy who cannot possibly be accepted as king. . . .

"And yet there has to be a king. When Hastings . . . died
. . . there were nearly riots in the streets, people thinking
we were back to the successive wars again." He went to
the windows overlooking the spot where Hastings had
been killed. Snow was falling, straight down and becoming
heavy. *"Oh,"* Richard said. "Hastings's mistress . . . she's
still in a cell. There just isn't any limit to the people need-
lessly hurt by this, is there." He turned back, shaking his
head, his shoulders very bent. "What are we going to do
about the boys?"

Cynthia said "Does their mother know?"

"No."

Dimi said "Can you communicate with her at all, without Hastings or Mancini?"

"Oh, we found her sanctuary." Richard looked at Dimitrios. "It wasn't in the Pantheon at all; they were in a cellar of Warwick's old inn—certainly not a place I'd have
looked early. Master Mancini was leading you on a dragged
scent."

Dimi nodded, disappointed and a little angry. Then he
thought of the two Mancinis he had seen, just before the
trail went cold. "Your pardon, sir, but I wonder. Suppose
Mancini were going to a meeting, but not with the Queen."

Richard looked thoughtful. "You want Buckingham,
don't you, brother?"

"Yes, my lord, I do."

The door opened; a woman and a child came in, with a
man behind them. The man was James Tyrell. "Annie!"
Richard said and went to put his arms around his wife,
while his son looked up curiously. Dimi turned away, saw
Cynthia looking at Duchess Anne with a vaguely concerned expression.

Richard broke the clinch, looking only slightly embarrassed. "Tyrell, I was going to fault your timing, but it's
perfect as always." He knelt. "And how fare you, my lord
of Middleham?"

Dimitrios looked at Tyrell, and was surprised: he had
never seen the man look so uncomfortable. Sir James had

a wife, Dimi knew, and sons. Surely he was not so put out by little domesticities. Or maybe he was just homesick.

Richard looked up. "You may not have Buckingham, Dimitrios. He is still a duke, and more things that we have hastily made him, and he requires Royal justice."

"I understand, Your Grace. And is the wizard—"

"I'm not done with Harry Stafford yet. Nothing is emptier than justice passed on an absent party. Hunt him down, Captain, and fetch him back. I know it isn't nearly enough, but it's what I can give you. As for the wizard, no obligations of nobility apply, but he's not worth losing anyone to his curse."

Edward of Middleham said to his father, "Mama said we were going to see the King get his crown. When, Papa?"

Richard looked at Anne, whose expression was first simply unknowing, then apprehensive as she saw Richard's face.

The Duke patted his son's shoulder. "Soon, Edward." He stood up. "Tyrell, get a coach for my family; they'll be staying with the Duchess."

Anne said "Is something wrong, Richard?" Her voice was thin, and a little shrill.

"You like staying with Mother, don't you? I've never heard you say otherwise, and you know how Edward is about her picture books." Then Richard said suddenly "The King's got a cold. The doctor"—he indicated Cynthia—"says it'll be all right, but it's catching like fire, he's already given it to Dick of York."

Anne looked at Cynthia, who sat uncomfortably on a straight chair with her jade-handled stick against her knee. If anything passed between the two women, Dimi could not detect it.

Anne said "Well, then, dear, we'll be going. Say goodbye, Edward, and Sir James will take us to Grandmother's." Dimi could see that she did not believe her husband, supposed he wouldn't have, either. Richard simply wasn't a very good liar, and Dimi felt he had seen enough expertise to judge.

Edward bowed gravely from the waist, said "Good day to

you all, my lady and gentlemen, and to you, my noble father."

When they had gone, Richard said "And now . . ." He
held up his left arm, felt the spot where he had been bled at
York. "And now we begin breaking oaths."

The last of the fir branches about the image of Janus had
crumbled to the littered floor of the temple cubicle. Even
the minor, half-forgotten gods were getting offerings now,
with the Coronation coming, but this temple was utterly
forgotten.

Except, Dimi thought, that one of the wall mirrors was
clean of dust.

"This one," he said, "you two cover us," and stepped
clear. His two crossbowmen braced their backs against the
opposite wall, aimed at the panel. The two spearmen
raised the butts of their weapons and smashed the glass.

Beyond was a passageway, large enough for a crouching
man, light flickering at its end.

There was a muffled explosion across the room, and the
sound of glass splintering. One of the crossbowmen cried
out and dropped his bow; the quarrel slipped from its notch
and the spring thumped. The man fell, folding over. At the
small of his back was a red crater. A set gun, mounted in
the wall behind one of the mirrors, had cut him almost in
two from zero range.

"Sir, is there more o'such . . . ?" one of the spearmen
said. "Probably," Dimi said, drew his long sword, and
started into the tunnel.

He emerged into a circular room, larger than the first,
hung with red velvet and white silk. On a wall between
red draperies and a pair of wildly flaring silver sconces
was what Dimi at first thought was a doorway, but it was a
mirror, framed like a doorway. There were elaborate carv-
ings, like knots, in the posts and lintel.

In the center of the floor was a whitish circle with the
sheen of metal, carved with two entwined dragons, one
light and one dark.

"All right," Dimi said, letting his men on in, "tear it apart."

"That isn't necessary," a voice said, and the Duke of Buckingham appeared from behind the draperies. There was a lighted red taper in his left hand. He wore a robe of red China silk, with the tail and head of a dragon embroidered over the shoulders: he was apparently naked beneath it.

"No, I'm not a sorcerer," he said, almost jovial. "But you'd be amazed by how much help they ask for sometimes, creating their effects. . . . Not that these effects are minor." He ran his toe along the edge of the floor disc.

"Is Morton back there?"

"No. I suppose he's home at Holborn. Home is a good place to be. Home and warm, home and dry." His voice pitched up. "Home upon the quartered wind, round the earth and home again, lodestone of the heart is turning, open, way, and home by morning." He blew out the candle and ran for the mirror in the wall.

Dimi started to move, to call for a spear to crack the glass.

Buckingham collided with the mirror. He gasped. Cracks radiated around his head, one of his knees; his nose was bleeding.

"Morton!" he howled.

Buckingham staggered back from the broken glass. He turned, saw the soldiers, then turned again and made, awkwardly, for the draperies where he had first appeared.

Dimi put his sword away as Buckingham stumbled by; he drew his boot knife, raised his arm.

Buckingham began to push the curtains apart. There was a door beyond. Dimi's knife went through the broad sleeve of the Duke's robe just above his right arm, nicking the skin, nailing the sleeve to the wooden door. Buckingham groaned and sank down, his weight pushing the door open, while his pinned sleeve held his arm straight up.

Beyond the door, Dimi could see alchemical glassware, smell acids and hot metal. It smells like a battlefield back there, he thought, and it took one moment more to realize it was because of the scent of decaying flesh.

"Morton, damn you," Buckingham was muttering, as Dimi pulled his knife free and hauled the Duke to his feet. "None of it was ever for me, was it?" He turned to Dimitrios. "Tell Richard . . . to hold on tight to the crown, now, and watch like Heimdall for the man the East sends to collect it."

"My master is not the King," Dimi said, more for the curious troopers' benefit than the Duke's.

"You're not an idiot, Ducas," Buckingham said, with coarse good humor still showing through. "Of course he'll usurp the crown. What other choice did we give him?"

The two boys were on the floor of the Royal apartments, shooting marbles on the carpet.

"That's a keeper."

"No, it isn't. It's only a keeper if it stops on one of the white places."

"That's white."

"No, it isn't, it's silver. We need more light."

"More light makes my eyes hurt, and besides, silver is white."

"No, it isn't."

"Is too. You don't know anything about heraldry. You didn't even know the doctor's name meant silver."

"I—"

"Look."

The King of England brushed his gold hair out of his reddened eyes and stood up. The Duke of York rose to his knees and looked the visitors up and down, running a livid tongue over his lips.

How much easier if the legends were true, Gregory thought. Anyone could throw a bat on the fire, and wolves were shot down almost as habit. But here were just two children playing. And then if it needed just a scratch from a silver edge, or a handful of mustard seeds over the grave, why, the town fool could rid the world of vampires.

"Hello, Sir James," Edward said. "And who are you, sir?"

"This is Sir Gregory of Bavaria," Tyrell said, as Gregory put his bag on the table and unlaced it. "A German knight-doctor."

Edward said "Uncle Richard said Doctor Argentine had to go away to Italy, but we would have a new doctor. Are you the one?"

"Richard said the doctor was a lady," said the Duke of York.

"You don't know anything. That was the other doctor, the one Uncle Anthony brought to Ludlow. I liked her."

"It was she who sent me," Gregory said, which was only the truth. Doctor Ricci was tired of killing his kind, she said. *Tired*. As if she knew what it meant to be tired.

"Have you brought some blood? We haven't had any blood for a day and a half. There were some birds outside the window, but when we killed one once it tasted awful, and Doctor Argentine said it was bad for us. Anyway, Uncle Richard says we can't go into the courtyard, because of the men at work."

The Duke of York peered close at Gregory. "You're one of us, aren't you? A Perfect, like Doctor Argentine."

The perfection, to feed on humankind alone. "Yes."

"You see?" York said triumphantly. "I *do* know something." He looked up at Tyrell. "Did Uncle Richard send you to feed us, Sir James? We haven't done that with anyone but Doctor Argentine, but he said it would happen very soon."

Gregory saw the sweat start on Tyrell's forehead, thought his high leather collar and gorget must be choking him. The henchman said nothing, but held out a gloved hand.

Edward said "You go first, brother."

"Oh, no, Your Grace."

"Yes, do." Then he whispered "King's Taster!" and the two boys laughed.

Edward said "You would know this, Sir James: do dead people bleed?"

Tyrell said "It depends, my lord . . . but usually they may, for a little while."

Told you, York mouthed, and went toward Tyrell.

"Then when I'm King, with my crown," Edward said, "we'll take all the dead murderers, after they've hanged, and give their blood to everyone who's hungry. And when someone has his head chopped off for treason, that will be just for the Lords. . . . Doctor Argentine said they don't even do that in Byzantium."

"No," Gregory said, "even in Byzantium that is not done."

Tyrell said "I have him now, Sir Gregory."

Edward's eyes widened. "What are you doing, Sir James? Let my brother go. I order it! Doctor, make him let York go!"

Gregory thought perhaps town fools should be recruited for this work: they were capable of great singleness of purpose, and if they ever thought of their own mortality it did not worry them.

"Bite him, brother!"

"Tyrell is dressed in steel and thick leather," Gregory said, "and biting me will not change anything." He closed his hand on Edward's shoulder, drew the scalpel, thinking all the while of Cynthia.

He told her she could never understand what it was to drink at another's life until it was all gone, the omnipotent pleasure of it. Because he had known, every moment, what he was doing to Dominic Mancini. He had always feared that hunger would make him mindless, but the actual horror was that it had not.

"I suppose I cannot understand," she said. "That's why I can't do it, and you must. You do know. And because of that, you're the only one who can do it without hating them."

In that she was right, he thought, as he made the second stroke, and the boy shuddered in his arms and was still. There was no hate in it. Perhaps that was actually the important thing, that there not be hate.

How else explain that he still lived?

* * *

John Morton strolled between his strawberry vines, pausing to pinch back a leaf or adjust a wire on a stake. He reached into the greenery, plucked out a berry two inches across; he scrubbed it with his thumb and took a small bite.

Above him, snow was falling heavily, and outside the garden walls it was four inches thick on the ground. There was no wind, but a few yards over Morton's head the flakes were suddenly whipped aside. Only in a far corner of the garden did the snow come through, and in the last feet of its fall it thawed, to land as gentle rain.

"Magister Maleficarum Johannes Mortoni," Richard of Gloucester announced from across the rows of vines, "you are under arrest for the practice of injurious and criminal sorcery—"

"There are problems with 'criminal sorcery' as a legal concept, you know," Morton said calmly. "One doesn't accuse a false coiner of 'criminal metal-pressing,' or a man who steals city water of 'criminal plumbing.' " He took another bite of fruit.

"Dcotor Morton, you are not a man who deserves warning, but I warn you to take care."

"There *is* 'criminal trespass,' of course. That's what you're doing, my lord of Gloucester, with your armed men there. But it's not hard to mend: Come in, Your Grace, and your company. And you are innocent! This is mighty sorcery indeed, don't you agree?" He swallowed the last of the berry, went to a row of small trees bearing green fruit. "I'll have blood oranges in a week or so. Sorry now I wasted the space. But it would have been a nice variation on the berry jars: cut one with a silver knife and instead of juice . . ."

"Will my lord wizard walk to the Tower, or be dragged there in irons?" Richard said furiously.

"Neither, I think." He plucked one of the unripe oranges, turned it over, displaying a blemish on its rind. "There is only one thing to be done with a rotten fruit, my lord Protector." The orange began to shrivel up in Morton's fingers, until it was as black and wrinkled as a peachstone;

then that crumbled to dust. "Who will you have kill them, Richard? James Tyrell? Or the Greek mercenary? I've wondered, if I sent his name to the record-keepers of the East, what reply I would get; the Ducai were an Imperial family."

He chuckled. "Does it surprise you that I should know such things? It's the essence of magic, you know, deception and misdirection until the unexpected wonder is produced. The same is true in a court of law."

He reached into his armpit, produced a green orange, showed the same blemish on its side.

"I know what you're thinking," Morton said, "and without putting my fingers into your mind. It's another fruit, and I made the bruises myself, with my thumb. Which is entirely possible, but you have no way of proving it." He tossed the orange aside.

"Now, you have two blemished fruits plucked from the tree of English nobility. But you also need something to show England, so the nature of the blemish never becomes known.

"I have a contract of marriage between King Edward the Fourth and Lady Eleanor Butler, antedating by some years the marriage of Edward and Lady Elizabeth Woodville. It's quite valid, witnessed and sealed by Stillington of Bath, and best of all, never annulled."

"Eleanor Butler's dead," Richard said.

"But *after* Edward's marriage to Elizabeth Woodville. Now, indeed, if Edward and his overt Queen had ever repeated their vows since Eleanor died, their children would be as legal as . . . oh, your son, say. But I happen to know that they did not. Doubtless Edward felt marrying Elizabeth once was enough for even his full life. And so the boys in the Tower, or wherever you've stuck them, are as bastard as . . . well, your first two.

"Now, I assure you that you will not find the document by searching me, or Holborn Hall, or every rabbit hole in England. But I will consider a general pardon by *supersedas*, and a safe-conduct to no specified destination, fair exchange for it." He smiled benignly. "I am not a man who craves personal wealth, as you know."

"Damn your exchange," Richard said evenly. "We'll get Stillington's oath."

Morton shook his head. "He's a shaky old fellow, mind and body. And remember, many of the population you have to convince haven't even a bigamous marriage about their births. No, it's Edward's duplicity you have to prove, and for that you need the paper."

Richard looked pensive. Then he said "I don't think so. It sounds . . . petty." He turned, called to the garden gate. "Doctor, what did you determine to be the condition of the Prince of Wales when you examined him at Ludlow?"

Cynthia pushed back her hood and stepped forward, her cane sinking into the soft garden soil. "A nodular inflammation of the arteries, Your Grace. Certainly fatal, perhaps within only a few months."

"And did this disease cause the Prince's death?"

"In my trained opinion, to which I am willing to swear publicly, the disease began the chain of physical events which led to his death."

"And the Duke of York?"

"One of the Prince's complications was communicated to the young Duke. Had I been . . . available, I would have made clear the hazards of keeping the children together."

Morton applauded. *"Bravo! Bravissima, Signorina Dottorina!* You see, Richard, the value of the surprise witness: you have me completely helpless. Now, how ever will I save my life?"

Richard said "Buckingham swears he turned Hywel Peredur over to you, alive. Where is he?"

"Ah, my lord wizard Peredur. When I saw the lady, I thought we might come around to him." He turned to Cynthia, bowed slightly. "And may I say, Doctor Ricci, I am quite pleased to see you alive. The troopers were quite confident they had killed you . . . but tell me, how did you survive? You did not suffer too greatly, I hope?"

Cynthia said "It is a long story, my lord wizard, which I would not give you the pleasure of hearing."

"You wrong me, madam," Morton said, and the hurt in his voice was startlingly authentic. "I am a pure thaumaturge; nothing I do is for its spiritual sake, but for a practical end. It was not I who had a man drowned in wine, or sent a woman to the rack for being a dead king's mistress." He reached out to his vines, picked a scarlet berry. "I do not prune my vines because I hate the leaves, nor water them for the pleasure of drowning insects, and if I sometimes sow the . . . strawberries of discord, then others willingly serve them at their tables."

"Then tell us where Hywel is," Cynthia said, wondering if a person could completely lose track of when he himself was lying.

"You know I cannot do that. Not now that I know it's what you want." He looked at Richard. "I'm not on speaking terms with Nimue."

Richard said, controlling himself, "Are you really in any position to bargain?"

Morton offered the strawberry to Cynthia, who did not respond; he shrugged and took a bite. "We're back to the doomed boys. You still haven't any case the commons will understand; the reputation of a Ricci of Florence means nothing to them, nor will rare diseases. You see," he said, very gently, "their children die every day, without ever seeing a doctor. The highly born have doctors, a sort of engineer-priest who cures. It isn't true, of course, but they really don't believe your children die." He sighed. "And as many of them believe this lady is not even mortal, they will not believe the explanation she proposes."

"They'll believe me," said a voice from the gateway, and a man came forward, tossing off his cloak. Beneath it he wore velvet and silver and steel, and the daylight through the whirling snow made highlights on his yellow hair.

Morton opened his mouth, but could not seem to find his voice. Finally he managed one word: *"Rivers?"*

"Surprise," Anthony Woodville said.

"I heard your death ordered of the steadfast James Tyrell," said Morton, recovering rapidly. "Is there no one in England a man may trust?"

"Fortunately, the messenger to the steadfast Sir James was the headstrong Squire Bennett, and Tyrell decided to deliver me to Richard instead of Pluto.

"Look now, Doctor, I understand better than Richard how it is between rival scholars, but I agree that you ought to tell us where Doctor Peredur is."

"Oh, I dare not, sir; it is all my life is worth." There was a fluttering motion in the air above, and all looked up: a red and gold cloak fluttered down, batlike, and alighted on Morton's shoulders. He wrapped it around himself. "I have been confined before. I suppose you will torture me, as much as you dare. But I warn you, when you do it you will be thinking of what Peredur may be suffering in exchange, and eventually you will torture yourselves into letting me go."

He began to walk toward the garden gate. As he passed Cynthia, he paused and said, "When you accused me of an unnatural passion of spirit, did you know that Anthony Woodville was here?"

Just outside the gate, a group of soldiers was waiting. Two of them held cold iron chains ready.

"Not here. Please," Morton said, looking back at his vines and fruit trees, at the dome of deflected snow above. "Later, of course you must, but not here . . . I don't want to see it, when they all die."

London was alive with lights, from lanterns and scented wax candles down the scale of cost and smoke to tallow-dips and rushlights, all shining off the crisp snow and the low pink clouds. Partly it was for Iambolc, the February light festival, but mostly it was for the Coronation.

As with any fairytale event, there had been a string of omens and ominous appearances by villain and hero figures. The Duke of Buckingham was attainted traitor on numinous (and, it was said, unspeakable) grounds, and then took a fall down Tower stairs that cheated the heads-man of his neck. The fell sorcerer Morton being confined securely, the population of North-West London tore his house and gardens to pieces in search of treasure or human bones. Finding neither, a farmer brought some blighty wheat and sowed it in the garden, salt being too precious for such a use; and *John Morton!* joined the names used for counting-out rhymes and scaring naughty children.

And then there were the Princes. Aldermen and dung-carters, shoemakers and priests of aloof Thoth all wept when Earl Rivers told of their end. None of them had a wish to see the bodies of two dead of a confinement disease, knowing childbed fever and the bloody catarrh and galloping flux well enough.

But they did talk. Rumors appeared about Richard and the children's death as if they were being coined by a machine. It was a good cause to brawl over, tied as it was to how you felt about Northerners or the loose atmosphere of Edward's court (and bed-chamber), Hastings's death or Clarence's or Humphrey the last Protector's if you were old enough to recall that and still brawl.

There was a need for a crowned king, even if you did not believe the talk that the land was wounded without him. And the ceremonies had developed a momentum, which like that of a charging body of cavalry could not be stopped, but only deflected. And so the crowns and robes were resized and the formal documents rewritten from Edward V to Richard III.

There were few other differences in the result. It was a Coronation, time to reaffirm hope and life and joy.

In many of the windows, lights were going out.

"I'm sorry," Dimitrios said. "A man with any honor or wit would have understood the invitation for what it was. Your thanks are sufficient, and accepted. Good night, Mistress Shore."

"Wait, Captain . . . please wait."

He stopped in the doorway.

"It is . . . difficult to know what to tell a man who has rescued one from a dungeon."

Especially, Dimi thought, when that man helped to put you there. He turned. She sat on the edge of the bed, framed by the gold-tasseled canopy. Her sleeves were unbuttoned, and her hair was loose . . . though it had been severely cut.

She was smiling.

Dimitrios said "Dungeons aren't very . . . conversational places. I know."

"No. There is no weather down there, nor any news, except what they think will persuade one to confess. And 'are you well?' is the cruelest thing that they say." She looked at the ceiling, struggling with some memory. "It was not that they hurt me so much," she said, quite calm. "As you see, my limbs are all still in place. And they showed me the whip with metal ends, but used only the leather. It was . . . it was that they were always hurting me, so I could not rest from it or . . . or do anything. I never even had time to hate them."

Then she laughed, astonishingly without bitterness or fear, but a pleasant and bell-like sound. "Ah, my. Like Ishtar I am come out of the pit. Maybe I will be a little wiser for it. . . . Sit down, Captain, you look like something of wood, there to prop up the door. No, don't sit there—here."

She offered a hand, and he took it. There was a linen bandage on her wrist, all day old and a little soiled, still smelling faintly of cold unguent. His own wrists were too toughened by leather bracers to have been marked in the short time he had been shackled. But she was not made for such uses.

"Here we are again, where we were just a moment ago," she said. "Shall we try again? I was thanking you for releasing me."

"What I should have said . . ." Was good night and fare you well, he thought, but said ". . . is that I am not a very successful savior."

"Why? Even Galahad accepted ladies' favors for saving them." She tugged gently at his collar. "And he could not have carried so many scarves as that."

"Say rather . . . what I rescue is often lost again." As she touched his cheek, he felt his nerves awaking, but knew that he could lose even that.

"Oh. Then I should say that I am not a very successful

lover, because what I have loved is all lost: my Edward, and kind Will Hastings . . . and Master Shore, who was to me what a candle in the window is." She looked past him, at the candle in the bedside holder, and its images danced in her liquid eyes.

She said suddenly "They could not have broken me otherwise," and was at once far away from tears. "But they said my lovers were all dead, and I confessed it as I must, and in the lawyers' papers that was witchcraft." She looked at her toes. "Am I redeemed, Captain?"

"The King has granted you a full pardon."

"I do not mean a pardon at law. Am I redeemed, for my losses?" She looked him eye to eye. Her breath warmed his lips. "Are you redeemed, for yours?"

She struggled to smile again, as someone moving a great weight. Then, with a quiet humor, she said "If we are neither to be redeemed, then there is only one solution. Promise me that you will not try to save me, Captain, and I will promise not to love you."

"I . . . promise, my lady."

She did not draw back from him. "We have a truce, then?"

"A truce?" Then he understood. "Yes, my lady."

"Thank Lady Freya," she said. "I could not have been at war much longer."

Her fingers encircled his unscarred wrists as he kissed her cropped hair.

The warm spiced wine was halfway gone, and half the candles in the room were put out. "What did Morton mean," Cynthia said, "when he asked about . . . you, and pain?"

Anthony Woodville leaned forward in his chair, winecup in interlaced hands. "You aren't easily shocked, I think, Doctor. . . ."

"I'll tell you when it happens," she said evenly. She supposed that he would not shock her. Disgust, perhaps. Disappoint, certainly.

Rivers stood, turned his chair, sat down again facing

away from her. He pulled a brooch, and his gown slipped down to drape over the chair's arms and back. Then he tugged open his shirt lacings and let that too slide down.

She judged that the newest of the scars was at least five years old; some seemed far older. It was apparent that they had been quite deep cuts, but that was not the disturbing thing; mere enthusiasm could make the scourge bite deep. It was the regularity of the marks, precise in angle and spacing: the work had been done with care, with science. With love.

"Someone . . . did this to you," she said, though nothing could have been more evident. She wished that she had not drunk so much.

"It was something I had done to me."

"But why?"

"At first it was because of someone I killed," Rivers said. "Then it was worship, when I discovered those gods. But soon enough I discarded that, and it was done because it pleased me that it be done."

"Why?" she said. "Why you?" And it was not shock, or disgust, or disappointment; it was despair, where she had not even been aware she had had any hope.

"It is no longer my ruling passion," he said, and his shoulders drew tight, the lattice showing redly.

"But still your . . . your . . ." She felt choked. "Would you ever have noticed me, if you had not seen me first with a knife in my hand?"

Rivers gave a small, very tight groan. He pulled his clothing up to cover his shoulders, stood up, turned to face her. "You are a most well-favored woman, Doctor, and I hope I shall have the pleasure of your conversation many times after this. But I would not ask for anything more, knowing that you would doubt the reason." He went to the hallway door. "Especially when I would doubt it as well."

His movements were relaxed, supremely dignified. She watched him go, thinking that she must do nothing, for if she forgave him this there would be nothing she would not forgive him.

Or perhaps all it meant was that there was true forgiveness in her.

She grasped her stick and pushed herself up from the chair. It would not do to go hobbling after him. "Anthony," she said, calmly, and he paused.

She had been an expert witness many times in the Florentine courts, her services being especially desired in cases of rape. As the death penalty was not rare if the victim were noble, certainty was required: and she had found no sign more certain than the withdrawal from, the fear of love, and not merely of physical occupation.

Now she needed to know how frightened she was.

Anthony said "What would you have me say, Doctor Ricci? That roses have thorns? I am a better poet than that."

"I am not English, but I have been told that the word of an English knight is an antidote to doubt."

"Do you . . . pity me, madam?" The feeling was all forced out of his face, but she could hear the traces in his voice, knew that he had despaired too.

She wondered how she could ever have confused this man with a fanatical little wretch in a Florentine apartment, when the difference between them was the difference between shame and glory.

What did you want, Ricci? she thought. We're all damaged.

"On earth we're all earth," she said, "and flesh must touch." Now she needed to touch, know if it was all right for her.

He caused her some pain—she was old to be starting this, she knew, and the tissues were thickened, not to mention her hip—but at his sob and soft murmur she knew he had not meant it, and then she knew that it was all right, and then it was more than all right.

Gregory von Bayern watched from his window as the lights of London went out. It was a good night, he thought, to be at peace with the world. His room was dark, except for a circle of white light thrown by the lamp on his worktable.

In the light were some sketches, his bullet molds, a small pan of congealed lead over a cold spirit burner, and some tiny glass jars labeled in German, all around a spanlong cylinder of wood, with a hole at one end and slots along its sides.

He opened a drawer and took out his small metal gun, checked its load. Then he picked up the cylinder, pushed its end over the muzzle of the gun; the front blade sight slid in a key-way, and a quarter-turn locked the two parts together.

Gregory thumbed a bit of sawdust from the cylinder, checked its vents for excess traces of glycerine and powdered metal. When a thing can only be done once, he thought, that is the time to do it perfectly.

It would be, he thought, a sort of final triumph of German technology over Byzantine: the Eastern Empire had never mastered the channeling of high-temperature products that made German projectiles and infernal devices the best.

The device on the end of his gun, when ignited by a gunshot, would according to design create a roughly eggshaped zone, two yards high and one across, for eight seconds at the temperature of boiling iron. He wished the circumstances permitted a fire of longer duration, that he might vanish except for some lumps of metal . . . and his teeth, probably. Teeth were surprisingly refractory. He knew an alchemist in Westfalen who was trying to master a synthetic tooth coating.

But the fire he had constructed was sufficient for himself.

Gregory stepped to the center of the room, away from objects which might cause secondary fires. There had never been any thought in his mind of writing an explanatory letter. There was no explaining to them the taste of their blood in his mouth.

He primed the gunlock, held the weapon close to his chest, pointed upward.

His door opened. A man was standing there, dressed in Tower livery and holding a spear: Giles, the feeble-minded porter. He held out a large key of black iron.

"Very well," Gregory said, and followed Giles, thrusting the gun into the belt of his gown. He wondered if the true nature of his damnation was that he should always be interrupted just at any moment when he had ceased to hate himself.

Giles, and then Gregory, stopped in front of the cell door. From within there was a sound, long and wailing.

Gregory knew very well that no ordinary scream could carry through that door. John Morton was no ordinary man, of course, but von Bayern did not believe in demons summoned from the Pit.

He took the gun from his belt, turned the cylinder on the muzzle to unlock it, but did not take it off. He nodded to Giles, who put the key in the lock.

As the door opened, the cry came again: then Gregory saw that it did come from Morton, but it was not a human sound.

Cold intruded on Cynthia's warmth like the blade of a knife. She gave a small, shrill cry, and reached for Anthony. She found him stirring; the room was dark. Then the cold touched her again, fingers upon her shoulder.

"I am sorry to do this, Doctor Ricci," Gregory von Bayern said from the darkness above her, "but you must follow me at once. It concerns the wizard Morton." He struck the candle.

It took a time for the words to make sense. Anthony Woodville was listening, blanket drawn up to cover his back. Finally Cynthia said "Will he confess where Hywel is?"

"No, Cynthia, I do not believe he will." There was a maddening nothingness in his voice.

"Is he sick, then?"

"For his sake, Doctor, I hope that he is dying."

She dressed in a shift, robe, and slippers, Anthony in a

heavy gown; halfway to the cells, he gave her a scarf to cover her hair.

Giles the porter stood, dull as always, outside the cell: the door was open wide, and she thought that Morton must surely have tricked them all, cast a glamour of sickness and walked from the Tower laughing at them. But that was not the case.

"Burning God," Rivers said, and tried to hold Cynthia back. "Don't go in there! What if it's . . . catching?"

She went past his arm. "This isn't a disease," she said. "Get the hall lantern in here." She reached out to touch the twisting, howling thing on the floor. "This bone's shooting spurs like a hedgehog, and this one . . . just seems to have gone . . . liquid." She felt bile in her throat. *"What in the Lady's name?"*

Rivers seized the partizan from Giles, brought its butt down on a small green blob that was crawling away from Morton, all on its own, trailing gall. Rivers reversed the spear, and aimed its point at the Morton-lump.

Gregory returned, leading Dimitrios and a woman, apparently also taken in the act.

"Who *is* it?" the woman said.

"John Morton, the Holborn wizard," Rivers said. "Edward's killer."

The woman pressed forward, enough for a good full look: there was an awful strain in her face. Then she said "No one could deserve this," and turned away.

Then, from the corridor, she cried out.

Giles the porter walked past her, past Dimitrios and Rivers, casting his shadow across the Morton-thing on the floor.

His hose were torn—or rather, they were tearing, ripping seams at his knees. A line of already loose stitching at his shoulder popped completely. He staggered against the wall of the cell, half sitting, half collapsing, and reached down to pull off his shoes with hands that seemed to have no knuckles. Freed, his toes grew another inch, poking through his hose.

Something like chicken fat fell from his face, and tufts of

spiky white hair. He put his face in his long hands, tilted it upward, running his fingers over his piebald scalp. He sighed and coughed, a little blood showing on his lips.

Hywel Peredur rested one eye and one dark socket on the people gathered in the cell.

"Oh, it's good to see you all," he said, in not much more than a whisper, "see you and know all your names again."

Morton's body was trembling now, and he no longer cried out. Cynthia said "Hywel . . . you didn't do this . . . surely not?"

"He did it to himself," Hywel said. "Sixty years of magic lies there, all caught up to its worker." He shook his head. "But in a way it is my doing. He was worried; he tried to check on me with his mind . . . and I made him let me out." He shook his head. "That's a dangerous event."

Cynthia reached to the lump again. "His heart's still beating."

"You can't save him. Not even as that ruin . . . and Mistress Shore is right: no one could deserve to live as that." Hywel crawled forward, bent over Morton. "Will you rest now, John? There won't be any pain. Nor curses, eh, John?"

Morton's face slouched over, eyes like grapes in oatmeal.

A twisting wind whirled up dust in the room. Cynthia was knocked on her side, crying out at the pain in her hip. Hywel was grasping at the air, small lights flickering around his hands. The wind pushed into the door, buffeting the others; Dimi grasped Jane Shore to keep her steady. Then the vortex was gone, up the hall, funneling up the stairs.

"It was so cold," Cynthia said, as Anthony helped her stand. Hywel was still crouching, looking at the ceiling. "It was a death," he said, distantly. "Only one, but a strong one."

"Whose?" Dimitrios said.

Hywel raised his hands. "I can't catch it!" Gregory took a step, gripped Hywel's left hand in his own, held out his other hand. Dimi took it. Jane Shore joined the chain, then Rivers, then Cynthia, and back to Hywel.

Cynthia felt a tingling in her hands, almost painful; then something was being sucked up from within her, like life itself draining. She could feel her great vessels like lines of fire within her.

"*Siôn, dewin,*" Hywel shouted, "what's it *for?*"

And then there was quiet in Cynthia's mind, and body; she still held hands, knowing she would fall if she did not.

She knew—and, as a story around the circle, saw they all knew—

"Anthony," Hywel said, "will you come with me? We've known him longest."

"Of course, Peredur."

"I'm his man," Dimitrios said.

Hywel said gently, "Not for this, Dimi. It doesn't want a warrior-brother to tell a man his only son has died."

As they went from the room, Jane Shore took Dimi's arm firmly in her own, said "He'll need you soon enough." Dimitrios nodded. Jane pointed toward the cell, said "What about . . . that?"

Cynthia saw Gregory take his small gun from his belt; there was an object fixed to its muzzle. "I will attend to it," he said, and when she was almost out of hearing, she heard "*Mehr Arbeit für den Todesmann.*"

PART FIVE

Ends of the Game

But shall we wear these honors for a day?
Or shall they last, and we rejoice in them?
   —ACT IV, SCENE 2

Chapter 13
DRAGON

FEBRUARY was melting into March, but the atmosphere in London was still deep winter: Coronation had promised to heal the country, but now the King was grieving and the land was wounded.

Richard sat in his chair after the councillors had departed, plain gold crown straight on his forehead, rolling a scepter over in his hands.

Dimitrios said "My lord, I don't think they're as disaffected as they may sound. But they want leading."

"A leader has to have someplace to take his followers," Richard said dully. "And something to offer them once they arrive. I have no heir. And we've used up everyone else, haven't we? My father, all my brothers and all their sons . . . even the desperate claimants like Harry Buckingham."

Richard Ratcliffe came into the chamber, a rolled paper tight in his hand. "We may have something, Your Grace. There's been a man spreading sedition—"

Richard held out his hand for the paper, unrolled and read it. It was a printed broadsheet, done in crooked, hand-whittled type on a basement press. Dimi read:

When Northern men lay England waste
Her noble Tree of Kings erased
Her wise Lords carpentered in Haste—

When Lyons are by Boars displaced
Soon comes *dies irae!*

Richard handed the sheet back. " 'Carpentered in
Haste.' Witty, too. What of it?"

"My lord, we found the man who printed them, a William Colyngbourne."

"I'll endow him a chair of letters at Cambridge."

"Richard, please listen. In Colyngbourne's house we
found type half-cut for more broadsides, proclaiming a
Henry Tydder as rightful King of England. And we found
these."

Ratcliffe held out two objects. One was a robin's eggshell
on a ribbon. The other was a medallion, showing two
warring dragons.

"The Tydders are an old and notably rebellious Welsh
family," Hywel said, turning the medallion over in his fingers. "Owain Tydder, managed, somehow, to acquire
Henry the Fifth's widow as a wife. They had a son, but
Owain was killed not long after and his brother Jasper
raised the boy . . . here and there and on the run."

"This Owain is a famous wizard, isn't he?" Dimi said.
"When we were north, I heard stories—"

"Oh, no," Hywel said, "that Owain was Glyn Dŵr. He
had children, but neither magic nor war bred strong in
them. But his memory's stronger than life, you know how
that is, and it's certain that young Harry Tydder will
shout Glyn Dŵr's name every chance he has." Hywel
turned to Ratcliffe. "Has Colyngbourne said anything
more?"

"He's said the last he will, my lord wizard."

"What?"

"This morning, by the King's order, he was hanged. And
quartered."

Hywel said quietly, "So speaking one's mind is death,
and everyone in London knows it. We could have better af-
forded prison for him."

Not quite apologetic, Ratcliffe said "Some of the papers

we found upset Richard no small amount. The one that said Queen Anne was struck barren, for the Princes' deaths . . ."

"Yes, I know," Hywel said. "That's exactly their purpose: to excite people to rash and irrevocable acts. That paper in particular I wonder if Master Colyngbourne even wrote."

Cynthia appeared in the doorway, leaning on her green-headed cane. "Hywel, may I talk to you?"

Hywel said to Dimi and Ratcliffe "Excuse me, now . . . and please try to have a thought before acting. If Anthony Rivers were dead, where would we be now?"

Hywel and Cynthia walked through the upper apartments, above the level of the outer walls; from Tower Hill came a sound of thunder, the Duke of Norfolk's men practicing with Gregory's quick-drill artillery.

Cynthia said "Have you heard from Anthony?"

"Very little. He's as well liked in Wales as any Englishman, I think, but there's no good will from the people he's after. . . . Do you miss him?"

"I'd call you jealous, but you wouldn't laugh," she said. "The fact is, I'd like to visit Mary, if there's any chance of it."

"Not a social visit."

"No." She tapped her fingers on the head of her cane. "I'm trying to think of something to do for Anne. She can't be convinced that some women just aren't made fertile—and being in the shadow of the prolific Woodvilles hasn't helped. She's offered to change her faith, and have surgery, and everything between: I think she'd die gladly to give Richard another son. Not," she said distantly, "that I'd allow her to . . . but if we could get her to the point, I think we could carry her home." She laughed, once sharply. "She'd be carrying, of course. What am I saying? I must be tireder than I think."

"We all are," Hywel said casually. "And I won't argue this time. We'll go. And if we're to do Anne and Richard any good, we'd best go before Tydder gets sailing weather."

Still in his high boots and spurs, James Tyrell clumped into the throne room, bowed to King Richard the Third.

Richard said "What's the news from the coast?"

"Tydder's sailed. Three days ago, from Brittany."

Dimitrios said "But the weather's been foul—"

"There's a sorcerer in the boats with 'em," Tyrell said, "and the coast-watches say he opened a hole in the squalls and sailed through. Where's my lord wizard Peredur?"

"By now," Dimi said, "halfway to Wales." He turned to the King. "If I rode after . . ."

"There's not time," Richard said, "even assuming you could pick up their trail. Dick: where's Tydder planned to land?"

Ratcliffe said "Pembroke, according to the Colyng-bourne papers. But it's a lot of coast to cover."

"True . . . but it's not Wales he's after, is it. He'll march for England, picking up his dragon rebels as he goes. . . .

"Then we're for Nottingham. And when he whistles for his robinhoods...we'll feather him." The King banged his fist into his palm.

"What in the Lady's name *is* this mess?" Cynthia said.

Hywel said "Dragon spoor."

Along the roads was the detritus of an army: broken belts and drums, rusty weapons, torn knapsacks spilling rotten food. There was something bright on the crown of the road, and Cynthia bent to pick it up. She turned the medallion over in her hand, and over again, and again.

For the next mile, she carried it, and neither of them spoke. Then Cynthia stumbled, and looked at the disc, and then snapped her wrist and threw it into the scrub. She leaned heavily on her cane.

"I almost . . . wanted to follow it," she said haltingly. "Wherever . . . wherever it led."

"And if you had carried one for months now," Hywel said, "you would have followed it. Did you notice your leg?"

"No, I . . . No. I didn't. I lost my limp, didn't I?"

"You did not feel it . . . but I could hear the bones grinding."

"Why didn't you . . . why weren't we taking them from people when we were here? We chased those damned things for two years, and we should have been shouting what they were!"

"No. The people who cast them, who invested them with power, *wanted* them seized. The more, the better. Had we done that, the ones remaining would have been even more tightly held . . . or the folk might have made their own, and a bond the subject forges for himself is the hardest of all to break."

"Still, we could have done something."

"We did," he said, smiling. "Anyone who was healed by the lady known as Rhiannon, or who traded medals with her wizard companion, will not get far with the army before deciding he or she would be happier at home—"

Hywel stopped still, looking up at the northern sky, at the white bulk of Mynydd Troed.

"Hywel, what is it?"

"It's . . . I don't know." His voice was very small. "Mary's house is warded against . . . so much . . . I can't see."

She touched him. His hands were trembling, and his forehead was damp. "Let's hurry," he said, without any need.

The sun was high when they reached Llangorse, and the village was peculiarly silent. There was not a single horse on the street, or a mule. There was a message at the inn, written right on the door in chalk: GONE TO FIGHT FOR WALES.

"Rhiannon, aid my son!" a woman's voice called from behind Hywel and Cynthia. A woman in a widow's black dress was running toward them, dropping to her knees. "Rhiannon, Gwydion, aid my son."

"I am not a goddess," Cynthia said, in the commonest Cymric she could manage, "but I am a . . . healer, and if your son is sick I will be glad to help him."

They passed more old men and women as they followed

the widow, and signs were made at them, and some of the people bowed or knelt as they went by. There were a few younger women, working furiously at gardens or tending babies, and young men who either did not meet their eyes at all or looked right through them.

The widow's son was perhaps twenty, sitting on a stool in the back-kitchen of the house. He wore a leather jack, almost worn through, and a baldric hung with an empty scabbard.

He sat absolutely still, back straight as a poker, hands folded loosely in his lap. His eyes were open, fixed on nothing. He had the warm, meaningless smile of an idiot.

Cynthia turned to Hywel, said in Italian, "Is *this* what you meant by—"

"No."

She chewed her lip, nodded. To the widow she said "How long has he been like this?"

"He came in last night," the woman said. "He'd'a gone out on that morning, with his friends. Proud, he was, to be wearing his fa's sword, and his gran'fa's coat from the French wars . . . but he come back without the sword, and I can't reason it. Do you think . . ."

Cynthia reached inside the young man's collar, brought out a leather cord with one of the dragon medallions. She lifted it over his head. He continued to stare.

Cynthia threw the medal out the kitchen door.

Nothing happened.

She touched the man's forehead, said clearly, "War's over. Why don't you go home?"

The son blinked, stood up, said "I'm going to rest now, Mother, and later I'll hoe the garden." He walked out of the kitchen.

"My!" the widow said.

"I don't know," Cynthia said to Hywel, bewildered. "But maybe—" She turned to the widow. "You say he's been . . . ill since last night. Have you gone to the Jeshite healer? Mary Setright?"

"Oh, my, no, Lady," the widow said, terrified. "No, we wouldn't do that—please don't punish him on that! Why, his gran'fa' fought them in the French wars, and his faith's good—"

Cynthia limped out of the back-kitchen, leaned against a fence-post. Hywel came behind her, carrying her cane.

"No," she said, sick. "You said she was safe, Hywel . . . Hywel, *what did you see on the road this morning?"*

"Nothing clear," he said, and they started down the road, leaving the widow shouting praises after them.

There were at least a dozen men and women around Mary's cottage, all quite still, eyes open and staring. Some sat in the grass, intent on clouds passing; some lay on the ground and contemplated a single turd.

One had been kneeling by the brook, evidently to drink, and had never taken his face from the water. Another squatted beneath the corner of the roof thatching; there had been a torch in his hand, and the thatch was sooty. But the torch had burned down, all the way past his fingers and away to nothing.

Cynthia stood in the yard, looking this way and that, leaning on her stick each time she became dizzy, thinking about the knife in its hilt.

"Cynthia," said Hywel, from the open door to the house.

She took a step, saw his face. "You don't want me to go in, do you."

"No."

"Is Mary in there?"

"Yes."

"Then I'm going in."

"I know."

She went inside and saw Mary. A tearing sound came from Cynthia's throat, and she lifted her stick, to smash it down on the townswoman who sat numbly before the fire, mallet still in her flaccid hand.

But it seemed that someone caught her hand and held it, and she held very still, until she said "Her curse, Hywel? Is that what's happened to them all?"

"Her blessing, I think. We forget that anyone who can curse can bless. I think . . . she told them to find . . . peace."

"Absolute peace?" Cynthia said, looking hard-eyed at the statue people. "Until they starve, and blow away to dust?"

"Possibly."

"I like that. Now help me find something to draw these nails."

They buried Mary a little distance into the woods, pounding the cold earth down. Cynthia made holes in the soil with her cane stiletto, and sowed thyme and rosemary as a lasting marker. They agreed that Mary would want the cottage left standing, as shelter for anyone in need.

"And them?" Hywel said, pointing at the people caught in peace.

Cynthia looked at them for a long time. Finally she said "I don't suppose I have a choice, do I?"

"I think you do. I think that's why you can release them."

She shivered in a nonexistent wind, went to a man who sat with his back against the woodpile, a medallion in one hand and an axe in the other. Cynthia threw his medal away. "Go home now," she said, softly. "We forgive you."

The man blinked, looked up at Cynthia. He let the axe fall, then stood and walked unsteadily toward Llangorse village.

Cynthia cut a neck cord, let the disc fall. "Go home, it's over." "Go home, rest." "Go home, you're forgiven. . . ."

King Richard was in the castle tower at Nottingham, looking east: not south at the town, with spearpoints bristling in the streets and bodies on gibbets, not north at Sherwood, with small fires still rising from it, and not west at all.

"What does he have, now?" Richard said, working the fingers of his left hand.

"A few exiles, some of his relatives," Tyrell said. "And the outlaws who've filtered to him. That amounts to his household guard: maybe a hundred, all good. Then the Bretons, some mercenaries, minor nobles mostly, calling Tydder 'Arthur come to free their land.' "

"They believe that in Brittany too?" Dimi said, not very surprised by it.

"He was the Breton savior before Badon," Richard said, distracted. Then he said to Tyrell "And?"

"And the Byzantines."

"Definitely them?" Dimi said, before Richard could speak.

"They're wearing eagles and floating banners. There's a full century of lances, and they do glitter."

"Every army needs something to leave a legend behind," Richard said. "I wonder if Tydder's aware he's not it? But I'm sure he'll be grateful."

"It'll be in his contracts that he's grateful."

"Guns?" Gregory said.

"There they're light," said the Duke of Norfolk, sounding concerned. "We know they have not more than six of the serpentines, and the scouts swear not more than one hand-gunner to twenty spears."

Dimi said "That's not Byzantine organization."

"Or English," Richard said. "Their ships must have been sinking full: could they be short of powder and shot?"

No one spoke for a moment; then Dimi realized everyone was looking at him. "It's not impossible." he said, "but I don't think it's the reason. . . ."

"And?" said the King.

"There's only one reason to abandon a weapon," Dimi said. "Because you don't expect to need it, because you have something better."

"There is the dragon, my lord," Tyrell said.

Richard nodded. "Yes," he said, sighing, "the dragon. What about the light foot, Tyrell?"

"Their numbers vary with every report. If it isn't bad scouting, which I do not think, he seems to be both gaining and losing men."

"And losing," Richard said softly.

"If neither flow changes, he'll have some ten thousand with him when he enters England, somewhere near Shrewsbury. We have about the same."

"Twenty thousand men," Richard said, "away from the

fields at spring planting . . . Well, gentlemen, it had better
be a short war, or it could be a very long winter."

Something crunched within Richard's hand. He opened
his fingers, let bits of pale-blue eggshell sift down to the
floor.

"Cynthia!" Rivers said. "When did you get here? Hello,
Peredur. God, you must have flown." He looked sidelong at
Hywel.

"Horses of flesh, not air," Hywel said.

"Did you find the healer?"

Cynthia said "No."

"Well . . . after tomorrow, there'll be time to look
again." He shrugged. "Or there won't be need. Anne's upstairs."

"Here?"

"They wouldn't leave each other. Am I going to fault
them?" Anthony's eyes met Cynthia's for just a moment.
"But the trip was hard on the Queen. You'll want to look
at her."

Cynthia nodded once, hiked her pannier on her shoulder, and went up the inn stairs, cane tapping.

Rivers said to Hywel "Can you walk a little farther?"

"As far as you need."

They went out of the inn, into the village of Sutton
Cheney. From the village, a hill stretched west for about a
mile; it was a few hundred yards north to south. At its
western point, a group of men were silhouetted against the
low sun, a shadow banner fluttering beside them.

"What's this place called?" King Richard was saying.

"Ambien Hill," Tyrell said. "And the plain below is
called Redmoor."

"And more red when we're done, I dare say."

"Rivers, there you are. And Peredur, it's a relief to see
you. . . . You've come up from South Wales? Around
Tydder?"

"Around, sometimes through."

"Then you've seen the Red Dragon?"

"This was no time to tickle its tail. But we saw what

happens in its path." He told them briefly, what had happened in Llangorse.

They stood around, silent, expressions shadowed out. Dimitrios shook his head slowly; Rivers turned back toward Sutton Cheney.

Richard said "And men are supposed to fight that?"

Hywel said "The central absurdity of magic is that it can only do what men can imagine; and anything a man can imagine, a way may be devised of doing, without sorcery."

Dimitrios said, straining for humor, "Even raise the dead?"

"Had you ever been dead," Gregory said, eyeglasses flashing like copper coins, "you would not ask that."

"Peredur, I don't need your mysteries now," Richard said, somewhat irritated. "I need a victory. What can you do, against their wizard? Can you give me a White Dragon, to meet the Red?"

"That would be exactly their wish. *Now,* the *Ddraig Goch* is no more than a banner for them. But if we meet it on its own terms, it becomes . . . real, in a sense, because we have acknowledged it as real." Hywel pointed toward the setting sun, Tydder's army somewhere beneath it. "Remember, everyone drawn into this through the medals *knows* the Red Dragon can defeat the White."

"So what are you going to do tomorrow?"

"I will watch for a chance to do something, and when the chance comes, I will do it."

Exasperated but blackly amused, Richard said "Isn't there a saying about meddling in the affairs of wizards? Well. This is where we'll meet them; let them come."

Rivers was looking to the southwest. Sixty yards from the base of the slope there was a patch of bog, still half frosted over. "Do you think," he said, rubbing his chin, "that they might be coaxed to come that way, instead of from the north slope? Would they run between the hill and the bog?"

Dimi said "You said Tydder's never led men?"

"So far as we know. Though he's got his uncle Jasper,

who's an old hand, and the Earl of Oxford." Rivers said the
last name with particular venom.

"And they'll be leavened well with the Breton serjeants," Dimi said. "I suspect you know they're sharp. And
the Byzantines . . . I'd say, coaxed never, but a hot enough
fire might drive them. Gregory . . . ?"

Gregory examined the ground, held up a device like a
mariner's quadrant and took sightings in the bad light,
said "Quickly sustained fire with fragmenting balls cre-
ates a zone in which, in theory, nothing may live. But as
you experienced soldiers doubtless know, by prostrating
oneself and uttering a prayer to the Goddess of Artillery,
this scientific law is suspended." His voice was absolutely
level, and it was too dark to see his face. "However, the
Goddess of the Engineers has been known to outvote her
daughter. I shall need several of my lord of Norfolk's engineers, and men to hold the lanterns."

"You'll have the best," Norfolk said.

"No. The second best. The best will be needed tomorrow,
awake."

"Don't drink that!"

Rivers put down the pitcher of hot spiced wine. "What's
the matter, Cynthia?"

"That's for the Queen . . . there's a strong sleeping
draught in it. The wine hides the taste."

"Oh. Isn't that rather cruel, to her and Richard tonight?"

She stood still for a moment, then said "I suppose it
might be. But she needed the rest . . . she's feverish.
Sweating sickness, I think; Lord Stanley's complaining
too."

"With you it's always the patient first, isn't it?"

"Yes. There's more wine; I'll get it."

"That's not necessary."

"Maybe not for you." She brought the wine and sat
down, resting her stick against the table. She gripped the
armrests of her chair and pulled hard, feeling the muscles
and sinews loosen in her arms and shoulders.

"You might let me do that," Anthony said.

"All right."

He worked through the joints of her arms and hands, squeezing out the aches, watching her face intently for signals. He made her wince, then said "Sorry," and moved on to the next point. Finally she lay face down on the bed, and he slid her skirt up and began massaging her hip.

She buried her face in the crook of her arm for that, because she did not want to show him quite that much feeling.

He said "I'm glad you'll be here tomorrow, with the Queen."

"I don't plan to be."

"How can you leave her?"

"She'll be sleeping, well nursed after, and there's going to be a battle; have you forgotten? Or are you going to handle battlefield surgery as well as men on horseback?"

He moved his hands up to her lower back. "Do you know who the Earl of Warwick was?"

"Anne's father, of course."

"Yes. Well, I saw how he died. He was in a battle that had turned against him—turned badly, because Tydder's good friend the Earl of Oxford deserted him. Warwick was fighting in armor but on foot, because of some matter of a woman's honor. You've seen, in the yards, how little a good armor impedes a man, and Warwick's was the best stuff; but still a bunch of common soldiers caught him, and knocked him down, opened up his visor and stuck knives in.

"He was a man in his prime, Cynthy, and you couldn't run away from a plow horse—"

He had one hand tight on her hip, one on her shoulder, quite pinning her; she felt something hot on the back of her neck and realized it was a tear.

Then he shook from shoulders to waist, and helped her sit up on the edge of the bed. He showed no sign of tears.

"I'm sorry," he said, smoothing her gown. "Again."

"Anthony," she said, trying to think if she had missed him at all, when first he and then she had gone without the other to Wales; she was unable to remember. "Whatever is the matter with our being friends, who love?"

"Because I am the best knight of England," he said, going to the door, "as the penny-a-page poets will have it; and you insist on being real." He smiled, not bitterly at all. "Good night, friend Cynthia. Be careful, in the battle."

"Good night . . . friend Anthony." Her voice rose: "If I hear you fought on foot I'll never speak to you again!"

They were both smiling as the door closed between them.

There was a thin fog, haloing the bronze cannon and the mounted troopers' shining helmets: the sunlight was a thin gilding on polished steel.

Norfolk's guns were on the western lip of Ambien Hill, poised to rake downward. Nearby, Gregory von Bayern worked an optickal range-gauge; a few feet from him was a box, cubical and about a yard on a side, made of heavy old wood black as lead.

A little to the rear were Richard and Dimitrios, and Earl Rivers, with the main body of cavalry. Behind them was the Earl of Northumberland, leading packed bodies of Northern pikemen, and a small cavalry rearguard with James Tyrell in command.

Almost a mile to the north, but clearly in sight, Sir William Stanley waited with a flanking force. His brother, the sweat-sick Lord Stanley, was similarly placed to the south.

About half a mile from the front, on the southern slope of the hill, the engineers had built a wooden penthouse near a well: there Cynthia waited, with a tiny company of surgeons and some young village men who swore they had strong stomachs.

Leather creaked and chains jangled. Pikebutts shifted with a sound like heavy whispering. A horse whinnied and a man began to cough.

The Red Dragon came out of the west.

Its broad body was a quarter-mile long, the swinging tail that long again; the neck rose into the air three times the four-hundred-foot height of Ambien Hill. Its eyes were lanterns and it drooled fire.

The dragon advanced through the little men around it like a man walking across a fur rug; some of the army seemed to scurry around the feet, but none was kicked aside or trampled.

And, as the dragon moved, it changed.

The scales were now copper, now red opal, now garnet, now something the color of dried blood. The ridge down the dragon's back grew prongs; forked them; scissored, raked, and folded them. The legs showed corded muscles, and then had no rigid form, and then were driven by belts and chains. The head grew and changed and lost horns and whiskers and fangs and tongues, split into many heads and fused again into one. Only the beacon eyes burned on, constant.

Hywel sat beneath a tree some distance to the north, his horse cropping grass nearby. He held his eye, one of the finest English glass, cupped in his palm, and in its glowing pupil he watched the dragon move.

He saw the wizard in his eye, carried on a litter just beneath the dragon's backside. He was a little man, bald on top, dressed in voluminous robes of velvets and China silk. His legs were folded up beneath him.

And Hywel saw Henry Tydder, in a gold back-and-breast with a dragon enameled red upon it, being led from beneath the dragon's belly toward the forefeet.

The armies were now only a few hundred yards apart.

The gunners on the hill touched off their pieces, with a chain of smokes and a rippling roar. Hywel felt the first twists in the pattern, the first hard tug on his heart.

"Look!" one of the gunners cried.

The large round shot from the serpentine guns flew surprisingly slowly, enough so that they could be followed by eye. Now the balls were seen to twist their path, soar upward.

The dragon inhaled them, spat them back.

One of Norfolk's guns was blown to pieces. A gunner rolled down the hill, screaming.

Gregory replaced his glasses, trying to calculate the kinetic force involved in the trick.

The gunners were recharging. Gregory was not their commanding officer; he had no say in the matter.

Richard said "Why doesn't he show himself? He can see me, can't he? Raise the banner higher!"

As the gunsmoke blew away, Dimi could see the Byzantine mercenaries on Tydder's left flank. A century of lances: a hundred riders, each with two footmen for support. There would be no question of getting them into the bog on the opposite wing. But if they should lead the attack up this slope—

If they should do that they would be murdered, and such fine men should not be murdered by infernal machines of some bloodless serpent's devising.

Tydder's first wave, carrying the Earl of Oxford's colors, was starting up the western point of the hill. The guns spoke, and a man in the first rank was beheaded, but the other balls went up the dragon's snout and were spat out again, crashing into the earth, knocking two more serpentine cannon from their wheels.

"Retire!" the gun commander shouted. "With your pieces, in good order, damn you!"

The gunners picked up their cannon by the trails, began pulling them backward. From the rear, Norfolk's pikes and handgunners moved up, opening ranks to let the guns pass through them.

Apparently ignoring them all, Gregory went to the wooden box, opened its side. Within was a mechanism incorporating three large mainsprings, clock escapements, vials of fulminate, all at the center of a spiderweb of carefully knotted and primed quick-match.

Gregory pulled three pins and pushed a pointer on an engraved brass dial. The springs groaned, and the works began to whir, quietly and smoothly.

Buried in the earth of the north slope were more than three dozen ground mortars, some flame, some blast, some splinter. In twenty minutes, just the time it would take Tydder's men to reach the ground, the mechanism would put fire to them all; even if two of the mainsprings should fail, the third would still ignite the works.

Gregory did not know if the result would drive the enemy down to the southern slope; but they would be that many fewer, and the instant-fuzed mortar bombs would not feed the red dragon.

There would, he thought suddenly, be a great deal of blood.

There was a gunner with his arm off in the penthouse, and a man with a crossbow quarrel through his armor and his thigh. Cynthia left the bowshot man to another surgeon and began cleaning the gunner's stump. He was clear-eyed, deep in shock, quite calm because of it.

A man stepped quickly through the door. "Doctor Ricci."

"Sir James, close the door and stop scattering dust."

"My lady, the Queen requires you."

"What can have happened to her?"

"I don't know, my lady; I've just the message, and a horse to take you there."

" 'S'all right, ma'am," the gunner said, "you see to the Queen," and his head tipped over and he died.

Without removing her bloody apron, she followed Tyrell out.

Hywel watched the men within the dragon. They pushed forward, bearing it on: for of course it was them, all of their desire for freedom and victories and power.

It was made from them, and if he destroyed it he would in a way be destroying them. And for what? A crown, a throne. More power.

The dragon showed only one bright eye. Hywel blinked to clear his sight.

* * *

A messenger ran, stumbled, nearly falling, reached Earl Rivers.

"Richard, Doctor Ricci's been . . . called to the Queen."

"What?" Richard said, as if he had not heard. *"Annie's dead?"*

"No, Richard . . . she's ill. That's all—"

"That's your death, Tydder!" The King turned. "Come, Anthony, Dimitrios, brothers, and we'll ride for him, and make him give us combat, him and his uncle and Oxford." Richard smiled. "No more than five will die."

"Richard," Rivers said clumsily, "Anne's not dead. But Cynthia may need help with her . . . she may need to do surgery." Rivers swayed in the saddle. "Dimitrios can take my command, and I'll go to her. I've helped her work before."

So Woodville *was* a coward, Dimi thought hazily.

"Go on, then," Richard said, choked. "Go on, Galahad. Lay on your bloody hands, and heal with your rotten purity."

"Thank you, Sire." Rivers pricked his horse and rode, back through the ranks of his own puzzled men.

"I knew you wouldn't do it!" Richard cried after him. "I knew you'd never fight in any fair tournament!" He turned to Dimi. "Well, brother Balan. This time we charge together, eh?"

"No," Cynthia said, "don't try to straighten her limbs. Just hold her gently. We're only trying to keep her from hurting herself."

The woman restraining Queen Anne looked at Cynthia, doubtful and a little frightened. Anne's back arched again, almost a foot off the bed. Bloody flux, Cynthia thought, I'm frightened too. "Please be calm, Your Grace," she said softly, and Anne, who by the quantity of drugs in her system should have slept through an amputation, cried out long and thrust her body upward and sweated great cloudy drops. The other women knew the symptoms as well as did Cynthia, being all midwives; if they had not known, they should not have been so afraid.

Anne of England cried like Death come calling, and twisted again in labor, trying to give birth to a child she did not carry.

Norfolk's and Oxford's footsoldiers were colliding. Some had swords out, and pikemen and halberdiers held each other at their long weapons' length, but the real business was being done with maces, or studded bats, or sticks with bits of flailing chain, to crack armor and smash bone and pulp soft tissue. *Goedendags*, Dimitrios had heard them called: And good day to *you*, sir.

"I see him," Richard said eagerly. "There, with the dragon on his chest. Do you see me, Dragon? I am the White Boar, and you may scorch me with your fire, but I will gore your soft belly to the heart."

Dimitrios looked at the Byzantine cavalry, some way distant but curiously clear in his sight. He thought that they looked very splendid; he was seeing them not on this cold English hill, but in a beautiful French valley, hooves splashing through a stream while the sun made the grape-vines around them to prosper.

Or perhaps they were on the Greek coast, the Aegean a sheet of blue crystal, passing in review by their coronal's white, white villa. Hooves echoing . . .

He was not aware that Richard had begun to charge until his serjeants, and Rivers's, began to call his name. "Captain Ducas! Captain, shall we ride?"

"No," he said, "not here, not now," and then repeated it in English, for of course these men knew no Greek.

Richard's horse advanced, at the trot, down the northern slope of Ambien, toward the Byzantine horsemen.

Gregory watched the pointer crawl from one mark to the next. There were only ten minutes remaining now: and then there would be fire, and death, and blood in rivers. And no one at all would know he had fed, for the dead may bleed but they do not speak.

He looked up from the box, and saw something wrong. Men were crossing the mined slope, much too soon, and coming from the wrong direction . . . no, he thought, not "wrong." It was elementary dynamics that directional forces were not incorrect, merely unaccounted for. One merely adjusted the vector diagram in response to the situation. Gregory looked again at the men in his field of destruction, at the colors they carried. He did not recognize them, though it vaguely seemed that he should.

No, no, no. He must not allow false parameters into the diagram, corrupting it. Physics was above such things. Physics was the purest of the sciences, the cleanest.

Gregory pushed the pointer eight minutes toward zero.

Hywel was admiring the internal structure of the dragon, its viscera and nerves, as it were. The power of each man was linked into a sort of hub, and drove the catching of cannonballs, the sparks of light that burned arrows to slag and carbon, and of course maintained the illusion of the beast.

Illusion? he thought. The dragon was there, it walked, it breathed, it ate. When Owain Glyn Dŵr was crowned in Harlech, men really bowed to him. When Herbert burnt Dyffryn Conwy for the sheer joy of it, the smoke really filled the lungs. These were actual things that they did, and it was time he, the only heir in power of Glyn Dŵr, joined in reality.

In his held eye, he saw Lord Stanley away to the south, sweating and scratching and certainly not advancing to King Richard's aid. And now William Stanley's men on the northern flank were dropping their White Boar banners and tying on red brassards.

So the reality Hywel would make for Wales would be made for the North as well.

Dimitrios saw Richard's men on the slope, colliding with a force of footmen. He looked farther, to see what the Byzantine century was doing: they were advancing on Richard's flank.

That was a good tactic, flank attack.

He looked north. William Stanley's men were coming

now. Dimi supposed they meant to take the Byzantines in the flank, creating one of those confused melees where no one quite knew who was on whose spearpoint.

The thought of such disorder displeased Dimitrios. Stanley could be met with on better terms. Dimi called a charge in every language he knew, and whispered to Luna beneath him, and with a magnificent cheer of "Richard, Richard, the Boar, the King!" they made for the space at Richard's rear.

Richard? Dimi thought, the Boar? The *King?*

He had never wanted to be a King. *Never.* And Cosmas Ducas had known it. His father would rather have seen him with one horse and one sword, and the honor of his faith, than Emperor of the World.

Dimi's head snapped up with a jolt. Richard's men were just to his left, Lord Stanley's troops straight ahead. In seconds Dimi's charge would impact on Stanley's, and Richard's rear area would be in total disarray. "Left wheel!" Dimitrios shouted, knowing as he did that it was much too late to stop the momentum of four hundred charging cavalry. But they did wheel, as much as they could, and the two bodies collided at an oblique angle.

Stanley in turn had tried to wheel right, and now tried to halt his men; they stretched out like cheesecloth pulled at the ends. But still there was energy left over, so that leveled spears and shrieking horses smashed at full gallop into the flanks of the trotting Byzantines.

Then Dimi saw the direction of charge that Stanley had intended, and the colors the men wore on their sleeves, and suddenly the shout was *Down Traitor!*

Dimitrios looked up, at the Dragon striding over all of them. So the enchantments had failed somehow: so all the power of Empire had failed to find the Ducas gone for a soldier. But the strayed Ducas had found the enemy . . . and the purpose, and the self, he had thought forever lost on the Scottish border.

Men and horses were piled together and upon each other; spears stuck in the earth and through bodies. The smell of blood was as strong as smoke from a fire. Dimi reined

Olwen in, drew his saber. So it would be murder after all, but at least not murder for its own sake this time.

He saw Richard, began cutting his way to the King's side. Olwen stumbled; Dimi looked down, saw one of Gregory's wire-wrapped eggs in its nest, all ready to hatch out death.

Gregory leaned on the fuzing box, fingers arched, staring with aching eyes at the scene of horses and men cut down. The wind carried him the scent. He could not remember ever having been so hungry . . . but today it was a quiet sort of hunger. The feast was being prepared before him.

Then he saw the white horse, red-spotted now, with Dimitrios white-armored on its back, and there was a flash in Gregory's mind like silver-match burning.

He swallowed back gluey saliva, and thought, with exhaustion pulling at his slow heart, that he was damned in fact to be called back whenever peace of any kind was in his reach.

The box whirred. Gregory dropped to his knees, shoved the pointer back from the mark, but the escapements were already freed, the friction wheels spinning against the flints. Having nothing else, he reached with both hands deep into the mechanism. Gears closed on the webs of his fingers. A razor-sharp spring broke and whipped past. A striker ground out white-hot sparks.

But the net of quick-cords was not burning.

He began, slowly, to free himself from the machine. He felt no particular pain, though he could see the watery blood and pale skin on the sharp brass.

It did not matter. He was a vampire. He would heal. He would continue to live, and in time he would heal.

"Am I in time?" Rivers shouted, bursting into the bedroom. "Oh, no, she's not—the Queen's not dead, Cynthia." He took Cynthia by the shoulders, shook her.

"She's asleep," Cynthia said, trying to pull away. There

was a wholly mad look in Rivers's eyes. "What's wrong, Anthony?"

"Don't you feel it? This . . . *heat* in the air? I heard the Queen was sick, and you were called, and I thought you might need my help. . . ." He leaned against the wall.

She took his hand. "It's all right, Anthony. You can see the Queen is well." She led him to the bedside, where Anne slept quietly, smiling, hands across her chest in a cradling pose.

Rivers ran his hand over the disordered bedclothes. "Did she—try to charge off after something, too?"

Cynthia nodded.

"What did you do?"

"I told her her child was healthy and well."

Rivers put his face in his hands. "But . . . why did I come here? Why didn't I charge into their midst—or ride for single combat, as Richard wanted? Oh, God, I must get back to him."

Because it was the answer that would hurt him least, she said "That's why, then. They wanted to separate you."

"But you never . . . felt it at all."

"No." She leaned on her stick, placed her thumb against the hollow of her hand. "I was . . . warded, I think."

"Then it was Peredur's doing."

"Yes," she said. "Yes, it would not have happened without him."

The dragon had stumbled.

The Byzantine mercenaries had never contributed much to the beast, but they had consumed a great fraction of its power, keeping their mounts fresh, their brass shiny, their spirits charged.

But when Stanley's men struck them unexpectedly, the pattern was suddenly upset: some Byzantines died, sending throbs of energy back into the dragon's nerves, and others began grasping for more, fearful of treachery and more fearful of dying. Stanley's men had tried to join the dragon as well, but now they were more like a lamprey, fastened to its side and sucking.

None of this, Hywel knew, was deliberate. The men were only confused or afraid or dead. The Byzantine on his litter in lotus was doing his best to balance all the lumps and threads and packets of power, and his best was indeed very good. Hywel looked into his eye and saw where only a tiny pull was required to bring the dragon's body back into equilibrium.

Hywel put the eye back into his head, sighed.

He pushed.

The dragon howled: it was not sound, but something that bowed across the nerves like psaltery strings. Soldiers collided with one another, and fell down, and got up fighting the first man they saw. One of the litter-bearers dropped the Byzantine sorcerer, and he tumbled over on the ground, breaking a bare toe on a stone, and his cry was sound, but inaudible by comparison.

The dragon's tail whipped up, and its head curved back. Hywel waited. Again, he could pull where a push was wanting; but he knew the consequences of that, and was not willing to cause them.

It happened anyway, as the Byzantine wrapped a bit of silk from his robe around his toe, pulled it tight.

The dragon's mouth enveloped its tail, and began to swallow it. Scales sloughed and melted, and claws broke off, and piston-rods snapped. Debris fell, burning with a fire that did not consume realer things.

Byzantines and Bretons began to kill one another, with anything to hand, bare hands if there was nothing else. Young Welshmen stared at the junk they had carried as weapons and began to drift away from Redmoor, toward the west.

The Red Dragon tightened into a torus, a spinning vortex, eating itself. Hywel felt himself sorrowing for the thing, not for any beauty in it, but for the power going to nothing: did all the people on the plain realize that they had given months and years of their lives into a fading whorl of crimson light with darkness at its center?

Hywel felt his heart begin to swell up into his throat, a

deep pain in his left arm and his back. He leaned against the tree, his horse nuzzling him curiously.

The remnant of the dragon reached down to him, searching for a vessel to fill. The dragon, he knew, could open his congested heart, or give him a heart of living bronze, or do away with his need for a heart at all. All he need do is allow it.

Cavalry could no longer move on the killing ground. Dimitrios, on foot, looked for Richard, who was searching on foot for Tydder. The dragon had driven them all, he knew, and he wondered if he were truly free of it yet.

The smoke was thick; as the dragon began to collapse both sides had employed their handgunners. And everywhere Dimi stepped there was a corpse, or two, or three in a human barricade.

"Richard!" he called.

"Who's there?" A figure came stumbling through the mess.

"Richard? Is that you?"

"Aye, and who wants to know? If it's Tydder, no answer but to fight."

"It's Dimitrios, Richard. Ducas, brother *miles*."

"Eh? Oh, well met, brother. Together we'll take him back to London in a cart."

"Would that be fair, Gloucester?" A man stepped into plain view. He wore battered, cut armor, but the golden breastplate with the Red Dragon was still bright. Tydder's vizor was raised, but Dimi could not clearly see his face. "Two on one, Richard?" Tydder said. "Is that knightly?"

"What sort of knight are you?" Richard said. "Well, you've cost me everything but crown and honor today, Sir Nothing, and I think we'll keep those. Stand aside, brother."

"And if you're killed, my lord?"

"You swear allegiance to me, of course," Tydder said.

Dimi said "No. If my lord orders, I will give you my throat to cut, but nothing more."

Tydder peered at him. "Who are you, fellow? Some

glory-seeking exile?" He pointed at Richard. "Here's glory: kill that man and you are Duke of Gloucester."

Dimitrios spat on the ground, stepped closer to Richard. The King said "No use, Sir Nothing. We are Balin and Balan, the best of brothers." He said aside to Dimi, "Somehow I've forgotten to knight you. Well, it's done."

"These cannot be Balin and Balan," said a voice a little distance away, "for in the story one brother wounds the other. These are more Gawaine and Gareth. Or should it be Agravaine? I forget."

Earl Rivers held a spear in a casual grip.

"Anthony," Richard said uncertainly, "I forgave you once, but not again."

Dimi saw Rivers's arm recoil, almost lazily. He took a long quick step in front of Richard, putting himself between the King and the spear. From the corner of his eye he saw another movement, of bright metal, and he heard Tydder say "Out of my way, you stupid—"

Tydder's sword entered his armpit; he felt it through his body like a sudden breath of cold air. Something flashed past him, and there was a tremor through the steel piercing him. He heard Tydder fall, with Rivers's spear through his open vizor, and knew that the Earl had been innocent of the tournament. A guilty man could never have brought himself to master the tainted weapon so well.

Dimi turned, feeling the coldness spread inside him. He wanted to see Richard, but he could not. He felt himself embraced, but he could not see anything at all.

And then he saw the wheels of fire, and waited for the whirlwind, and his father's face.

There was still a little halo in the sky as evening fell, a crimson rose on pink, with a dark center.

The thing in the sky was the Empire, Hywel thought, a city of light built of wasted human lives, with nothing but void at its heart.

It would not be killed so easily as the Red Dragon, he knew, but it must be vulnerable, perhaps in the same ways, and it must die.

It must.

Hywel turned around. Richard was sitting by Anne's bed, holding her hand; she was still asleep. Tomorrow, Cynthia said, she would wake, and when she called for her son they must tell her she had dreamed.

"Was it worth it, Peredur?" Richard said. "So I am now undisputed King. Do I have a son, or brothers? Is the land renewed? Shall I decree happiness, on pain of death?"

Hywel did not reply.

"What, wizard . . . not even a riddle for me? Well. We'll say it was a great day, and soon enough we'll believe it. 'This is the day the kingdom was saved.' Maybe I should be known as Dragonslayer . . . *Ricardus Tertius Rex, Draco . . . Dracocide?*"

"*Nemesis Draco,*" Hywel said, without really thinking.

"That sounds appropriately dark."

"Good night, Richard, Sire."

"No, Peredur, not that title, please. . . . Good night, wizard."

In a room down the hall, Cynthia was adjusting the cushions under Dimitrios's upper body. She poured tea for herself and Hywel.

They looked at Dimi on the bed: pale, in white linen gauze, he looked very fragile. There was a startling wrongness to the picture: he could be seen as gloriously dead, but not alive and so frail.

Hywel said "Will he recover?"

"Anthony applied the pressure at once and perfectly, and I don't think his other lung was nicked, or his heart. But if I'm wrong, he could bleed out within . . . so fast it would shock you." She looked at Hywel. "Even you." She sipped her tea, smiled faintly. "But he won't die of loneliness, you know."

"Where will you go now?"

"Oxford University, I think." She laughed lightly. "Though Anthony says Richard will offer me a larger endowment at Cambridge."

Hywel said "I had thought, perhaps, Wales. . . ."

"With Anthony? Or . . . to the cottage? No. I'm not the

woman for either job . . . except, perhaps, once in a while, when there's need." She put her cane across the table, between them. "Or did you mean with you?"

"I'm not going to Wales."

"I didn't think you were."

He stood up.

Not looking at him, she said, "Hywel . . . why are we so terrible to one another?"

"We're what the world makes us. And half the world is Byzantium, while the other half looks East in wonder."

She turned her face upward to him. "Kiss me once, Peredur, for Mary's sake."

There was, Hywel thought, more Goddess in her than she would ever know. He kissed her. It was entirely silent.

Gregory had the horses loaded and ready in the courtyard. The moon was just rising, very gibbous, illuminating knife-thin layers of clouds, and stars were coming out in scores.

As Hywel mounted, he said in German, "Was there anything you wanted to say to them?"

Gregory pushed back his hood with a bandaged hand. "No." He faced Hywel. "Do you find that it helps?"

"No. Not really. Shall we go?"

"A man must keep busy."

Without any noise, they rode away, and soon were lost to sight.

Now have appeared, though in a several fashion,
The threats of majesty, the strength of passion,
Hopes of an empire, change of fortunes, all
What can to theatres of greatness fall,
Proving their weak foundations.

—*from* PERKIN WARBECK

Historical Notes

IN this best-documented of all possible worlds, Byzantium was extinguished in 1453 C.E., when Constantinople fell to the besieging Turks. There was nothing else left, and the City itself was a shell: in 1404 the infamous Fourth Crusade had achieved its one success by sacking and looting the chief stronghold of Christianity in the East.

As many fictional time-travelers before me have discovered, changing history is not a simple process. Some alternatives seem to damp out, while others oscillate in ever-widening arcs. But which are which? There are any number of theories: Toynbee's, Wells's, Marx's, mine.

Perhaps it is really all a matter of people on white horses; or perhaps they have nothing to do with events except to label them with their presence. But one has to start somewhere, and people are inherently more interesting than blind, impersonal forces.

The Emperor Julian, called *Apostata*, has been used as a historical marker in many histories and fictions before this one, at least one of them a masterwork. We have more information about Julian than any of Constantine's heirs (there were five, and before you could say "fratricide" there were none) or any Emperor after him until Justinian. This helps explain the attention, but the facts are clear that Julian did not do much in a lasting way.

Of course that doesn't matter. What matters is what Julian almost did: he literally took on Heaven, and *almost*—well. One's view is unavoidably colored by one's feelings about Christianity, even if (especially if) one confuses the modern forms of that faith with the ones Julian was dealing with. (How many Arians do you know?)

The best evidence of Julian's character supports neither the view of him as a modern agnostic humanist nor as the instrument of Satan. If he had been more extreme, in fact, he might have succeeded; certainly other faiths were reduced to the status of cults, a cult being, like a war crime, an asocial practice of the losing side. As Edward Luttwak comments, a better man than Julian might have reestablished paganism. And so I have made him.

About the Emperor Justinian I there are two principal views: that he was a great leader and raiser of works who, with the aid of his wise and comely Empress Theodora, brought New Rome to its apex; or else that he was a venal booby of vile personal habits, who rose on the achievements and backs of others, egged on by his harlot wife.

Both these pictures are the work of the same man, the historian Procopius, who while he was writing volumes of praise for his Emperor was also keeping a notebook of vicious and rather pornographic "Secret History."

Again steering between the extremes, it is a fact that Justinian recaptured Italy and more from the "barbarians," and a fact that he did not secure his gains. Justinian had the resources, which is not the same as the ability, but he really needed a little more time, like all of us. He died old, but short of consolidating the expanded Empire, perhaps by ten years. And he had already lost his Empress, who we know stiffened his spine when the "Nika" rioters were about to force them from the throne. (Justinian's stiffened spine was a fearful instrument: his army trapped the rioters in the Hippodrome and slaughtered thirty thousand of them.)

I have allowed Justinian his time—and Theodora as well—by a mechanism which should be apparent from

Chapter Three, and not too different from some of the reports of Procopius's Secret History.

Lorenzo de' Medici was described by the great Italian historian Guicciardini as the pleasantest tyrant Florence could have known. It seems a fair enough analysis. There is no doubt that he was the city's absolute ruler, that he ran it to most Florentines' satisfaction, and that he was tyrannical. He used his power successfully against another business family, the Pazzi, and as so often happens, it came back to haunt him.

Lorenzo, like his father, was afflicted with gout (an extremely common term for what may have been a whole group of diseases); there were several dietary cures, of limited efficacy. Colchicine was known only as a poison, which of course it still is.

On 26 April 1478 conspirators led by the Pazzi murdered Giuliano de' Medici at Mass; Lorenzo escaped, narrowly. The "Pazzi War" had the support of Francesco della Rovere, Pope Sixtus IV, a man of great heart and rotten soul who thought the Sistine ceiling insufficient monument to himself—but Sixtus knew how to limit his losses, and the Pazzi shortly learned that when you aim at a king, you dare not miss him.

Lorenzo died in 1492 C.E. A few months later, the power vacuum in Florence was filled by a hellfire preacher named Girolamo Savonarola. He was, very like Julian the Apostate, either a reformer or a terrorist, depending on your point of view. After six years, the Florentine population changed theirs, tortured a confession of heresy from Fra Girolamo, and burned him.

The career of George, Duke of Clarence, was essentially as I have presented it, including his turning coat against his brothers (and turning it back again) and the judicial murders of his wife's servants. There may have been a document of Exemplification; it is mentioned in period papers, including the Bill of Attainder, and it is highly possible that at least one fake was prepared. None, true or false, has been discovered, however. As to his end ("wine enough"), George's daughter Margaret Pole wore a model wine cask on her wrist ever afterward, which gives the tale some credence; certainly it would not have been the most bizarre execution of its time.

Anthony Woodville was a Renaissance Man before the Renaissance had quite started: poet, musician, author of the first book produced on an English press, amateur philosopher (and patron of the arts and sciences), and perfect gentle knight. Edward IV entrusted the upbringing of his heir apparent to his brother-in-law Anthony, and he seems to have served the Prince well. Richard Plantagenet seems to have had a personal grudge against him; why, we do not know. It would matter, at the end.

Anthony had inherited his father's earldom when his father and brother were executed by the Lancastrians; his sister was Queen of England *and* a Lancastrian's widow; there seemed to be a Woodville for every vacant office. The Woodvilles were not so much a dynasty as a political party, and, like anything big enough, they made an easy target. Which is not to say that they were not intriguers; that went with the territory. And when control of England (and, it must have seemed, survival itself) hinged on possession of the young King Edward V, Anthony Woodville was the lone player carrying the ball.

He was beheaded, along with Vaughan and Grey, at Pontefract in 1483. The executioners were surprised to discover that the fair-haired, smiling figure of knighthood had worn a hair shirt under his clothing.

John Morton is an amazing example of the political survivor. He served in Henry VI's court until Edward IV took the throne, was exiled to France with Henry and Margaret of Anjou, returned for their Readeption, and at the end of that year stayed on as one of Edward's diplomatic corps. Richard III had him arrested along with Lord Hastings (possibly over a bowl of strawberries from Holborn) and given to the Duke of Buckingham for safekeeping; but he helped persuade Buckingham to try and seize the throne himself, and in the confusion escaped to France.

He returned again in the train of Henry Tudor, and spent no more time in exile or prison. Henry VII made him Archbishop of Canterbury, then Lord Chancellor (does one hear the sigh of Becket's ghost?). He would be created a cardinal, and finally Chancellor of Oxford University. In his latter years he wrote a history of Richard III, which was translated from Latin by a young man in Morton's household. The young man was Thomas More, and the argument about whether Morton told him anything true will probably never end.

Morton died in 1500 C.E., at about the age of eighty, leaving behind a form of legal extortion known as "Morton's Fork" (though it was probably invented by his assistant Richard Fox) and a number of dead kings of all persuasions.

As was said in the prolegomena, this book does not attempt to provide a "solution" to the "problem" of Richard III. Even when such problems are not wholly synthetic, the solutions fall into the abyss of all deductive reasoning, namely that one cannot deduce from data facts that are not inherent in the data. In the supposedly crucial "Mystery of the Princes," we have various pieces of evidence—Dominic Mancini's account, James Tyrell's confession, Thomas More's history, *et alia*—and various reasons to consider each reliable or unreliable (not the same as "true or false"). And we have opinions, because we cannot reason without theses and hypotheses . . . and ultimately it is the opinions that determine what evidences we use to form a judgment.

There have always been those who portrayed Richard as a good man and king, and until lately this usually meant clearing him of his nephews' deaths, sometimes by the most remarkable chains of reasoning. Today we are less particular. We have assimilated Machiavelli. We have even come to admire a little ruthlessness in our leaders, especially a theatrical ruthlessness; power, after all, exists to be used.

Richard Plantagenet, Duke of Gloucester, King of England, was killed in battle 22 August 1485 at a place called Redmoor Plain, near the village of Market Bosworth. Until recently, many historians dated the end of the Middle Ages and the beginning of the Renaissance from Richard's death, as if he were personally standing in the way of History.

Our revels now are ended, the airy constructions fading. Only the music remains, as it always remains, waiting for another improvisation of life.